Printed in the United States
97086LV00001B/60/A

9 781847 481245

In his second historical novel, John Pollard has researched the second-best-known classical period – that just before the Trojan war. Although Hercules is the centrepiece, we learn of the early lives of Theseus, Jason, and those who accompanied him on the expedition of the Argo, and of Priam who, as king of the doomed city, ultimately presided over the destruction of Troy by Agamemnon and Menelaus and their Achaean army. The seeds of later tragedies can be seen to have been sown here and perhaps there are lessons also for us today in the treatment by the conqueror of those who collaborated with a vicious despot. Although the conventional wisdom is that all males were slaughtered and the women and children sold into slavery, this was not practical if the conquerors did not wish to annex the conquered city. In this novel, John Pollard suggests that frequently, in Hercules' time, most of such people were allowed time to repent and embrace the new order. Only a few were considered too badly tainted to participate and put their skills at the service of a freed people.

John Pollard's writing is driven by his background of a scholarship in classics to Oxford, where he achieved a law degree, and a lifetime of work in business, local government and charities. Early retirement from full-time work has enabled a return to his first love – the classics – and the opportunity to visit the historic sites in Greece before the recent disastrous forest fires.

This is another well-researched and thought-provoking book which sheds light in many dark corners. John Pollard is planning further literary excursions into the same era.

John Pollard's first historical novel was entitled Helen, Queen of Sparta.

HERCULES

HERCULES

John H Pollard

ATHENA PRESS
LONDON

HERCULES

ISBN 10-digit: 1 84748 124 8
ISBN 13-digit: 978 1 84748 124 5

First Published 2007 by
ATHENA PRESS
Queen's House, 2 Holly Road
Twickenham TW1 4EG
United Kingdom

Printed for Athena Press

Acknowledgements

To my wife, for her continuing and unfailing support; and to the ancient Greeks for their incredible ingenuity, artistry, humanity and determination which never cease to amaze and stimulate me.

Author's Note

In *Hercules* I have tried to record what, after research, I think probably really happened to the Hercules I have chosen as my subject. It is clear that there were many ancient heroes called Hercules – several classical writers refer to a number of people of that name – but the Labours were attributed only to the most famous of them. The confusion caused by the large number of 'Hercules' meant that I was forced to sieve carefully through the many exploits attributed to the hero and extract only those I could be reasonably confident were achieved by the Hercules who lived in the middle of the thirteenth century BC, dying in his late forties or early fifties, a few years before the Trojan War.

I have, however, started from the premise that legends, in general, are basically truthful, if frequently exaggerated. In this belief I follow humbly in the footsteps of the explorers from the late nineteenth century to today, starting with the erratic and egocentric Schliemann who stirred the world's imaginations with his discoveries at Mycenae (1876), Tiryns (1884) and Troy (three major excavations over the period 1870–1881). Of those who were active in archaeological writing in the twentieth century, I have been most impressed by Werner Keller (*The Bible as History* – first published in English in 1956) and the discoveries of Michael Wood, one of whose books *In the Footsteps of Alexander the Great* (BBC Books 1997) I found particularly stimulating. I enjoyed his other books too! Both these authors confirmed to me what I had always suspected: if you go and look at the sites of these ancient events you will still find in remote places – even now –hard evidence of these 'legendary' events, sometimes supported by local oral traditions. Both the authors I have named experienced this.

My conclusion is that most of the surviving ancient legends contain a basic truth. The problem is to tease out the real facts from the myth. This I have attempted to do both in this book and my previous one on Helen.

I have used the ancient words for measurements, except for the height of one mountain where I thought it would be confusing. Unfortunately, the Greeks and Romans both used the words 'stadium' and 'cubit' to mean slightly different things. I have used the ancient Greek version in which the stadium is worth roughly one-tenth of an English mile and a cubit is the equivalent of eighteen inches.

The gifts made by the writer to Queen Alcmena and by Iolaus to King Menestheus are based on items of the relevant period found in excavations over the past 150 years or so and now on display in the Mycenaean section of the British Museum in London or the National Museum of Athens.

The spelling of names is a constant problem. The Greek name for the hero is, of course, Herakles, which makes the derivation relating to Hera clearer than the use of the Latinised form of Hercules, which I have used simply because it is the better known version. The Latinisation of classical and ancient Greek names became embedded in the eighteenth century and the definitive classical dictionary by Lemprière, first published in 1788, uses Latin names throughout. As this involves calling Zeus, Jupiter and Hera, Juno, I rejected this approach and have generally adopted what is the modern practice of using the Greek versions.

The 'Cades' where Hercules lifted the cattle is of course now known as Cadiz, and the town of Alesia, where Hercules wintered the cattle and his men with Queen Galata and her people, still exists. Now a small village on the edge of the main Burgundian vineyards and known as Alise-Sainte-Reine, it is incorporated into Venarey-Les-Laumes. It is well worth a visit as it was the site of the last resistance of the Gauls (continental Celts) against the Romans. The Gauls under Vercingetorix were finally defeated here and the ruins of the town and traces of the Roman siege walls can still be seen. Napoleon III erected a huge bronze statue of Vercingetorix on the site in 1865.

The Acropolis today's visitors to Athens see is quite different from the one depicted here. Around 750 years passed after Alcmena's death before the remodelling initiated by Pericles started in 447 BC. The work was not completed until 395 BC, thirty-four years after Pericles' death in 429 BC. At the time of this novel, the main city and the King's palace was on the rock. The foundations of 'Theseus' Palace', partly under the Erechtheion, and the 'Porch of the Caryatids', are still pointed out to modern tourists.

A brief not on the maps on pp.15–16. These are indicative only, mainly to identify a few places which could not be found on a current map. Some modern cities, which did not exist at the time of Hercules, are shown for reference only. The port of Phaleron, which the writer and Iolaus used on their visit to Athens, was at that time the port of Athens. It was close to where Piraeus now is, but not on the same site. Paraitonius in Libya is where the town called Mersa Matruh – a place much in the news during WWII – now is. 'Libya' is what the Mediterranean peoples of Hercules' time called the whole of North Africa – from the western borders of Egypt to the Atlantic coast.

Contents

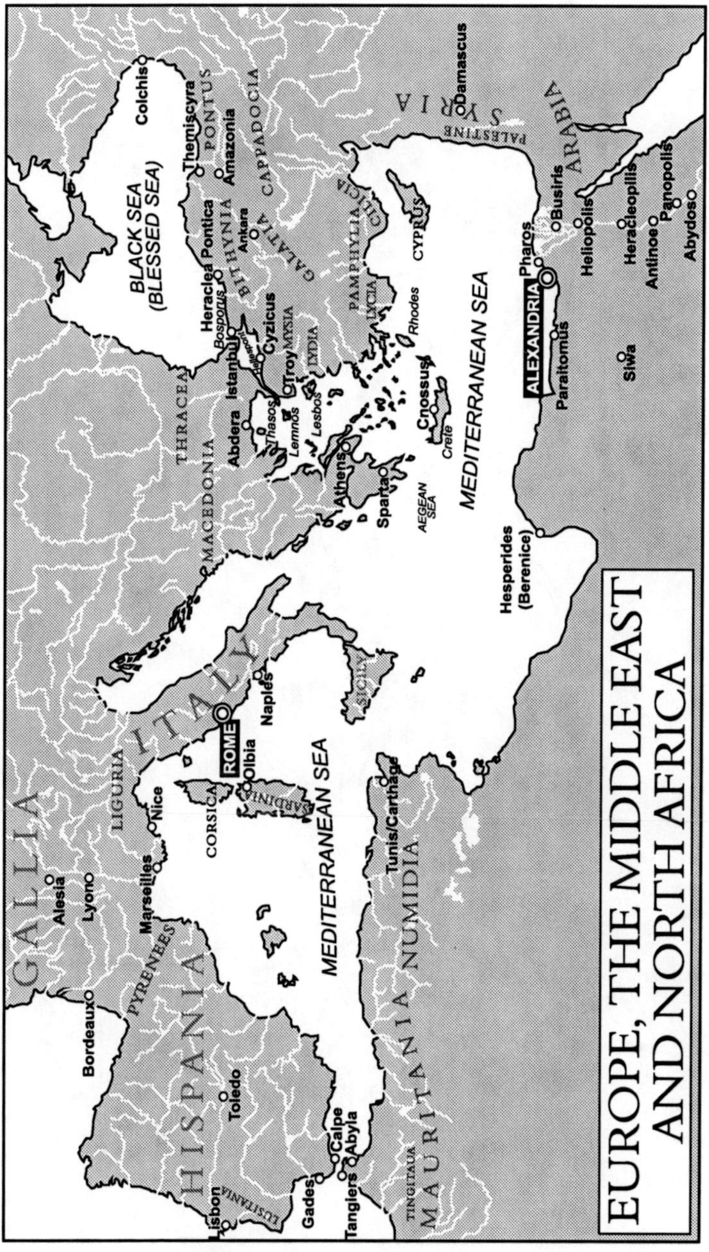

EUROPE, THE MIDDLE EAST AND NORTH AFRICA

GREECE, CRETE AND WEST ASIA MINOR

Introduction

As I grow older, I feel more and more drawn to the study of those whom our ancestors considered heroes. The more I learn, the more I am impressed by the deeply embedded wisdom of their age – particularly the time when they first dissociated themselves from the concept of human sacrifice as the most precious thing they could offer their gods. This was the beginning of civilisation. The greatest forefather of the human race, Abraham, realised this around 1950 BC. It took others many more years to appreciate this. The priests of Apollo appear to have brought this concept to Greece around 1450 BC, after they fled from Crete following a series of major natural disasters, commencing with the Santorini tsunami and culminating in a massive earthquake some 150 years later, which destroyed their temple and the Minoan Culture. But the Mayans in Central America were still practising human sacrifice around 1100 AD.

The Hercules (or Herakles, which is the Greek form of his name) I write about in this book was born when the cult of Apollo was gaining popular support. It was a time of great change, both in thinking and practice. Many ancient writers found it hard to believe that one man could travel so far and achieve so much. Most of them did not know of the exploits of Alexander the Macedonian. What he achieved, with the tools of his time, is unbelievable – or would be, if we did not have the thoroughly reliable eye-witness account of Callisthenes and many local legends of 'Iskander', as Alexander was known in some parts of the old Persian Empire he conquered.

That there were many men of achievement called Hercules is beyond doubt. After the Hercules' death, it would have been a popular name, if rather hubristic. There is also little doubt that some of the greatest human stories have some apparent similarities: Moses killed a man and went into the desert as a herdsman for many years before God called him to lead the Jews out of Egypt. Hercules was similarly banished out of harm's way and became a herdsman until he matured. Moses was treated by the Jews as favoured by God, appearing with Christ in the Transfixion. Hercules, as was the practice of the people of his place and time, was elevated to being a god himself.

I have always believed that there was more to Hercules than the blustering, vacuous bully portrayed in many of the versions of his legendary deeds. He had phenomenal strength, there seems no doubt, but he had a gentleness of spirit. He was terrible when drunk, which occurred on several only too memorable occasions, but some were jealous of him and tried to exploit his weaknesses. Some important people, astonishingly, tried to renege on contracts they had made with him – and paid the price. But he was a musician of quality as well as a warrior of outstanding ability and his time as a herdsman in his formative years gave him a rapport with animals that was undeniable. Finally, there is evidence in the writings of a Greek writer, Lucian, that the Celts revered Hercules, in the form of their god Ogmios, as an orator – not as a derring-do fighter. The Celts considered eloquence the most important accomplishment. This is surprising, considering the reputation of the Celts (or Gauls, as Julius Caesar called them) for aggression. Certainly the old legends do underline this quality in Hercules. At the age of eighteen he successfully defended himself when charged in court with the murder of his tutor, Linus.

But my studies of the old Herculean legends indicate a much more intriguing secret. He was instrumental in changing the structure of kingship in Greece from a matriarchal to a patriarchal base, and had a major impact on the development of written language by introducing an expanded alphabet.

I hope you enjoy this book as much as I have enjoyed writing it.

The Beginning

I first met Iolaus at the harbour. We were both there on business, awaiting the offloading of cargo from a boat that had arrived late the previous evening. Now dawn had come and gone. The wharf was busy. The Captain was anxious to clear the cargo, receive payment and load up for his next voyage. We both quickly learnt from him that our valuable cargoes – silver for my jewellery business and precious stones for his wife – were in a remote, secure part of the hold and could only be accessed after most of the other cargo had been removed. So we decided to dismiss the staff we had brought to protect us and summon them back when the Captain alerted us our property was about to be unloaded. In the meantime, we would patronise one of the many wine shops around the harbour, which gave us a good view of the boat and its Captain. We told the Captain where we were going and he undertook to send over one of his sailors to tell us when our valuables were about to be unloaded. Whilst we were settling the charges, our staff would be recalled.

And so Iolaus and I had time to get to know each other. I knew, of course, that he was the son of Hercules' twin brother, Iphicles, and that he had served Hercules for many years as his charioteer. I knew also that towards the end of his life – tragically brought to an end by his own wife's love for him – Hercules encouraged Iolaus to leave him and seek his own destiny by establishing colonies in Sardinia. This Iolaus had already done, with outstanding success, before our first meeting. He had led a combined force of Thespians and Athenians and taken over the whole island very quickly. He divided the island into provinces, planted olive trees and founded the bustling city and port of Olbia, where we now were. The Athenians were encouraged to found their own cities elsewhere. This division of responsibility and territory was achieved amicably and, once the newcomers' military superiority had been asserted, without serious local opposition. This was a little surprising, as there already was an established local culture, which manifested itself in the curious dome-like structures they had built and to which they retreated in time of danger. However, they were not established everywhere on the island, which was generally sparsely populated at that time, and the inhabitants were not very skilled in raising crops or animals.

Indeed, possibly because of their fear of being attacked – which had led them to develop their defensive building techniques – the best land for growing crops was mostly uncultivated. And so, as many of Iolaus' soldiers had farming experience, the land's fertility developed rapidly and there was soon surplus produce for the original population to share, with much left to export and exchange for other goods we needed. With the added advantage of Iolaus' force guaranteeing security, the scene was set for a harmonious life for all. I had been attracted to Olbia by the security and wealth that had been created, which had enabled my business to flourish. I told Iolaus this.

'Kind of you to say that,' he said. 'I value peace and tranquillity, probably more than many, because of my life's early experiences. I saw much violence when I was serving Hercules although, at heart, he was a kind man. The problem was that people were jealous of him, misunderstood him or, the cause of many a tragedy, misled or tried to cheat him. The last he could not grasp; he always kept his word and never understood when others did not. Of course, he was so strong that nobody could stand up to him physically and it always amazed me when a promise to Hercules was not honoured – usually by a person in authority. Retribution from Hercules was not always immediate but it was inevitable and ruthless!'

'How very interesting!' I rejoined. 'I had always understood that he was quick-tempered, violent – brutal even – and very unpredictable.'

'Yes,' responded Iolaus, 'that was his reputation. It is true, to some extent, particularly when he had drunk too much. But he was also kind and very patient. Not many would have put up with the treatment he had from his cousin, the High King Eurystheus.'

'Ah!' I replied. 'You are talking of the famous Labours of

Hercules. I have heard so many different stories about them, many pretty incredible. You were with him on all of them, weren't you? What really happened?'

'Yes,' replied Iolaus, 'I was with him on most of his expeditions, but that is a long story. I think we had better postpone our discussion as I see the Captain is now ready for us.'

He was right. The Captain, on the prow of the boat, was waving to us that he was now about to unload our goods. We acknowledged his signal and sent a messenger to recall our servants. We then made our way to the boat and, while our servants were returning, checked our goods, paid our dues to the Captain and took possession of our property. But, before we went our separate ways, we agreed to meet again at Iolaus' magnificent house in the main town square this day week when he promised to answer some – not necessarily all – the questions I wanted to ask him about Hercules. I couldn't sleep that night. I was so thrilled at the prospect of hearing the true story of Hercules, the greatest man of our age. Who knew that? Possibly not even Iolaus, but he was an excellent starting place.

The Meeting

At last came the day for my meeting with Iolaus. I could hardly contain my excitement. What would he tell me? What dare he tell me? I knew, of course, that Hercules had passed on several years ago and was now one of the gods. Temples to him had sprung up all over the Mediterranean. Every city and nation claimed that he had performed some feat of strength or daring in their territory and called him their own. His popularity was rivalling that of Apollo and Athene. I doubt they were very pleased!

When I arrived at Iolaus' house, his doorkeeper – one of his old soldiers, I was told later – met me courteously and showed me into a side room, where I was told to wait. As time went by, I suspected that Iolaus had regretted his offer and was thinking of withdrawing it. But then I thought of what he had said about Hercules' standing by his word – which Iolaus clearly felt was one of Hercules' main virtues – and I could not believe that, although the promise had been so lightly given, Iolaus would as lightly withdraw it.

And so it proved. Within minutes of my coming to this conclusion, he came to the door of the room himself, full of regret.

'Please accept my apologies for keeping you waiting. I was pressed earlier to deal with some urgent business. I tried to postpone it but quickly realised that if I did not deal with it there and then we would be interrupted and I did not want that. Anyway,' he continued, as he led me into a large room at the rear of the house, 'I have told Auturgus – you met him at the door – not to disturb us. He was a loyal soldier to both Hercules and, later, to me and is totally reliable. He will only come in if there is an earthquake or an armed party is at the door! Now then, what do you want to ask me?'

'Well,' I said, 'I would like to start at the beginning, but, as you are the son of Hercules' twin brother, you will not know much about that!' I smiled.

'Quite right!' he responded. 'I was not there, of course, and even my grandfather was unable to recall what actually happened! There were an amazing number of people who were there to witness the most famous incidents in the earlier days of Hercules' infancy, judging from the number of first-hand accounts I hear.' He smiled and continued. 'I suppose that I had better start with the stories about his birth.

'You probably know that his mother, my grandmother Alcmena, refused to marry her promised husband, and my grandfather, Amphitryon until he had avenged the killing of her eight brothers by a cattle raiding party of Taphians and Teleboans. As you probably know, they came from islands just off the west coast of Achaia near the entrance to the Gulf of Corinth. They even then had a reputation for piracy. My grandmother's precondition to her marriage became all the more poignant after Amphitryon had managed to find the stolen cattle whilst Electryon, Alcmena's father, was searching for them and the thieves.

'Unfortunately, to resolve the matter quickly and amicably, my grandfather paid to get them back from the innocent new owner and expected Alcmena's father, Electryon, the High King of Mycenae, to refund the payment he had made. Electryon was recalled from his campaign to find and punish the thieves by a message from Amphitryon, saying that he had found the cattle but needed Electryon to confirm that they were indeed his. Electryon was not pleased to hear that any money had been paid for his stolen cattle. In the course of the ensuing argument between them, Amphitryon, in frustration, threw his club at one of the cows, which had strayed from the herd. The club hit one of the cow's horns and rebounded to strike Electryon on the head, killing him instantly. My grandfather was, of course, devastated. But, as there was now no prospect of Alcmena's father avenging her brothers' deaths, Alcmena, who was present at the accident and instantly forgave Amphitryon, nevertheless repeated the ultimatum I have already mentioned. But now, of course, he first had to atone for the accidental death of his father-in-law-to-be, and, when he was banished from Argos by Electryon's brother, Sthenelus, who also seized the High King's throne, he returned to

Thebes with Alcmena, where he was purged of his guilt by King Creon. He then went in search of the killers and duly found and despatched them, returning to Thebes, and Alcmena, as he had fulfilled his challenge. The delayed wedding then took place and the happy couple retired to their bridal chamber.

'It is said, in order to account for the astonishing strength and power of Hercules, that he was the son of Zeus but that his twin, Iphicles, my father, was the son of Amphitryon. All agree that they were both the sons of Alcmena. Whilst Hercules was certainly outstanding in many ways, as I shall recount, he was a man and a mortal, my uncle and, I have no doubt, the son of his father, Amphitryon. The excuse for the story may lie in the form of the marriage ceremony, or the crowning ceremony for a king, when the male takes on the attributes of a god – for one night only. Anyway, this whole business was very sad for my grandfather: not only did he lose his father-in-law, his wife lost her father and they lost the throne of the High King of Mycenae. Had Amphitryon not been involved in the death of his father-in-law, he would have followed him as High King. But there were many who had eyes on that throne – the Taphian cattle raid was sponsored by a potential usurper, Pterelaus – but Sthenelus had a better claim than Pterelaus and was able to settle the succession for a number of generations, by what some suspect was a trick. But there was a curse on that line, as I expect you know?'

I did know. He was referring to the terrible stories told of the reigns of the sons of Pelops – Atreus and Thyestes – who were appointed joint kings of Argos (which then excluded Mycenae and Tiryns) and who later vied for the High Kingship. But I was not interested in that story now.

'Yes,' I said, 'I am aware of some of those awful stories. But tell me about the serpents that attacked Hercules and Iphicles when they were very young.'

'Ah, you have heard that story?' Iolaus enquired. 'I once asked Hercules about it. He was very dismissive and thought it was made up. Of course, he had no personal recollection – he was only a few months' old at the time. But there is another part of the story to tell first.

'Although Amphitryon had lost his right to be High King, the grounds for this loss were very dubious. After his atonement at Thebes, he should have been reinstated. But it appears that Amphitryon was offered the throne of Thebes by Creon, as his successor, and, as he was closely related to the Theban Royal Family anyway (Creon, in reality, being a usurper), he apparently preferred to accept the throne of Thebes peaceably rather than fight for the throne of the High King of Mycenae, on which a number of people had set their ambition. It appears that my grandfather agreed privately with High King Sthenelus that whichever of them should first produce a son, that son would be declared the heir to the High Kingship of Mycenae. Sthenelus reluctantly agreed – probably only because Amphitryon promised not to challenge Sthenelus' right to be High King if he did agree. Now it happened that Sthenelus' wife, Nicippe, became pregnant at about the same time as Alcmena. I am not quite sure what actually occurred, so I will stick to the facts as I know them. Alcmena's children went to term, but Nicippe's son, Eurystheus, was born two months premature, a day before Hercules and my father, Iphicles. Divine intervention was blamed, but I look no further than the Royal Physician at Mycenae who, I am told, produced some potion to bring forward the birth of Eurystheus at Sthenelus' request, and at great risk to the unborn child and its mother. Anyway, both survived. Amphitryon and Alcmena were naturally upset but, as they had not expected anything for themselves and as their children, particularly Hercules, were strong and healthy, I understand their disappointment gradually subsided.'

'Interesting,' I commented. 'Before you tell me the story about the serpents, what is the truth behind the talk that part of the bargain Amphitryon made with Sthenelus included the subservience of the second-born son to the first – making Alcmena's eldest son, Hercules, servant to Nicippe's son, Eurystheus?'

For the first time in our discussion, a flash of anger passed across Iolaus' face. 'You know nothing!' he almost shouted at me. He paused, drew his breath and apologised. 'I am sorry for that outburst – it was most unfair of me. Of course, you don't know. Perhaps I care too much for the truth. I will answer your question fully, and calmly, later. The truth will surprise you, I can promise you! The short answer is that, no, there was no such bargain and, anyway, contrary to what many seem to believe, it was my father, Iphicles, who was the firstborn. This was partly because, being the smaller, it was easier for him to be taken first out of the womb, to be followed by the larger Hercules. But, as the story of Hercules and his exploits became well known, it was assumed that he was the elder and my grandparents did not bother to correct the mistake. As I shall tell you, the Labours of Hercules were a crusade concealed as a penance. Quite a complex business and not at all as people think. If you don't mind, I would like to stop now – it is proving more exhausting and emotional than I thought! I have never before told the whole story – so far as I know it – to anybody, but you have convinced me that I should tell now what I know, as much of it will die with me. I was very fond of my uncle and he was not as many have portrayed him. He was incredibly talented, sensitive and loving and gave himself totally to the cause without any thought for himself. His friends and family suffered much because of that. Let us meet tomorrow to talk more about my knowledge of his childhood and the cause to which he devoted his life.'

With that, and a brief expression of thanks from me for his frankness, we parted, to meet again at the same time the following day.

The Youth of Hercules

On my arrival at Iolaus' house the following day, early in the afternoon, he met me himself at the door and conducted me to the same room we had used the previous day. After we had both sat down, he asked if I would like some wine and told me that he had much to say. If I had no objection, he said, we could be together for some hours. I confirmed that I had no other appointments and would be pleased to share a simple meal later with him, as he offered, if he was able to continue the story into the late evening. I also accepted his kind offer of a glass of wine, which his servant brought into us. By this time, I was even more excited than I had been the previous day.

'Before I tell you about the Cause,' Iolaus commenced, 'I will tell you all I know about the story of the two serpents. I cannot guarantee that it is true!

'My father and Hercules, when they were only a few months old, were put to sleep together on a large bronze shield, which, incidentally, Amphitryon had won on killing Pterelaus, the instigator of the cattle theft I have already told you about. Covered by a lamb's fleece, because it was winter, the twins were snug and fast asleep. Around midnight, two large serpents slid into their room and, sensing the babies' presence, circled the shield and raised up their heads to see what was inside. Their hissing woke the babies and my father kicked off the fleece, screamed and rolled out of the shield on to the floor. The noise awoke Alcmena who immediately awoke her husband – by giving him a dig in the ribs, I expect – and told him to go and see what the problem was. Pausing only to grab his sword out of its sheath, he raced into the room to see my father rolling on the floor screaming whilst his brother Hercules, chuckling, was sitting up in the shield with one chubby hand round the neck of each serpent. As his father ran towards him, he threw the serpents down at his father's feet – stone dead! Meanwhile, Iphicles had crawled into his parents' room to be comforted by Alcmena, who later asked the soothsayer Teiresias what was the significance of it all. Teiresias foretold Hercules' future and advised Alcmena to cleanse the palace, burn the serpents, scatter their ashes and sacrifice a boar to Zeus. This last part of the story was true, at least, because it was then, and still is, the custom to sacrifice a boar at the midwinter festival, which occurred at about that time.

'I cannot tell you much about Hercules' upbringing, but it was very thorough. As you know, I was his charioteer for many years and he would often talk to me about his own youth. I suppose he was rather ashamed that he had taken me away from my family at such a young age – I was barely sixteen – but I felt as if I was a man, of course, and could hardly understand then what he was grieving over! I now see that he was regretting the loss of my youth. He had spent all his youth learning many skills. Did you know that he was one of the best singers and players of the lyre of his time? Some old men who heard him said they had never heard better.

'But, like so many of his achievements, there was a human cost linked to it. Hercules' first music teacher was Eumolpus and he was taught to read and write by Linus. Now Linus was also an accomplished musician – some say that it was he who added a string to the lyre, although that is generally attributed to Apollo – and, when Eumolpus was temporarily absent, Linus took it upon himself to teach the young Hercules to play the lyre. Unfortunately, Linus was very rigid in his approach and his style of playing the lyre was quite different to that of Eumolpus. So, when he tried to teach Hercules, he was telling Hercules to ignore what Eumolpus had taught him and play it the way he, Linus, played. When Hercules persisted in playing the way Eumolpus had taught him, Linus beat him with a stick – which was a silly thing to do. Hercules lost his temper and hit Linus such a blow with his lyre that it killed him instantly. The death of such a well-known person could not be hidden and, as Hercules was by this time considered an adult, he was tried for murder. He went to court and defended himself. I am told by eye-witnesses that he presented his case brilliantly. He claimed that he had the right under a law of Rhadamanthus to defend himself against an aggressor and produced evidence of Linus' violent assaults on him. The evidence he produced showed that the final assault by Linus was not the first. Hercules was acquitted.

'However, his father, Amphitryon, was very concerned at Hercules' hot temper and physical strength and decided it would be safer for everybody if he sent Hercules away from the city to work with cattle in the distant countryside. Hercules often told me how much he had enjoyed being in the open air, away from the city, and he seemed genuinely fond of animals. Certainly, his experience with cattle came in useful later, as you will hear. He honed his archery skills, too, at this time. He must have spent much of his time guarding the cattle against predators, who would have provided him with legitimate targets, and it seems he also acquired a deep knowledge of the stars at that time. I suppose being in the open air at night – away from the noise and lights of the city – would have made this easier, and he would have had less to distract him! I haven't heard that many young ladies pestered him then as they did later! He was also quite a philosopher. He taught me a great deal. How he acquired this knowledge I know not, but he would have had plenty of time to think. I am afraid there is not much more I can tell you about Hercules' early life, but his mother, Alcmena – my grandmother – is still alive, living in Athens under the protection of the King of Athens. Although she is now an old lady, she may be prepared to talk to you – but you would have to go to her. She is too frail to travel to Sardinia.'

'That sounds an interesting idea,' I replied. 'Do you think she would see me? A visit to Athens might be a good business opportunity for me, anyway. I have had it in mind for a little while.'

Iolaus smiled. 'I can see where your heart lies,' he teased. 'From what I have seen of the ornaments you manufacture, their design is unusual and could appeal to the Athenian women. They like to be distinctive! I would happily give you a letter to introduce you to my grandmother; indeed, I might even come with you, as I have not visited her for some time and I doubt she will live much longer.'

'That would be extremely kind of you,' I responded. 'So we

can leave Hercules' youth now and move on to his later life. But, first, tell me about "the Cause" you mentioned when we last met.'

Iolaus again smiled at my eagerness to continue with the story. Considering the gap in our status, I was being a little discourteous and some would have been angry at my behaviour. I vowed to be more restrained in future. But I need not have worried. My haste to hear the story proved to be an amusement to Iolaus rather than an irritation, as he made plain in his response.

'Well, well,' he said. 'We are in a hurry! I suppose I have only myself to blame for holding up this mystery in front of you without any hint of what it is all about. I am sure my curiosity would have bettered my manners, too!' Here he raised his hand to stifle my protested apology. 'I know you meant no disrespect,' he continued, 'so I take no offence – unlike Hercules! My experiences with Hercules exposed me to so many unfortunate events, most of which could have been avoided or prevented if the parties had spent a little while understanding each other, that I have acquired a thick skin and a slow-burning anger. Mind you, when I am really angry, I can be pretty fearsome! Be warned!'

The Cause

'Now, you may already know some of what I am going to say,' Iolaus commenced, 'but I would appreciate it if you would let me tell this part of the story in my own way. Do ask questions if anything I say is not clear, but try to do that when I come to a natural break in the story. I ask this because I will need to concentrate hard to make sure I tell you everything in its context and do not forget anything important.'

I said that I quite understood and settled down in my chair to listen to what he had to say.

'You must be aware that, until recent times, kings were selected in a very primitive way, and many had a limited time to be king before they were put to death – in one way or another.'

I nodded.

'These practices were basically religious in origin and centred on mother-worship. I suppose there were two strong, practical, reasons for this: first, that only the female of most species, including man, could produce offspring and, second, that because of this association it was felt that the driving force behind all new life, and, indeed, of our world, manifesting itself in the miracle of spring and the productivity of the earth must be female. This meant that early religions focused mainly on female gods, who, being mostly devoted to domestic matters, were worshipped much more by women than men. Indeed, some religious groups would not allow men to be involved in any of their religious ceremonies or functions at all. This is still the position today, although the emphasis is somewhat different.

'There was one other crucial factor. It was early recognised that, to avoid unnecessary bloodshed, it was vital to have a clear system for settling succession. When a leader died there had to be an accepted way of choosing the successor. As females dominated early society, for the reasons I have already given to you, the people decided that the succession should be only through the female line. This was made even more complex because of the limited period during which a woman can have children. And so, instead of the now generally accepted rule that the crown descends through the eldest son, in the matriarchal society – as I shall call it – the crown descended through the youngest daughter to give the maximum time for her fecundity. I don't think too many older sisters liked this very much!

'The men didn't like it either, largely because the system required eligible men to fight for the right to marry the heiress and they were ceremonially killed after, at most, a reign of just a few years. The women arranged horrific deaths for their discarded kings, which I prefer not to explore!

'I suppose that, so long as communities were fairly isolated, it was very difficult for any man to challenge this system. Certainly it was not seriously challenged for a very long time. It was not, actually, a particularly local tradition – it seems to have been common over a large area, possibly the whole of the world as we knew it. Then, not many years ago, rumours began to circulate of tribes where the men had taken charge, male gods were supreme and kingship descended from the king to his eldest son. This was denied at first, and then there were the scare rumours: you only knew who the mother of a child was, you could never be certain who the father was. So, you could have a "false" ruler if the system was changed, which you couldn't have with the matriarchal system. Then the women argued that they would not produce children under a regime that favoured men but this was abandoned when the most extreme set up their own state, whom some call "Amazons", and which the majority of women deplored.'

Here he paused momentarily, so I ventured to ask a question. 'You visited them with Hercules, I believe?'

'Yes,' Iolaus replied. 'I will tell you about that when I come to talk about Hercules' Labours. But I will recount now some of the Amazons' practices. Being an all-female society, they had no men to help them produce children, without whom, of course, their tribe would die out. They had a simple answer to that little problem. They worshipped the moon goddess – which some say is the source of their name, though others say it reflects their practice of burning off the right breast when young so that they could throw spears and shoot arrows as accurately as men. Every year over the three or four days of the celebration of the moon goddess' festival, those Amazons who wished to have children would visit selected men of neighbouring countries, stay with them for the duration of the festival and generally return pregnant. Boy children born were either killed or had their legs broken when in childhood so that they would not grow up strong enough to challenge the female regime. Males were tolerated so long as they were content to do menial tasks, but those who wanted more either had to escape – and some did – or they were slaughtered. When this became generally known, this helped to swell the numbers of those who wished to overturn the matriarchal regime, which was becoming more and more associated with the extreme practices of the Amazons. To be fair, many women did not like it either, so there was popular support for a major change.

'But change did not happen easily. Before Hercules was born, there had been a number of attempts to replace the matriarchal system with a patriarchal one. There had been some small successes, but many defeats. The story of Oedipus is, really, the story of a failure to change the system in Thebes; the old king had to die because he had come to the end of his term and a younger man was due to take his place and his bed. Substituting the son for the father in the marital bed was supposed to cause revulsion, alarm and a change of the system, but it was misinterpreted and the attempt failed. And so, by the time Hercules was well into manhood and his reputation as a strong, intelligent and honest man established, this need to overthrow completely the matriarchal system had become a "cause" for many. Of course, one of the most significant events that propelled the Cause was the coming of the Cult of Apollo to Delphi.

'Prior to the arrival of the Cult of Apollo, Delphi was the shrine of the Pythian – a sacred serpent – and the earth goddess, Gaia. It is disputed where Apollo came from – some say the island of Crete on the back of a dolphin, others from the island of Delos. I believe there was a religious cult of Apollo in Crete many years ago and the Cretan priests fled to Egypt on the mainland after the disastrous events many years ago when the north of the island was flooded by a huge wave and the whole island itself was covered, to the depth of many feet, by grey dust that killed all plants and made the land sterile for over one hundred years.

'Now, some believe the Cult of Apollo actually originated in Egypt, where there already was a system of kingship succession by male primogeniture, whence it was spread by the priests to Crete. There is also a tradition that Apollo came to Delphi "from the north". It is possible to reconcile these stories by supposing that the Cretan priests fled north and ended up in Delos. There they consolidated their cult in a new environment and, when they were ready, they landed in Thessaly and approached Delphi from the north by land, thus surprising the guardians of the shrine. From what Hercules told me, the Cretan priests of Apollo had become aware on their travels of the mood for change on the mainland of Greece and decided that to champion this cause would be a popular way to establish themselves permanently. Delphi was targeted as it was a stronghold of the matriarchy, but not well guarded, and was in a central geographical position. The priests were also tired of their insecure, nomadic, life and wanted to return to the stability they had formerly enjoyed in Crete. Delphi was a good choice. The shrine lies in a naturally protected spot, nestling against a tall mountain with excellent all-round views and supplied with a reliable flow of pure water from a natural spring. As you know, one of the words used to describe the shrine is by reference to the *omphalos*, or "navel-stone", which has been placed in the shrine from the remotest times, and represents both mother power and that Delphi is considered by many to be the centre of the civilised world.

'Anyway,' continued Iolaus, 'whatever the history, Apollo's priests took over the shrine and killed the serpent that guarded it for Gaia. Then, strangely, the Cult decided to atone for the "murder" of the serpent by putting the Chief Priest at the service of Admetos, a king of Thessaly, among the Pelasgians, for eight years – some say longer. I think he just wanted to be out of the way to see what reaction there would be to their invasion and takeover of the shrine at Delphi. In the meantime, the priests quietly established an excellent reputation for the Cult.

Volunteering for atonement showed that they accepted the rules for mortals and the Cult was quickly associated with the fine arts, music, medicine, poetry and public speaking – all of which soon became recognised as the pursuits mainly of men! When the Chief Priest returned to Delphi, the Cult of Apollo was established as the patron of the peaceful, manly arts. This attracted male support and the unwarlike attributes also helped to assuage the female opposition to the attempts to introduce into mainland Greece the patriarchal system already established in Egypt and Crete. At least, most of what I have said was Hercules' view.

'Now, Hercules never admitted what I am going to say now. The accepted story is that Hercules, having completed a successful expedition against the Minyans, returned to Thebes – whose liability to pay a crippling tribute to the Minyans had been extinguished by Hercules' defeat of them – and was greeted as a hero. King Creon gave him his eldest daughter, Megara, in marriage and my father married the youngest daughter, Hecale. Unfortunately, the defeat of the Minyans was not the end of the matter. Some time later their friends and neighbours, the Euboeans, marched against Thebes, led by King Pyraechmus. Hercules assembled and led the army of Thebans and supporters to an absolute victory over the Euboeans and, to dissuade others from attacking Thebes, he ordered Pyraechmus' body to be torn apart by two colts and left unburied. He was later quite ashamed about this episode and, ever afterwards, he became known as one of the few warriors who allowed the enemy to bury their dead.

'After this episode, a strange melancholy took over Hercules – usually blamed on the gods! I think he was probably drugged, whether by himself knowingly or unknowingly, or by others who were jealous of him or who had a grudge against him I do not know. His violence could be terrifying, and I – then only a young boy – was one of the first to experience it first-hand. I had just begun to get to know my uncle and we were on very friendly terms. When Hercules came out of the palace, I was practising swordplay with wooden sticks with his young sons and my brothers. So, when he came towards me with a drawn sword in his hands, I thought he was just going to join in and teach us some tricks. As soon as he saw me, he went for me with his sword. I ran and saved my life. His sons and two of my brothers did not realise what was happening until it was too late. Eight young people were killed that day and later burned on a funeral pyre by Hercules himself. Just as the fire was burning itself out, Hercules recovered his reason and, realising what he had done, fled to a dark room where he remained for several days without food. I think Megara took him some water, but even she could not calm his despair. Suddenly, without any warning, he emerged from his room and declared that he was going to see King Thespius of Boeotia to be purified. I don't know if I have mentioned this, but Thespius was the king who, some years' previously, had encouraged Hercules to bed his fifty daughters – some say in one night but others over fifty days. From this activity, fifty-one sons were born, including two sets of twins. One daughter had declined the honour and, instead, became the celibate priestess of a temple to Hercules at Thespia. This story is of particular significance to me because all these sons came with me to Sardinia many years later, have settled here and are such loyal friends, as you can imagine!

'So Hercules stayed with King Thespius for some time, discussing what he should do. Thespius advised him to go to Delphi to consult the Oracle of Apollo, as the crime he had committed was too great to be remitted locally by the purification Thespius had given him. Hercules returned to Thebes and told Creon and Megara he was going to Delphi. They insisted that he took an armed escort. There was a suggestion that I should go with him, as I was the living witness of what had happened. I was too scared of him at that time to accept – and I am sure no one could blame me for that! I now wish that I had gone. It would have been a wonderful opportunity for me, but I did not at the time realise the significance.

'All that most people heard about the visit was that the Pythoness, as the priestess spokeswoman at the Oracle is still called, announced through the interpreter priest that, to expiate his crime, he would have to serve his cousin, Eurystheus, High King, then based at Tiryns, for twelve years and carry out whatever tasks he was given. According to the stories circulating at the time, Hercules was devastated at having to serve a person he considered a usurper, a cheat and a weakling. This was certainly the impression they both gave when in public – mutual loathing – but, in my later private conversations with him, and there were many over the next twelve years, he originally expressed some admiration for his cousin and appreciated the subtlety of his support. Unfortunately, this relationship began to deteriorate later as Hercules' extraordinary strength and charisma became apparent and aroused Eurystheus' jealousy.

'Now I do not know precisely what the Pythoness said, although I don't think that is the most important thing. He told me later that he had many conversations with the priests of Apollo, including some in private with the Chief Priest, who told Hercules that he had been selected as the man most likely to change the world and establish the new order. His task was to extinguish, or at least undermine, the most extreme female cults and establish male cults in their place – his own and that of Apollo. Hercules already knew he had a large following, amongst men as well as women and, clearly, those behind Apollo had marked out Hercules as the man who could succeed where others had failed. As I shall tell you, they were right!'

By this time, evening was upon us. We accordingly adjourned for a light meal and a relaxed talk about the progress of the Sardinian economy and how the Nuraghic peoples, the original inhabitants of the island, were reacting to his recent invasion. Their building skills and knowledge of finding, extracting and working stone had been vital in developing the port of Olbia and had complemented Iolaus' supporters' skills in agriculture to mutual benefit and appreciation. A sound augury for the future of this community, we both thought.

The First Three Labours of Hercules

We continued talking through the meal. By this time, I could see that Iolaus was keen to tell of his experiences working with his uncle, Hercules, but there were earlier episodes in Hercules' life about which I wished to hear.

'I can see that you want to tell me about the Labours,' I said, 'but, before you recall your exploits with Hercules, I wonder if you can tell me about the stories of Hercules being one of the Argonauts and what happened at Troy?'

'Yes,' Iolaus admitted, 'there were some other stories about Hercules and what he is supposed to have done before I was born or when I was very young. He did tell me a little about these himself during the time we were together. He was actually a very modest man and I am not sure whether his understated versions were any more accurate than the exaggerated versions one hears now. I suspect the truth lies somewhere in between. If you don't mind, I will tell you now my first-hand experiences – which relate almost exclusively to the Labours – and perhaps talk about his other exploits, and what I know about them, at a later date.'

I agreed.

'Thank you,' he said. 'The first I knew about the tasks Hercules had been set by his cousin, Eurystheus, was when my father called me into his chamber. We were living with my grandfather, Amphitryon, at Thebes at the time. When I answered my father's summons, I found Hercules already in the room, talking earnestly to my father. They broke off their conversation as soon as I entered the room and Hercules immediately stood up and walked over to greet me with a handshake and a warm embrace – not too warm, fortunately! I am afraid that I was a little reticent, as the last time I had seen him he was killing my brothers and cousins during his drugged rage.

' "Come and sit down, both of you," said my father. "We have much to talk about. My brother has just returned from Mycenae, where he has spoken to High King Eurystheus. He has given Hercules some tasks to complete in order to atone for his crimes. Hercules has asked for my help and, if you agree, would like you to accompany him as his charioteer."

'At first I was very reluctant to get involved closely with my uncle, but I was curious, young and considered myself a very competent charioteer. As you know, flattery often wins when other argument fails. It did not take them long to talk me into accepting the offer. What I didn't tell you earlier was that Hercules' name was originally Alcaeus. At least, that was the name by which I first knew him. It was only during this discussion with my father that I learnt that my uncle's name was now Hercules. So, with the impudence of youth, I asked why he had changed his name. Hercules told me that, when he went to Delphi to consult the Oracle of Phoebus Apollo, he was told to adopt this new name, as part of the penance. I am sure this is true. However, the reason given for this change was only half the truth. I am not sure that my father actually knew the whole truth – I never asked him – but he never told me. I found out for myself later, as you will hear.

'Although I was young and eager, I was not completely foolish. I asked what being his charioteer entailed, how long would I be in his service and how dangerous were the duties. My uncle made it clear that he had ten Labours to complete, which he expected would take several years, maybe as long eight years – the period Apollo himself had spent in atonement for the killing of the sacred python at Delphi – and possibly longer. He added that he would ensure that I would not come to any harm as he would tackle the tasks on his own, or with help from trained soldiers. The terms of his slavery – for that is what it was, in reality – were that he must perform these tasks on his own. This had an unexpected consequence as, because of the help he had from me on one occasion, and of a claimed irregularity on another, two Labours were disregarded and the original ten Labours became twelve. But I am anticipating.

'My father pressed me to accept and promised that the experience would be good for me. He also said that this was how Hercules hoped to make up to me for the terrible things he had done to our family. As my father had clearly forgiven him, and expected me to do the same, how could I refuse?

'So I accepted. My uncle and I then made our preparations for the First Labour, which was to kill the Lion of Nemaea. Now this was very close to home for High King Eurystheus because Nemaea was only some twenty miles from Mycenae and about thirty from Tiryns and Argos, the principal parts of his Kingdom. This Lion was supposed to be ravaging all the neighbouring countryside. I later discovered that, although an animal of some ferocity did exist, and Hercules killed it, there was a savage cult of Selene, the moon goddess, in the area who, dressed up to look like lions, would go out at night preying on and killing the flocks of men who would not acknowledge the superiority of their goddess. Sometimes men who opposed them were also killed. Before setting out to find the Lion, we stayed overnight with a shepherd who himself claimed that his son had been killed by the Lion. We learnt later that the son had been well known as an opponent of the Cult of Selene. In deference to Hercules, the shepherd offered to sacrifice a ram to Hera – the name "Hercules" means "The Glory of Hera" – but Hercules advised him to wait until after he had fought with the Lion. If the Lion was killed and Hercules returned the sacrifice was to be made to him; if he failed to return after thirty days the sacrifice was to be made to Zeus.

'I was not allowed by Hercules to see what happened. He went into the hills with a small force of soldiers to find the Lion's lair. The whole area had been depopulated, allegedly by the activities of the Lion, and there was nobody who could tell us where to find it. So I was told to wait with the other soldiers. We waited a long time and I grew more and more anxious. At last, after twenty-nine days, the party emerged with Hercules carrying the carcass of a dead lion on his shoulders. The story I was told was that Hercules had strangled the Lion with his bare hands. I think this was probably true. He was certainly courageous enough to attempt it and strong enough to succeed. I asked him afterwards to explain why some of the soldiers' swords were bloody and why he had not sanctioned the sacrifice to Hera – after whom he was now named. He explained the first by saying that some "wild women" had attacked the soldiers whilst he had been wrestling with the Lion. I later realised that his mission was to destroy the Cult and their mascot, which he did. He did not answer the second question at the time. I had to find out the answer to that question later.

'The next task was to return to the shepherd, where we made a sacrifice to Zeus. Hercules' previous suggestion that a sacrifice should be made to him if he returned successful appeared to be a joke. We then took the Lion's body to Mycenae. And so we returned to Mycenae to report to High King Eurystheus that the First Labour had been accomplished. The current story is that the King was terrified at the sight of Hercules wearing the lion pelt over his shoulders with the gaping upper jaw framing his head. I have seen many statues of Hercules depicting him thus. The truth is that Hercules did this as a joke and Eurystheus pretended to be frightened, also as part of the joke. When, soon after this incident, stories began to circulate about Eurystheus' fear and his exploitation of the great Hercules, it was decided to encourage this, as it provided an excellent cover for what they were actually doing. Eurystheus produced a brilliant idea to reinforce this public perception. He ordered a large vessel of bronze to be made so that he could hide in it when Hercules came back from his Labours with his trophies, sometimes bringing back live wild animals. In fact, this was originally all play-acting to conceal their common purpose, which, of course, was to destroy the main female cults in the Peloponnese and elsewhere, which were the major supporters of the matriarchal order.' He paused.

'Was that why Apollo changed your uncle's name to Hercules – to confuse people into thinking he was on the side of the female goddesses and the matriarchal system?' I enquired.

'Yes,' replied Iolaus. 'That was all part of the deception. Of course, Eurystheus was also involved right from the beginning. He was receiving his instructions on the Labours to allocate to Hercules direct from Delphi. As you will see, some of the Labours were clearly anti-female cult; for others the true target was more obscure. However, with a little help from Hercules, both during and after our exploits, I was able to make sense of most of it and will include this in my story.

'Well,' he continued, 'after our initially friendly interview with the High King, Hercules was given his next task: to "kill" the Lernean Hydra. Now, the Hydra was not an animal at all, as even now some storytellers maintain. It was a killer all right, but, as its name implies, it was a waterborne killer. The truth of the matter was that Lerna is a country not far from Argos, and by the coast there was a lake and a grove of trees sacred to a Cult of Demeter, the goddess of corn and harvests. The same Cult had been ejected from Delphi by Apollo's Cult. This local Cult of Demeter was a particularly vicious one. Assisted by the priestesses, the local women would murder their husbands and throw their severed heads into the lake. As you can imagine, there had been several attempts to disband this Cult, but, until Hercules came, they had been unsuccessful.

'Part of the legend was that the Hydra had many heads. The story was told that for every head that was cut off several new ones would appear. There were two versions of how many heads the Hydra had. One said that it had seven, and the other that it had fifty. In fact, the first related to the number of streams that issued out of the lake and the second to the number of priestesses at the Shrine of Demeter. Now, apart from the practices of the local wives, the streams also were killers because they frequently, and unexpectedly, changed their courses. When they did, a huge volume of water would be released and it would sweep away everything in its path. As the plain was very fertile, it was intensively farmed and, as these floods generally occurred when the ground was being prepared for planting crops, there would frequently be people working in the fields when the torrent rushed through. Many men were regularly drowned, and the Cult encouraged the men to think that this was part of the goddess' judgment on them, although in fact it had a natural cause.

'As Hercules and I discovered, the main problem was that the ground between the lake and the underground channels from the lake to the streams' outlets was unstable. At that time, there were frequent ground tremors, which, of course, added to the mystery of the place. My understanding is that these earth movements occur in many places and I do not accept that there is not a natural reason for them. I do not know what that is, but I am sure that they do not occur to order, as some priests would have people believe.

'Hercules and our party managed to trace the general course of the underground streams from the lake to the outlets, but, because of the rough nature of the ground and the thick vegetation, we were unable to trace them accurately. So Hercules ordered me to set fire to the undergrowth in carefully limited areas, so that the land could be cleared and we would be able to work safely in this inhospitable terrain. Now we knew that our presence would have been reported to the Cult priestesses, and, as part of the Cult worship related to the worship of the spring that fed the lake at the other end, and the sudden death from the changes in volume and direction of the outflow was all part of the Cult's hold on the local people, we guessed that we would not be allowed to interfere with the outlet streams without opposition. We had deliberately not made any contact with them before we started work as we wished to put them at a disadvantage.

'Still, we were not prepared for the ferocity of their reaction. Just as I was setting up the first fire, a swarm of priestesses in long white flowing robes, wielding swords and spears, came charging at us from two sides. We had no choice but to stand and fight. Fortunately, we had Hercules on our side and he was magnificent. I had been warned to keep my arms and shield with me when I went to start the fire, so I was able to defend myself and join Hercules and the few soldiers we had brought with us and fight back to back against the priestesses. It was over remarkably quickly. All the priestesses who attacked us were killed and we had no fatal casualties – a few had minor scratches. Hercules was unscathed. We counted the bodies. There were forty-six. So Hercules set off with a few soldiers to the Sanctuary to find the four missing priestesses and sack the Sanctuary whilst I, guarded by the rest of the soldiers, carried on with my interrupted preparations.

'Hercules and the party soon came back, accompanied by some of the male villagers, delighted to be released from the tyranny of the Cult. They quickly armed themselves with the dead priestesses' swords, spears and shields and some of our soldiers were greatly amused to be asked to give instruction in their use to the villagers who, under the Cult regime, had not been allowed to possess arms or even learn how to use them.

Meanwhile, I continued with my preparations and lit the first fire. This was very successful and cleared the ground around what we thought was the main outlet. Whilst the fire subsided and the ground cooled, I lit two more fires, which were equally successful. By this time some of the villagers had tired of practising their swordplay and came across to where Hercules and I were working offering to help. We accepted.

'In fact, they did know more than we had credited them with. We had thought the mystery of the Cult had dulled the local villagers' interest in the problem of the flooding, but they were able to show us where the streams had previously run, tell us the time of the year when the changes had occurred and how long before the changes each stream had dried up. It became clear to us that the drying process triggered the change: the longer the dry period, the greater the chance of a change and the fiercer the new outflow. The solution was to reduce the number of outlets and to clear surface channels from the lake to the sea so that the water would not need to find a subterranean route. This we did, reducing the number of outlets to three at points convenient to the farmers and filling in the old subterranean channels, where we could find them, as best we could with soil and rocks.

'I later heard from Hercules that his party had found the missing priestesses, who had been as ferocious as their sisters and had been duly despatched by Hercules. The Sanctuary had been completely destroyed and set on fire. Indeed, we could see the smoke rising in the air from it when clearing the routes for the new streams. This work took several days. At last, we could relax and watch the water running through the new channels we had cut. The villagers themselves then made new conduits from the new channels to lead the water to their fields. The level of the lake at the entrance to the new streams remained much the same and the streams down the new channels, after the initial burst, settled down to a steady flow. Those villagers whose fields were furthest from the new streams complained that they were not getting a fair share of the water – with some justification because a few had been close to one of the original seven streams. It was pointed out to them that they would have to get together and agree how to manage their new water supply, as it would vary with the weather and the streams now flowed down different channels. A system of linked conduits with sluices was suggested so that parts could be closed off at preselected times and the water diverted to other parts, ensuring a fairer distribution overall. At least, Hercules pointed out to them, they could now be reasonably sure that the water would continue to flow down the new channels whilst, before, they could not guarantee how long the water would flow in any particular direction or how long there would be no water at all from one stream or another. Also, now that the channels were above ground, they could see when they were running dry and, if necessary, make the new channels deeper or put some sort of control at the entry points from the lake so that the water would flow down the channels at different lake levels. They had not thought of that. And so we left them to manage their lives in a new environment. We heard from one or two of the men that their wives had been very subdued after our intervention! I have returned twice since our original visit and the land is better managed and more productive and the women have accepted a more balanced regime. Indeed, by common agreement, they have erected a Temple to Hercules and men and women alike consider him their champion. An excellent result.

'And so we returned to Mycenae. Eurystheus had heard of our exploits from others by the time we returned. His welcome was restrained, if not slightly hostile. It was certainly different from his original warm welcome. I realised later why. He was jealous of Hercules' success and beginning to see him as a rival who would, with popular support, throw him off the throne and take it for himself. This was a pity because Hercules would not have done that, but, by becoming increasingly unpleasant to Hercules he alienated him and his followers and friends. This ultimately led to the outcome he most feared.

'The tone of the interview was quickly set when Eurystheus announced that, because I had helped Hercules by setting the fires, he had not completed the task by himself, as required under the terms of the contract, and so it would not count as one of the ten tasks. Hercules simply shrugged his shoulders at this and asked what the next task was to be.

'The Third Labour was to capture the Ceryneian Hind and

bring her alive from Oenoe to Mycenae. Now I knew that this Hind was sacred to Artemis, Apollo's twin. She also represented the domination of the female sex and, again, the rituals associated with her worship at Oenoe had become more and more extreme over the years. Apollo's priests at Delphi had decided it was time to close it down.

'This was a much more difficult task, as Oenoe was some distance away to the north, across the Isthmus of Corinth, and this time he had to bring back the animal alive. In view of the decision of Eurystheus on the validity of the previous task, we agreed to be much more discreet on this occasion. We clarified with the High King that Hercules could have support from others in defending himself against attack from robbers, for example, and even in being transported to where the task was to be carried out, but he was not to have any assistance in carrying out the task whatsoever, or it would be declared invalid. Hercules' plan was to chase the Hind until it stopped running, out of exhaustion, and he did not need my assistance in this. So, I drove him in the chariot to the foot of the Geranian Mountains in the Kingdom of Corinth and left him there to return to Thebes to await his call.

'It was a long time coming. I knew the Hind was a strong animal and would test even Hercules' stamina and strength, but over a year had passed before I had a message from him to say that he had finally captured the Hind and was on his way to Mycenae and that I was to meet him there in a month's time. When I arrived with the chariot, Hercules was already there and had delivered his charge. Eurystheus really didn't know what to do with the Hind. It was a magnificent animal, but scarcely domesticated. After a few days' thought – time for messages to pass between Mycenae and Delphi, I guessed – he ordered Hercules to take the Hind away and release it back to the wild. This we did and then returned to receive the orders for the Fourth Labour.

'During our ride out to release the Hind, I asked Hercules what had happened.

' "Well," Hercules replied, "I first had to find the Hind. This did not prove to be as difficult as I had thought. Many knew why I was there and were so sure that I would fail that they had no hesitation in telling me where the Hind's favourite grazing places were. On my arrival at the third one, there she was – a truly magnificent beast, as you can see for yourself. As soon as I approached with my net, she was off – streaking away to the north – and I followed. At the beginning, I tried all sorts of tricks to catch her: creeping up on her from downwind with my net attached to a spear ready to throw it over her; trying to catch her when she had settled down to rest at night. But every time she jumped up and ran away just as I was about to catch her. In the end, we made a sort of truce. We were well matched: I could run as fast and for as long as she could. Then we both tired. I respected her need to eat and rest and she respected mine. Only once did she move away when I was asleep and I soon found her again. I must confess – but don't tell Eurystheus! – local people did occasionally help me by watching her while I slept and waking me when she decided to move on. So I was not entirely on my own. Eventually, after what must have been a year, she suddenly decided she had had enough and I managed to fire an arrow between her legs with rope attached which tripped her and I was then able to tie her legs together and lift her, trussed, on to my shoulders and bring her back to Mycenae."

' "What about the Cult?" I asked him.

' "Yes," Hercules replied. "I had forgotten about them, and was stupid enough to carry the bound Hind along the road close to the Cult's temple. Suddenly I was surrounded by an angry mob of men and women demanding that I release the Hind immediately. Unfortunately I was on my own and quite tired and did not want to become involved in a fight. So I reasoned with them, explaining that I had to do this task, that I had not hurt the Hind and did not intend to and would ask that she be released when I presented her to the High King. Some, who I guessed had heard what had happened at Nemaea and Lerna, were keen to despatch me directly but others were more cautious, arguing that whilst they might manage to overpower me eventually, I would take many of them with me and that if I had wanted to destroy their temple, I would have done so already. In addition, the Hind could be killed in the fight and what was the purpose of that? Finally, if I escaped, I would surely return and destroy them all –

which was true. Why not trust me to do as I promised: the Hind would return and they would not have angered my gods by interfering with my mission. I could not have put it better myself! And so they let me go, and you are aware of the rest of the story."

' "Not quite," I said. "I thought your main task was to destroy these female cults. So why are you not destroying this one also?"

' "A good question," Hercules replied. "I wondered about this myself. But my instructions were clear. I was only to capture the sacred Hind, not to kill it. I interpreted this to mean that Apollo only wished to demonstrate his superiority existed, not to enforce it on this occasion. The High King took the same view and, indeed, the response from Delphi about the release of the Hind confirmed that I was not to go back to Oenoe – which I took to mean that he did not want that cult destroyed. I know not why. As I said earlier, men and women appeared to support it so perhaps it is a unifying cult, not a divisive one."

'So,' concluded Iolaus to me, 'you now know as much as I about this strange episode. But I have had enough storytelling for one day so, if you don't mind, I would like to stop now.'

I agreed. It had been a fascinating way to spend an afternoon and most of the evening and he had left me with much to think about. Iolaus and I talked about local matters for a little while and then Iolaus returned to Hercules.

'Before you go, we must agree another day for us to meet so that I can finish my part of his story. But, I have been thinking. You really ought to go to Athens to see my grandmother, Alcmena. She can tell you about Hercules' early life and, of course, if Theseus is still at Athens – but I am a little doubtful – he has a particular reason for being grateful to Hercules, as well as being close to the Argonauts, although he did not go on that expedition himself, whereas Hercules did – at least for part of it. It is time I visited my grandmother and I would be very happy if you would come with me. I am sure that she would be very pleased to talk to you about old times and I am also sure that you would find a market for some of your jewellery. If you agree, I will send a message to her with the next ship and see what she says.'

I was very happy to agree to his suggestion. We arranged to

meet a week later to continue the story. I calculated it would be at least a month before we would receive an answer from Athens, which would give me time to design and make some special items to sell to the ladies of the Athenian court. And so we parted.

The Fourth Labour: The Capture of the Erymanthean Boar

A few days after this, I received a message from Iolaus asking that I come to his house a little later than had been arranged. Iolaus explained that he had to attend an important meeting earlier in the day, away from Olbia, and he wanted to be sure that he had returned home well before I arrived. In compensation, he offered a meal and an uninterrupted session to cover the rest of Hercules' Labours. As I had already arranged to leave the afternoon and evening of that day free, and had planned little of importance for the following day, I was pleased with his offer and replied immediately with my grateful acceptance.

At the appointed hour, I presented myself at Iolaus' house to be warmly welcomed by him personally. After enquiring after my day and saying a little about his, he took me in to the same room at the rear of the house we had used before at our previous discussions. This time, although it was only late afternoon, there was a table in one corner of the room laid up for a meal for two, Iolaus explained.

'I thought that we would break for a meal when it suited us. The food will be ready in an hour or two, but I did not want the staff busying about, laying the table whilst we were talking. And, some of what I shall say I would prefer that they did not overhear. When the food is ready, Auturgus will come and tell me and then we can call for it when we wish to stop. We can, of course, continue with the story over the meal. Indeed, if we are to cover all the rest of Hercules' Labours before the end of the night, we may need to continue over the meal. As I will be doing most of the talking, I will not expect to be able to eat much,' he added, smiling, 'but, don't worry, I have had a good meal already today and it won't do me any harm to go a little short this evening!'

'I have no doubt that I will want to ask you many questions

about what you are going to tell me,' I responded, 'so, whilst I thank you for putting my mind at rest in advance, I feel reasonably confident that you will be able to eat something tonight!'

'Thank you for that,' he rejoined. 'Now, when we broke last time, I had just finished the strange story of the Ceryneian Hind. The next Labour, as I expect you know, was to capture the Erymanthean Boar.'

I nodded.

Continuing, Iolaus said, 'Although Hercules told me a little about the reasoning behind the need to capture this dangerous animal before we went in search of the Boar, and I questioned him about it on a number of later occasions, I must confess that I do not fully understand what this was all about, and I suspect that neither Hercules nor Eurystheus knew the full story. Some years later I heard a rumour that the Boar was involved in inflicting some terrible injury to a son of Apollo, but when I asked a priest of Apollo if that was true he denied it, although his face indicated that there was a connection somewhere. Still, as I said when we started, I can only tell you what I know.

'Now the Boar was to be found up on the slopes of Mount Erymanthus near Psophis in the north-west corner of Arcadia in the Peloponnese. When Hercules and I left Argos in our chariot, it was halfway through one of the coldest winters I can remember in the Peloponnese. The snow, having been driven off the slopes of the mountain by the high winds, had created dangerously deep drifts in the valleys. It soon became clear that we were not going to be able to make any progress in a horse-drawn chariot and would have to find another method of transport. Mounted or walking, we quickly sank into deep snow drifts, some deeper than we were tall. It was a frightening experience for me, but, of course, Hercules, who loved a challenge, revelled in it. But even he realised that we would both tire quickly in this environment and could easily freeze to death if we could not reach shelter by every nightfall.

'However, before we reached the mountain we were attacked by a vicious highway robber, called Saurus. His favourite trick was to tie his captive's feet to one bended tree and his arms to another and then cut the ropes securing the trees, so that the captive's body was torn apart by the force of the trees returning to the upright position. Not a fate I coveted, I can tell you, so I was happy to hide behind Hercules, who soon despatched this odious character. Nevertheless, we were a little shaken by this incident and decided to visit an old friend of Hercules, the centaur, Pholus. Despite what you may have heard, centaurs are normal men, but, when they go into battle they wear baggy leggings and a towering helmet, which looks like a horse's head. They are also very fierce fighters and, as you will hear, are easily aroused. Their reputation for drunkenness is well known. Together, these characteristics have been amalgamated to produce some ridiculous stories about them.

'It soon became clear that it was a big mistake to make this visit. Hercules, as you may know, was no mean drinker himself and, as we sat down to eat the meal Pholus had prepared for us, Hercules asked where the wine was. Pholus started to say that he didn't have any wine of his own – only what belonged to the whole colony of centaurs. Hercules rather rudely reminded him that, many years ago, some very special wine had been given to them at a Festival of Dionysus "for the entertainment of a great warrior". Hercules, not unreasonably, claimed that his existing achievements confirmed he was that warrior and required a reluctant Pholus to find and open the wine jar. The commotion aroused the others and, when they smelt the wine, they wanted to join the party. Unfortunately, instead of asking nicely, they arrived in full war gear and with any weapon they could lay their hands on. I was terrified, and joined Pholus in a discreet hiding place until it was all over. Hercules told me afterwards what had happened. Apparently, he was gaining the upper hand against this rough band when it started to rain heavily. This both made it difficult for Hercules to stand up and also allowed the string on his bow to stretch, thus making his arrows ineffective. But his superior strength enabled him to overcome the onslaught and those centaurs he did not kill fled the field and are probably still running.'

'That was a good outcome, then,' I interjected.

'Well, no, it wasn't in the end,' responded Iolaus. 'Hercules' old tutor, Cheiron, took no part in the fight, but one of Hercules' poisoned arrows flashed right through the arm of one of the belligerents and, sadly, pierced Cheiron's thigh, causing him considerable pain, despite the application of an antidote that Hercules had with him and that he gave him after withdrawing the arrow from his friend's body. But the poison was so powerful, it could not prevent Cheiron's death, which caused much sorrow to Hercules.

'In the meantime, unknown to us, a further tragedy awaited. We had left Pholus behind when we went to tend Cheiron and he decided that, without waiting for our return, he would bury those of his companions who had lost their lives fighting Hercules. When we returned to the battlefield, we saw Pholus lying on the ground in his death agony. Just before he died, he managed to tell us what had happened. He had pulled a poisoned arrow out of the dead body of one of the centaurs before burying him, and was puzzled why, as the arrow had only pierced his arm, it had killed the centaur. As he was musing on the reason, the arrow slipped from his grasp and the point buried itself in his foot, thus poisoning him. He died within minutes of our return.

'Hercules was too distraught at these disasters to continue the hunt for the Boar – at least for a while. We retired to a settlement at the foot of the nearby range of mountains and buried Cheiron and Pholus in a moving ceremony that brought tears to my eyes. A solemn sacrifice to Apollo followed. As I was to discover over the ensuing years, the unjust actions of other people against Hercules frequently resulted in tragedy – to those who instigated the actions and, too often, to Hercules' friends who found themselves unwittingly caught up in the events.

'After this experience, Hercules decided – with my full agreement – to proceed on his own to track and capture the Boar. He told me later that he had trapped it in a long valley and had chased it into a deep snow drift, where the snow had helped him to overpower and tie up the animal. He then brought the Boar back to where I was waiting for him.

'The remainder of this episode is quickly told. The Boar was delivered alive to Eurystheus' palace, as directed but, without waiting for Eurystheus to climb out of his hiding place in the bronze vessel, Hercules, having heard that the famous Argonaut expedition was about to leave, decided to go and join them.

'Now, all the strongest and best went on this expedition – no place for me! So, with Hercules' blessing, I went home to Thebes for a rest. Hercules promised to tell me later about his exploits, which he did, and I was to await his call when he resumed his tasks for Eurystheus. In the meantime, I puzzled over the meaning of the last task he had performed, intending to ask for his explanation when he returned. The position was made more complex when the Boar, after Hercules had left, was killed. My understanding was that, like the Hind, the Boar was only to be caught, not killed. Perhaps, there had been new instructions from Delphi. I resolved to find out.'

The Argonauts

'At this point,' said Iolaus, 'I suggest that, to keep our chronology, I'll relate what Hercules told me about his participation on the Argonauts' expedition. It has some relevance to the rest of the story about the Labours and you may know that Iphitus, the brother of High King Eurystheus, was a member of the expeditionary force.'

'No,' I replied, 'I had not realised. How very interesting.'

'Yes,' responded Iolaus. 'I thought so too, particularly as Hercules had not mentioned it to me when he went off to join the expedition. But I am certain he knew the names of every single member on board. After all, it was a very dangerous mission and you needed to have absolute trust that everyone would be looking out for you if the going became difficult, which, of course, it did.'

'I am not very clear on the reasons for the expedition. Could you please perhaps fill in some of that detail before you tell me Hercules' part in the story?' I asked.

'Certainly,' responded Iolaus. 'Where do I start? Like a number of old stories, its origins lie in a failed marriage and sibling rivalry. Athamas, King of Thebes, married Ino, the daughter of Cadmus. Now Cadmus was the original founder of Thebes, then called Cadmea, although it was only a small citadel at that time. Thebes today is much enlarged from Cadmus' original. Anyway, Athamas and Ino at this time had been married for only a short while, and had not been blessed with children. Possibly fearing for his own future under the matriarchal system that operated at that time in Thebes, Athamas decided to divorce Ino and marry a rather strange lady called Nephele. They had two children, a son, Phryxus, and a daughter, Helle.

'Shortly after the birth of Helle, Nephele began to have recurrent fits of madness and Athamas soon tired of this, divorced her and remarried Ino, by whom he quickly had two sons,

Learchus and Melicerta. But this, of course, was considered too late for Ino's children to inherit. Nephele's children, being born first, had a prior claim to the throne of Thebes. Ino was furious at her children, the grandchildren of the famous Cadmus, being deprived of what she considered to be their birthright, and plotted the downfall of Phryxus and Helle. Her opportunity soon came. There was an early spring drought and the crops began to fail. Prayers were said and sacrifices made, but there was still no rain. Ino blamed this pestilence on Athamas and shamed him into consulting the Oracle of Apollo at Delphi.

'Now Ino's father, Cadmus, had brought the priests of Apollo to Delphi some years before, probably from Delos, although others claim they came by sea direct from Crete. Whatever the truth of the matter, Ino had strong, and secret, connections with the priests at Delphi, and so she was able to have a very considerable influence on the response given to Athamas' enquiry of the Oracle. The Oracle pronounced, in very clear terms, that the cause of the pestilence was the continuing existence of Phryxus and Helle, and the only way to get remission was to kill the two children by sacrificing them to appease the gods by bricking them up in a vault with enough food and water for a few days, so that they would die of starvation and lack of water. A terrible death, but a way often used in those times so as to avoid the accusation of murder.

'But Ino's plot had been uncovered by Phryxus. Presumably a servant warned him what his stepmother was doing. So, pausing only to gather up his sister, Helle, he fled to the court of Aeetes, King of Colchis, to whom he was closely related. To cover up the source of the warning, a story of divine intervention was invented and the story included Phryxus' and Helle's flight on the back of a winged golden ram, the fleece of which was preserved under guard in a sacred area near the palace of King Aeetes. Colchis, as I am sure you know, is a country on the far-eastern coast of the Black Sea – what we called the Blessed Sea – bounded on the north by the Caucasus mountains. A very long way from here in Sardinia and a difficult journey even from Thebes. Indeed, Helle died on the way there, probably drowning accidentally by falling into the sea from the ship they travelled on. Tradition holds that she met her death near the entrance to the narrow waterway giving access to the Black Sea. This is now called, in her memory, the Hellespont – the "Sea of Helle". Phryxus paused there, at a place called Pontos, and, having recovered his drowned sister's dead body from the sea, buried her there with an appropriate ceremony, vowing to make a sacrifice to the gods for her safe passage to the underworld when he arrived at Colchis.'

'So Phryxus sacrificed a ram for his sister on arrival at Colchis?' I interjected.

'That is right,' said Iolaus. 'When Aeetes heard that Helle had drowned on the way to Colchis, he immediately offered Phryxus whatever animal he wanted. A ram was chosen because it is sacred to Zeus and also because Phryxus' companions on the ship had suggested there should be a "cover story" for the miraculous flight to safety. One of the crew also knew that it was the practice in the Colchis area to dip the woolly fleeces of sheep in the local streams to clean them after they had been stripped. He also knew that in certain streams this was a way of harvesting small gold pellets being washed down by the stream as the pellets stuck to the wool of the fleece.

'Now, Helle had beautiful golden hair, and Phryxus thought it would be an appropriate memorial to her to hang the purified ram's fleece in a well-guarded holy place, after it had been used for collecting gold in one of the nearby streams. And so this was done, and the story of the Golden Fleece became a legend.'

'And the Argonauts knew nothing of this?' I asked.

'I don't think so,' responded Iolaus. 'Not at first, anyway, but I am not so sure whether Hercules knew. I think he certainly knew later, but probably not when he agreed to join the expedition. But now I need to tell you why the expedition was mounted.

'Once again, the root of the story is a wrong – or, rather, several wrongs. Although he had at first been welcomed by King Aeetes, Phryxus soon managed to upset him by becoming more popular with the King's subjects than the King himself. And so, Aeetes decided to get rid of him. He had him found guilty on a trumped-up charge of sedition and killed.

'As was the custom then, those killed for treason were left unburied, which meant that his soul could not pass to the underworld. This series of events was well known back in mainland Greece, but nobody was prepared to take the risk of going all that way to make amends, particularly as they knew that they would not be welcome. So, several years went by.

'Now some years before Phryxus arrived at Colchis, a man called Pelias seized the throne of Iolchos, a city state in eastern Greece in Magnesia near Mount Pelion, from his half-brother and the rightful heir, Aeson. Pelias was warned by oracles that he would be killed by a descendant of Aeolus, Aeson's father. So, when he heard that Aeson's wife was expecting a baby, he made arrangements to kill it, should it be a son. A son was born, and called Diomedes, but his mother knew of Pelias' intentions and went into mourning immediately after the birth of her son, pretending that he had died in childbirth. As soon as Pelias' interest waned, she had her baby son smuggled out of the palace to safety in the country and he grew up a stout warrior and handsome young man. He did not know his real identity, believing he was the son of the herdsman at whose humble home he had been raised. But, as he grew towards adulthood, he realised that he did not belong where he was. So he was advised to consult the oracle at Delphi, whose intelligence network had already told them who he really was.

'The Oracle told him to go to Iolchos, his native country, covered with a leopard skin and dressed in the clothing normally worn by a native of Magnesia. On his journey, he was delayed as he had to cross a major river in spate, following an inundation. In the process of crossing the river, with, some say, divine assistance, he lost a sandal and was unable to replace it before reaching Iolchos. Now Pelias had been told in another oracular revelation that he must beware of a man arriving at Iolchos with one foot shod and the other foot bare. Diomedes was tall and handsome and his presence caused quite a stir in the marketplace. Pelias soon heard about this handsome stranger's arrival in his kingdom and went down to the market place to see him. When he saw that he matched the description of the stranger to beware of, Pelias was terrified and invited him into the palace. When the stranger revealed himself as Diomedes, also known as Jason, and the son of Aeson, and demanded the throne as his father was now dead,

Pelias was even more terrified. Pelias was in a difficulty: he knew that Jason had made a very good impression on the people and that he himself was a usurper, but he did not want to give up the kingship tamely to this young upstart. So he asked Jason what he would do in the same situation. Jason responded, as he had obviously been prompted to do, that he would set the young man claiming the throne the task of going to Colchis, avenging Phryxus' judicial murder and bring back his soul and the Golden Fleece. A relieved Pelias promptly agreed to this and Jason left the palace to raise the crew he needed to carry out the tasks he had set himself.

'As I told you earlier,' continued Iolaus, 'Hercules had released me from my service to him for the duration of the expedition of the *Argo* to Colchis. He did not, however, go unaccompanied, but recruited, from a small country called Dryopis in Thessaly, as his squire a young man called Hylas. As you will hear, the gods were on my side when that decision was taken!

'Anyway, fifty men were eventually chosen to man the *Argo*, every one of whom was expected to man an oar with a colleague. The *Argo* was powered by twenty-four oars and, of course, a sail. Two crew acted as helmsman and lookout, but also took turns at the oars. A man called Argus was responsible for the design and building of the ship and he accompanied the expedition as an oarsman. Obviously, the building of the *Argo* – from timber felled on Mount Pelion – gathering the crew and provisioning the ship took time. It was well over a year before all was ready and it was at this time that Hercules appeared and was immediately invited to take charge of the expedition. He was very flattered and pleased to be asked but, although he knew that Jason was relatively inexperienced, he recognised that Jason should be in charge, so he declined the honour but agreed to join the crew with, I have said, his new squire, Hylas.

'And so, after making a sacrifice to Apollo at the dockside for fair winds and weather on their hazardous journey, they set sail. Their first landfall was at Lemnos, a strange choice as there had been rumours of serious trouble on the island, but it was thought to be the only friendly place near the entrance to the Hellespont, where the *Argo* could take on fresh water and food. The Trojans dominated the communities on either side of the entrance to the Hellespont and the nearby coastline. The Trojans had already refused a request from Jason to be granted safe passage, so it had been decided to land first at Lemnos to find out how difficult it would be to slip past into the Hellespont unnoticed. As the Lemnians were believed to be friendly, the Argonauts expected some help and advice, bearing in mind the nature of their quest.

'Much was their surprise when, as they drove the *Argo* towards the beach, a heavily armoured group appeared on the beach to oppose their landing. Echion, one of the crew with diplomatic experience, suggested the *Argo* remain off-shore whilst he waded through the sea to explain to the hostile crowd that the Argonauts' purpose was peaceful and they merely wanted to purchase food, water and information. He was allowed ashore to talk to their leader who, after a long conversation with him, asked him to return to the *Argo* and for the *Argo* to remain off-shore until a Council meeting had been held to discuss whether or not they should be allowed to land.

'So Echion returned with the message, together with the astonishing news that the armed crowd appeared to comprise women only! Not a man had he seen and he had considered it unwise to ask where the men were. A crew member then recalled he had heard a rumour about a quarrel between the men and women on the island, which had resulted in most, if not all, of the men leaving to go to mainland Thrace. However, another crew member, who had relatives in Thrace, said that the Lemnian men would not have been welcome in Thrace, as they frequently raided the settlements on the coast and had recently kidnapped some young girls who had not been seen since. The Argonauts apparently discovered later, but not until they had left Lemnos on the next leg of their journey, that the Lemnian men had made derogatory comments about their wives' personal hygiene and had taken Thracian girls as their bed companions instead. The Lemnian women were so outraged that, encouraged by their warrior priestesses, they had killed all the men and their Thracian concubines. Only their king, Thoas, had been spared, being smuggled out of the palace by his daughter, Hypsipyle, and put adrift on the sea in an open boat. It was Hypsipyle to whom Echion had spoken and who was the new ruler.

'The Council gave permission for the Argonauts to beach their ship and disembark, and they were allowed into the city of Myrina. It had originally been suggested by the Queen that the Argonauts should be offered food and wine, but should not be permitted to enter the city for fear that they would find out about the murders and seek revenge. But another member of the Council pointed out that, without men, their race would eventually be extinguished. Here was an admirable opportunity to mate with some of the strongest and most skilful young men in the whole of Greece and create the foundation for a new virile race! This argument won the vote, but the Argonauts were not told about this. But Hypsipyle did admit to Jason that the Lemnian men had been forced to emigrate by the women and she invited Jason to stay in Lemnos, marry her and become king. This offer Jason gracefully accepted, but said that, before he settled down with her in Lemnos, he must complete his task. However, it was not long before his companions were suborned by the overtures of the Lemnian ladies. Jason led the way and moved into the palace with the Queen. Following his example, each of his companions (apart from Hercules and a small group still aboard the *Argo* as guards) paired off and settled down with a pliant lady Lemnian. Many children were born as a result of these liaisons, including twins to Jason and Hypsipyle, called Euneus and Nebrophonus.

'Meanwhile, Hercules, on guard on the *Argo* off-shore and unaware of what was happening ashore, waited patiently for his companions to come back to the ship so that they could continue their journey. After many months without any decision to embark, he stormed into the city and found the streets deserted. So he banged on the doors of the houses with his club and demanded that his companions came back to the ship to resume the voyage. Tumbling out of bed they obeyed Hercules' call and trailed back to the *Argo*. Without further ado, the *Argo* set sail for the island of Samothrace, some thirty miles to the north, where they picked up food and water, as they had been too busy at Lemnos on other matters to remember to load up there! It was later said that had Hercules not been on the expedition and roused his companions from their beds, the *Argo* would never have left Lemnos, let alone reached Colchis.

'Whether that is true or not, they next landed at Samothrace and were very kindly treated, but without the special comforts they had enjoyed at Lemnos! Here they secured the stores they needed and made appropriate sacrifices to the gods for the success of their mission. They also learnt that the best way to get past the unfriendly Trojan outposts was to sail through at night, as the Trojans and their allies did not think it worthwhile to mount a night patrol. And so they did, gliding through the narrow entrance to the Hellespont under sail with a firm following wind just when the modest tide was enough to neutralise the flow of water from the Black Sea. Arriving in the Sea of Marmara, they were clear of the Trojan influence and rowed heartily through the dawn to the peninsula of Cyzicus, where the King of the same name gave them a warm welcome. As it happened, the King had recently married and the Argonauts were invited to join the wedding feast. Despite all the time lost in Lemnos, they accepted the King's invitation and were enjoying the hospitality when a messenger arrived from the harbour to say that the guards on the *Argo* were being ferociously attacked by armed bandits and, if they wanted to save the ship and their companions who were guarding the ship, they had best attend the harbour immediately, which they did.

'On arrival at the dock, they found a fierce battle raging. The guards were clearly outnumbered, but the arrival of their colleagues put new heart into them and dismayed their attackers. Before long, the attackers were defeated and disappeared into the darkness. Fortunately, there were no serious injuries to the Argonauts – only minor scratches – and, although it was believed that at least one of the attackers had been killed or seriously wounded, there was no sign of any body. The attackers must have taken the body away with them. The King expressed his sorrow at the incident, saying that the attackers were probably wild men from the interior. Those who fought most closely with the assailants said that they were huge men and quite unlike the King's men, who were of smaller stature.

'This unpleasant incident reminded Jason and the others of the need to continue with the voyage with reasonable speed and, as dawn was already breaking, they made the ship ready and rowed out into the harbour on their way to the Bosporus, the gateway to the Black Sea. The sail was hoisted and the *Argo* began to make good progress. Suddenly, the wind veered from south west to north east. Now they had to haul down the sail and row into the wind and flow of the sea. After several hours of toiling, little progress was being made and the evening was approaching. Tiphys, the skilled helmsman, who was always on duty when the sailing was difficult, advised Jason that the ship should be turned round and they should run for Cyzicus for shelter and overnight there.

'This was agreed, but darkness had fallen long before they came close to land. And so, the *Argo* was beached in a cove on the east side of the peninsula. As soon as the *Argo* hit the beach a heavily-armed group attacked them. The fighting was fierce with casualties on both sides. And then, just as suddenly as they had arrived, the assailants left. Soon after, dawn broke, and Jason realised to his horror that the body lying at his feet – the person whom he had killed – was none other than the King himself! The Argonauts learnt afterwards that the King had seen the ship approaching and alerted his warriors thinking this was an invasion by their enemies, the Pelasgians. A sorrowful Jason led a cortege with the dead King resting on a hastily made wooden bier back to the palace, which, not many hours before, had been the happy scene of a wedding banquet. The dismal procession was greeted by a distraught and weeping widow, Cleite. Jason promised Cleite a magnificent burial with funeral games for her deceased husband in expiation for the murder he had unknowingly committed and was as good as his word. Sadly, Cleite could not be consoled and, before the Argonauts could resume their voyage, had hanged herself. So she was interred with her husband. Jason and the Argonauts erected a temple on the nearby Mount Dindymus in their memory, dedicated also to the local goddess, Rhea, the mother of Zeus.

'Hercules then heard dark rumours that King Cyzicus' fate had been decreed by the priestesses of Rhea because he had unwittingly killed an animal sacred to her on the slopes of Mount Dindymus. At this time, the unfavourable north-easterly wind, which the local inhabitants said was unusual for the time of year, was still blowing hard. There was no sign that it would drop or ease westerly. So Jason and Hercules agreed to make a sacrifice to Rhea, as well as to Apollo, for a favourable outcome. Immediately the wind changed to south-west.

'Without any delay, the Argonauts resumed their voyage. Perhaps overanxious to burn the recent unhappy events out of their minds, Hercules offered a challenge to his colleagues: he would out-row them all. They all agreed. Hours later, only Jason and Hercules were still rowing – all the others had stopped, exhausted. Then, just as the *Argo* was passing the mouth of a river, Jason fainted. Shortly after, much to his annoyance, Hercules' oar broke. Hercules was declared the winner and his exhausted companions dipped their oars back into the water and drove the *Argo* on to the beach near the river mouth. Everyone disembarked, found a soft place on a nearby grassy bank and lay down to rest.

'Hercules, of course, had to replace his broken oar. So, leaving his companions resting, he went off alone to find a tall fir tree. After an extensive search, he found what he sought: a tall and stout fir, standing on its own at the top of a slope not too far away from where the *Argo* was beached. He lopped off the branches and dragged the uprooted tree trunk back to the camp, intending to carve it into the shape of an oar. He found most of his companions were awake and starting to prepare a meal. Looking around, Hercules could not see his squire, Hylas. On enquiring, he found that Hylas had left some time ago to find water and Polyphemus had gone to look for him. Fearing that some accident had occurred, Hercules immediately went back into the woods from which he had just emerged, calling Hylas by name. He soon caught up with Polyphemus, who told him that he had heard Hylas calling for help some minutes previously and had searched for him in the direction from which the call had come. He had found the pond that Hylas had been told to use and, abandoned on the bank, was the container Hylas had taken to fill with water. There was no sign of a struggle and there were no footmarks of wild animals to indicate that Hylas had met with a violent end or been carried off.

'Hercules refused to give up the search for his friend and he and Polyphemus spent the rest of the day and the following night in a fruitless search for Hylas. Dawn came and, with it, a strong favourable wind. But Hercules and Polyphemus had not returned to the shore and the *Argo*. After an hour of shouting their names, with no response, Jason and the majority decided they would wait no longer and set sail leaving them behind. Hercules and Polyphemus eventually gave up their search for Hylas, but it is said that Hercules extracted a promise from the local inhabitants that they would continue the search after he had gone.

'As the *Argo* had left and there was little prospect of catching up with the expedition, Hercules decided to return home by land, but Polyphemus, finding the local Mysians friendly, settled there near the pond. He founded the city of Cius but perished later in battle. Hercules' trek along the coast was, he told me, uneventful and he managed to secure passage on a trading boat in Thrace back to Argos. Summoning me to join him at the court of High King Eurystheus, I hastened to Mycenae, where we heard what the next task was to be.'

The Fifth Labour: The Cleaning of the Augean Stables

'I wonder if, before you resume your story about Hercules' Labours, you could explain the religious significance of the Fourth Labour, the capture of the Erymanthean Boar?' I enquired.

'Ah, yes,' replied Iolaus, 'I did leave that rather in the air, didn't I? Well, that was how it was until I had the opportunity of raising it with Hercules some time later. If you don't mind, I will defer making comment on that until we come to it naturally in its context. Are you happy with that for the time being?'

'Of course,' I responded. 'I am puzzled about the connection and was perhaps a little overanxious not to miss the explanation.'

Iolaus laughed. 'You really are hooked like a fish on this tale, aren't you?' he said, not unkindly. 'I promise I will tell all – all that I know, that is – at the right time. Now, I was about to recount what happened when we met Eurystheus to receive our orders for the next – the fifth – Labour. I can only tell you what I gleaned from Hercules later, as I was not present at the meeting. Hercules told me that Eurystheus was very angry that Hercules had gone off on the Argonauts' expedition without getting his permission first – and without even telling him. Hercules was never impressed by that sort of domineering behaviour and simply pointed out the importance of the mission to the Greeks as a whole and to future trading in that part of the world. Having said that, he refused to discuss it further and asked for his instructions. Although we knew that Eurystheus had been seriously embarrassed by having a huge wild animal simply left on his doorstep when Hercules went off, he apparently did not raise this with him at this time. It was only later that Hercules found out that the Boar had been killed because Eurystheus apparently simply did not know what to do with it. The people were growing restive: they feared it would escape from the temporary cage it was being kept in and, as Hercules was in distant lands, there was nobody available to restrain it should it escape. I rather sympathise with their view!

'Enough of that for now! The Fifth Labour was to clean the Stables of Augeas, son of Eleus, the king of Elis. Now, Elis, as you know, is a city in the west of the Peloponnese, about 200 stadia north of Olympia. Augeas kept a large herd of cattle and, whilst horse manure benefited the growth of crops and helped retain moisture in the dry weather, cattle manure was of no use at all. In fact, I was told that, instead of providing warmth to the crops, cow manure was "cold" and hindered growth rather than aided it. And so, as Augeas was lazy and had lazy servants, the dung kept accumulating. I believe his Stables had not been cleaned for many years when we arrived.

'We had no difficulty in finding the Stables. "Follow the smell!" we had been told on asking the way when we reached the country of Elis. They were right. The stench of the dung could be smelled many miles away, depending on the direction of the wind. As we approached the Stables, the stench was overpowering and even Hercules paled in the face of it. Augeas, however, who came out to meet us, seemed completely oblivious to the atmosphere around him and for which he was responsible. Still, he readily agreed to engage Hercules to clean the Stables on condition that he would accomplish the task "within the day". Should he do this, Augeas promised, with his son Phyleus as witness, then Hercules would have one tenth of their cattle for his own, amounting to some 300 animals. I was amazed at the bargain Hercules had struck. Even a man as strong as Hercules would have to work for more than twenty-four hours to clear out these filthy Stables!

'But, of course, as usual, I had underestimated Hercules' cunning.

' "Come on!" he said, taking my arm, "we haven't much time." Leading me over to one side of the Stables, he pointed out how the land sloped away to the south and that, by a careful routing of a strong water flow, a stream could be forced through all the Stables from one end to the other. I still did not believe it to be possible, but accepted his instructions to break down a small part of this wall here and build a barrier there until the whole of the Stables had been covered.

' "Right!" said Hercules. "Now we must divert the stream down the channel we have prepared for it."

'And so, without delay he walked over to the River Peneius, digging a trench as he went with the butt end of his fighting club. The surplus earth he piled on the side so that the channel was some four cubits deep. When he reached the riverbank, his channel was several feet below the water level. Warning me to stand well clear of the channel he had dug, he breached the bank. The water flooded down his new channel into and through the Stables. I stood amazed at the sight, as did Augeas who, by this time, had begun to realise what Hercules' plan was and that he might lose his wager. He was not too pleased at that!

'During the rest of the day, Hercules and I were kept busy, making sure the flow of water did not slacken and that every corner of the Stables had its cleansing stream. As dusk came and the river flow reduced to a trickle, it was clear that Hercules had completed his task. The Stables were clean and glistening in the final glow of the setting sun.

'Unfortunately, Eurystheus had sent a servant, Copreus, to watch what happened and report back to him. This servant then told Augeas that Hercules had already been instructed by Eurystheus to clean the Stables and, accordingly, the wager was invalid. And so, Augeas promptly told Hercules that he would not honour his oath – for both he and Hercules had sealed the wager with an oath in front of Augeas' son Phyleus – because Hercules had already been under contract to carry out the work and because he had not done it himself, but had used the waters from the river. Hercules, predictably, responded with his "cool" rage to this disgraceful act and shamed Augeas into denying that he had made an oath at all, which was foolish because his own son had witnessed it. So Hercules demanded that a court be set up there and then to resolve the dispute. Augeas had no option but to agree and, when his son gave evidence to the court confirming that the oath had indeed been sworn, and the court could see with their own eyes that the task had been completed, they had no hesitation in finding in favour of Hercules and awarded him the cattle that Augeas had promised.

'Augeas refused to accept the verdict and the award. He sent his own son, Phyleus, into exile from Elis and ensured that we were seen off his kingdom under armed escort – without any cattle. Hercules was surprisingly relaxed about the whole affair. He told me later that he didn't want the cattle anyway – he had nowhere to put them, he said – and an offer he had made to Phyleus to kill his father and install him as the King had been turned down by Phyleus. Despite Augeas' despicable behaviour, Phyleus did not want to be the cause of his father's death. Hercules applauded this and helped Phyleus establish himself in Dulichium, an island in the Ionian Sea.

'We then went north, to the court of King Dexamenus who ruled over the port of Olenus on the Gulf of Corinth to the west of Patra, where we were made very welcome by the King and his family, which included his daughter, Mnesimache, of whom I shall be telling more later. Dexamenus was not particularly surprised at Augeas' behaviour, which he felt should have been punished severely. He agreed with Hercules, however, that, as Phyleus was the most severely injured person and he did not want his immediate restoration as heir to the throne, it was preferable to do as he wanted. However, Hercules felt strongly that it would cause more trouble for everyone in the future if those who abrogated their oaths were not brought to account for it.

'We now made our way back to Mycenae to see what Apollo had next in store for us. On the way, Hercules and I called in at Olympia where Hercules had founded a temple to Zeus some years earlier. I was surprised how modest the temple was and Hercules confessed that it was as he himself had built it. The three priests there when we arrived were very pleased to see him and were particularly profuse in their thanks for his cleaning of the Stables of King Augeas. They said that the stench frequently was borne by the wind to the temple and this had discouraged visitors. Prior to our visit, they had received no visitors for over six months, although they admitted that, as we were now in mid-winter, they did not usually expect many visitors at this time of the year.

'Even in mid-winter, the site was impressive – under the shadow of Mount Kronos and watered by two rivers, one on either side. The rivers' flow of time past had created a large flat plain between them, which would surely some day be a site for something more impressive than the present small temple to Zeus.

'When I expressed these views to Hercules, he sighed and said, "This is how it is, I am afraid. Despite my strength, and the support I can command, there is only so much that I can do. And some people won't do things unless they can take the credit for it – sometimes they want to take the credit for what other people have done. I have suffered all my short life with others being jealous of me and my achievements. I have done these things not for my own glory, but to benefit mankind and improve his understanding of the gods and the world we live in together. I want to be remembered for the contribution I have made to our life here and, when I die, I want people to appreciate what I have done to help them and those like them. This temple will grow and be famous one day, I am sure. But others will take the credit for that – probably rightly so. My fame will give this beautiful site a recognition it would not have had otherwise. I believe I have chosen wisely a site for the king of the gods."

'I agreed. As we took our leave of the priests, I asked Hercules about the religious significance of the last two Labours.

'Hercules paused a while before replying.

' "Quite frankly," he said, "I am rather more puzzled now than I was immediately after I had captured the Erymanthean Boar. I know that Mount Erymanthus is sacred to Artemis and the boar is a symbol of the ancient matriarchal rituals, representing the king who has to be killed by his successor. I also know that the mountain takes its name from a son of Apollo, who, according to legend was killed by another goddess, Aphrodite, who claimed he had watched her whilst she was bathing in a pool nearby. Apollo is supposed to have avenged his son's death by either taking the form of a boar, or more likely, arranging for a wild boar to injure fatally Aphrodite's human lover, Adonis. As the boar, in this context, is the "friend" of Apollo, I can't understand why Apollo would want to do it any harm. On the other hand, if it is a symbol of the matriarchal system Apollo now wishes to discredit, I suppose it does make some sense.

' "But," he added, "on my return from the expedition on the *Argo*, I learnt that the Boar had been killed. My instructions, presumably from Apollo, were only to capture it. So the Boar's death would appear to be contrary to the wishes of Apollo. The only other explanation I can think of is that the instruction from Apollo was to kill the Boar, but Eurystheus changed his instruction to me out of malice, knowing that it would be much more difficult to capture the Boar than kill it. Another explanation has also come to me which I will give in a moment after I have commented on the last Labour."

'He then asked if I agreed with his thinking, which I did, although I was also intrigued as to what his other explanation could be.

'And so Hercules continued: "Now we come to the Stables of Augeas. I can see absolutely no religious significance here at all, which is why I think we may have to seek another explanation for both of these last two Labours. There is no doubt, though, that the job needed doing and, as we heard from the priests at Olympia, many will be relieved that the Stables are now clean. Let us hope they will be kept clean in future."

'What about your "other explanation"?' I asked.

' "Ah! Well, I think I will say nothing about that just now. I am intrigued to know what the next task will be first before I discuss this further. It may shed some light on what is really going on."

'With that we drove on in silence until we reached Mycenae.

'As we expected, Copreus had arrived long before us and had given an account of what had happened in the Stables at Elis. Eurystheus immediately denounced the manner in which Hercules had performed the Labour – he had obviously expected Hercules would have been forced to move all the dung by hand, a nauseous task – and promptly disqualified it on the grounds that Hercules had not done it as a task for him, but was contracted by Augeas and he had not carried out the task himself but had employed a river to do it for him. Hercules, I understand, simply held his peace and asked what the next task was. This proved to be more local and dangerous: to kill the carnivorous Birds of Lake Stymphalis in Arcadia.

The Sixth Labour: Killing the Stymphalian Birds

'When Hercules came out of his discussions with Eurystheus, I could see that he was both delighted and relieved at the new task. Realising that he would not want to tell me his feelings until we were alone, I merely discussed with him what arrangements he wanted me to make for him, and when we were likely to set off for Arcadia. As it was still winter, Hercules made it quite clear that he was not in a hurry to travel into the mountains again. The lake was close to one of the highest mountains in the Peloponnese, Mount Kilini, not far from the city state of Nemaea. And so it was not until some time later, when we were alone and our conversation could not be overheard, that my curiosity could be assuaged.

'Hercules initiated the discussion with a faintly amused expression on his face.

' "I suppose you would like to know why the news I have been given by the High King has particularly pleased me?"

'On my nodding assent, he continued.

' "Well, do you know what the 'Stymphalian Birds' are?"

'I said that I understood that they were fierce, vulture-like birds who inhabited the marshes surrounding Lake Stymphalis and terrorised the country between Nemaea and Orchomenos in Arcadia. It was rumoured that these birds were so fierce that they killed and ate human beings, so the countryside around the lake was left uncultivated, although well watered and believed to be fertile. Hercules laughed.

' "That is what the locals want you to think!" he said. "In fact, it is a colony of wild, vicious priestesses who serve the goddess Artemis at the ancient temple near the north bank of the lake. Artemis, as you know, is the sister of Apollo and the goddess associated with hunting and the Moon. It appears that Apollo does not like the excessive aggressiveness of this cult and has decided that it should be destroyed. I also believe that the cult have prevented the marshes surrounding the lake being drained and that, in the summer months in particular, the marshes are full of pestilential insects whose bites make people very ill and many die. The priestesses put on leggings of birds' feathers and cover the rest of their bodies with feathers to make themselves look like birds to perpetuate the legend they have created.

' "I am pleased," he continued, "because it confirms the religious nature of these tasks, which I had thought was the true reason behind my Labours. I can now tell you my other theory about the last two Labours, which appeared to have little connection with religion.

' "The boar, as you know, is one of the symbols of Artemis. It is also traditional to kill a boar in mid-winter. I believe that Apollo's instruction to Eurystheus was that I should kill the Boar – for the traditional reason. Eurystheus changed this, merely to make the task more difficult for me. When I asked him about it, he was very evasive, but I did not get the impression that the priests of Apollo had told him that the Boar should be kept alive – hence my feeling that the original instruction was to kill the Boar. The cleaning of the Stables of Augeas had no religious significance at all, except that I suspect the priests at Apollo's temple at Olympia may have complained to Delphi about the vile smell emanating from them. So, apart from performing a useful function for the community, why was I asked to do it? I think that the priests of Apollo at Delphi are being quite cunning here. It was not difficult to see that the first three tasks were aimed at suppressing female cults, as we have discussed. As you know, I ran into trouble with the Ceryneian Hind as the Cult supporters appeared to be aware of my activities.

' "However, now that I have this next instruction, I shall not be surprised if most – if not all – of the remaining tasks I will be given will also have the suppression of extreme female cults as their objective. But the priests do not want others, especially the cults yet to be destroyed, to realise at this stage what is happening. If they do, they will establish some additional defences or seek to arouse popular support now, which could make their suppression in the future difficult if not impossible. Do you see now why the two apparently unrelated tasks were given me?"

'I agreed that what he said did seem to make sense of the situation, in so far as it had been revealed to us. As it could be several years before Hercules completed his tasks, there was much sense in concealing the true nature of them. Although the local cult supporters could soon switch their support away from the cult if someone from outside came in and destroyed it, while it was still functioning, popular support could be very strong. As he had recalled, Hercules had already experienced this when he captured the Ceryneian Hind. A crowd of Cult supporters had threatened him and it was only because he had been able to assure them that the Hind would be released unharmed that they let him go on his way. If they had thought that their Cult, temple and priestesses were to be destroyed, their attitude would no doubt have been quite different.

'And so we returned to Thebes for a short rest before venturing out to Lake Stymphalis.

'At the first sign of spring, Hercules ordered me to make the chariot ready. It was also my task to ensure that we had some basic provisions for the journey – food, wine and some water for ourselves as well as some fodder for the horses. We were normally well entertained by local people along the route – there were few who had not heard of Hercules and wished to be able to boast that Hercules had eaten at their table or slept under their roof. But the weather could still be unpredictable and we might need to be self-sufficient for one night or more. Frequently at this time of the year, summer and winter streams became raging torrents, swollen by the melting snow that amplified the seasonal rainfall. Although Hercules' great strength enabled him to cope with most natural disasters and trials, neither I nor the horses would be able to do so. I knew, of course, that Hercules would never abandon us. My main concern was that he would push himself beyond his limits to save us if we got into difficulty. I did not think that his time had yet come – he had much more to achieve – and I was determined that he should not risk his future to rescue me or the horses. I did not tell him my train of thought, and we never discussed it, but I think he guessed and respected me because of it.

'I asked Hercules what his plan was. "Well," he said, "I don't think we will approach Lake Stymphalis by the normal route. I suspect the priestesses will probably know of my task and will have spies posted on the obvious routes I might take from Thebes: by Corinth and Nemaea or from the north by the pass to the west of the mountain peak. Instead, I propose to cross the Gulf of Corinth by boat to the mouth of the River Sithas and follow the track up the river valley to a settlement halfway up the mountain. There I expect we will be able to find a herdsman to guide us through a high pass so that we can descend to the lake from the north and surprise the priestesses."

'I thought this was a good plan. He was right to assume that his task was known to the priestesses. Although Eurystheus was taking instructions from Delphi, this did not mean that he agreed with the strategy. It was clear that he was becoming increasingly jealous of Hercules' successes and feared that his own position as High King was now under threat from Hercules, who was waxing in popularity daily. Eurystheus was also a timid man and was probably beginning to realise that Hercules' exploits, when appreciated for what they were, could antagonise the female public and some powerful goddesses. He was bound to have every reason for paying lip service to what Apollo wanted whilst leaking advance notice to the victims in the hope that Hercules would be killed, or at least fail. Hercules agreed and said that, in future, he might need to keep the time period between Eurystheus' instruction to him and his action as short as possible. We both agreed to be vigilant and find out what rumours were already prevalent on Hercules' next task in the hope that we might be able to identify the source of any information being circulated. However, despite careful questioning of our friends and others, nobody seemed to be aware of our next mission. So, on this occasion, we were not successful in confirming any leakage – at least not in and around Thebes.

'Hercules confirmed to me that he had already found three friends with a large boat who were prepared to take us, two horses and a light chariot across the gulf at night. I was very concerned. At the point where we would be crossing the gulf, it was some 250 stadia wide. The horses would be terrified, particularly if they had to be loaded in the dark as well. Hercules calmed my anxiety:

he accepted that we would have to give the horses plenty of practice in embarking and disembarking in the dark before we ventured on our journey, but he reminded me that plenty of horses were transported across the gulf and he had never heard of a serious problem. Later that day, we met with the leader of the crew, who was also the owner of the boat. Diplomatically, he agreed with both of us! Many horses were indeed transported across the gulf by boat, especially small groups as they were more vulnerable to highway robbers if taken by a land route. But such trips were normally in day time, not at night.

'He then put forward a suggestion. At the eastern end of the gulf, there were some small islands, called the Alkionides, about halfway across the gulf. Several of these islands, he knew, were uninhabited. We could load up late in the afternoon and arrive at an uninhabited island he had identified as suitable at dusk and disembark. We would then reload three hours before dawn to arrive on the north coast of the Peloponnese at dawn. The horses would still have to load and unload once in the dark but the journeys would be shorter and there was less likelihood of bad weather causing a problem on two short journeys than there would be on one long journey. There was also the added advantage that we could practise sailing across to the island with the horses in daylight for several days to accustom them to both the boat and the landing site on the island before doing it in earnest.

'We applauded this suggestion. The next step was to procure suitable horses. This did not prove difficult and, over the next ten days, we practised loading the horses on to the boat from the mainland and sailing across to the chosen island, where we found several suitable landing places. We selected the one that had some shelter from the prevailing westerly wind and was also out of sight of both mainland coasts. On several occasions, we landed the horses and then, after a short while, reloaded them on the boat for the return journey to the north shore of the gulf. On the last two practices, the chariot was also taken and the loading on the mainland and the unloading on the island were carried out in the dark. We re-embarked before dawn, as we proposed to do for the final journey, returning to the mainland in the early hours of daylight.

'As I had expected, the horses were a little nervous at first. But they soon drew strength from our quiet confidence and, apart from one show of anxiety by one of the horses on the final day when being loaded pre-dawn on the island for the return journey, there were no problems. I noted that the anxious horse was reassured when he found that he landed on the mainland where he had embarked earlier. Although he would be landing the following day on the other side of the Gulf – for Hercules had decided that we had waited long enough – I did not think the horse would now be too concerned. Anyway, it would be too late by then!

'All went well the following day. We loaded late when nobody was about and sailed across a flat sea to the island, where we disembarked just after sunset. We sheltered in the remains of a herdsman's stone hut and the horses sheltered behind a windbreak of brushwood we had built for them on a previous visit. We decided not to light a fire. It was a mild and clear night and we did not want to draw attention to ourselves.

'As dawn approached, so did the sea mist. This was not entirely unexpected. We could hug the coast for half the last stage of our journey and only launch into the open sea for the last half. So we loaded as planned and set sail, the owner listening for the sound of the waves breaking on the shore and steering the boat clear of the rocks whilst the rest of us rowed hard to supplement the power of the light breeze in our sail. The horses appeared calmed rather than alarmed by the mist and the light wind accompanied a gentle swell. From our point of view, the weather was helpful for our enterprise. However, not knowing the coast as well as the boat owner, I was just a little anxious but suppressed it mainly to prevent any fear being transmitted to the horses, who can be astonishingly sensitive to human emotions.

'With the breaking of dawn the mist cleared. The coastline we were aiming for was visible and only a short distance away. Within minutes we had beached, had manoeuvred the horses, the chariot and our meagre supplies off the boat and sent it on its way back with its crew and our thanks. After giving the horses a feed and some water, we decided to move west along the coastal track immediately. This was partly because we were cooling off and stiffening after our exertions at the oars and partly because we wanted to warm up the horses who had been inactive on the boat for several hours and were eager to get going.

'And so we clattered at speed along the track towards the mouth of the River Sithas. Within a short while we passed through the small town where the obvious route to the lake branched off left, to the south. Although there were by this time quite a few people about, we were not conscious of any notice being taken of our passing. We had earlier decided that we would not stop here, as we did not wish to attract attention. Hercules was such a distinctive person, and by now so well known, that we felt he would be instantly recognised.

'We paused a little distance further along the track where, just off it, there was a welcoming grassy meadow by a fresh water stream that was just large enough to give the now tired horses some sweet grazing and cool, clean water. Hercules and I also welcomed the rest and the water, which eased the passage of the rather dry food we had brought with us. We discussed what lay ahead. Whilst I did not doubt that we would find a way through the mountain range on the route we had chosen, I realised that we had selected a difficult option. The peak was over 2,370 metres high, and a pass at even half that height was likely to be snow-bound at this time of the year, with the risk of sudden avalanches and torrents of water stimulated during the day by the snow melt in the gradually rising spring temperatures. At least we could expect reasonably mild daytime temperatures. By contrast, the cold at night at high altitude would be intense, particularly if there was a strong wind. Early morning starts would be on ice – the day-melted snow frozen by the night cold – turning gradually to feet-cloying slush as the sun's heat penetrated the cloud and mist. My predictions proved right – but it could have been much worse.

'We had little difficulty in finding the start of the track south to the settlement. It was relatively easy going for the horses, although so steep in parts that Hercules and I had to dismount from the chariot and walk alongside it to prevent it from toppling over. Pausing as need and opportunity presented, we reached the settlement and the end of the defined track well before midday.

Beyond the settlement the track split into a number of narrow paths going in different directions, each no doubt leading to a different summer pasture. There was snow in abundance here and the precipitous snow-clad slopes above us were a sobering reminder of the challenges that awaited us.

'Hercules was not recognised here – as he had predicted – and we experienced no problem in persuading a local goatherd to guide us over the ridge into the valleys beyond the mountain range. He was more than a little puzzled as to why we should want to go there, but the size of the reward Hercules offered him and the terms – half now and the rest at journey's end – dispelled his curiosity. The saddest part was that we could not take our horses and chariot with us. The goatherd was adamant that the path we would use was too narrow and steep for the horses, let alone the chariot. We had no option but to leave them behind with a friend of the goatherd who promised – also for reasonable reward – to feed our horses and guard our chariot until we returned for them. I like to think the horses were sorry to see us go: we heard their whinnying for some time after we left them to start the trek up the mountain.

'It was hard work, but Hercules' strength, the goatherd's knowledge and skills and my fitness ensured that, after several days' climbing, we came to the top of the pass. There, far below, was Lake Stymphalis glittering in the sun. At this distance we could not see any signs of life – no bird priestesses and no buildings. Unprompted, the goatherd had told us on our journey of the strange, man-eating birds that lived down by the lake and urged us to give them a wide berth. We told him that we would – we had also heard of their terrifying habits. We were also very understanding when he told us that he was too frightened to come any further with us. We knew from the way he had guided us up the mountain passes and shielded us from rock and snowfalls that he did not lack courage, so the tales of the man-eating birds must have had a very powerful effect on him and his fellow herdsmen. We bade him farewell and watched him out of sight before we commenced our climb straight down to the lake.

'The snow line on the south side was higher up the mountain than on the north, as we had expected, so we were soon out of the snow and moving over solid rock and small stones. At first, I was glad not to be walking on slippery, foot-grabbing snow, but I soon concluded that shifting small stones mixed with large unyielding rocks are also none too pleasant! Still, lightly loaded as we were – Hercules had only his lion's pelt, spear, shield, bow and arrows and I only a long dagger and some food and animal skins to help make us some shelter – it was not too jarring an experience. We carried no water, preferring to rely on melted snow and mountain streams. Nevertheless, as I had noticed before, climbing down steep uneven slopes is very hard on the knees and ankles. But Hercules hardly noticed.

'We were quite close before we saw them: about ten white-clad women walking through what looked like a sacred grove, less than ten stadia away. They clearly hadn't seen us, which was to be expected as by now we were moving carefully down through a jumble of large stones and stunted trees. The lake was now just the other side of the grove and, as we paused to look more closely, we could see movement on the northern shore of the lake. As we edged closer, it was an astonishing sight: at least thirty large birds, each well above the height of a normal person, with a small head and large protruding beak, were parading along the shoreline in what appeared to us to be military fashion. As we watched, they came to a large rock on the shore, walked around it and came back along the shore in the same formation. It was very impressive. Even Hercules was impressed.

' "I think," he whispered to me, "that the ones dressed in white are the priestesses on duty at the Sanctuary. There are probably twelve of them, although we have only seen ten so far. The ones dressed as birds, for I am sure they also are priestesses, are the guards. That makes about forty-two in all. I believe that there are about fifty in total, so we need to watch a little while and see if we can locate the missing ten, including the two in the Sanctuary, wherever that may be."

'For the next hour or so, we quietly moved closer under cover of the rocks and shrubbery and then settled down to watch what was happening. Hercules first spotted the Sanctuary: a quite small building near the western end of the lake, but difficult to see because it was built among the trees of the grove. It would not be difficult to approach it unseen from where we were. It appeared that there was an open space with few trees on the far side of the Sanctuary between it and the shore of the lake, which confirmed our suspicions that the Cult were not expecting an attack from the north. Hercules decided to attack the Sanctuary first and kill the priestesses in there, and then lie in wait for the other white-clad priestesses to come in search of them. He thought the priestesses dressed as birds were probably not allowed in the Sanctuary area so he would have time later to decide how to tackle them.

'As we approached the Sanctuary, two priestesses came out and walked the short distance to the edge of the stone-paved area around the west end of the Sanctuary. They were both carrying what looked like large cups for wine or some other liquid. As they reached the edge of the paving, they turned and faced each other, bowed, clashed the cups together, and then turned to face the grove whereupon they ceremonially poured the liquid from the cups onto the ground. They then brought the cups up level with their waists, turned towards the Sanctuary and walked sedately back inside – closely followed by Hercules. On his instructions, I stayed just inside the Sanctuary to give warning of the approach of any of the other priestesses.

'I heard a strangled cry and the sound of a metal cup hitting the floor and I knew that Hercules' short dagger had done its work. I waited for the second – but it did not come. There was the sound of talking – Hercules was having a conversation with the second priestess! On hearing a sound behind me, I turned quickly, dagger in hand. It was Hercules, accompanied by the second priestess who was introduced to me as Phoebe. Phoebe told us that she had been kidnapped some years earlier from Thebes and brought here to be trained as a priestess of Artemis. She had heard that we were coming and had been looking forward to it as she had hoped this would give her the opportunity to escape and go home back to Thebes. Taking cover in the portico of the Sanctuary so that we could not be seen from outside but could see if anyone approached, Phoebe then told us of the rituals and confirmed our assumption about the two different groups of priestesses was correct: the "Birds" never came into the Sanctuary; they were only allowed as far as the paved surround, which they called the precinct. Their role was to protect the Sanctuary and they were selected for their physical strength and ferocity. In Phoebe's opinion, they were not very intelligent.

'Phoebe told us that the priestess Hercules had killed was the chief priestess, who had established this Sanctuary many years ago, largely, it appeared, out of hatred for her husband who had deserted her for a younger woman. The Cult was based on hate and destruction. The lake was a source in summer of pestilential insects, and the activities of the Cult prevented the insects' breeding grounds being destroyed. The prevailing winds carried the diseases and the insects south and east away from the Sanctuary. One of the tasks of the "Birds" in the summer was to maintain fires that burnt foul-smelling wood. This had the double purpose of keeping the insects away from the Sanctuary area and spoiling the air for those living within many stadia of the Sanctuary. In the late summer, just before the crops were to be gathered in, the "Birds" would issue forth in a flock with a poisonous substance that they gathered from a secret source – even Phoebe did not know where it was – and scattered it over the crops to spoil them. Any farmers who happened to get in their way were slashed to death with swords, but the rumour was that the "Birds" had done it with their sharp beaks.

'With Phoebe to advise him, and the priestesses now leaderless, Hercules was able to kill all the ten remaining Sanctuary priestesses. At night, Phoebe said, the "Birds" disrobed their costumes for sleep, leaving only four fully clad "Birds" on guard. Phoebe added that there was a legend that the Sanctuary would be destroyed and all the priestesses killed if a rattle, hidden in the Sanctuary, were to be sounded at night. Phoebe showed us the rattle and Hercules told me to take it. By now, it was night and the "Birds" had retired to sleep. Hercules, assisted by Phoebe, who knew where the guards were posted, killed them all and sent Phoebe back to tell me to sound the rattle as loudly as I could. This I did, and great was the commotion as the "Birds" fled without their costumes, never to be seen again. Hercules encouraged them on their way with a few swishes of his sword, but only the four night guards were killed.

'In the morning, Hercules destroyed the Sanctuary building, buried the bodies of the slain priestesses and the "Birds" and Phoebe said a prayer over them. The abandoned costumes were buried deep by the lake and Phoebe accompanied us to the nearest village, where we gave them the glad news that the birds had flown and they could now take charge of their own lives. In their delight, they gave us three horses to ride away on. First, we returned to the settlement to collect our chariot and horses and we then all rode or drove back to Stymphalis, where we returned the horses the local people had given us. They were very pleased to see us and proudly showed us the progress they had made in the short time we had been away.

'Hercules then left us for Mycenae to report to the High King the completion of his task and hear of his next assignment, whilst I made my way back to Thebes to deliver Phoebe back to her family, who were overjoyed to see her again after such a long time. After two days' rest, I then drove the chariot in easy stages back to Mycenae to meet up with Hercules and find out what we were to do next.'

The Seventh Labour: The Capture of the Cretan Bull

'Hercules was in a strange mood when I met him at the main door to the High King's palace. This was where we had arranged some time ago we would meet at midday after a separation, if no other arrangement had been made. I decided not to anger him by enquiring into the problem. If he wanted me to know, or it affected my well-being, he would tell me, I knew that. Criticise me if you will, but I never did find out what was upsetting him that day.

'The bad news was that his next task was in Crete and that he had decided not to take me with him. This was a big disappointment, as I had only visited Crete once and had been enchanted with it. But Hercules was adamant. He explained that Eurystheus had again made the point that, whilst he could be accompanied and supported in his tasks, he was not to accept help of any kind in executing them. It was not clear precisely what he meant: it could be interpreted to mean that just Hercules himself, alone, must capture the nominated quarry, or it could mean that, by merely acting as lookout for him at the Stymphalian Lake, I had been "helping" him carry out his task. Whatever the interpretation, Hercules had decided that he did not need any assistance from me on his next task and thought it best to allay Eurystheus' suspicions by ostentatiously leaving me behind. I, of course, accepted his decision and asked what the task was.

' "To capture the Cretan Bull," Hercules said, "and bring it back to him at Mycenae. Apparently, the Cretan King has asked for help in capturing this troublesome beast and, although it is so fierce that nobody will go near it, I am promised – and apparently allowed under the rules to accept – some help from the local people, including the King, in fulfilling my task. Like cleaning the Augean Stables, this task seems to have no particular religious significance," he continued, "but I am not so sure. Most things do have some religious significance if you look hard enough!"

'He went on to say that the story of Crete was dominated by tales of bulls. He reminded me that Europa was kidnapped by Zeus (who had assumed the form of a bull) and taken to Crete, and King Minos had offered his guests the spectacle of "bull-leapers" – trained young men and women who leapt through the horns of a charging bull, did a handstand somersault on the bull's head, landing on their feet on the heaving bull's back, whence they jumped to the floor, making quickly for the exit, no doubt! Throughout Greece, bulls were associated with manly strength and particularly the god of war, Ares, but they were also identified with fecundity, being sacrificed to Dionysus as part of prayers for a good crop. The sacrifice of a bull also had significance in the older religious ceremonies. I recalled to Hercules that I had heard that the bull was linked with the moon goddess, the earth goddess and life-giving rain. Perhaps this was the female cult link? I suggested.

'Hercules dismissed my suggestion, although he did admit that this Bull had turned to destruction of crops and field boundaries – hedges and so forth – thus becoming the antithesis of a fertility symbol! Anyway, he said, a bull's bellow was sometimes likened to the rumble of thunder that often preceded rain. A dead bull would not be much use. I persisted in my argument. Surely the waywardness of the Cretan Bull's behaviour confirmed the futility of relying on such a volatile creature and its removal would underline, for everyone to see, the feebleness of the cult? Hercules conceded that I might have a point, but I could see that he did not wish to continue this discussion and so I fell silent.

'After a long pause, by which time we had reached the main gate, where I had left the chariot in the hands of a bystander, he suggested that we drove off into the country where we could discuss in private his plans. I happily took the horses' reins back from the bystander, paid him and, with Hercules beside me, we trotted down from the citadel into the open countryside. A little way down the road towards the coast, we came upon an attractive olive grove beside the road. As the sun was by now getting quite hot, we decide to dismount and unharness the horses, putting them on long leather leads so that they could browse in the short grass whilst we leant against a tree, eating some of the fruit I had brought with me.

'And so, relaxing in the early spring sun, I had perhaps one of my happiest moments with Hercules. His moodiness had left him and he talked about his childhood, his growing up as a herdsman – which he clearly enjoyed very much and from which he derived much of his love of animals – the influence of his teachers and, how, in his opinion, jealousy was the worst vice of man. In a burst of foolishness, I suggested that, for a man as well blessed by the gods as he was, it was hard for him to understand the jealousy of others, who were not so blessed. The moment the words passed my lips, I regretted what I had said. I realised that it would make Hercules angry. Much to my surprise, it did not. After a long pause, he turned to me, looked me straight in the eyes and, with a serious expression on his face, began speaking.

' "You know, I am glad you said that. You are quite right. Many will think that I have everything and have no reason to be jealous of what little they may have, whereas they are deficient and yearn to have just a part of what I have been blessed with by the gods. But that is very superficial, isn't it? I may be the strongest man, but I am not the High King. I may have been destined to be the High King, but I was born too late – albeit I was cheated out of my heritage. But I do not feel any anger. I look at the way my cousin Eurystheus lives – in fear and, now, consumed with jealousy. He is not happy. I do not envy him now and never will. I do not want to be High King. Although people may think that I am in thrall to him, I am freer than he is. I have been so well trained by the best in their calling. I have a good brain and the physical strength to do what many could only dream of doing. I have a greater fear of growing old and gradually losing my powers. But I do not wish to accumulate riches. I have seen rich men – they are not happy. Many of them live miserable lives, fearful that what they have will be taken from them or that they will be killed by a thief for an inconsequential trinket. I would be disappointed if, at the end of my life, I could not look back and feel that I had made the world a happier place."

'He paused, and a shadow passed across his face. He turned away to look out towards the sea, which was just visible on the skyline and then continued:

' "My great weakness, and the cause of considerable shame, is my occasional inability to control my temper. Sadly, you have seen it at its worst. I cannot explain or excuse those actions and I fear more will occur in the future. My increasing awareness of this problem helps me to contain it, but I know in my heart that I will never fully control it. May the gods help me to cope with it!"

'On this sombre note he paused and, a few moments later, we turned to discuss his forthcoming Cretan adventure.

'As there was no role for me, he merely outlined what he had been told, what he knew and how he proposed to tackle the task. What had turned the Bull wild had apparently not yet been discovered. Hercules thought that it was either mentally ill or had some physical pain that was causing it to react so aggressively. Bulls were naturally aggressive, but not usually without good cause. They would protect their territory and what they regarded as their property, such as a cow and their progeny, but they would not normally be destructive away from their territory for no reason. He aimed to get close enough to the animal, without upsetting it, to communicate a calming feeling to it and try to monitor its behaviour, in the hope that some clue would emerge to identify the real problem. I bowed to Hercules' greater experience in dealing with animals and their troubles and agreed that what he said was logical and probably correct.

'We then remounted and resumed our journey to the port, where Hercules enquired on a boat to carry him to Crete. He was lucky. A suitable boat was leaving on the late evening tide and we just had time to find ourselves something to eat before he had to board. He enjoined me to meet him at Tiryns on his return. He would send a message to me there from Crete before he left, giving the day on which he expected to land back at the port, and would call for me at Tiryns on his way to the High King at Mycenae with the captured Bull.

'And so we parted, and I commenced my long journey back to Thebes, intending to be at Tiryns some twenty days hence. Allowing for the two sea passages and the time it would take him to locate and subdue the Bull, Hercules calculated that it would take him at least that long to complete his task. On the third day of my journey, after a pause at Corinth, I arrived back home to be greeted by my family and the local news.

'The waiting days passed quickly. I awoke one morning several days after returning home and I could scarcely believe it when I realised that, if I did not leave that day for Corinth, I might miss my rendezvous with Hercules. I quickly said my farewells and rode off in the chariot to Tiryns, staying at Corinth and a hostelry near Argos before reaching Tiryns on the afternoon of the third day. Tomorrow was the twentieth day after Hercules had left, so I had fulfilled my part of the bargain. There was no message, so, after being feasted by friends of Hercules, who were also awaiting his return, I retired to sleep in the house of a friend, expecting to hear in a few days' time from Hercules the date of his return.

'Having feasted rather too well the night before, I was still in bed well after dawn, to be awoken by the bellowing of a bull and Hercules' calming voice. I later discovered that he had somehow overtaken his messenger at sea and had arrived before him. I had scarcely jumped out of bed when the wife of the friend in whose house I was being given hospitality came to tell me that my services were required by Hercules.

'I dressed with speed and was soon outside the main gate of the city to greet Hercules, who was standing there with a broad grin on his face, holding in his massive hands a thick iron chain, the end of which was attached to a ring in the nose of the biggest and wickedest-looking bull you have ever seen. Guided by Hercules, I approached them slowly and cautiously, making sure that the Bull could see my every move. He was obviously suspicious, but Hercules was talking to him quietly and, after a little while, I could see the tenseness leaving the Bull's frame. Hercules encouraged me to come right up to the animal and stroke him on the nose. The surrounding crowd, who, I must say kept a respectful distance away, thought that I was either foolhardy or enchanted. I was neither. Wary, I think, best described my state. Anyway, having been introduced, Hercules then suggested that we move slowly away from the city towards

Mycenae, Hercules leading the Bull gently behind him. Most of the crowd stayed at the gates of Tiryns, but a few followed at a discreet distance. Neither Hercules, the Bull nor I were concerned and, halting near some lush grass, Hercules allowed the Bull to graze while he told me what he now proposed to do: quite simply, he would deliver the Bull to his cousin, receive his instructions for the next task and leave with me for Thebes where he would plan with me his next expedition and my part in it, if any. He would tell me later how he had achieved the capture of the Bull and his adventures on the way.

'On arrival at Mycenae, the High King refused to see Hercules, hiding in his bronze urn in the hall of his palace until the Bull had been taken away outside the city walls and the gates shut firmly against it. Hercules and I thought this extremely amusing, but were careful not to show this to the servants, and certainly not to the High King! On this occasion, Hercules persuaded me to join him in the audience with Eurystheus, who treated me most courteously. Of course, he knew of me and my background and had every reason to want to be on good terms with the rulers at Thebes, which was a very important city, and to whom I was closely related. I was very careful to avoid saying anything specific about helping Hercules and, of course, could confirm that, on his latest task, I had not been involved at all – I had merely travelled down from Thebes to meet Hercules and drive him back to Thebes. This was just what Eurystheus wanted to hear, and, of course, what Hercules wanted me to say. It was accordingly a pleasant interview and the time passed quickly.

'When the formalities of the meeting between us were concluded, I was asked to withdraw. I waited in the anteroom for a short while before Hercules joined me. As I had supposed, Eurystheus had considered it inappropriate to give Hercules his orders in front of me. Virtually all that passed between them after I had left the room was that the next task was to capture the four wild Mares of Diomedes. I had never heard of them, and did not even know where they were to be found. Hercules, as usual, knew a great deal about them and promised to tell me when he had told me how he captured the Cretan Bull.

'As soon as we were outside the city, on the road to Thebes,

Hercules turned to me and, smiling, said, "I am sure you want to hear about my adventures in Crete! I had a fast crossing and on arrival it was clear that I was expected: I had hardly disembarked before a welcoming party of court officials came to greet me and offered to conduct me to King Minos' Palace. As it was some distance away from the harbour, I was driven there in a chariot. The King's welcome was warm and friendly, but I must confess that I was a little disappointed in the quality of the palace buildings. I had been expecting something rather grander. King Minos, I think, sensed my feeling of anti-climax and told me something of the history of the Minoan dynasty, which suffered a major catastrophe several hundred years earlier when a series of huge tidal waves struck the whole of the north coast of the island. These waves were accompanied by a huge under-sea explosion at an island many stadia north of Crete, where a large part of the Cretan navy was based. Over half the Cretan fleet was destroyed by these events, many people drowned and most of the principal buildings on the north coast of Crete were destroyed, including most of the palaces. Just as recovery work began, the heavens opened and over the next few days there was a very heavy fall of grey ash, some of it so hot that it burnt people alive and buried them several cubits deep. The fields also were covered with this grey dust and all the crops destroyed. However, much of the population survived this double catastrophe, but, except in the south of the island – which, as you know, is mountainous and not very fertile – no crops could be grown on most of the island for many years and those who stayed could not survive. The elderly died and the young emigrated to mainland Greece or to colonies elsewhere. With most of the fleet destroyed and many sailors killed, the pirates returned, making recovery through trade virtually impossible over a very wide area. The whole of the Aegean was badly affected for a very long time.

' "At last, about 150 years ago, the Achaeans brought respite from the pirates, settlers returned from the mainland and the earth miraculously became fertile again. The King told me that some even claimed that the land was more fertile than it had been before the ash fell – but he did not know how anyone could possibly know that! With life returning to normal, wealth was created and some new palaces were built, including the one in which I was now being entertained by King Minos. However, he had to admit that his immediate predecessors had not had access to the quality craftsmen available to previous dynasties: he suspected that the wall paintings and possibly even the columns and architecture were not yet to the original standard – or, indeed, to the standards encountered in much of the mainland. Still, he said, life on Crete had improved markedly under Achaean rule and trade had begun to flourish, bringing gold and silver back to the island. Then, only fifty years ago, the gods had shaken the earth and many of the new settlements were destroyed or badly damaged. The King's father had been fortunate: his palace had been built on solid rock, which had defied the gods and remained unshaken and practically undamaged. But, once again, the islanders had been forced to struggle to recover their hard-won prosperity. The King commented that, after many years of hard work and under the protection of the Achaean fleet, prosperity was at last returning to its previous level – according to those who had studied the past. I remarked that the harbour seemed busy enough when I landed and, apart from some buildings I had noticed which appeared to be semi-derelict, all appeared well. The King agreed, but he felt the prolonged period of struggles had adversely affected both his father's and his plans for the palace – they could not justify work on enlarging or improving the appearance of the palace while the people they ruled were struggling to survive.

' "The King then moved on to mention the problem I was there to solve: the manic Bull. He told me that the Bull, though a massive one, had behaved normally for many years. It had become unpredictable and vicious only about a year ago. Suddenly, and without apparent warning, one morning in winter, on being released from its night stable, it had rushed at its two regular handlers, gored them both to death and charged out into the countryside, bellowing loudly and destroying everything in its path. It was now ranging freely over a vast area of the western part of the island and none dared approach it. I asked if there was anybody I could speak to who knew the animal, preferably someone who had looked after it for an extended time. I could see that the King was a little surprised at my request and was unable to answer at first. But, seeing I was serious, he summoned a servant and asked that his chief steward be brought to speak to me, explaining that I wished to find out what I could about the Bull's character before I went to try to catch him.

' "Within a short while, Alexandros, the King's chief steward, was introduced to me. I took to him at once. A handsome, intelligent man, he immediately understood what I was seeking. He suggested that, as the two men he had in mind to answer my questions were likely to be working some distance away from the palace, and would like to have time to prepare themselves before meeting the great Hercules – I presumed he meant a wash and a change of clothes! – he would, if the King and I were agreeable, like to present them first thing in the morning. We confirmed that his proposal was quite agreeable, whereupon Alexandros bowed politely to both of us and glided out of the assembly room. The King and I then talked on a number of matters, which were of little relevance to my story. The King invited me to join him, the Queen and the courtiers at a banquet they had prepared for me. Before you ask, I was moderate in my drinking that evening! I excused myself and went to my quarters early so that I would be sharp and alert the next morning when I met the herdsmen Alexandros had promised to bring me.

' "I was scarcely dressed when Alexandros called, on his own. He very quickly gave me a description of the two herdsmen, who were awaiting his call in the anteroom adjoining my chamber. One, whose name I forget, we both thought would not be of much help and so I agreed to see him first. At my request, Alexandros remained during the short interview. We were right: the first man was a simple herdsman and could add little to what I already knew. The second herdsman, Epimenides, was quite different. He had known the Bull from his birth and gave as his opinion that the Bull had a naturally placid character and his reported present behaviour had come as a complete surprise. As it happened, Epimenides had known the two herdsmen killed by the Bull quite well and had discussed with one of them some days before the incident his concerns about the Bull's erratic behaviour. When I pressed him to explain further, Epimenides said that he had got the impression that the Bull was becoming increasingly restless, frequently tossing his head and foaming at the mouth and wouldn't let either of the herdsmen near him. Both herdsmen appeared quite frightened of the Bull but, when Epimenides suggested that they reported their unease, they declined to do so, thinking they would be ridiculed by the other herdsmen. Epimenides had not pressed the point. However, he had been rather upset when he heard a few weeks' later the news of the Bull's escape and the goring to death of his two keepers. By the time he heard of these events, they had occurred some time previously. The news had been delayed in reaching him because he was working in a rather remote part of the island and had not returned home for several weeks. On hearing the news, he had made a few enquiries to establish what had happened: the consensus appeared to be that the gods had made the animal mad. Epimenides, realising that nothing he could say now would bring the killed men back to life, had decided to hold his tongue.

' "Probing further and with, I must say, some help from Alexandros, Epimenides did add that he felt there could be a natural explanation for the Bull's behaviour. This is what I had felt as soon as I became involved. I asked him what he had in mind. He replied that he had once been in charge of a cow that had displayed similar behaviour. It too had attacked its herdsmen, though not fatally, and had escaped. He had chased it and managed to kill it with a spear before it had done much damage. When pulling out his spear from the carcass, he noticed that the cow's mouth had fallen open and that one of its teeth looked rotten. He prised it out with the tip of his spear and found that the tooth was completely eaten away inside and its roots had broken off in the cow's mouth. He recalled now that this animal had also foamed at the mouth in a similar fashion to the Bull and, just prior to the escape the cow had developed a habit of rubbing the side of its mouth that had the bad tooth against any solid object around, ranging from the sides of buildings to human beings. The Bull's herdsmen had described similar actions by the Bull before its breakout.

' "Epimenides' comments confirmed my suspicions about the reason for the Bull's aggression. Someone had suggested that it was to do with the mating season! This was, of course, ridiculous. The mating season does not last continuously for over a year, and there were no young cows in the area when the Bull escaped – nor had it attacked any cows, only crops, buildings and people. As for divine intervention, this suggestion was just an excuse to avoid facing up to reality. There had to be a rational explanation, which I felt we had uncovered. What worried me now was that, if I was right and the Bull had diseased teeth, he would be in even greater pain now than when he escaped. It was important to get to him as soon as possible and relieve his misery.

' "Fortunately, during my time as a herdsman, I had acquired a vast knowledge of herbal remedies for animal ailments. Unfortunately, I was not on mainland Greece but on the island of Crete, where the plants and animals were quite different. Having dismissed Epimenides with my great thanks for his help, I managed to find out from Alexandros who was the best local apothecary and where I could find him. Alexandros of course volunteered to summon him to the palace for my convenience but, as I was not sure whether what I wanted was available and I did not particularly want what I was doing to be bruited abroad, I declined his offer. Instead, I asked Alexandros if he could tell me where I could find the apothecary. I learnt that he was to be found some distance away, in a small town along the coast from the port where I had landed. I gratefully accepted the offer Alexandros made of a chariot and driver to take me there.

' "Pyrgios, the apothecary, dispensed his wares from the front room of his house in a street that led off the main square of a small town called Amphimalla. Although at the mouth of a river, and sheltered from the south and westerly winds, this town was not a thriving port and did not, so far as I could see, enjoy much trade of any sort. It had clearly seen better days. Pyrgios, who was well beyond middle age, told me that, when his father was a young man, it had been a thriving port. The earth shake of fifty years' previously had disturbed the flow of the river and severely damaged the harbour. Other ports had quickly restored their damaged facilities but the river at Amphimalla had changed its nature and brought silt into the harbour at such a rate that it had become uneconomic to keep the harbour open to the larger vessels. It was now reduced to being a small fishing port, providing a living for a few local fishermen but of no interest to the businessmen who used to service the formerly busy port. They had moved elsewhere. This accounted for the rather melancholy air I had detected when I arrived in the square.

' "Understandably, Pyrgios was more than a little curious about what I wanted. Although a few of his potions could be used for animals, he normally only prescribed for humans. I was in a dilemma: the remedy I needed for the bull would need to be many times greater in quantity and much more powerful than could possibly be needed for even the largest and strongest man. But I did not particularly want to disclose to a stranger precisely for what purpose I wanted the apothecary's help. He soon exploded my reserve.

' " 'You are Hercules, aren't you? Come to rid us of the Bull? What can I do to help you?'

' "He was a little shocked when I burst out laughing.

' " 'Why," he said, " 'surely you didn't think that I wouldn't recognise you – your fame precedes you, my dear young man.'

' "After that, there was no point in trying to hide anything from him. He made it clear that he was not interested in what he called 'street talk' – he had a job to do and integral to that was keeping his ears open and his mouth shut. I felt that I could trust him and explained what I was seeking and for what purpose. He confirmed what I had suspected: the particular herb I sought did not grow on Crete. He had inherited some from his father when he took over the business, but that had long since been used up or discarded. He had not attempted to purchase any more because, as he pointed out to me, the herb had a sharp taste that was not easy to disguise. Whilst a trusting animal might be prepared to take it from a well known handler or herdsman, a raging bull who had never seen me before might not. Before I could respond to his comment, he told me that he felt a combination of two herbs he had might work: one was a tranquilliser and the other a sweet-smelling soporific. Both would calm the Bull, even if only temporarily. Thinking of the long sea journey ahead of me if I was to bring the captured Bull from Crete to Tiryns and then to Mycenae, I felt that I would need herbs with these qualities and in some quantity. After some bargaining, I bought from Pyrgios what we both felt should be sufficient. The transaction completed, Pyrgios then remarked that he thought I might need his help later and told me to call for him if so. He would answer such a summons immediately and promised that a member of his household would always know where he could be found if he was not at home. I thanked him, promised to let him know when my mission was complete so that he would not await my call indefinitely and departed with his good wishes for my success ringing in my ears.

' "The return to the King's Palace was swift. On arrival I was summoned into the presence of the King, who was eager to know what I had discovered. He knew of my discussion with the herdsmen and my visit to the apothecary. I told him as little as I could and successfully turned the conversation on to how to find the Bull. The King had expected this question and Alexandros was summoned to give me a report on the latest sightings of the Bull. By good fortune, he had left the far west coast and was moving in our direction. He was still at least a day's charge away from the palace and would probably turn either south or west again before he got much closer. It would appear that my best opportunity to approach him was the next morning.

' "As you know, we were now approaching the end of winter. And so there was not much new grass yet, and the weather uncertain. The lack of food the Bull would be experiencing I intended to turn to my advantage. The package of herbs I had bought from the apothecary I would place at the centre of some sweet-smelling new grass I had harvested from a sheltered field near the shore. This, I hoped, would ensure that the rampant Bull would be somewhat calmed before I seriously attempted to capture him and find out what was upsetting him. I also managed to persuade some of the men the King had put at my disposal to follow me at a safe distance with some chains in case I needed them to secure the beast.

' "On my arrival in Crete, the weather had been unseasonably fine and sunny. Overnight, this changed dramatically and, as we started our search for the Bull, the sky opened and the rain fell heavily and continuously. We were all soaked through in minutes.

Nevertheless, we persisted in our search and after a few hours were rewarded for our zeal by stumbling upon unmistakeable signs that the Bull had passed our way recently. I was very impressed by the damage he had caused. Not only had he charged straight through a thick thorn hedge – leaving a hole a cubit wide – but we shortly came to the wreckage of what had been farm buildings. Small buildings that appeared to have been used to keep sheep or goats had been flattened and the animals gone. A large barn was on the verge of collapse, the posts supporting the corners of one end having been removed by the Bull. We knew that he could not now be very far away as parts of the barn were falling to the ground even as we came close. Warning the men with the chains to keep their distance and stay well away from the barn, I ventured on in the direction the Bull had obviously taken, guided by the path of destruction he had left behind him. I had just come to another thick hedge with a large hole in it when I heard a rushing sound behind me and turned just in time to see the damaged barn collapse to the ground in a heap. Turning round to continue walking in the direction I had been going, I almost came face to face with the Bull. He, too, must have heard the sound of the barn collapsing and it must have aroused his curiosity. Fortunately, I had not yet started to move again and I don't think he saw me.

' "I decided to stand still and see what he did. To my alarm, he came shambling towards me at a slow walk. At the time, I thought he was coming for me but, in fact, I think he was only coming to investigate the barn collapse. He was the wrong side of the hedge to get a clear view of what happened and, as if to confirm this, he sauntered up to the hedge and stopped just the other side of the hole he had made earlier – presumably to get a better view of the damage for which he was responsible. I remained stock still. After a loud snort, which I interpreted to mean satisfaction with the results of his labour, he turned slowly away and walked back into the field.

' "We had planned to approach the Bull's last known whereabouts downwind and, fortunately for me, the wind was still blowing towards me. That, and the noise of the falling rain, would have prevented any sound or scent of my presence from reaching him. But the wind did blow the stench of his snort from him to me and I noticed what appeared to be blood and mucus running out of his mouth. All these signs served to confirm my diagnosis – here was a sick animal.

' "The Bull was now settled into grazing the very poor grass that had survived the winter. I decided that there would probably never be a better time to try and capture him so I quickly gave the signal to the men that I had agreed with them previously to indicate that they should take cover whilst I made my first attempt to subdue him. I calculated that, if he charged me, I could reach the wreck of the barn before him and he would find it more difficult to chase me over the rubble than I would to evade him. At the worst, I would have to wrestle with him, but, apart from the personal risk in doing that, I did not wish to use too much violence on him if this could be avoided.

' "Now, during my time as a herdsman, I had developed a soft musical call that seemed to have a calming effect on cattle. It also aroused their curiosity and I often used it to herd them indoors for the night in winter. I decided to try this on the Bull, hoping he would come close enough for me to give him some of the herb enriched grass I had brought with me. My first attempt was a failure because, I think, the rain and the adverse wind flow prevented him from hearing it. I decided not to risk suddenly appearing in the field, as I was sure this would startle – and anger – him. So I waited in the pouring rain. I had by now got used to being thoroughly soaked; my main concern was that the Bull would see the cloud of steam rising above me as my body heat evaporated the water that had seeped through to my body! It may be that he did see this, because he raised his head to look in my direction and then slowly began to graze towards me. If I had not known otherwise, I would have thought that he was cleverly moving towards me without actually appearing to do so in order to catch me off guard. When his head was turned briefly away from me, I tossed a bunch of grass into the field through the hole in the hedge. It landed a cubit inside and was large enough to be obviously different from the normal surface of the field. After a little while, the Bull had reduced by half the distance he had been from me when I had first tried to attract him with my whistle. So

I whistled again. This time he did hear me, lifting his head and turning it in my direction when I whistled the first notes of the call. I continued whistling until the end of the first phrase, by which time he was trotting towards me and the hole in the hedge. As I stopped, he reached the bundle of grass I had thrown into the field. The combination of my stopping whistling and the appearance of something more appetising than the tired grass he had been eating caused him to stop and investigate. In the brief moment it took him to devour my offering, I was able to take a good look at him.

' "He was – or rather had been – a magnificent animal. A regal head with two beautiful, long, sharp horns stood proudly on a massive pair of shoulders. He had fallen away a little at the rear, probably because he had not been able to feed properly during the winter. He should quickly recover his condition with appropriate husbandry. But even in his present, reduced, state he was more than a match for most men. I was not surprised that he had killed two men when he escaped over a year ago. But his eyes, which I saw when he raised his head briefly from my gift, really alarmed me. They were bloodshot and fiery – but weary at the same time. They were the windows to a sad, lonely, bewildered and tortured soul. I felt really sorry for him. He had now finished his snack and it was time for me to make my next move. I knew that my next whistle would bring him through the hedge and then I would be exposed to him. I would need to have my wits about me. The apothecary had told me that the herbs would act quite quickly – in not more than a few minutes – so a short while after he had finished eating and gave the impression that he was thinking of moving away, I gave a shortened version of my call. He was alert at the first note and without a pause made straight for the hole in the hedge and for me.

' "I knew that, by this stage, he was aware that I was standing there. As soon as he reached the hedge I changed the whistled call to a wordless low speaking noise, which I had also found had a calming influence on cattle, particularly bulls. He stopped dead in his tracks, looked at me full in the eyes and bowed his head at me whilst emitting another snort, softer this time than the first one I had heard. I decided to take a risk, and slowly raised my hands, in which I held another bundle of grass, all the time making encouraging, friendly, noises to him. To my relief and delight, he came slowly forward, gently eased the grass from my hand and retreated backwards, keeping his eyes on me all the time whilst he ate it. We both then paused, looking at each other. I continued to 'talk' quietly to him, and he seemed to listen. The herbs and my talking gradually calmed him and, as he came towards me the second time, I thought a little of the frenzied fire had gone out of his eyes. This time I was not worried about lifting my backpack, in which I had put the grass mixture, up off the ground in order to offer him what remained of the portion I had brought with me. I still moved slowly and deliberately, ensuring that at all times he could see what I was doing and that it was not threatening to him.

' "I have often heard people use derogatory expressions about bulls and cows, implying that they are without, or have low, intelligence. Those who say these things usually have never handled animals of any sort and think that any animal that obeys a human's orders must be stupid. I know this is not true. Their intelligence is merely of a more basic quality than ours, related more to their own and their master's survival than some philosophical principle! Anyway, I knew that I had to convince the Bull that he needed human help and that I was here to help him.

' "By this time, I could see that the herbs were working. The Bull's body was more relaxed, his breathing was calmer and his eyes even less fierce and challenging. I had been told by Alexandros that the Bull came from a well-known Cretan docile strain and his rampage had come as a complete shock, so I was not surprised at his change of demeanour. I now had a problem. After over a year rampaging through the countryside, he had not a vestige left of his collar, so there was nothing that I could hold on to. I did not want to call up the men who had the tackle as I was sure that would antagonise him. He would feel that I had betrayed him and would not trust me again. At this moment, the rain stopped falling. He seemed to be as relieved at this as I was. So I decided to make physical contact with him, whistling and talking quietly to him all the while. He did not draw back or indicate any anxiety when I placed my hand on his shoulder and stroked him. I was nervous of touching his face until I knew where the problem was – a touch on the wrong spot could have had disastrous consequences. I moved gently around him for a long time. It was over half an hour before I felt that I could risk going behind him. I made sure that he knew where I was at all times. I was either in view or, if not, I was whistling and talking to him so that he could hear where I was.

' "When I placed the rope I had brought with me round his neck, he was so relaxed that he made no move even to acknowledge it was there. I had earlier decided that I would not try to take him back to his former home until I had established a rapport with him over several days. By this time, I had received a discreet signal from the men I had brought with me that the farmer whose barn had been destroyed was agreeable to the Bull being taken to a shed nearby that was large enough for the Bull to be housed in overnight – or for several days if that was what I wished. This was ideal and, short step by short step, I led the bull towards the shed that one of my men had identified for me. When we got there, I saw that the farmer had thoughtfully left some food out for him. No doubt, prompted by his own instinct for self-preservation, the farmer ensured that he and his family kept out of sight and hearing whilst I was completing the delicate task of leading the Bull into his temporary quarters.

' "He settled down quickly and seemed relieved to be under cover and with food to eat. I decided not to try to tie him up at this stage, although I wanted to leave him to brief the men and the farmer and to change out of my wet clothes. I had already decided that I would stay in the shed, or nearby, for several days, hoping that during that period I could do something about the Bull's physical problem. There was a stout door on the only entrance to the shed, which would probably prevent a normal animal from breaking out but this one would smash it to pieces with one blow of his rear legs! Still I had no choice: I had to leave him some time. Better now, whilst he was quiet and eating. The farmer had forgotten to give him any water, so I made a show of taking the empty water trough, which was there, and indicating to the Bull that I was going to get some water for him. He seemed to understand this and, when I moved to the door with the trough, he simply continued eating. I decided it was too early to shut the door on him, so I left it wide open. The farmer appeared at my side as soon as I rounded the corner and in a whisper I told him to fill it up with water and bring it back to me. Whilst he was doing this, I managed to signal to one of the men to come over and I instructed him to bring to me the spare dry clothes brought with us and leave a couple of men overnight with the chains and tackle at the farmhouse. I was not going to risk trying to chain him tonight! They also brought over some more of the grass mixture I had prepared and the men had brought with us. And so, approaching the shed door with the water in view of the Bull, whilst one of the men brought the food and my dry clothes around the other way, out of sight of the Bull, and placed them outside, I prepared for my vigil.

' "At first, the Bull was a little on edge when I returned with the water. He seemed rather restless, but, after I had talked to him quietly, he relaxed. Nevertheless I sensed he was still wary of me and wondering what I was going to do next. By now, the sun was setting and, although it was reasonably warm in the shed, the temperature outside was dropping. I decided that now was the time to change into dry clothes. The door of the shed was still open, so I moved slowly to the door, making sure the Bull could see me all the way. I was just wondering how to pick up my clothes, which, when I had last seen them, had been left in a waterproof bag against the door lintel by the hinge, when the bag appeared in front of me, held out by one of the men I had brought with me, grinning from ear to ear. He had been waiting for me to come for my clothes, realising that I would not want to be out of the sight of the Bull if this could be avoided. His thoughtful anticipation enabled me to collect my clothes – and some more of the grass mixture, which was also handed to me – without my being invisible to the Bull for more than a few seconds. Leaving the grass just to the right of the open door, where I could retrieve it without leaving the shed, I brought my clothes bag inside and, without delay, changed out of my wet clothes.

' "The Bull watched me change with, I thought, a rather supercilious look on his face, as if to pity me for being a mere mortal and not having as versatile a waterproof skin as he had. I suspected that he had seen a herdsman do this on a number of occasions as he did not appear in the least alarmed. I then flung the wet clothes out of the door so that they fell out of sight of the Bull and myself (which startled the Bull a little), knowing that one of the men would pick them up and have them washed and dried. I then made a bed for myself near the door out of hay in the shed and spread the bag in which my change of clothes had been held over the hay to reduce the irritation of the hay stalks on my skin when I lay down to sleep. All the while, the Bull watched me with considerable interest, but not hostility.

'"By now, it was quite dark. My men and the farmer had, however, managed to place a few burning torches around the yard without making any noise loud enough to startle the Bull, although I think he heard their movements. The light was sufficient to enable me to see, dimly, the inside of the shed and the profile of the Bull, whose eyes shone brightly, making an eerie sight in the darkened shed. I decided to bring the feed in and give it to him and then close the door. This I accomplished deliberately, slowly and in the Bull's full view. He still kept a wary eye on what I was doing, but I felt he was beginning to trust me. After all, I had given him food and shelter for the night – and some companionship – and had not seriously attempted to restrict his movements. The closing of the door was an anxious moment but his long experience of being enclosed at night, and possibly the fact that I was staying with him, reassured him. After a few anxious snorts, he accepted it and settled down to eat the food I had given him. Within a little while, we were both asleep.

'"I awoke before dawn with a shock to find the Bull standing over me and licking my face. His breath smelt terrible! Managing to conceal my alarm, I remained prone and reached out my hand to touch him gently on the left cheek. Even in the poor light from the torches, I could see that the right side of his face, which had generally been shielded from me, was swollen and was, I suspected, badly infected. He allowed me to stroke him for a few seconds and then, with a brief snort, trundled away, back to where he had lain down when we went to sleep. Now wide awake, I wondered why he had awoken me and concluded that he was probably hungry. So, slowly and carefully, I stood up, opened the door slightly and brought in some more of the food I had prepared. On taking this over to him, he almost snatched it from my hands but it was done with care so as not to catch my fingers. He was hungry but not so much as to forget his manners!

'"I decided now was the moment to see if I could find out what was wrong with his jaw. Dawn was breaking and, although there was a risk of losing him if he chose to rush for freedom, I gently opened the door to bring the rapidly strengthening light into the shed. He was still munching the grass and herb mix I had given him with a strange motion of his jaw. Instead of the normal circular motion, he was clearly favouring the right side of his jaw and using only the left side to chew. This must have made eating very awkward for him. He found my intense interest in his eating rather embarrassing and pawed the ground with his front feet in a veiled warning to me, so I deflected my gaze and no longer looked directly at him. Out of the corner of my eye I could see that the outside of his jaw was bleeding from a giant sore that I had not noticed before because of the mucus that had covered it. This mucus had either been wiped off his mouth by the straw or subsided whilst he had slept or, as the apothecary had inferred, the herbs he had given me had reduced the infection. It was clear to me that I could do nothing for him here. I would have to get him to some secure stables where he could be given a drug either to put him to sleep or that would remove all sensation from his jaw. The apothecary had anticipated this need and had given me a potion that he said would temporarily deaden the Bull's sense of feeling from the area over which it was spread. The problem, which the apothecary himself recognised, was that the Bull would react instantly and violently to being touched where the potion needed to be spread. He would have to be chained for the safety of those attending him.

'"Even so, there was still a problem for me. I not only had to capture him but sail with him back to Mycenae. It was essential that he did not associate me with pain – only with pleasure. This meant that I could not administer the potion myself, nor carry out any of the treatment myself. I was sorry about this but, with a long and dangerous journey ahead of me, it was best to preserve my present good relationship with him.

‘ “I was encouraged that, after his latest feed had been digested, his recent docility remained. I could not be sure for how long this would endure, so it was clear that the Bull would have to be led as soon as possible to some secure stables, where he could receive treatment. Again, I felt it was important that he should not associate me with what he might consider to be any ill treatment. So, I decided to lead him out myself with the rope I had originally used but had taken off when we arrived at the shed. As before, he hardy noticed when I placed the rope around his neck and willingly followed me out of the shed when I indicated by my body movements that it was time to go. I did not need to tug on the rope.

‘ “We had, of course, prepared for the need to place the Bull in a secure stable after capture, preferably not far away from where he had last been seen grazing. On our way to catch him, a suitable building had been identified and my men, when they saw me emerging slowly from the shed with the Bull on the end of a rope, guessed that I was trying to lead him there without chaining him. Taking a parallel route to ours and out of sight so as not to alarm the Bull, the men gathered up the chains and raced to the selected stable to set up the required restraints. Impressed by the effect of the special ‘grass’ I had fed to him, they also ensured that the manger at the stable was suitably filled with the magic mixture.

‘ “While we were a little way off from the stable, I sensed a change in the Bull’s demeanour: he became agitated and shook his head from side to side, as if he wanted to rid himself of something. I immediately talked soothingly to him and he calmed down. I suspect he had smelt the presence of my men and remembered being beaten about the head by his keepers when he escaped. He clearly associated people with being hurt, but I was not sure how he could reconcile this with the permanent hurt he now had in his head. Surely he could not attribute this to human beings?

‘ “Fortunately, all the men had followed my instructions to remain out of sight, although it was comforting for me to catch an occasional glimpse of one or two of them behind me as the Bull and I approached the stable. Surprisingly, considering the chains were fully visible on the walls of the stable, I managed to lead the

Bull straight into the stable. Of course, he could smell the food prepared for him and made straight for it. Whilst he was feeding, I managed to put a harness on to him to which the chains could be attached, without his becoming angered. I then had a dilemma. Should I risk putting on the restraints myself or leave it to others to do it, and preserve my reputation in the Bull's mind as his friend? My responsibility was clear. I was the best person to do it. Whistling and talking to him as he ate, I managed to link the chains to the harness and secure them to stout hooks in the wall giving the Bull sufficient length to move around the stable with minimal risk of entanglement. Having done this, I left to find the men and particularly the apothecary, who had promised to administer the ointment provided I would guarantee him protection against a raging bull.

'"Surprisingly, the Bull did not react to my departure. He was enjoying his food and had not really noticed when I had shackled him. This was in my favour as he might not associate me with his restraints. The apothecary had been summoned but had not yet arrived. So there was nothing now for me to do but wait. When the apothecary arrived, he told me of a slight change of plan. He had a potion that could put the Bull to sleep. He had not mentioned it before because it was dangerous for a human to take in large quantities and he had never before heard of it being used on an animal the size of the Bull. The quantity required by a bull of his size was certainly large enough to kill a human and he was a little nervous of using it at all. However, when he heard from me an outline of the Bull's condition, he felt it would be impossible to treat him without first making him unconscious. He then asked what I thought the weight of the Bull was. He explained that this was so that he could estimate how much of the special potion he could safely use on the Bull. I told him that I thought that the Bull weighed as much as twenty men. The apothecary, concerned that an overdose could kill the Bull, decided to limit the multiplier to fifteen.

'"Of course, as the Bull trusted me, I was asked to administer it to him in another bundle of grass, this time freshly picked and without any of the herb content. What could I do but agree? When I re-entered the stable to carry out my task, the Bull was still on his feet but looking decidedly groggy. The apothecary had told me that the volume of the herbal 'cure' he had been given so far could generate a sleepy feeling in the Bull, which was an advantage as far as I was concerned. As I approached, the Bull shook himself and heard the chains attached to his harness rattle. Before he could get over his surprise, I was offering him the fresh grass with the potion. Within minutes, he had eaten it and was stretched out on the floor. Unfortunately, he was lying on his right side and access to the right side of his jaw was virtually impossible. It took ten men with ropes some valuable time to lift him over on to his other side so that the apothecary could begin his work with a skilled herdsman, known for his treatment of animals. They had to work fast because the apothecary calculated that the Bull would only remain unconscious for an hour at most.

' "I stayed to watch, although, because the two of them were working on the Bull's jaw, I could see little and had to find out later what they had found. Five teeth in the lower right jaw of the bull were badly affected and three were removed. The infection had spread to the inside of the Bull's cheek and, as I had noticed, had spread through to affect the outside. They cut away the rotten tissue and bathed the areas they had cleaned before putting on an ointment to deaden the pain and speed the healing process. At the same time, they cleaned out his mouth generally to ensure that whatever had caused the infection could not spread elsewhere. Both the apothecary and the herdsman considered that the Bull must have been in very great pain for a long time. The herdsman, privately, told me what he thought of those charged previously with looking after the Bull.

' "As soon as we left the stable, the Bull stirred and got unsteadily to his feet. He quickly realised he was chained and that something had happened whilst he had been asleep. I imagine the pain of his infection must have been quite severe as, for some time, he bellowed, rattled his chains and strained to break free. I managed to watch him for most of the time while remaining invisible to him. At last, the pain seemed to subside and he grew calmer. At this point, I entered and gave him some food and fresh water, keeping well out of reach, as he still had a wild look about him. However, as I had hoped, he did not associate me with his pain and he showed no antagonism towards me.

' "Over the next few days, we watched his recovery and planned the next phase: the transportation to Mycenae. I discovered that the Bull, not unsurprisingly, had never been on a ship before. I also discovered that he had been mated successfully several times with a particular cow, who was still in the King's herd. Over the following days, I was allowed to take this cow down to the docks and put her on board the ship we had to take us back to Greece, go for a short sail and disembark, so that she could become accustomed to the procedures and the feeling of being at sea. I was relying on the Bull being sufficiently trusting of me and the cow to do as we wanted without concern. The day before I planned to sail, I sent a swift ship ahead of me to let you know when I expected to arrive with the Bull. I understand that my messenger has still not arrived?"

'When I confirmed this was so, he continued:

' "Oh, well, so much for advance planning! Anyway, with some help from the apothecary and a corps of ten strong men with a leather strap behind his haunches, we managed to persuade the Bull to follow his favourite cow on board the ship. He seemed unconcerned when we smuggled the cow off on to land and, as much for his safety as our own, secured him in the centre of the ship by his chains to rings bolted into the deck. The whole area, at my request, was surrounded by canvas so that he was sheltered from the wind and rains and could not see out. I spent most of the voyage with him, making sure he was properly fed and watered and that his rapidly improving jaw was kept clean.

' "The voyage took three days and nights and we were reasonably fortunate with the weather. Although we had some brisk winds – and choppy waves – we did not have a storm; or even much heavy rain. And so we reached the mainland at last. You know the rest of the story."

'I then asked him what he thought was the significance of the mission and what would now happen to the Bull.

' "As to the Bull's future," Hercules said, "I really don't know what the High King will do with him. The King and the people are clearly very afraid of him – his reputation has preceded him, I fear. But this time, the King dare not kill him because I believe that, on this occasion, for the reasons I shall give you in answering your first question, the instruction from Apollo was to capture, not kill, the Bull. As to the significance, I am sure it is related to the project we have discussed. As you know, the bull is a symbol for a number of things, mainly related to fertility. In Crete, bulls are sacred to the goddess Artemis, who, as you know, is Apollo's twin sister. In fact, they share the shrine at Delphi not only with Dionysus but also with each other. But, nevertheless, there clearly is some rivalry between them. I think that in this task Apollo is gently reminding his sister that she has failed to look after her protégé, that he has managed to save the Bull and is, therefore, her superior. Sibling rivalry, I think, but he means the Bull no harm, as he himself is known to be generally well disposed towards the animal."

'We later heard that the High King and the people were so frightened of the bull that they drove it off to the north, and, after roaming through Sparta and Arcadia, it was last heard of crossing the Corinth Isthmus on the way to Attica.'

The Eighth Labour: The Wild Mares of Diomedes

'Hercules and I then discussed his next task. This was to capture the four wild Mares of Diomedes. Hercules explained that these were to be found in Thrace, the best route to which, from Mycenae and Tiryns, lay by sea. But we decided to make for Thebes immediately and discuss how to achieve the task and what role, if any, I would play en route. During the journey, Hercules explained what was significant about the Mares, who were reputed to be man-eating, and how he thought he could capture them.

' "There is an old tradition," explained Hercules, "in the matriarchal system in Thrace that when the King's rule comes to an end – usually after a hundred moon phases – he is chased through the hills by wild women in horse masks and killed and eaten by them. This horrible custom was changed some years ago into a chariot race between the King and his challenger. The result was the same – the King was killed and the challenger took over if he won. Usually the race was fixed so that the (younger) challenger did win. Rarely, the King himself made arrangements so that the challenger lost. In those cases, he was killed and the King remained on the throne. To show his power over the old traditions, Diomedes some years ago caught and restrained in his stables four wild Mares and circulated a rumour that these horses were fed on the flesh of his unwelcome guests. This is contrary to the general custom that visitors and strangers should be treated courteously. It also reminds the people of the old, matriarchal, tradition. I think this is why Apollo has decreed that the Mares should be removed from Diomedes – Apollo must fear the old ways may return after Diomedes' death and wishes to prevent this."

'Hercules made it clear that, as Thrace was far away, it would be essential to go by ship and a sizeable force would be required to sail the ship and protect us against pirates at sea and robbers on land. As he wished to visit his old friend King Admetus and his wife, Alceste, at Pherae in Thessaly on our outward journey, he wished to take a chariot with him on board, preferring to hire horses locally as required. As we would be calling at the important port of Pagasae in Thessaly to disembark for the overland trip to Pherae, no difficulty was expected in finding horses there for the chariot and the mounted warriors who would accompany it.

'But first, a boat, crew and warriors had to be found. This did not prove to be difficult. Everyone wanted to be able to boast that they had been on an expedition with the great Hercules. Indeed, at one time, I thought that I might be left behind! Hercules decided that he would need an older, more experienced, warrior to accompany him on both the ride to Pherae and to be his right-hand man when we arrived in Thrace. And so he chose as his armour-bearer for this expedition a man called Abderus, a native of Opus in Locris, which was the port we set out from and where many of the crew lived. This was a fortunate choice by Hercules for me, as it later proved – but not for Abderus!

'The first part of our journey was uneventful. We negotiated the veering winds and tricky currents of the channels between the mainland and the huge island of Euboea with its many kingdoms and, a short distance before we came to the open sea, we turned north into the Pagasaean Gulf, at the head of which was the sea port of Pagasae.

'As we sailed up the narrow channel leading to the port, Hercules asked me for my first impressions. I had no hesitation in telling him that I was impressed. The large clear area in front of the imposing dock warehouses spoke of a carefully planned and well directed enterprise. There appeared also to be a healthy boat-building business occupying nearly half the visible area of the docks. When I remarked upon this, in my ignorance, Hercules told me that the famous *Argo* – which, he reminded me, had sailed into the furthest corner of the Black Sea in search of the Golden Fleece – had been built there and that he had first met Admetus, then the heir to the throne of Pherae, in the building yard here, helping to supervise the *Argo*'s construction. Admetus was one of those young men who accompanied Jason in his quest and Hercules had already told me how he himself had travelled with them for part of their journey. The paths of Hercules and Admetus were crossing again in their lives' stories.

'It was a disappointment when Hercules decided that I should stay in Pagasae with the crew to guard our boat while he and a small heavily armed band rode off to Pherae, Abderus acting as both armour-bearer and charioteer on this occasion. I would have liked to meet King Admetus and hear tales of the Golden Fleece expedition but Pagasae was an interesting, bustling port with much activity of interest to a young man like me, particularly as I had friends among the crew with whom to share experiences. I think Hercules realised that I would enjoy their company better than his and those of the older warriors he had taken with him. Perhaps he also wanted to talk to his old friend Admetus of youthful indiscretions without a young, potentially critical, audience. He never told me his reasoning, so I can only guess. However, I am sure that I did not miss the long dusty journeys to and from Pherae and I also found the night life of Pagasae most pleasant and relaxing!

'However, as the days passed I did begin to become rather tired of the limited pleasures that Pagasae could offer and yearned to be on the road again. Disturbing rumours of problems at Pherae for the King and Queen emerged to upset me further. But I remained confident that, whatever fate had to throw at them – and there was no suggestion in the rumours that Hercules himself was threatened – I was confident that he would help in a resolution of whatever difficulties he found at Pherae. Still, as the days lengthened into weeks, my concern grew. At last, we had news that Hercules was on his way back to Pagasae. This came with his instructions to prepare the ship for sailing as soon as possible. I set about this immediately, as Hercules' trusted assistant. I was a little discomfited with the change of plan. Originally Hercules, I thought, had said that he would travel overland from here, although I personally had doubts of the wisdom of this because the party would be vulnerable to being waylaid on the journey, possibly even by Diomedes' warriors, as we must presume that he had already heard of the expedition. At best, if we travelled overland, Diomedes would be certain to get considerable advance warning of our approach. We had a long distance to cover to reach his palace. I guessed that Hercules had come to the same conclusion – possibly his friend King Admetus had advised him.

'There was, however, at first, no information on the reason for the delay, but we then heard that Alceste had died but had been brought back to life by Hercules! These market rumours grew until people were speaking openly in the market about how Hercules had wrestled with Death and prevented Him from taking Alceste to the Underworld. Just as these stories were taking hold, Hercules arrived, dusty and dishevelled, holding the reins of the chariot while an exhausted Abderus relaxed in the back. The rest of the party staggered in after him and led their horses and chariots away to their stables. Hercules' horses were out on their feet and, at a gesture from Hercules, I unhitched them immediately from their chariot and summoned help to manhandle it – with Abderus still on board – and put it away under cover whilst I led the horses to their stable where I fed, watered them and washed them down. I could read the gratitude in their eyes for the welcome gentle treatment they received!

'By the time I emerged from the stable with the horses resting in a secure enclosure, Abderus had recovered and Hercules had washed and changed into clean clothes. He looked different: leaner, fitter and slightly wearier than when we were last together. He had quickly become aware of the rumours in the market about his activities and was extremely amused, as I knew he would be. Curbing my impatience, I waited for him to open the subject. He first wanted to know about the preparations for sailing and was pleased when I told him that I thought the ship would be ready within two days. Anticipating my questions, he explained that he had thought of travelling overland but, for the reasons I had already deduced, had abandoned the idea after Admetus had spelt out the risks, the most important one being that he would lose the advantage of surprise. He then outlined his strategy privately to me and Abderus. We would sail close to the borders of Thrace and land secretly at night at a secluded cove. A small, heavily armed party, including Hercules and Abderus, would ride swiftly along the coast to Diomedes' city, arriving before dawn. I would stay behind with the ship, the chariot and the majority of our force. My task would be to ensure the ship was off the coast of

Diomedes' city, preferably just visible on the skyline, immediately before Hercules attacked at dawn. Hercules would approach from the landward side. If the lookouts were observant, and expecting an attack, they would probably assume the ship carried the attackers and prepare a defence facing entirely the wrong direction. On a more dismal note, Hercules emphasised that, whatever happened, I was not to bring the ship within reach of Diomedes' force. If ships were launched against us, I was to take the ship out of reach, returning three days later to the cove where the party had originally disembarked. There the horses and his party would embark. I was not, for any reason, to beach the ship and land our force to assist him. If immediately successful, he would embark straight away. Although he was confident of success and a safe escape, he did not want me to take unnecessary risks. Concern for my safety was, I am sure, one of his motives, but I suspect he also had no wish for this task to be disqualified for excessive outside help, and he honestly felt safer, if things went wrong, if he had fewer peoples' safety to worry about.

'The next two days we were all very busy and I completely forgot about the story of Alceste running through the market, even though I noticed that whenever Hercules appeared the general populace visibly shrank from him in awe, despite the beaming smile he gave them all. We were loaded and at sea before Hercules and Abderus satisfied our curiosity.

' "You have been remarkably patient," Hercules remarked to me with a huge grin when the ship had rounded the headland and was scudding its way east towards Thrace. "But then, you know my ways – and my temper! You must be dying to know what happened in Pherae and so I will tell you. As soon as we got to Admetus' palace, I could feel something was wrong. Admetus was not on the palace steps to greet us after Abderus and I had descended from our chariot, which was taken away promptly enough by the palace grooms, nor was their any sign of Queen Alceste who, as you know, knows me personally. The Chief Steward was there to welcome us, and a rather muted welcome it was. Knowing that my friend Admetus did not have a quarrel with me, I saw no reason to prevaricate and asked straightway what the problem was. The Chief Steward, who by now had tears in his eyes, said that the dear Queen was dying and the King was distraught. Apothecaries and soothsayers had been summoned but could offer neither medicine nor solace. I was minded to leave at once as it was wrong to intrude upon my friend's grief. However, I decided to suspend my judgment as the King had ordered that I, alone, be brought to him on arrival. And so I was ushered into the presence of my royal friend, King Admetus.

' "He was so downcast that I was most upset. He was pleased to see me and apologised for the shabbiness of his welcome, which, of course, I said was understandable in the circumstances. Enquiring after the Queen's health, I did not receive a clear response. After much pressing, he told me the story, some of which I had heard and which was one of the main reasons for my visit. For some years a powerful group of matriarchs had been trying to overthrow the, relatively new, patriarchal system that had been established in this part of Thessaly. This was partly backed by a popular reaction to the events at the city of Iolchos, at which you and I were present a few years ago." '

The Return of the Argonauts

Seeing my puzzled expression, Iolaus added: 'I think that I had better explain now what this was all about, as, otherwise, you will not understand the context. When Jason and the Argonauts returned to Pagasae with the Golden Fleece, intending to deliver it to Pelias (who, you recall, had usurped Jason's father's throne) and claim back the throne, they found this part of Thessaly practically deserted. While the Argonauts were deliberating what to do, Hercules and I arrived, by chance, on our way back to Thebes. There were rumours that Pelias had ravaged the land and killed his twin brother, Aeson, and his wife, Polymele – who, of course, were Jason's mother and father – in order to consolidate his position as King of Iolchos. Pelias had apparently heard that Jason's expedition had been successful and was intent on reneging on the agreement he had made with Jason to renounce the throne in Jason's favour if he brought back the Golden Fleece. Understandably, Jason and the majority of the Argonauts were extremely angry and resolved to attack Pelias' palace and kill him, if what they had been told proved true. Hercules advised caution. The stories might not be true and, anyway, the Argonauts would be no match for Pelias' forces, who would vastly outnumber them. One of the Argonauts, Acastus, pointed out that he was Pelias' son and could not join in any such expedition against his own father. It was agreed to keep the news of the *Argo*'s return a secret for the time being and Acastus excluded himself from any further deliberations, whilst also taking an oath that he would keep silent about the *Argo*'s return.

'The Argonauts, with Hercules and myself joining them, then debated what to do. After a long discussion, a consensus emerged that the Argonauts should each return to their own countries to raise an army to subdue Pelias and regain the throne for Jason, the rightful King. But Medea, Jason's fiancée, a daughter of King Aeetes of Colchis, and who had given Jason much help in gaining the Fleece, gave the council her advice, which was accepted. She agreed with Hercules that the Argonauts were not a large enough force to challenge Pelias' army – and the rumours might not be true. It would also take time to raise an army and many innocent people would be killed. She volunteered to enter the city, disguised as an old priestess, with her twelve handmaidens, carrying an image of Artemis they had brought with them. Her aim would be to penetrate the King's palace and, if the rumours of him were true, to kill him. If she was successful she would arrange for burning torches to be in lit on the palace roof as a signal. In the meantime, the *Argo* should be sailed a short distance round the bay, beached and concealed in a secluded place within sight of the city. The Argonauts should wait there until summoned by the burning torches. Whilst the crew did as asked, Hercules and I assisted Medea and her "priestesses" get ready – so far as we were allowed to do. The tasks we were allotted were mainly to garner vegetation and despoil garments with soil so that Medea and her party looked thoroughly unkempt. Medea told us that they were posing as Hyperboreans, claiming to be Celts and from a magical far-off land to the west. She transformed herself from a beautiful young princess into an ugly old crone, hobbling along with the help of a stick. She was very convincing!

'At Medea's request, we found a young lamb, which she concealed in the statue of "Artemis", having given it some drug to keep it quiet. We had no idea at the time what she intended to do with it. When all was ready, this strange procession launched itself towards the distant city, at a slow pace, with Medea in the lead, followed by one of the priestesses carrying the statue, who passed it one to another during the journey. Hercules and I kept a discreet distance behind them, taking advantage of what natural cover there was. We heard the shrill call of Medea demanding entry from the gatekeepers and they threw the gates open at her demand without delay. Within a few minutes we could hear uproar within the city as Medea's plan to inspire the inhabitants to a religious frenzy took hold.

'What I will now tell you is what I learnt afterwards. I did not witness any of it.

'The commotion in the city soon caught the attention of

King Pelias, as Medea had intended. He must have found the sight of these ragged religious fanatics led by an ugly, bent, old crone carrying aloft a large statue and proclaiming good fortune if they were well received more than daunting. I understand that he was very nervous of what it all meant and, having a guilty conscience, he was obviously keen to have as much good fortune as he could get. Still, he hadn't managed to seize the throne from his twin brother and hold off his nephew from his rights without being a reasonably resolute man. So, before he would offer them any hospitality, he wanted some indication that they were above the ordinary. Now, it so happened that his brother, Aeson, was still alive and had been released a few days earlier from his confinement by Pelias – he had not been killed, despite the rumours. This was because sickness, disappointment and years of harsh treatment had aged him prematurely and Pelias was no longer in fear of him. He, too, had been aroused by the commotion caused by Medea and came out of the palace to see what it was all about.

'Medea soon understood who he was and saw that he was very run down in health. Medea had great knowledge of herbs and of their healing properties. She had brought some with her from Colchis and gathered more on the journey to Pagasae. Before Pelias could stop her, Medea approached Aeson and offered to treat him for his ailment. Within a very short time, she had him stretched out on a couch, surrounded by her attendants and made a great show of letting his blood and giving him a potion. He was then left to rest for a short while and, to Pelias' (and, I imagine, Aeson's) astonishment, Aeson awoke to find his youthful vigour returned and gave his profuse thanks to Medea for this transformation. Pelias was not too happy but, in face of this magic change in his brother, could hardly deny that the visitors seemed to have some magic powers.

'He did not need to ask for more proof of Medea's prowess. She was eager to show him, all as part of her plot. She demanded of Pelias an old ram, which was duly brought in. Medea announced that she would bring back Pelias' youth for him in recognition of his gracious reception of the deputation she had led but wished to give final proof of the powers vested in her by

Artemis. Ordering a large cauldron to be filled with water and brought to the boil, she cast off her grimy clothes revealing herself to be young and active – which of course she attributed to the goddess Artemis. By now, Pelias could scarcely believe his good fortune – he wished to recapture his youth and sire more children to secure his dynasty. Medea had told him that his son, Acastus, had lost his life in the Argonaut expedition, and so he thought he no longer had an heir other than Jason, his nephew, who he could not deny if he had no sons of his own, although he did have four adult daughters.

'When the water in the cauldron was boiling, Medea brought out a huge sharp knife she had hidden in her clothes, slaughtered the ram and carved it into thirteen pieces, one for each lunar month. As you know, Artemis was associated with the moon and its worship. The pieces were cast into the cauldron and were gradually dissipated in the boiling water. The statue of Artemis, carried into the city by Medea's attendants, was then brought to her and waved over the bubbling cauldron. Accompanied by a clash of cymbals, which the attendants had hidden in their clothes and brought out at the appropriate moment, Medea apparently drew a young lamb out of the seething cauldron, to the gasps of the watching crowd, including Pelias, who had been joined by his four daughters, Alceste, the eldest, Pisidice, Pelopea and Hippothoe. Pelias, with his daughters' support, was eager to be similarly rejuvenated and, when Medea invited the daughters to kill their father and cut him up into thirteen pieces, as she had dealt with the ram, only Alceste declined. On Medea's instructions, the pieces were thrown into the bubbling cauldron. It was now early evening and Medea then, apparently to enhance the spell she was to cast on their father's body parts, required the daughters to light torches and take them on to the palace roof whilst invoking the blessing of Artemis, the moon goddess. This they did. Seeing the pre-arranged signal, the Argonauts, Hercules and I made our way quickly to the main gate of the city. We had no difficulty entering as the gatekeepers were all in the city main square outside the palace, enjoying the performance.

'By the time we reached the palace square, Medea and her attendants had vanished, leaving the city without a ruler. The citizens had quickly realised that Pelias and his daughters had been tricked. The drugs given to Aeson by Medea had by now begun to lose their power and he was relapsing back into his former condition. Realising, on seeing Jason, that he probably had something to do with the killing of Pelias and that he had returned to claim the throne, Aeson greeted his son warmly. Pausing only to confirm his suspicions about his brother's death and that Jason had brought back the Golden Fleece, he retired to his room, drank poison and died quickly. Jason immediately realised that Medea could not return as queen but he could not abrogate his oath to her. So he announced to the people that Pelias' son, Acastus, was alive and had returned safely from the expedition. He now proposed to hold funeral games in honour of the dead King Pelias, after which he would leave Iolchos to allow Acastus to become King in place of his father, Pelias. This decision was warmly welcomed.

'Shortly after the funeral games, Alceste made her way to Pherae to marry Admetus, to whom she had been engaged before the Argonaut expedition. Her sisters were banished from Iolchos by their brother, Acastus, for complicity in their father's murder but, I believe, after a suitable period of atonement for their involvement in their father's death, they were accepted as purified and made happy marriages. Jason and Medea sailed to Corinth where, by happy coincidence, the man whom Medea's father, Aeetes, had appointed to act as his regent had just died, as had the usurper, Corinthus. Medea's claim to the throne was accepted by the people and she and Jason settled as King and Queen of Corinth. Later, as you probably know, all ended in tragedy.'

Admetus and Alceste

'But now it is time to go back to our story. The relevance of the episode I have described is that, perhaps not surprisingly, Medea's "visit" as a priest of Artemis reawakened interest in the worship of Artemis and, by association, of the matriarchal culture. Medea herself used it to claim the throne of Corinth – but through her father's right of inheritance, not her mother's. Some in Thessaly were so impressed by the stories of Medea that, although many felt she was a false prophetess, in the end there were enough influential mature women in many cities to spark a religious revival over a wide-spread area, which brought with it a desire to throw out the "new" patriarchal cult and return to the matriarchal.

'Hercules told me that one of its most serious manifestations was at Pherae. He reminded me that one of the main features of the matriarchal system was that a "king" was replaced every eight to ten years, usually by some form of armed combat, or a chariot race involving a younger man who would take the existing queen to wife on the old king's inevitable death. If he didn't die as a result of the combat, another way would be found.

'Hercules continued to relate the story. This is what he said.

' "After several happy years as King, Admetus became aware of a movement to make him abdicate after eight years' reign so that his wife could choose a new consort. Alceste denied all knowledge of this – indeed, she opposed it. As she was herself not of the royal family of Pherae, but of Iolchos, the campaign was misdirected. But it appeared deep-seated and Admetus and Alceste were extremely worried and did not know what to do.

' "They decided, first, to consult an oracle. Unfortunately, they chose Delphi in the autumn when the priests of Dionysus, not Apollo, were in residence. The clear message was that Admetus had to die, although whether by disease, by his own hand or by the hand of another was not clear. There was, however, a hint that someone of similar rank would be acceptable to the gods in substitution. Alceste was adamant that Admetus should not die before his time and offered herself as substitute. Admetus refused and, distraught, asked his father and mother, who were both still alive but by now very old and weak, whether they would die so that he could live. They both indignantly refused. They were both in retirement enjoying relative comfort without responsibility.

'"By now, spring was approaching and the pressure for a decision was mounting. A few days before my arrival, the Chief Priest of Apollo from Delphi called at the palace at Pherae. He was on his way from Delos, where he had passed the autumn and winter, to Delphi, where he spent the spring and summer. He had heard of the problem and urged Admetus on no account to sacrifice himself. This would do untold damage to the cause of those who wanted to stabilise the patriarchal system. Unfortunately, the priest had left before I arrived. Admetus, perhaps wrongly in my opinion, told Alceste what the priest had said. Her resolve now to die in place of her husband was resolute. She supported the move away from the matriarchal system, with its long tradition of violence and human sacrifice, to the more humane approach of the patriarchal system. Her sacrifice would further the cause she favoured and damage the cause she opposed. Alceste's resolve was unshakeable and she took poison just before my arrival.

'"After much persuasion, Admetus took me into the room where his wife lay dying. Although she was still breathing, I could see she had not long to live. Smelling her breath, I recognised the poison she had taken and I knew that I had brought an antidote with me. It is a common one and I frequently carry it with me. I urged Admetus to clear the room and arrange a bier to carry Alceste to the family tomb where a place had already been prepared for her. Whilst Admetus was busying himself following my instructions, I managed to administer the antidote to Alceste, who was just conscious enough to swallow what I gave her. Now I knew that, despite the antidote, Alceste would soon be unconscious, from which she might not ever recover. It was important to get her out of this room, which was hot and stuffy. The stone-built, vaulted tomb would be a perfect place for her to recover, if that was what the gods willed.

‘ “As Alceste slipped into unconsciousness, the bier arrived carried by weeping servants. Admetus, seeing the apparently lifeless body of his wife on the couch, broke down and wept copiously over his wife’s body. All were convinced that she had passed away. It was easy for me to take charge. I ordered the servants to transfer the body of their Queen on to the bier and carry her out through the courtyard to the burial chamber, which was a little distance away. I accompanied the bier and made sure that her, possibly last, journey on this earth was comfortable. I was particularly concerned that she did not slip off the bier on to the ground; contact by her head with the ground would be fatal and prevent anything I could do from being successful.

‘ “Queen Alceste was gently carried into the tomb and, at my instruction, the servants laid her bier on the prepared stone slab in the middle of the floor. I asked the steward in charge of the servants to leave me alone with the now-presumed dead Queen but send back a servant with some fresh water, wine, honeyed bread and figs. I undertook that, when I left shortly, I would seal the only entrance to the tomb. My requests were met, the steward himself returning with the food and drink I had sought, accompanied by Admetus, still overwhelmed by the loss of his beloved wife. Placing the supplies in a niche in the wall of the tomb, clearly visible from the stone slab on which the Queen’s bier was set, I comforted Admetus as best I could.

‘ “While he calmed down, I had to decide how I was to explain Queen Alceste’s recovery, if my antidote was successful, whilst protecting Admetus from the double grief of losing his wife a second time if my attempt to save her proved unsuccessful. I decided to say nothing about my administration of the antidote but to offer to go down to the Underworld and try to bring her back alive. By now, Admetus, who had earlier been forcibly restrained by me and his senior steward from killing himself, was calmer and resigned to his loss. He heard out my proposal and tried, rather feebly, to dissuade me from risking my life in such a forlorn attempt – as he put it. However, it was not difficult to persuade him to agree to support my venture, although I made it clear that I would go alone and that during my absence nobody should enter the tomb, which I would personally seal. He agreed and then, at my request, left me alone in the tomb with Alceste. Now the tomb was quiet, I could listen to see if she was still breathing. Although the tomb was lofty, made of stone throughout and resonant, I could hear nothing. I feared the worst. I moved right up to the bier and bent my head down to within touching distance of her face. Listening intently, I heard the slightest whisper of breathing and, at that moment, felt a surge through my body as I realised that she was still alive. At the same time, I also realised that for my deception to work I had to leave her sealed in this tomb for at least two whole days. If Alceste were to live, she would undoubtedly wake up whilst I was 'away' in the Underworld. I had arranged for food and drink to be available and it was clean and cool inside the tomb, which should guarantee that she could survive several days without outside help. Clearly, I needed to leave her a message to explain what was happening: that I would return and release her in a short time as well as making arrangements with someone outside I could trust to open the tomb in three days in case something happened to me to prevent my planned return to rescue her.

' "The first task was quickly performed, as I had brought writing materials with me. To ensure Alceste saw it as soon as she awoke, I marked the floor with chalk arrowheads pointing to the food and drink and propped the message against the receptacle holding the wine. On completion of this task, I left the tomb and, using the stones and cement provided, with a modest addition to the cement mix of my own to slow the drying process, sealed it. On returning to the palace, I informed Admetus that I would be leaving virtually immediately, after I had done two things: firstly, I needed a new substantial club made of an olive tree for my visit to the Underworld – and here I asked for Admetus' help in identifying a suitable locally available tree that I could uproot – and, second, write a sealed note on what should be done should I fail to return within three days. Admetus was in such a state that he did not think to ask what was in the note but agreed to keep it safe until my return and open it and do what I asked should I fail to return by the appointed time. While I wrote my note, Admetus' staff made enquiries for a suitable olive tree, and, when I delivered the note to Admetus, the chief steward was waiting to conduct me to a nearby olive grove where I could take my pick of several trees that were thought to be appropriate. The olive tree was, I thought, an excellent choice, as the tree is known to ward off evil spirits and would lend credibility if my mission was successful. The chief steward's information was accurate and I found amongst the trees in the grove one of the ideal size and weight. I quickly uprooted it and trimmed off the branches and, after a brief explanation to my companions – who were more than a little dismayed at developments – bade them farewell, resisting their persistent attempts to accompany me. As I only intended to walk as far as the next valley and hide up there for a day and a night, I did not need any company!

' "All went according to plan. I had taken a little food and drink with me to avoid talking to anybody. It was important, for my ruse to work, that nobody recognised me. And so I kept to little-used tracks and away from pasture. I found a long disused shepherd's shelter by a derelict sheep pound, where I slept an uncomfortable night on some bracken I gathered in the gloom, but I am sure that I was not seen. I stayed there the rest of the following day until night began to fall, when I began my return journey to Admetus' Palace. Both on the outward journey and the return, I had employed the olive-tree club to help clear the path I took of undergrowth, mainly to make the club look 'used'! Fortunately, Alceste's tomb was in a grove outside the town and a little distance from the palace, so I only needed to make a simple detour to reach it. The night was half over when I arrived close to the moonlit tomb. Before I approached it, I needed to know if there were any guards posted. I had found out by discreet questioning before I left the palace that it was not customary to guard tombs, even if they were royal tombs and outside the city wall – which this one was – but I had not asked Admetus directly what he intended because I thought that, if I put the idea into his head, he just might do it. Worse still, he might have said that he would not put a guard there but change his mind after I had gone. So, I had thought it would be best to leave it all to chance, particularly in the light of what I had understood was local custom. I lay quietly in the grove a short distance from the opening I had sealed two days before. After a long wait, listening to the night calls of men and beasts, I concluded that no guard had been mounted.

' "My next problem was to open the seal without making too much noise, and without alarming Alceste – as much for my benefit as hers. Although I did not want to startle her, I particularly did not want her to cry out and attract the city night guard. In anticipation of this problem I had put an ingredient in the cement I had used to seal the tomb that would slow down its hardening. I had also said in my note to Alceste that I would return at night and would knock in a certain way on the sealing stone so that she would know that I had returned to release her. I suggested that she returned the signal but added that her failure to do this would not deter me from breaking the seal and entering the tomb to release her.

' "I duly knocked on the tomb wall and waited. There was no response. I knocked again and, to my delight and relief, I heard a faint answering knock from inside the tomb. Now I could not wait to tear down the sealing stones and release the dear lady from her enforced confinement. My cement ingredient had worked and the cement had not yet hardened sufficiently to make it more than difficult to remove it. But there was not much night left when I finally managed to remove enough of the stones to enable me to climb in and greet a very relieved Alceste. Motioning her to be silent, I helped her through the gap in the sealed entrance and roughly resealed it so that it would not be too obvious that someone had tampered with it. Leading Alceste away to a nearby empty building, being silent all the while – which was a huge effort for us both as we were literally bursting to talk – it was not until we were inside and with the doors shut that I allowed us to communicate other than by signals.

' "I had forgotten what a charming lady Alceste was. I had first met her at Iolchos, when she bravely refused to participate in Medea's terrible scheme to kill her father, Pelias. The dignity she displayed then showed an exceptional strength of character, which had already attracted many suitors, including Admetus. We talked quietly through what was left of the night and she listened intently to what I had to say about her husband's reaction to her apparent death and how I suggested that she reappear alive. She was in good spirits, grateful for the victuals I had provided for her, and very chastened when I told her how distraught her husband had been when he thought that she was dead. Her gratitude to me personally for giving her the opportunity to undo her decision to commit suicide was clear from the look in her beautiful grey eyes.

' "I explained that I would claim to have rescued her from the Underworld, but neither she nor I could talk about the experience. This was a condition of our release. To forestall initial questions, I would publicly introduce her back to her court as my lady companion in need of Admetus' protection whilst I was away on my next task in Thrace. Alceste would need to be veiled at this introduction to avoid recognition. Once in the palace, she would reveal herself to her husband by removing the veil but would not speak until the third morning after her return in accordance with, what I would claim, an undertaking we had given to the gods of the Underworld. It was now morning and soon the servants would be bustling about. We had to re-enter the tomb without being seen, collect and destroy my note, wipe away the chalk marks and remove or destroy anything else that could disclose what had really happened. I also had to tear and dirty my clothes and face, and generally look as if I had been in a doughty struggle! Alceste had, as part of her burial clothes, a piece of cloth which could be used as a veil and was able to reverse her layered clothing so that her outward appearance was totally different to the 'corpse' introduced into the tomb two days before. This was accomplished without being seen. Leaving the tomb deliberately, but not too obviously, unsealed, we walked to the palace. By the time we reached it, the servants were busy about their tasks. I was instantly recognised by the door guard, who summoned a servant to take us indoors. They made no comment on my appearance, but they did not appear to know of my mission. They had no idea that my companion was their Queen.

' "After a short interval, we were ushered into the presence of the King. He was surprised to see me and, as he did not recognise my companion, but saw how unkempt I was, instantly assumed that my mission had failed. This I neither admitted nor denied but stuck to the story I had agreed with Alceste. Admetus was very reluctant to take this unknown veiled lady into his custody.

He could tell that she was a young and personable lady and appeared to fear being compromised, but, even more seriously, of being seen to be disloyal to his deceased wife. Alceste must have been overwhelmed by hearing his reasons why he did not wish to take on the responsibility of looking after this stranger, as they all reflected his great love for her.

' "Eventually, out of regard for me, he agreed to invite her into his private apartments and, as we had previously arranged, on doing so, Alceste removed her veil. Admetus, after initial shocked surprise, could scarcely believe his wife had returned from the dead. As she did not speak – I explained the reason for this – he took a little time before believing the evidence of his own eyes. His joy was then a pleasure to see, even more so when I told him that she now very much regretted the action she had taken and the hurt this had caused him. He, of course, was equally repentant and grateful for the outcome. I thought the timing was right for me to leave and, after a bath and a change of clothes, I bade them both farewell and returned to my companions, who were as delighted to see me as was I them!" '

Undertaking the Eighth Labour

'And so, at last, we boarded ship and set sail for Thrace. In the spirit of the instructions from Eurystheus that Hercules should achieve his task by himself, we had on ship only one chariot, planning to purchase horses locally. The sea journey was too long and dangerous to risk having frightened horses on board anyway. The curling and unpredictable winds of the Bay of Pagasae, despite having aboard sailors who claimed much experience of these waters, unexpectedly delayed our entry into the open sea until dusk was approaching. We had agreed that, to reduce the possibility of Diomedes having knowledge of our approach, we would sail eastwards across the open sea to the island of Lemnos and then turn north towards the mainland, using the east coast of the island of Thasos as our landmark. By approaching from the south, rather than the west, we hoped that our ship would be identified as coming from one of the settlements on the mainland of the eastern Aegean rather than Hercules from the west. We also felt that, by keeping out of sight of the mainland, Diomedes' spies – and we were sure that he had them – would be unable to track us and give their master an estimated time of arrival at his city, called Tirida. However, this was essentially a fine-weather plan. Unfortunately, the weather gods had not read it, or, if they had, were determined to show who was mortal and who made the decisions!

'As soon as the prow of the ship rounded the island at the head of the Bay of Pagasae, we were hit by a squall that bowled us sideways towards the rocky mainland shore to the west of us. We had been warned that, when the wind was in the east, this experience was not uncommon. So we were prepared for it, but not the ferocity. Most of those on board had sailing experience – for some it was their livelihood – but even they would not normally have been able to right the ship and reduce the sail quickly enough to prevent the ship either capsizing or being driven on to the rocks. Hercules, as usual, was outstanding, ably supported by the strength of the warriors he had recruited. I was terrified. I could hear and see the waves crashing on the rocks a few cubits from where I was sitting. At one point, I was tempted to think about leaping from the ship to the rocks, the distance was so short. Gradually, with the help of Hercules and his warriors, the oarsmen and the helmsman managed to turn the ship's prow into the wind and manoeuvre us into the shelter of a promontory to the east of the port of Oreus on the island of Euboea. There we anchored close to the shore and waited for dawn, it now being pitch black with no moon visible.

'After a fitful sleep, I awoke to a cold, grey dawn. Still, the wind appeared to have abated and Hercules, with advice from those sailors who claimed to know these waters, decided to raise sail and make another attempt to pass through the strait separating the island of Sciathos from the mainland. To my surprise, the wind had veered west overnight and within a short while we were racing across some mildly turbulent water towards Sciathos and, then, we burst into the open sea. Sciathos appeared and soon sank behind us with surprising speed. As the sun began to set, the small island of Irresia appeared. We had hoped to reach this the previous day and had planned to stop there to meet the local inhabitants, who were known to some of our crew. The islanders were mainly elderly and the island rarely had visitors. Our information was that they were very unlikely to send a message to Diomedes about our whereabouts even if he had paid them to do so. I was told that there was nobody on the island with the skill to sail a boat as far as mainland Thrace and no boat either! Although the island was fertile, it had a bad reputation: it was remote and landslides into the sea were frequent. Lives had been lost through sudden and unexpected landslides in the recent past, so now only a few old people lived on the island all the year round. Most of the young people left as soon as they could and never came back.

'I found it a charming island, remote, yes, but peaceful. The few islanders made us very welcome and we shared what we had with them. They did not know who Hercules was and were not curious about why we were there. He loved the lack of notoriety and spent most of one evening talking to an old man who had been a herdsman on the mainland, discovering, to his delight, that the old man had an ear for music and could still play the lyre. Hercules had great pleasure in bringing his lyre from the boat and I could tell that they both learnt something from each other.

'We set sail early the following day, wishing to take advantage of the westerly wind that blew strongly and consistently all day. Occasionally, I felt we were running a risk by not reefing in the sail a little – we seemed to be travelling too fast and in danger of capsizing. But the experts told us not to be concerned. Hercules was keen to move quickly as he was sure that Diomedes would have had news of his departure from Pherae and would not have known of the diversion and lay-up we were forced to make on the first day, although he would presumably have been told of the adverse wind conditions. We made such good progress that, by the middle of the day, we had reached the west coast of Lemnos. Hercules decided that we should waste no time but turn north directly in the hope of reaching Thasos by nightfall. Although the wind was still in the west, we were able to use it to progress on a northerly course without much loss of power. But I think we were all a little relieved and pleased when we saw the coast of Thasos appearing on the skyline well before dusk.

'Now the main port and principal city is on the north coast of the island and is also called Thasos. It faces the mainland of Thrace. We knew that there were strong commercial and family links with the mainland. It was possible that someone in the city would be aware of Hercules' mission and that he would be recognised. We had no obvious reason for being on Thasos, we had no goods to sell and we would not be offering to buy anything except personal necessities. We decided that, although we wanted to anchor as far north on the island as possible so as to reduce the time it would take to reach the mainland, it was too risky to sail into the port, where questions would be asked. One of our crew knew of a quiet cove a few stadia south of the port of Thasos, where the ship could be safely beached on sand. It was also close enough to the port for some of us to go there and listen to wine shop gossip. Hercules accepted the first part of this proposal but not the second, reasoning that the appearance of strangers, particularly those asking questions, would attract attention, whereas we were unlikely to learn anything useful unless we were extremely lucky. Possibly the best we could hope for, Hercules argued, was that Diomedes was expecting our imminent arrival. Well, we had guessed that already! His eminently sensible argument was accepted – one supporter even arguing that a member of the crew could be followed back to the ship and a message sent overnight to Diomedes, whilst we could be launched and away by dawn without anyone knowing if we did not draw attention to ourselves.

'And so it was. We beached the ship, posted lookouts in watches through the night and made a small fire in a cave that faced out to sea, where we ate a hot meal and some of us slept. Before dawn we were awake and had launched the ship and raised the sail before the sun broke through the early morning mist. The lookouts had reported nothing and I believe that our short stay on Thasos was only witnessed by ourselves.

'The sea was now calm and there was only a light breeze, and that from an unfavourable quarter. Still, with a combination of oar and sail we made good progress across the short stretch of sea separating the island of Thasos from the mainland. As planned, we landed east of the mouth of the River Nestos, where a dense wood ran down to the shore. Here we concealed the boat and several small parties went in different directions to buy horses for the chariot and the party that would accompany Hercules. Each of the four parties was accompanied by someone who knew the area and could speak the local dialect. The River Nestos was an important navigational aid and there were many thriving ports on both banks. All had horse dealers with good horses for sale, many of the horses having been brought down by river boat. The most difficult task was to buy four chariot horses – there were not likely to be many of them for sale and open negotiations could bring unwanted attention. Abderus and I were asked to join the group responsible for buying these animals and we were accompanied by a Thracian who claimed to know where they might be purchased.

'But first we had to cross the river. This proved to be more difficult than I had expected but we eventually found a river trader who would carry us across for a small fee. In the hope of a return passage from us, he even helped us find a horse dealer, who, alas, did not have quite what we wanted. The sun was low in the sky when we finally reached agreement on the purchase of four horses, which were claimed to have some experience of drawing a chariot and which both Abderus and I felt were probably suitable and certainly the best on offer. My one concern was that the price was high and I was fearful that our willingness to pay such a high price might cause gossip. Abderus was not concerned but agreed that we should share my concerns with Hercules when we returned back to where the ship was hidden.

'On our return, the first thing Abderus and I did was to take the two horses we thought would be the best and harness them up to the chariot. We then took turns in driving them, changing the pairing until we felt we had the best combinations. My concern about the price we had paid was a little dissipated by the unexpectedly good quality of the horses and I was pleased to report back later to Hercules our satisfaction with our purchases. It was important that he had reliable horses for his chariot and, in retrospect, he realised that he had taken a significant risk in assuming that he would be able to buy them in Thrace, on Diomedes' territory! He now was prepared to admit that he had been rather foolish and accepted my warning that, although the purchase had been made across the river – and the border – it was still possible that someone close to Diomedes might hear of our unusual purchase. Hercules decided not to delay, but mobilise his force to move out that night. But first we would have a rest and then, after a brief discussion, set to our tasks. As dusk approached, we relaunched the ship. This we could not have done after the raiding party had gone, as there would only have been a minimal skeleton crew left to sail the ship, which had been made even heavier by the four metal plates and restraining posts we had installed in Pherae and to which we hoped to tether the horses. Our council was held on board, two of the sailors being detached to look after the horses who stayed on land and keep a general lookout for approaching strangers.

'Hercules briefly outlined his strategy. The raiding party would make their way quietly inland of Diomedes' city and split into two groups. The role of the smaller one, under Hercules, was to locate the stables where the Mares were kept, overpower the guards and drive the Mares to the shore. A signal would be given to us, in the ship offshore, to approach close in, so that the Mares could be embarked, which would have to be done quickly. In the meantime, the remainder of the party would attack the city to cause a diversion from Hercules' activity, but, after the signal to the ship had been given, their role would be to form a protective screen around the embarkation area to ensure that the Mares were safely boarded and the ship withdrawn to safety at sea. Then the whole of the raiding party would make their way to the cove nearby to the west, which we had already identified, to meet the ship and, it was hoped, themselves embark. There would be no room on board for either the chariot or the horses and these would be abandoned on the shore. If Diomedes' force was in too close pursuit to guarantee enough time for a safe embarkation, the party would ride on westwards to the river where it was hoped we could meet up and embark the whole party safely. Such was the plan. As you will hear, events did not go quite to plan, as they often do not!

'The first part – the departure of the raiding party some time after nightfall and our sailing out to sea – went to plan. As I was on the ship, I knew little until later of what happened to the raiding party. For the purpose of telling you what happened, I will now include what I learnt much later about the adventures of the land party. We on the ship fulfilled our task and, as dawn broke, we could see Diomedes' city and would have been visible to those on shore. We earlier noticed some activity on the ramparts of the city and it appeared – as was later confirmed – that our ruse had worked and our attack was presumed to be from the sea.

'According to what I heard later, the land party arrived at their planned position on the landward side of the city walls well before dawn. All was quiet. Hercules knew that the stables where the Mares were kept were outside the walls of the city to the east. A brief reconnaissance by him and Abderus located them a short distance from where they had taken up position with, surprisingly, only one guard awake, although there was a guard house nearby where it was presumed others were sleeping. In order to confuse Diomedes' warriors, Hercules moved the main part of the party – the decoy assault force – further west, to make it appear that we did not know where the Mares were kept and draw the defenders away from the stables whilst Hercules and his small party raided the stables and secured the Mares.

'I understand that the ruse worked: even the guard at the stables left his post on hearing the alarm raised in the city at our approach and Hercules had no difficulty in capturing the Mares and leading them, tied to his chariot, to the shore where he gave us the signal to approach so that they could be loaded. At this point, Diomedes realised that he had been tricked, immediately broke off the fight with our decoy force and led his troops to the shore to recover his Mares and defeat Hercules and his small party. Hercules had perforce to leave the Mares in the custody of Abderus and defend himself from Diomedes' violent onslaught. Fortunately, the battleground was a flat expanse of sand and the tide was coming in driven by a brisk wind. Hercules spotted that the ground over which Diomedes had to pass to reach him was at least six cubits below sea level and the sea was being kept at bay only by the ridge on which he was standing with Abderus and the Mares, awaiting our arrival. Quickly identifying the weakest point in the ridge, he dug a deep ditch in the sand and the sea flooded in just as Diomedes' force entered the false sand plain. He was halfway across before he realised what was happening and, by then, Hercules had driven another ditch through the ridge at the opposite end so that the sea water was flowing in from two directions at once. Diomedes turned and fled but Hercules chased and caught him and dragged him back through the rising water to the comparative safety of the ridge. Here he found, to his great dismay, that the wild Mares had broken their bonds and had killed Abderus by kicking and trampling him to death. Diomedes suffered the same fate. I later saw the bodies of both of them and can honestly say that, in all my life, I have never seen two bodies mangled as they were. I can understand why the story grew that the Mares ate their victims. I saw no evidence of that, but they could certainly be vicious.

'By this time, Diomedes' force had fled back to their city of Tirida and we had beached the ship on the sand bank. The Mares were amazingly quiet – all the fight appeared to have departed from them – so, with some misgivings after seeing the evidence of what they could do, we loaded them on to the ship with little difficulty and secured them on the prepared metal platforms. Hercules then approached the city walls with a small unarmed party carrying the remains of their king, Diomedes, on one temporary bier and of Abderus on another. The main gate was opened and Diomedes' widow emerged with her young son, supported by a party of unarmed warriors equal in size to our own.

'I was not present at the discussions that then took place, but, from subsequent events, it appears that agreement was reached that Diomedes' son would succeed his father as King of Tirida, that his mother would act as Regent during her son's minority, that there should be separate funerals for Diomedes and Abderus and that Abderus should be honoured by being buried on a prominent hillock nearby. Funeral games in honour of Abderus would be held and a promise made that a new city would be founded, to be called Abdera, around the place of his burial. The Tiridans would also hold their own memorial games for their dead King. With this settled, the Mares were disembarked and temporarily accommodated on land, but not in their original stables, until we were ready to depart.

'The funerals and the funeral games were held and, after three days, we were ready to take our leave. As the Tiridans had accepted their defeat, Hercules decided to drive the Mares back overland to Tiryns. Amazingly, he harnessed them to the chariot in turns, two at a time with the two unharnessed Mares attached by leading reins to the rear of the chariot. I went with him, accompanied by four of the warriors on horseback. It was a long but uneventful journey back to Tiryns. The news of our passing went before us – as did the reputation of Diomedes' Mares – and strangers (including brigands) kept their distance from us, the combination of Hercules and the Mares being very intimidating! It was a little disappointing when I learnt that Eurystheus had no better solution than to order the Mares to be released on Mount Olympus where, so far as I know, they and their progeny roam still.'

He paused and appeared to invite me to ask questions – several of which had come to my mind during Iolaus' long discourse. The one I really wanted to ask, how his marriage to Hercules ex-wife, Megara, came about was one I dare not ask. As she was much older than Iolaus, I presumed that she was now dead and he would probably not want to be reminded of his loss by a stranger, which was, I had to admit, my present status. Anyway, chronologically, this was a future event: it did not occur, I thought, until after the Twelve Labours were completed. But I still did not fully understand the connection between the Mares of Diomedes and the matriarchal cult, so I asked Iolaus to expand on this. He did so in Hercules' words:

' "As I explained to you before," said Hercules to me, "the old Thracian custom, under the matriarchal system, was that a king who had served his time was chased and killed by a pack of women. In their, presumably drunken, frenzy they not only killed him, they ate him. Traditionally, these women wore face masks resembling horses and so the legend was that the king's body was eaten by flesh-eating horses. This was the tradition being perpetuated by Diomedes, although he ensured that he retained the throne, any challenger being forced to take part in the successor ritual of a chariot race, which required him to bridle the Mares – who, of course, overpowered him and killed him before the race even started. You saw yourself what destructive animals they are and it is not hard to see how the rumours arose that they ate their victims. I cannot understand why Diomedes used the matriarchal legend to keep himself on the throne, but I can understand why Apollo wishes to eradicate the practices Diomedes had established. It remains to be seen if what we have done will prove successful in the future. I hope so. Certainly, his widow and son and the people of Tirida seem to be relieved to be rid of the tyrant and his barbaric ideas.

' "Incidentally, I suppose you know," he added, "that we did not have the usual chariot race as an event at the funeral games for poor Abderus?"

'I hadn't, and said so.

' "Well, you see," continued Hercules, "to have had a chariot race would have undermined the point of it all: the fixed chariot race was the successor trial to being chased by the wild women in order to kill the king and bring in a younger successor. I felt it better not to remind them of this."

'I could see his point!'

The Ninth Labour: The Golden Girdle of the Amazons

'I now awaited news from Hercules of his next task. This was soon forthcoming: to bring to Eurystheus' daughter, Admete, the Golden Girdle worn by Hippolyte, the Queen of the Amazons. This was very exciting for me. Who had not heard of the Amazons, the legendary all-female race whose main kingdom (or queendom!) was on the southern coast of what we called the Blessed Sea? But I was to be disappointed again: Hercules would not need me on this expedition and indeed felt – although he did not say so in as many words – that he would be better off alone. He did, however, agree to let me accompany him for a large part of the journey and to wait close by for his return.

'It was not difficult to see the connection between this task and the matriarchal Cult. The Amazons' mere existence was a great support to the Cult as it appeared to be proof that a large state run only by women could not only survive, but be highly successful. If women could do this, why should not the governance of all states be in the hands of women? The Amazons appeared to have solved the problem of the lack of male partners to propagate their race, using their neighbours to provide the appropriate assistance in much the same way as the matriarchal cult "used" the male kings for as long as they wanted them and then discarded them when no longer required for a younger, more virile, man. I expected to hear much more on their way of life from Hercules on his return, so I deferred my questions and concentrated on making preparations for our early departure to the east.

'As news of Hercules' next task circulated among his many admirers the pressure grew to let some of them accompany him, not to assist him achieve his mission, but, rather like the expedition of the *Argo* some years earlier, because many young men were seeking adventure and to widen their experience of the world. No doubt the prestige of being with Hercules and the perceived additional security his presence offered were also significant factors. In the end, Hercules had to go back to Eurystheus to seek his permission to take a fleet of no less than nine ships overall. This was granted on condition that, however he secured the Girdle, he did so on his own and without anyone else's assistance at the time. This prohibition did not extend to his journey there or his return. Eurystheus had to recognise that, with such a valuable prize on the return journey, he would be a target for every cut-throat, robber and pirate in the universe. Some armed protection, even for Hercules, had to be permitted, and so Eurystheus agreed.

'With such a large expedition in prospect, and Eurystheus' acceptance of it, Hercules became much more relaxed about my presence and my role changed. Hercules used me to deliver messages to those who wished to accompany us to Themiscyra, the Amazon capital city and port at the mouth of the River Thermodon, and to bring messages back. This time was the origin of my long friendship with Theseus – Argonaut, friend of Hercules and Prince (later King) of Athens. Hercules admitted him early to the long list of those famous warriors who joined our expedition.

'As I said earlier, by the time we were ready to sail, our fleet was nine ships strong. We had room for chariots and horses and could safely have cruised along the coast, as few would have dared to impede the progress of such a force. But, for his own reasons, which he never communicated to me, Hercules decided that the various ships in the fleet would make their own way from their home ports, meeting for the first time at Paros, after which we would sail together to the entrance to the channel to the Blessed Sea, which began at the Hellespont. Our ship arrived first at Paros. We thought we were expected and would receive a friendly welcome. We beached our ship in a secluded cove and two sailors were despatched to find some water so that the crew could wash and cook the evening meal. They had only been gone a short while when we heard shouting and screaming coming from the direction in which they had set off. Without hesitation, Hercules grasped his club and raced off in the same direction. I, and a few others, followed a little distance behind and arrived in a grove in the trees just in time to see a furious Hercules standing over the dead bodies of our former companions, striking out ferociously at four heavily armed young men, who were clearly responsible for the massacre. Hercules gave them no chance: in a brief moment the four warriors were stretched out on the ground dead with their heads smashed in by Hercules' club. Fearful that we now might be attacked by the, apparently unfriendly, local inhabitants, we rushed back to the ship, pushed it out to sea with a few crew on board whilst the remainder of us, mostly warriors, armed ourselves and hurried off in the direction of the grove and beyond.

'We had not travelled far before we came upon a track and, on the skyline, the walls of a small city – which we later discovered was the main city, Paros. Although we first met with some resistance, it was quickly realised by them that we were not to be trifled with and they fled in terror inside the city. A herald soon appeared and enquired who we were and what we wanted. Hercules explained who he was and that he had only come to their island, as a peaceful stranger expecting hospitality not aggression. When the herald realised what had happened, he immediately apologised and told us that the four young men were, in fact, the King's sons.

'We were led to the palace by the herald across a most magnificent stone-paved square surrounded by two-storey buildings glistening in the sun. I later discovered that, under a thin layer of productive soil lay a deep slab of marble, which was in much demand as light could permeate through it to a depth of almost half a doron. With the famed island of Delos not far to the north, the islanders of Paros had not found it difficult to sell their remarkable stone for the adornment of temples and royal palaces. The King's Palace itself had some magnificent examples of the use of the local marble. The walls of the inner court where we met the King were roofed with a thin layer of it so that the sun streamed through, but in a subdued way. The marble was also an excellent material for carving statues and there several good examples in selected niches around the walls of the inner court and the main portico to the palace, through which we had gained entry.

'The herald introduced us to the King, Alcaeus, who entered the inner court from the room behind, which appeared to be a passageway leading to the throne room and the private rooms. After mutual introductions the King, I presume in deference to the status of Hercules and the reason for our visit, remained standing. He told us how he sincerely regretted what had happened and offered recompense by allowing Hercules to choose two of his people as slaves to replace the slain sailors. Hercules chose to nominate the King himself, Alcaeus and his brother, Sthenelus. Alcaeus agreed without demur, accepting graciously Hercules' offer of the rest of the day to put his affairs in order and nominate a regent to cover his enforced absence. The King concluded by compensating for the ignorance and misbehaviour of his sons by offering to entertain Hercules and his most senior officers at his palace until departure. Hercules accepted the offer for himself and the four senior officers on our ship and, from what Hercules and the others told me later, they enjoyed their time being entertained by Alcaeus and his household, although the circumstances giving rise to the invitation were a cause of much regret by all concerned.

'I returned to the ship with the remainder of the party. Those who had been left behind were very relieved to hear of the quiet outcome and astonished at Hercules' demand that their King himself and his brother should take the place of our slain comrades. They were even more astonished at the King's acceptance! Some suspected a plot to kill Hercules and our officers while they slept and I privately admitted that this was a possibility. But, when accepting Hercules' offer of a delay in the departure, Alcaeus and his brother had both sworn an oath to honour their agreement and called upon their citizens to support them, which they had done in open assembly in the square by acclamation before we returned to the ship. When our companions heard this, they were a little more relaxed, but it was decided to leave the ship anchored offshore and post lookouts inland, supported by the rest of the warriors in the crew who set up a temporary camp on the shore. The sailors and I remained aboard.

And so we spent a slightly anxious night until we heard from our lookouts early the following morning that Hercules, the King and his party were approaching with a small, armed escort.

'A signal was given to our comrade sailors and the ship was rowed ashore to make embarkation easier. The first to come aboard were Alcaeus and his brother, followed by the officers and our warriors. The last to board was Hercules, who gave farewell greetings to one of the escort, who I took to be the regent appointed by Alcaeus.

'By this time all but one of the eight "missing" ships from our fleet had arrived in the bay and we understood from them that the ninth ship was only a short distance behind. We therefore resolved to sail out to meet them. As soon as we had passed the shadow of the island of Antiparos, we saw them approaching and, reefing in our sails, waited for them to join us.

'I will not bore you with a tale of the usual seafaring problems we encountered on our way from Paros and into the Blessed Sea. Sufficient to say that all nine ships passed through the straits of the Hellespont and the Bosporus safely, although there were some accidents, disabling one sailor and killing another, both not on our ship. The dead sailor was buried at sea with appropriate ceremony and the disabled man was landed at our first main port of call with the promise that, if he wished and he was fit enough, we would collect him on our return journey and take him home. He was grateful for that and disappointed that the nature of his injury made it not possible for us to take him with us.

'Our first port of call was at Mariandyne, a city in Bithynia, the eastern part of which is known as Paphlagonia. Here we met Lycus, the exiled King of Paphlagonia, who very civilly entertained us all. Hercules listened to Lycus' problems with a tribe known as the Bebryces, who, although originally from Thrace, had settled to the east of Paphlagonia in a country known as Pontus – which, incidentally, was where the Amazons had settled and was our destination. It appeared that the Bebryces had invaded Lycus' kingdom and evicted him, for no justifiable reason. Flushed with wine and good nature from Lycus' hospitality, Hercules there and then offered Lycus his (and our) help in restoring him to his throne. I don't think Lycus had any expectation that his story would excite such a response and he was quite overwhelmed by Hercules' offer. He cautiously accepted with a great show of gratitude: the reason for his caution became clear in the morning when he quietly consulted some of our senior officers on the expedition, before Hercules was awake, to make sure that they had no objection to Hercules' offer. Knowing Hercules' reputation for plain dealing, he realised that Hercules would not withdraw an offer once made; Lycus made it clear that he would decline if the officers had any reservations. Fortunately for Lycus, the majority of our officers supported Lycus and appreciated the way in which he had handled a difficult situation. Those who were slightly unhappy about a delay for the expedition felt that a successful campaign against one of the Amazons' neighbours – in a just cause – could further our own cause: the measure of our success against the Bebryces could be that the Amazons would decline to fight and give us the prize we sought without a battle.

'By the time Hercules awoke, the decision was made: Lycus would be restored to his throne by his forces with the support of Hercules and his force. As Lycus, and we, had expected, Hercules fully recalled the offer he had made and reaffirmed it. He was delighted that his decision received the full support of the force he was leading and accepted what was hoped would be only a modest delay in descending upon the Amazons.

'The combined force took the Bebryces completely by surprise and, a few days later, much of their main army was destroyed, trapped in a narrow defile in the mountains of Paphlagonia. Lycus was restored to the throne and promised to allow Hercules to found a city near Mariandyne and which later became known as Heraclea Pontica. He was as good as his word. To this day, the city has flourished at the expense of Mariandyne, which declined and is now a ruin. Lycus' future, however, was not so untroubled: a few years later, he lost the throne again and was killed, and his kingdom was occupied by a number of different peoples.

'At last, we sailed into the mouth of the River Thermodon. Unsure of our reception, Hercules had decided that his ship alone would proceed to the quay in the port of Themiscyra, a little inland from the coast, while the others remained at anchor in the strait, visible from the shore. The women at the quay were friendly enough, particularly when they saw the physique of the men aboard – their eyes opened wide with astonishment when they glimpsed Hercules! – and assisted expertly in tying up the boat at the quayside. A herald was despatched to deliver friendly greetings to Queen Hippolyte and he, and a small entourage, were helped and accompanied on their way by a guard of Amazons attired in military uniforms. A similar Amazon group "attended" at the wharf where we were berthed. The impression we received was that our arrival was neither unexpected nor unwelcome. Hercules was prepared to fight if forced to do so to achieve his objective, but he hoped he could do this peacefully. He made it clear to all of us that we should at all times be courteous and civil and only to resort to violence if the Amazons attacked us first.

'Now you have probably heard all sorts of stories about what happened next?'

I nodded.

'Well,' Iolaus added, 'the story that relates how jealous gods stirred up the Amazons to attack us and how Hercules and his force destroyed the force the Amazons threw against us, killing all their leaders (including Queen Hippolyte) and many of their warriors, is untrue. I think this tale was sired by the same source that invented the story about the Amazons later invading mainland Greece and attacking Athens when Theseus was King there, with Hippolyte, his Queen. That last part was true, but the story of the failed attempt by the Amazons to conquer Athens is a fabrication, probably invented to support the first untruth, that Hercules was not welcomed by the Amazons.

'In fact, the Queen sent a message back by our herald that we were expected and that she would shortly visit the harbour to meet with Hercules and his companions. We quickly realised that she was giving us time to put our ship in order so that it would be fit to welcome a Queen. Because of the battles against the Bebryces and our rather hasty departure from Lycus' new dominion, the ship was more prepared for sea than for a royal visit. We were very grateful that the Queen delayed her arrival until the sun was setting – we had arrived shortly after dawn – to give us time to clean the ship overall and drape appropriate fabrics in the makeshift cabin in the stern. The speed with which the Queen arrived almost as soon as we had finished our work was, I was sure, not coincidence: I had noticed from time to time one of the Amazon guards slipping away in the direction of the palace and early came to the conclusion that this was not to obey a call of nature but to inform the Queen how our preparations for her arrival were proceeding.

'With a brief sound of trumpets, we were made aware that the Queen was approaching. Although there was some sort of carriage in the procession we saw wending its way down the hill from the palace to the quay, it was clear that the Queen was not in it – she was leading the procession on foot, and she was wearing the Girdle!

'There was only time for me to get an impression of the Queen as she passed me on the way to be greeted by Hercules who stood on the quayside by the boarding plank. I expected to see a strong, muscled, tall lady, more of a warrior than a woman. I had heard that she was a fierce warrior and I can confirm by later experiences that this was certainly true. But what I saw was a beautiful, mature lady with flashing grey eyes enhanced by the deep blue of her tunic, the movement of which was slightly constrained by the dazzling Golden Girdle around her narrow waist. Even Hercules appeared a little overcome, and his greeting to her was the more sincere for that. She gracefully accepted Hercules' invitation to board and they walked together to the stern of the ship, where some food and drink had been prepared for them. The obvious cordiality of our welcome took us all by surprise. We later learnt that, not only had they received very graphic accounts of our handling of the perfidious Bebryces – with whom the Amazons themselves had had some inconclusive encounters – the timing of our arrival was also most opportune, as this was traditionally the season of the year that the Amazons sought out breeding partners. The news that nine ships of young and healthy Achaeans were arriving off their shores imminently had elicited an expectation and excitement that had easily banished the incipient, and automatic, aggression of a few. Hippolyte, too, was tiring of her isolation in this outmoded society – she foresaw the forthcoming demise of the dominance of the Amazons in this region and their subsequent dispersal into distant lands. She had at that time three able deputies who each ruled a part of her kingdom and she felt that she could leave the future of her nation – such as it was – safely in their hands. This was what Hercules later told me although not much of this was obvious to me, or our crew, at the time.

'This later explained to me the open friendliness of both the Queen and her entourage towards Hercules and all of us. Despite this, there were some of the crew, whom I will call the "pirate element", murmuring amongst themselves that, with Hippolyte aboard wearing the Girdle, we had what we had come for and should up anchor and away before those on shore realised what was happening. I should explain that to fill the ships' complement we had been forced to recruit some who, prior to being recruited for this expedition, had spent much of their sea time prowling for booty. I then had some sympathy with their view: if we acted swiftly, there was no prospect of being stopped and little chance of any pitched battle, which would surely result in many casualties on both sides. The only problem was with Hippolyte herself and the few ladies who had come aboard with her, none of whom appeared to be armed. However, somehow a message to this effect reached the ear of Hercules and he was quite emphatic in his response: we were to do nothing but await events.

'And so, somewhat reluctantly, we awaited the outcome of the discussion between Queen Hippolyte and Hercules. We did not have to wait long. A short while after Hercules had given his clear instruction to do nothing, he ordered a signal to be made to the other eight ships of the fleet to raise their anchors and proceed to berth at the quay alongside us. As he spoke, a few fishing boats occupying spaces along the quay nearby were unhitching from their moorings to move elsewhere, presumably to give all our ships room to come alongside. This confirmed to me that all was well: it would have been simple to pretend that our ships would have to moor where there was space available, thus dispersing us and making a coordinated attack or defence more difficult for us. By berthing us together it put us in a stronger position to defend ourselves, or even mount an attack. This could only mean that the

Amazons' intention towards us were friendly. This proved to be an understatement!

'What happened next, I will leave mainly to your imagination. As you know, the Amazons were virtually an all-female society. There were some males, but they were all virtual slaves, many of them disabled in some way. This was done deliberately, shortly after birth, to prevent any male group from challenging the authority of the female hierarchy. This left the problem of the future of the race: without the participation of men, no children would be born and the race of Amazons would quickly die out. I have already told you how they evolved a system, supported by their neighbours, whereby each Amazon who wished to conceive would, at a set time in the year, leave Amazonia to stay with a selected male from a neighbouring tribe, returning after a few weeks when she knew she was pregnant. It so happened that we had arrived just before the annual "mating" and the Queen, unknown to us, had been petitioned to make us welcome as those who wished to be involved in the current year's "programme" made it clear that their chosen partner would most likely come from our warrior group in preference to the rather docile tribes with whom they had traditionally had relations in the past. When this became more generally known to my colleagues, the previous reservations were banished by an eagerness to participate in these strange Amazonian customs. Hercules decided that I was too young to be drawn into all this and, strangely, he also stood aloof, nominating Theseus as partner to Queen Hippolyte. This appeared to be by mutual agreement, and later developed into a loving partnership after Theseus and Hippolyte returned together to Athens as man and wife. In gratitude for this, Hippolyte gave the Girdle to Hercules.'

'So that mission was accomplished and you all sailed home?' I interjected.

'Not quite,' responded Iolaus. 'We first had to wait the outcome of the "programme" as I have described. But Hercules and Theseus became impatient and they decided they were not prepared to wait. So, in the end only two ships, Hercules' and Theseus', set sail for Greece, leaving the others to make their way home when they felt ready. Although of no concern to us, as they were all freemen hired for the expedition, whose objective had been achieved, Hercules did tell me later that he had kept himself informed about what had happened to them. Some decided to stay in the area, though obviously not in Amazonia, a few were killed in various border clashes fighting for one side or another in the hope of reward but most managed to return to their homes. I believe two ships were lost overall, but the others were loaded with tradeable goods and earned their crew a tidy sum.

'We called in to see Lycus on our way home and saw that an impressive start had been made on the new town, to be called Heraclea Pontica and which, you may recall, Lycus had agreed to found in gratitude for Hercules' help in subduing the Bebryces. After a short stay, we progressed back through the way we had come, calling in at Troy. Here we found a most extraordinary situation: the King's beautiful daughter, Hesione, bound, naked, to a stake on the shore! Thus yet another set of unforeseen, disastrous consequences was set in train. Hercules was, of course, horrified and scandalised by what he saw. He immediately released a very relieved Hesione and, handing her over to Hippolyte to comfort her, stormed up to the gates of the city demanding to see the King and be given an explanation for this appalling event. I was with Hercules when we met the King, Laomedon, whose craven and shifty attitude did not impress me one bit. Nor was Hercules impressed.

'The story that a human sacrifice had to be made annually by chaining a young maiden to be devoured by a sea monster to atone for a slight offered to the gods by Laomedon himself is now well known. This year, the choice had fallen on the King's daughter who, though terrified, had accepted her fate with courage. Hercules immediately undertook to kill the sea monster and ransom the city of Troy from its tribute. A grateful Laomedon offered Hercules six of his prize mares in compensation, an offer Hercules accepted.

'The Trojans then built a wall around the sacrificial site so that the sea monster would not be able to see there was no victim and also to give Hercules some invisibility. Nobody was allowed to watch what happened, but I learnt later that Hercules had surprised the monster and killed it after a battle fought over two days. Some have said that Hercules jumped down the creature's throat and did not emerge until the third day with every hair on his head burnt off. That story, I can confirm, was an exaggeration. Hercules was exhausted and bruised but his hair was intact, if rather dirty and dishevelled, which was hardly surprising! Of course, King Laomedon and the Trojans were delighted to be at last relieved of this regular tribute and, at Hercules' insistence, celebrated by making animal sacrifices to the gods they had upset in the first place. Whether Hercules' presiding over the sacrificial ceremonies was the key factor or not I do not know, but I believe that, from that day to this, the gods did not seek to renew their demands on the city.

'Unfortunately, the King and the leading citizens of Troy were trading people. Now that the threat had been removed they saw no need to honour the agreement they had reached with Hercules to give him six of the King's best mares in compensation but tried to fob him off by offering inferior animals. Hercules was incredulous but his protests were ignored. The mood of the citizens had turned nasty and Hercules did not think it right to involve his and Theseus' crew in a personal matter. But he made it clear that he was bitterly disappointed that Laomedon had reneged on his agreement, declined the inferior animals and said that he would return to claim the agreed reward. This drew jeers from the citizenry, by now safe inside the walls of the city with the massive gates shut. I will tell you the remainder of this story later.

'We now returned to Greece, sailing direct across the sea, the time of year and the weather being appropriate for open sea voyages. Arriving at the port for Tiryns, we made our way with the Girdle to Eurystheus' palace. Despite his obvious jealousy of Hercules, he was pleased to see us, if only to gloat over the prize we had brought him. He was a little disappointed that we had managed to obtain it without a battle, but Hercules pointed out to him that a battle for it had not been part of the contract! Eurystheus was not amused by this comment.'

The Tenth Labour: The Cattle of Geryon

'The King and Hercules then withdrew for Hercules to be given his instructions for the next task. This took only a short while and we were soon on our way out of the palace to a secluded place where we could discuss the next task and our strategy for achieving it. This was a huge task: to kill the monster Geryon and bring back his herds of man-eating animals.

'I was dismayed when I heard this. Hercules himself looked a little shocked but I later discovered this was not genuine. We both knew that the legendary Geryon lived at the farthest westerly point of the known world, beyond what became known as the Pillars of Hercules after this task was completed. It was not only difficult and dangerous, it would also take a very long time to drive the huge herds all the way from the far west to Mycenae. Again, I had difficulty in seeing the relevance of this to Apollo's supposed scheme to destroy the matriarchal cults.

'Hercules enlightened me: "This is not about destroying the matriarchal cult. Apollo appears to be moving on to challenging other male cults that he does not like. This king, who has adopted the name of Geryon – his real name is Chrysaor – has three sons, Geryon, Echidna and Chimaera. Each son, under their father's authority, rules a kingdom on the western boundaries of our world. The father's real name, which means 'golden sword', identifies their loyalty to the old gods, and Kronos in particular. The sword was originally his symbol, although, like many other old symbols and practices, they have been transferred or adopted by the newer generation of gods. The symbol of the golden sword has now been assumed by Zeus.

' "Geryon and his sons all ruthlessly enforce the old religion of Kronos, which encouraged human sacrifice. This must be stopped. Geryon and his sons must be destroyed and the old religion banished for good. The removal of the Cattle is to discredit their gods and impoverish these kingdoms for a generation to allow the new, more humane, religious practices to take root. High King Eurystheus has accepted that I cannot drive such a huge herd from the far west to Mycenae without substantial human assistance. This time I can accept as much assistance as I need. The only restriction is that I must not ask Geryon for the Cattle nor pay for them. I can and will, of course, simply take them without asking."

'Hercules then outlined his plan to me. He would raise a large army in Crete and transport it by ship along the Libyan coast close to its most westerly point where he would sail across to the south coast of Spain. Here was Geryon's kingdom, the cattle being grazed in a large fertile valley on the mainland near the coast, opposite a large island on which Geryon himself lived with his family, including his sons. I was to travel to Crete and on the expedition, including the long cattle drive back to Mycenae.

'On this occasion, we would take his favourite chariot with us on the boat, in pieces, to be assembled when we landed but would buy all the horses we required locally.

'Within days, we were in Crete. It took almost a month to recruit the numbers we needed, including skilled seamen, herdsmen and, of course, fighting men. Whilst Hercules was arranging this, I was charged with hiring a fleet of up to twenty ships to carry the force. As Hercules found with his recruitment, getting the first few was not difficult. The real problem seemed to arise when we were halfway to our target. In the end, although Hercules managed to recruit practically all the people he set out to get, I failed to secure more than fifteen ships. Hercules was quite relaxed about it. He pointed out that we now had sixteen ships overall, including the one we had sailed over in from Greece. These would just accommodate all those he had recruited and those we had brought with us. We had only a short voyage from the south of Crete to the coast of Libya and it was his intention to split the force so that some would travel by land and the rest by sea. Anyway, he gruesomely pointed out, no doubt we would lose a few on the journey through pestilence, disease, desertion and we could not expect a hero's welcome everywhere and might have to fight for a night's rest! He was right.

'I had encountered some difficulty in persuading ship owners to lease out their ships for a dangerous voyage of indeterminate length, but at least they would get their ships back once we reached our destination. The crews, too, could look forward to sailing back home with the ships after arrival and Hercules had decided he no longer had need of them, but the herdsmen and fighting men were required for the whole mission. This would include driving a very large herd of cattle a very long way. I think many joined the expedition fired with the enthusiasm that the personality of Hercules instilled into practically everybody he met. Once the voyage got under way, the huge size of the challenge began to dawn on the recruits. Some had overstated their previous experience just in order to be able to say later that they had served with Hercules. They soon found that this was not a distinction to be lightly earned. Hercules was right. We had not gone far before the numbers shrank – for the reasons he had given – to a comfortable level. But the further we sailed from Crete, the less easy it was for anyone to turn back. Most of the defections occurred shortly after we landed in Libya. Those who left later did so for mainly unexpected reasons, including one poor sailor whose wife had died just after he left Crete, leaving him a widower with four young children to look after. Hercules was very touched by his problem and paid him as if he had completed the trip so that he would take something back for himself and his family.

'Now I did not know this at the time but Hercules had chosen the route because he expected to travel some of it again soon. The perhaps overlarge force accompanying us was a deliberate statement by Hercules to impress on the locals that he was not to be trifled with, meant them no harm (although he had the ability to inflict it) and they should not obstruct him. He also showed his compassionate side. The inhabitants of several villages we passed by entreated us to help them stop the depredation of wild animals on their meagre herds. Hercules, without hesitation, enquired carefully where these predators might be, engaged several local villagers as guides and, with a volunteer force of villagers and some of our own warriors, led expeditions to find and destroy these unwelcome pariahs. These expeditions were invariably successful. The amount of goodwill these activities generated was enormous, and we all benefited from these celebrated victories. As one of the warrior officers cynically observed to me privately, it certainly kept the fighting men fit. It did – as well as providing an outlet for their natural aggression, which might otherwise have been turned on their companions. I was grateful for these excursions as Hercules did not expect me to accompany him, preferring to "blood" another of the force to drive his chariot. As he used a different one each time, I had no reason to be jealous or fearful of my status. I am sure that Hercules chose a different charioteer for each expedition not only for training purposes but also partly to avoid hurting my feelings. He was a sensitive man and could recognise sensitivity in others, which was one reason why he was such a good leader of men, as well as being a very brave and stout warrior. It was unusual for such a strong man to be such a thoughtful leader, but then Hercules was exceptional in so many ways.

'The evening before we reached the point at which we would cross to Spain near where the Cattle were, Hercules and I had a private meal together. He had already spoken to the whole force in an open assembly to explain that, for the sailors, their part in the expedition was close to its conclusion but that for the rest of us the serious part was about to begin. He had said that, within two days, we would be in southern Spain and the battle to secure the cattle would be joined soon, to be followed by the long drive home. Any of the herdsmen or fighting men who wished to leave should make their wishes known now so that they could be allocated places on one of the returning ships. The only ships that would not be returning immediately were our own and two other well-armed ships for company and which would track our return journey along the Spanish coast for the first few days. They would then leave us to return to Crete, our ship sailing on to its home port near Tiryns.

'No warrior or herdsman stepped forward to indicate a wish to leave the expedition. This pleased Hercules, as it confirmed the soundness of his selections. It was comforting to know that all supported and had faith in the venture, each other and Hercules himself.

'During our private meal, Hercules and I had discussed our

tactics once we had sighted the Cattle. After landing in the early evening, I was to take a small party of warriors in a direction that Hercules would identify for me. My task was to confirm where the cattle were and how easy (or difficult) it would be to remove them. The location of natural obstacles, such as ditches, streams, deep hollows and rocky ground that could slow down movement were to be carefully identified and I was to draw a sketch with my estimate of distances on a piece of papyrus he would give me, so that he could plan the best approach and escape routes. On no account was I to get involved in any fighting if this could be avoided. The warriors were only accompanying me for my protection in case of attack. Preferably, I was to complete my task without being seen. He suggested, but left it to me to decide, that I might choose to leave the warrior guard hidden in the lush undergrowth he believed I would find there, taking perhaps only one of them with me as a bodyguard and lookout, to enable me to concentrate on the task he had entrusted to me. Naturally, I was very proud to be trusted with this important mission. I then realised why he had, since our landing in Libya, excluded me from the excursions, encouraging me instead to look at the terrain where we were, draw it and identify the best defensive positions to resist an attack. I though he was merely being cautious. In fact, he was testing me to see how accurately I could identify the main features in a landscape. Hercules saw this thought dawn on me, whilst he was giving me his instructions, by the change in my facial expression – which I could not hide. He was very amused and we both laughed until we cried.

'This incident seemed to establish an even closer relationship between us than we had enjoyed previously. Thereafter, when the opportunity arose to have a very private conversation, he would tell me amazing things. Some were political, some personal – all were fascinating. Much was too esoteric for me to appreciate fully at the time. I think that, even now, I would have difficulty in understanding all he told me. He was a very able and clever man – far too clever to be a king!

'What we talked about that evening until late was the importance of language, how humans communicate by speech and in writing and, finally, what mechanics we use to communicate. By "mechanics" he meant the words we used and the various combinations of letters and signs we used to form those spoken and written words. In some countries, he said, there was no direct correlation between the written and the spoken word: you could not translate from one to the other so they were really two different languages. In his opinion, those languages that had a direct correlation were infinitely superior and would ultimately supplant the others.

'At the beginning of our lengthy conversation, I had little idea what he was talking about. But, as our discussion developed, I began to realise just how important this subject was. Using examples from history, he showed how misunderstandings of a written or spoken word had caused terrible wars or unjust slaughter. Greater care in word use and expansion of the vocabulary to allow more precise descriptions or define various levels, rather than just one level, of satisfaction or dissatisfaction assisted arrival at the right conclusion. Of course words can be used deliberately to confuse, as can the absence of words, as in the case of so-called "tacit" assent, but most men from their general experience or of a particular person can usually elicit the correct message. With strangers we must rely on our first impression – or what we have been told about them by persons we trust. We are impressed by an "honest face" – as if the face is always the window of the soul. By the time I had begun to grasp what he was talking about, Hercules had moved on to discuss the actual letters we used for words – what is now called the alphabet.

'Most languages, Hercules said, used words made up exclusively of consonants. Most words, even in languages that employed a number of frequently used vowels, could be understood even if only the consonants were given. The main advantage of using vowels was that many more words could be invented and nuances of meaning developed by subtle changes in the placing and use of different vowels within the structure of a word consisting entirely of consonants. I wasn't clear where this was leading, and I can see that you are confused, too! Hercules then explained that part of his task in Spain on this mission was not just to overthrow the regime but also to replace their barbaric – and limited – thirteen-consonant alphabet with one of fifteen consonants that he had invented himself some years ago. This was now being adopted throughout the whole of Greece. The introduction of new words with the new letters and their new associations would enable the old words and letters associated with the worship of Kronos to be banished from this region for ever. In effect, what Hercules was saying was that this was not an expedition to steal some cattle, it was for conquest and religious reform.

'I asked how he proposed to achieve his religious objective. I also wanted to ask who was behind this and how and when had he received his instructions, but I dared not ask these questions at this time. Perhaps an opportunity would arise later. Hercules glanced at me with a quizzical look. He knew what my unasked questions were and was a little unhappy that I did not trust him enough to ask. So he addressed those first.

' "You would like to know more about the reasons for this expedition than you have been told? I don't blame you. You are risking your life for them. I cannot yet tell you the whole truth, but I can see that you are intelligent enough to realise that this is a far bigger and more important task than it appears to be on the surface and that you can be trusted to keep a secret. Unfortunately, this particular secret you wish to know is one that I am not yet authorised to divulge to anybody. When the current tasks are over I will seek permission to tell you. For now, I will do my best to answer the question you have asked."

'Hercules continued: "I will not insult your intelligence by denying that conquest and religious conversion are the main objectives. I personally abhor human sacrifice. Gods that demand this are not worthy of veneration. King Geryon is a very powerful man. He and his three sons terrorise the large area they actually control and have a deleterious effect on an even wider area than you can imagine. Trade routes lead north from their land, which is called Erythrea, to the lands of mists and fog where there live an isolated people eager to learn from us. We want them to learn the best things from us, not the worst, so the conversion of Geryon's kingdom from their barbaric religious practices is particularly important. Now, you will have realised that it will not be possible to make these sweeping changes in a day. The King and his sons can be despatched quickly but the introduction of a new language and religion will take time. You will not be surprised to know that some of the warriors accompanying us have been recruited on the basis that they will be expected to settle in Erythrea in support of the work of the two priests I have brought, under the guise of herdsmen, to convert the people and destroy the old religion. I intend to remain a little while after we have taken control to satisfy myself that those I have appointed to perform these tasks are able to do so and to allow our colleagues time to settle. I have promised that anyone who wishes to stay here rather than return home with us will be accommodated, although I hope that not too many will take up this opportunity!"

'This reply reassured me. I was happy that Hercules had divined my unease and had clarified the situation for me. A few days remaining in Erythrea before moving off with the cattle would be a welcome diversion before what promised to be a long, gruelling and difficult journey back home. I had little doubt that that would also be the reaction of the others who were expecting to start shortly the work for which they had been engaged.

'The following day we sailed westwards again, hugging the southern coastline so that we would appear to any observers to be aiming at rounding the coast and then sailing southwards. There were some sailors on board who had served in the Phoenician fleet and had traded down the west Libyan coast – which they called Mauretania. The coast we were sailing along looked very inhospitable and I wondered what sort of welcome we would have on the other side. Suddenly, I became conscious that the shores on both sides were retreating away from us. We were now steering towards the middle of the straight, which was becoming wider all the time. As soon as we were out of sight of land, Hercules ordered the fleet to sail north-west. It was not long before land came into view again. This time, it was the coast where we would be landing. The captain of our ship, who knew these waters, consulted with Hercules and the fleet was stood well clear of the land, keeping it just in view to the lookout posted at the top of the main mast. Clearly, we were not going to advertise our arrival, although a fisherman at sea could see us and hurry home to tell of a large fleet of ships just offshore. From what happened subsequently, I don't think that our approach was noticed at all.

'As sunset approached, Hercules became much more animated. Following what appeared to be anxious discussions with the Captain – presumably just to decide the right time to change course – the order was issued to sail practically due north, towards the shore. With our ship leading the way, we sailed directly into a sheltered cove which could have been created just for us. Beaching the ships, the warriors raced ashore in bands to secure the heights overlooking the cove. Reports quickly came back that the countryside was deserted and our arrival almost certainly unmarked. I did not believe at the time that this was coincidence. Hercules later admitted that "friends" had arranged an important religious festival locally so that it was unlikely that our arrival would be seen.

'When the area was secure, and sentries posted, all the herdsmen disembarked, bringing with them their designated warriors' personal effects. As each warrior was on sentry duty, a herdsman had been allocated to each warrior to take charge of disembarking those belongings that he could not take with him on duty. By early evening all that was to be landed had been. Hercules gave the order to the Commander of the major part of the fleet that he could set sail for home. Within a short while, all but the three ships we were retaining had disappeared in the gathering gloom and had started their long journey back to Crete.

'Hercules then decided that it was unwise to light fires and, as it was a mild night, this did not cause undue hardship, although it would have been pleasant to have had some hot food. We had to make do with a cold meal helped down with some good warming wine. After a reasonable sleep, I was awoken by Hercules, who was accompanied by a well-armed warrior – my bodyguard. Leading me to the crest of a rise overlooking the cove harbour, he showed me the landscape to the west. Opening up before me was a vast plain with a large settlement, partly on an island, to the left, and lush pasture land in front and to the right. Even from this distance, I could see that there was a huge herd spread all over the pasture. As my eyes adjusted to the scene, I could also see that the pasture was divided into fields, some with hedges as the boundary, others with ditches or streams with bridges over. Quite a complex layout and I could understand why Hercules needed an accurate map drawn.

'Hercules explained that this system had been designed to prevent over-grazing. As soon as a piece of land reached the stage of needing to be rested, the cattle would be driven off that land on to a new piece. The layout would make our task of taking the whole herd – which I estimated to comprise at least 2,000 animals – quite difficult. It would take time to move them on to one piece of land close to the driving route northwards and it might not be possible to do that quietly, as cattle usually make a great deal of noise when being moved. Having expressed these thoughts, Hercules asked me to ignore that detail and leave it to him. What he wanted me to do was simply to draw a rough sketch of the whole area, showing clearly the entrances and exits from each piece of land, the means available at each obstruction for cattle to cross it – particularly if there appeared to be none as this would require the movement of some type of bridging to be brought from elsewhere, which would take time – where there were larger pieces that could be used as pens for the cattle until we were ready to move off and where there were unobstructed exits (apart from moveable gates) towards a route north that we could use to start the drive. Hercules could be so demanding!

'It took me most of the day to sketch the layout. I had to go down into the plain several times to confirm where there were bridges over the streams. Some of the streams were fordable but not all. I also managed to locate where the herdsmen sheltered and what looked like an important herding ring, near where I thought was the best route out of the area closest to the direction we wished to take. One helpful discovery was that the Cattle were herded fairly close to each other and, fortunately for us, most were not far from the herding ring I had earmarked as the most likely place for us to begin our drive. Despite these unexpected aids, I still felt it would take many hours to herd all the cattle and start their enforced migration.

'When I made my report to Hercules, he was very impressed and complimentary, and agreed to my recommendations on the exit route and the location of the herding ring. Calling in his chief herdsman, we then discussed in detail how we should manage the "lift". Copies of my sketches were made, and one set given to the leader of each herdsmen group. It was decided to start by moving the animals closest to the herding ring I had identified. They would be herded into the corner of the ring furthest from the entry point. When these were on the move, those further away would also be moved, leaving until last those that had the furthest distance to travel. To me, this seemed to mean that it would take longer than necessary to clear the whole herd into the herding ring, but one of the experienced herdsmen said that some cattle move faster than others and we did not know these animals at all; some would not like to find their route blocked by slower animals and would start jostling and making a lot of noise. Our objective was to move out the whole herd, if possible, before anyone was alerted. This made sense to me, as did the connected point that it would be far more difficult to fight the King and his warriors if we had to do so amongst moving cattle. At least, by moving them in groups in sequence we were less likely to trap ourselves in this way.

'The next question was what to do with the local herdsmen. The warrior leader suggested a dawn raid to kill them all but our herdsmen and Hercules felt this was too drastic and unnecessary. They were not a threat to us unless they were given time to raise the alarm. The dawn raid was agreed, but the herdsmen were to be tied up and left together in one of the shelters I had identified.

'The following day, after a full briefing the previous evening, an advance group of the warriors captured and tied up the herdsmen without a struggle and then, joined by the others, took up defensive positions on the town side of the pastures. Our herdsmen swept down on to the plain and set about their task of rounding up the Cattle and moving them to the herding ring. All went unbelievably smoothly. It was not until the last group were being driven into the herding ring and the whole herd were being readied to drive off that the alarm was raised. Geryon, his three sons and a force of armed men, some still buckling on their armour, came streaming through the city gates towards the pasturage. Hercules and our warriors were ready for them, concealed in the trees and ditches on the city side of the pasture.

‘The surprise was complete. In an instant, Geryon and his three sons had been slain by Hercules, together with many of Geryon’s warriors. Those who approached late on the scene saw what had already happened and fled before joining the battle. They knew it was lost.

‘A herald advanced towards us from the city and took the news back that Hercules had arrived, the King and his sons were dead and a new regime was to be installed. I was not involved in the subsequent diplomatic exchanges but, from what I have learnt since from Hercules and other sources, a new city council was elected and Hercules’ nominees were appointed to the most important posts to supervise the changes Hercules had told me about. Hercules himself stayed on for some days while the cattle drive got under way. He caught us up later. Our ships’ captains were advised of our success and were instructed to shadow the herd along the coast, which they did.’

I interrupted at this point.

‘Before you tell me about the cattle drive to Greece, could you say a little more about Geryon’s herdsman and his dog? And also, I have heard conflicting stories about the Pillars of Hercules. Where and what exactly are they?’

Iolaus smiled.

‘Yes. Two very good questions and this is the right point in the story to ask them. On the first question, I have generally only recounted my own experiences. I saw no dog and no special herdsman, but then I was not involved in the battle. My role was with the herdsmen and the Cattle, making sure that my plans were right and moving from group to group to ensure that they did not meet with any unforeseen problems – that is, not foreseen by me! I was very pleased to note that all my observations were correct: the bridges, fords and ditches were where I had drawn them and the herdsmen encountered no problems arising from my mistakes. Anyway, back to your questions.

‘Yes, Geryon was supposed to have one herdsman looking after the whole herd – what a ridiculous story! – a man called Eurytion, accompanied by a fierce dog, called Orthrus. I did hear that one of Geryon’s herdsmen captured by our warriors did not surrender tamely like the others and was killed. When we finally started the drive, some of Geryon's herdsmen – who we released immediately after the surrender of the city – volunteered to come with us and I remember one of them talking to a herdsman of ours about their dead herdsman. Apparently he was a bully, full of himself – being tall and strong – and not much liked by the rest of them. He could have been Eurytion although I never heard that name at the time, only much later, when the storytellers started to embroider the Legends of Hercules after his death.

'As to the dog, I, too, heard the story well after the event: how this fierce dog, Orthrus (or "Orthos" as he is sometimes called), had two heads and was born of a union between Echidna, a monster – half woman and half serpent – and Typhon, also a monster, who was supposed to be of gigantic stature, breathe fire from a hundred mouths and to have so scared the gods that they changed shape and went into hiding! Still, so the story goes, the gods returned and imprisoned him at the base of Mount Etna in Sicily, which is why that mountain still sends sour air and flames into the sky. I expect, if it existed at all, Hercules simply killed it with one blow of his club!

'Now, your second question is much more interesting – or rather, the answer to it is. As you imply, there is a dispute about where and what are the Pillars of Hercules. One story is that they are tall mountains, or cliffs, one on either side of the western entrance to our sea (the Mediterranean) and which were created by Hercules on this expedition when he, with one blow of his mighty club, opened a passage so that ships could sail into the ocean beyond. I can categorically deny the truth of the latter part of that story: we had no difficulty in sailing past where these "Pillars" are, as was the experience of the many who passed that way before us. The Phoenicians had, long before we arrived, been trading with lands and peoples to the west, south and north of Geryon's land, which itself was beyond the "Pillars". I think that you can safely say that Mount Calpe, on the north and Mount Abyle on the south have come to be considered as the "Pillars". If you sail beyond them, you sail into the unknown. So they came to be identified as the end of the known world.

'However, there is at least one other claim, which I think is reasonably valid. You remember that I said that Hercules and some chosen people stayed a little while in Geryon's city, now called Cades?'

I nodded.

'I also told you that a number of them stayed there to run the city and introduce important religious and literary reforms?'

I nodded again.

'Well, whether at Hercules' request or not I do not know, two bronze monuments some eight cubits high were erected in honour of Hercules, close to the port of Geryon's city and inscribed with the new fifteen-consonant alphabet invented and introduced by Hercules. I believe there later developed a ritual that sailors gave thanks at that spot for their safe return from a voyage. Much later, a temple to Hercules was founded further west, at a place called the Sacred Promontory, and I believe that the bronze monuments were moved there. Does that answer your questions?' he asked kindly.

I acknowledged that it did and asked him to continue with his story of the drove. And so he did.

'Our journey, first along the coast, later inland, was a hard, slow and unrelenting toil. Still, there was great comradeship among those of us on the expedition and Hercules was always ready to listen to suggestions. There were a number of incidents, but not as many as you will have heard, to be sure! One of the saddest occurred just as we were crossing the high mountains that separate this part of the world from us. A lady called Pyrene, the daughter of King Bebrycius of that part of the country next to the kingdom of Geryon, had been much attracted to Hercules when we had passed through her father's territory, with his prior permission of course. The attraction was mutual and her father gave consent for Pyrene to accompany Hercules back to Greece.

'We had just reached the mountains, as I said, and were camping by the shore before making an assault on a mountain pass that would lead us to the other side of the range. It was early morning. Pyrene suddenly emerged screaming from her tent and ran off into the woods nearby. It appeared from what she was screaming that she had found a snake in her tent and was terrified. Hercules and some of the others went after her to bring her back to the camp but sadly when they finally caught up with her she was dead, probably killed by a mountain bear, which are quite common in those parts.

'We were all very upset by the incident and Hercules gave Pyrene a funeral feast on the promontory nearby, where he also built a shrine to her. The promontory is called to this day the Pyrenaeum after her and the mountains the Pyrenees, in her memory.

'After we had crossed the Pyrenees, we came down to the plain beyond. This was a great relief because we had been many days in the mountains where grazing was scarce – and, what there was, poor – and the nights very cold. We also had to battle, especially at night, to keep the bears and wolves away from the herd, who, having spent all their previous life in lush pastures close to a city, were not used to protecting themselves against such crafty predators in the wilderness. But, although we were relieved to be out of the mountains, it soon became clear that we were not welcome on the plain. Hercules had warned me earlier that the locals here had a custom of killing strangers, which is of course quite contrary to our practice of welcoming strangers. Hercules was resolved to teach these unfriendly people some manners. This he did, as the many corpses of those who attacked us without provocation or excuse along our route sadly testified. As many deplored the custom, but had been afraid to oppose it openly, Hercules' actions brought us the admiration and support of most of the local population. We also responded kindly and generously to those who treated us well. All of us enjoyed friendship and hospitality from many of the peoples we passed through on our long journey.

'Now it so happened that a lady called Galata, the tall dark-haired Queen of the Mandubii, a nation to the north, was visiting one of the kingdoms we passed through, just before we reached the biggest and widest river I have ever seen. It was clearly impossible to drive the Cattle across it and to try and find a fleet of boats large enough to transport the whole herd was not feasible. So we had no choice but to divert north until we could find a crossing place. So when Queen Galata very kindly invited us to her kingdom, which was, she said, above the place where the river could be crossed without difficulty, Hercules accepted and we drove the herd due north.

'Many days later, we reached Queen Galata's kingdom. Whilst it was true that the river here was fordable, it was clear that we had come much further north than we need have done. Galata freely admitted that she had deceived us, justifying it on the grounds that she wished to join with Hercules in founding a new city and nation. She felt that she and Hercules were made for each other. Fortunately, Hercules had already come to the same conclusion, and so they founded Alesia (which means "wandering"), to celebrate the long distance they had travelled together.

'After many months driving the Cattle, virtually daily, over long distances, the men and the Cattle were ready for a lengthy rest, particularly as winter was now fast approaching. The Queen made it transparent that she and her court ladies expected Hercules and his handsome lusty warriors to remain at Alesia for at least the whole winter. As this was a major decision for us, Hercules summoned a council to debate the issues. Some general conclusions were reached, whereupon, as the outcome depended to a large extent on what Queen Galata and her people could offer, she was invited to join the meeting. The main conclusion was to accept the Queen's invitation to winter in Alesia, provided she would guarantee food and accommodation for the cattle and ourselves – for we knew that the winters here were generally very cold. We also sought some guarantees on help with manpower to look after the cattle if some of our herdsmen wished to return home for the winter. The Queen agreed to give us these guarantees.

'Following Galata's withdrawal from the council, there was a long debate over the wisdom of letting anyone go home. Some council members thought that anyone who left now would never return. Hercules agreed that this was a real possibility. However, he thought that a subtle blend of measures might solve the problem. Those who went would only receive one quarter of what they had been promised and another quarter when they returned, not more than half of those from one village or town would be allowed to go – the remainder would have to stay – and all members of one family would not be allowed to go unless there was a very compelling reason.

'Selection would be based first on family circumstances. Married men with children would have preference over all others and those with sick relatives, or a recent death in the family, would also be granted priority. The maximum number allowed to go would depend on the Queen guaranteeing substitutes for up to half of the total force, divided into herdsmen and warriors. All the leading herdsmen and warriors accepted that they would have to stay, as they were virtually irreplaceable. If more wanted to go than could be allowed, the issue would be decided by lot. As a final incentive, those who wished to go home and not return or later found when they got home that family circumstances had changed so that they no longer wished to return, could retain their right to payment if they sent a substitute capable of carrying out their duties.

'This proposal was put to the men, after Queen Galata had given Hercules the specific guarantees he sought. Rather to my surprise, most of our men preferred to stay. Of those who did leave, some failed to return but very few failed to send a substitute. One, we heard later, had been killed in a drunken brawl and another in an accident on his way home. Their relatives and those who had sent a substitute were sent the promised payment on our return.

'We now settled down to life in a growing town, with the weather getting colder by the day. In the beginning, Hercules encouraged all of those not on duty to help the local people build their new city. I found this very exciting. Wood was available in abundance in the local countryside and I spent some time cutting and preparing timber and, later, constructing houses and a public meeting place. By the time winter was fully upon us and all outside work had to stop, we all had reasonably comfortable quarters, if a trifle crowded. Shelters for some of the Cattle were provided in large dwelling houses under the living accommodation. I found this a very convenient arrangement, as the heat from the cattle rose to the living accommodation above and kept my colleagues (and me) warm throughout the winter. It was not so good in the spring when the smell of the accumulated waste began to permeate through the floor!

'At last, spring arrived. The men returned from their long

journeys home bringing us news of friends – and enemies – and expectations now that the last part of our long journey was about to start. It did start, but without Hercules. During the winter he had been very busy. The Queen and many of her female courtiers were pregnant. When weather conditions had permitted, he had paid visits, generally with the Queen, to most of the tribes through whose territory we would pass to reach Liguria on the Mediterranean coast, where we expected trouble. I do not know what agreements Hercules and the Queen reached with these tribes but we encountered no difficulties whatsoever from them on our passage south from Alesia, although we must have caused them a great deal of inconvenience at best.

'When on the move, we visited the local tribes several days before we were due to pass through their territory to discuss and agree with them the actual route they would like us to take with the herds, the locations of the watering places we could use and what feed we could take from the fields and meadows, with the fee they required for these vital services. We also agreed with them how they would like us to phase our passing through – all together or in small groups spread over a number of days. Some preferred the latter, although most preferred the former.

'We had been advised to set out as soon as the spring arrived in Alesia. This was because we still had to cross the Great River, which had various names given to it by the local tribes, and which flowed from the snow-clad mountains in the east to our sea in the south. We were told that, once the spring sun reached the mountains, the snow would melt and the Great River would change overnight from a broad, shallow and fordable stream into a raging torrent, several cubits deep. When in that state, it would be impossible to cross, even with boats. And so, after a relatively restful winter, came a frenzied spring.

'Within a few weeks of leaving Alesia, we were guided to what we were told was the easiest crossing of the Great River. The water came in a steady flow across a wide area. Apart from a few scattered pools, some of which were quite deep and easily seen and avoided, it was shallow. The water rarely rose above the hocks of the Cattle or the men's knees. Many of the herdsmen and warriors were mounted, some on horses and some on donkeys, who, although much smaller than the horses, were more nimble and less fearful than the horses. Even so, it took a full, long, day to complete the crossing.

'During the night, while we were encamped well up from the riverbank, a huge storm blew up with torrential rain, thunder and lightning. The animals, particularly the horses, had been unsettled before the storm broke, thus giving us advance warning of the deluge. We therefore had time to ensure our encampment and the animals were on the highest ground in the area with direct access to a ridge of higher land, leading away from the Great River. This precaution proved to be our salvation. By dawn, the river had overflowed and water was lapping at the entrances to our tents. Although the rain had ceased, the storm had merely passed further up the valley and its contribution to the flow of the river was continuing. Without delay, we struck camp and, within minutes of realising what was likely to happen, the whole herd was on the move along the ridge we had identified earlier. We made for the higher ground. To our horror, the water stealthily and relentlessly followed us. At one time, it seemed to be moving towards us faster than we were moving up hill. At last, the incline defeated the rising waters, which gradually receded from us as we progressed ever higher.

'By the time we felt we were safe from the rising water, and could halt and rest, we were some distance off our agreed route. We did not know in what tribe's territory we were now in, nor did we know whether the tribes downstream, who had agreed to our passing through their territory, had survived the overnight flood. We held a council and debated our situation. The overwhelming view was that we should aim to get back to the agreed route as soon as possible. This would avoid trouble with the local tribes. Although we had a strong, fit and well-armed warrior force, and could possibly defeat any force a local tribe could put against us, we would certainly suffer casualties, thus depleting our force with no realistic possibility of recruitment, and would give the other local tribes the impression that our intentions were not as we had told them – merely to pass peaceably through with our cattle – but violence and pillage. We also felt that the effects of the recent storm would subside in a few days and the water level of the Great River would return close to what it had been when we crossed the previous day. We should therefore rest where we were, sending out heralds to make contact with the local tribes to explain what we were doing on their land and that we would move on as soon as possible. Heralds were also sent to advise the tribes expecting us that we had survived the storm, to see how they were faring and offer our help if they needed it.

'The heralds all returned safely within a day or so. It was all good news. We had indeed strayed into the land of a tribe who had not agreed to allow us to pass through, but they fully understood the reasons for this and the gift of a few talents of silver (with which our heralds had been thoughtfully provided) soon persuaded them to allow us to stay until the waters subsided, which they said should only be a few days. The tribes downstream, who were expecting us, had realised what could happen as soon as the storm had started and had moved to higher ground away from the Great River. They expected their villages would have suffered some damage from the flood, but declined our help. They indicated this happened fairly frequently and their dwellings were made of wood and grass, which could easily be foraged and their homes rebuilt. They, too, thought the floods would subside in a few days and our original route would be open to us a few days after that.

'In the event, it was almost two weeks before we could recommence the drive, one week for the waters to subside and another for the ground to dry out sufficiently (in our opinion) so that our driven herd would not damage too much the ground over which they passed. This time delay also gave time for the pasture land, to be used by the cattle, to recover.

'We experienced no further problems for the rest of our drive down to the coast. We followed the east bank of the Great River and enjoyed the lush pastures adjoining it. The weather conditions were glorious – sunny with a light breeze during the day and cold enough at night to discourage biting insects. The Great River and its small contributory streams provided a constant supply of fresh water and there was plenty of dead timber to collect for evening fires for cooking and warmth. As I recall now, this was the most pleasant and relaxing part of the whole journey and, apart from where I live now, the place I would most like to spend the rest of my days.'

Iolaus sighed with nostalgia, and then continued:

'As it approached the sea, the Great River split into a number of branches, creating wide marshes and hidden pools of uncertain depth: a death trap for the unwary. Hercules had warned us to keep well clear of this area and had sent guides to meet us where we should turn due east. Shortly after the guides met us, we were reunited with Hercules. He knew about our problems with the flood and congratulated the council for their wise handling of the situation. He was particularly pleased that we had completed this part of our journey without upsetting anyone.

'We now entered mountainous terrain, turning east to pass north of the western end of a range of mountains with a white, crystalline appearance, and which rose abruptly from the plains. Then, after two days' drive, we crossed a large river, which I believe was a tributary of the Great River, and which had long ago broken a passage through these mountains, which were now to our north. As we drove the Cattle through the waters of the river and admired the soaring mountains on either side, we marvelled at the forces that had given us such an easy track through the mountain range. Emerging from the mountains we continued on a well-used track that followed the south bank of the river. This was another beautiful valley with abundant trees to give us shelter from the now burning sun and which provided a ready supply of pasturage, water and large camp sites.

'Hercules now held a council and warned us of the dangers ahead. During his absence since we left Alesia, he had confirmed with the tribal chiefs, whose land we had already passed through, that our aims were peaceful and he had paid in advance for the food, pasturage and inconvenience arising from our passage. Queen Galata had some emissaries sent some time previously to advise her nearest neighbours of our activities, the size of the herd, our probable route, our peaceful intentions and the size of our armed force, to deter any thoughts of piracy. This, Hercules said, had been very helpful. He had experienced no difficulties with those to whom the Queen had communicated this information. The remainder in the valley of the Great River had, after an initially suspicious greeting, accepted Hercules' assurances – and his money – and some, who had already heard of his reputation when dealt with fraudulently, told their people to honour the arrangement they had made with Hercules, as the consequences of not doing so would be dire! As most of the tribes we saw were relatively small groups, with more women, children and old people than young warriors, they clearly knew what was in their best interests and some could not do too much for us.

'So much for the past, Hercules warned us. We were now approaching an area controlled by much more war-like tribes. He told me later that he suspected these tribes had been bribed by Eurystheus to make our passage through difficult. At one point, several weeks' drive ahead, the mountains reached down virtually to the sea shore. However, there was a narrow track along the shoreline, barely wide enough for a chariot. This was virtually the only place anyone could gain access to the plains beyond, and it was here that he suspected an ambush would be made. It was the ideal place: the large herd could only be driven slowly as they would be fearful of the cliff on one side and the sea on the other. The track was only wide enough for two animals to pass at the same time, so the column would be extended over a long distance. If the warriors were divided, with half sent in front and the remainder in the rear, neither group would be able to bring support to the other if attacked. It was even less feasible to spread the warriors throughout the column, as they could then be picked off individually.

'Hercules therefore proposed two strategies. Firstly, to dig out a broad road through the worst part so that the passage of the herd would be safe and speedy and, secondly, to lead a strong armed party to tackle the forces of the Ligurians, who he believed would be ranged against our peaceful passage. The council agreed and, at Hercules' suggestion, also accepted that he should go now with a force of a third of our warriors. The remainder would be sufficient to protect us as we passed through the territory of tribes who had already shown themselves to be friendly.

'We were approaching the place at which we had agreed with Hercules that we would rest until he joined us when he suddenly appeared one evening, looking drawn and very tired. He was followed in a little later by the warriors. All had returned, but all were exhausted and more than half were wounded, several quite badly. Clearly, Hercules had encountered the resistance he had forecast. After a short rest and some food and drink, Hercules addressed a hastily convened meeting to tell us what had happened.

'Hercules reported that, as soon as they entered the mountains, they encountered stiff resistance from several bands of armed men. They clearly knew the terrain and had prepared ambush positions from which the bands, in turn, launched assaults on Hercules and his warriors. At one stage, Hercules found himself isolated and, with all his arrows shot, was reduced to foraging for stones to throw at the enemy to hold them off until some of his warriors, who were involved in separate battles some distance away, could come to his aid. Unfortunately, the place chosen by his enemies for the fight was a flat piece of ground totally devoid of stones. Calling on Zeus for aid, he made what he thought might be a final assault with only his club in his hand. Suddenly, the sky darkened and the air was full of what Hercules at first thought were small rocks. They were in fact large hailstones, each the size of a small stone. Miraculously, none landed on Hercules, but his enemies fled for shelter. By the time the hailstorm was over, some of Hercules' warriors had joined him and he was able to retrieve his arrows. The returning enemy were quickly despatched, only a few escaping to cause trouble another day.

'It was now believed that the main opposition had been defeated. On arrival close to the site of the battle, where the track we had been following narrowed considerably, the drive was halted. Working parties of warriors and herdsmen were drafted daily into the foothills away from the shore to make a road three chariots' width to drive the herd through. Deployed in well hidden and salient positions around the working parties were groups of warriors whose only task was to protect those working on the road. I spent time both on the road and as a guard. While the road work was hard, I preferred that to sitting up in the hills waiting for an arrow in my back! As it happened, there were no attacks. I later learnt that Hercules had sent selected warriors into the hills ahead of the workers to report on any attempted attack and, if the raiding party was small enough, to destroy them. This they did. It later became apparent that these "raiding parties" were actually bands of robbers who had been attacking and robbing all passers-by using the old, narrow pass, which our work, when completed, replaced.

'At last, we broke through the mountain and created our own pass! After the battles that Hercules and his warriors had fought, we were not sure what reception we would receive from the local people. We were therefore very surprised and relieved to get a very friendly reception at the first settlement we reached. When they explained that we had killed the mountain robber band and built them a new road so that they could now traverse the mountain in safety, I understood the reason for their friendliness. They were also pleased to be rid of the King's men who had been living in their village for some months, eating their food, drinking their wine and abusing their womenfolk. So they had good reasons to be grateful.

'Despite the stories you may have heard, the rest of our journey to Greece was relatively uneventful. Many years later I heard it said that Hercules had lost his way and drove the Cattle down through Italy with many adventures on the way. This is completely untrue: we drove the herd through Epirus to Corinth and across the isthmus to the Peloponnese where they were presented to Eurystheus. One story, that Hercules sacrificed a bull from the herd to Zeus, is correct, but this was in gratitude for his deliverance at the Ligurian pass, not at the toe of Italy as the story has it.'

The Final Two Labours: The Rams from the Gardens of the Hesperides and the Rescue of Theseus

'The next task set by Eurystheus was to steal the three Golden Rams from the Garden of the Hesperides. I knew where this garden was – we had passed close by on our trek along the Libyan coast at the beginning of our previous task. Suspicion grew in my mind that Hercules knew that this was to be his next task before he was told by Eurystheus, and he had cleverly already carried out reconnaissance and made local friends by conducting our expedition so sensitively through that part of Libya on our way to steal Geryon's Cattle. When we met to discuss how to mount this expedition, Hercules virtually admitted that he had chosen the route of the last task so that he would pass by the Garden. On one of the days I did not see him on the previous expedition, when we were close to the Garden, he had apparently visited the area and worked out a plan.'

I interrupted. 'But I thought that it was golden apples that Hercules had to steal from an apple tree given as a wedding present to Hera, the wife of Zeus?'

'Ah,' said Iolaus, 'I see that you have been listening to some story-makers! Do you seriously think that Hercules would get involved directly between Zeus and his wife, Hera? That would be unthinkable! The quest was for rams, the sacred beast of Zeus-Ammon. I will now tell you what others have said, and what really happened.

'Apart from the basic error of assuming a word meant "apple" when the alternative meaning – and the most sensible – was "sheep", some of the stories imply that Hercules did not know where the Garden was. They suggest he travelled to Italy to the mouth of the River Po or west again, back to near the Pillars of Hercules. He did no such thing. Others suggest that he engaged the services of the Titan, Atlas, to procure the apples for him and held up the world as his substitute while he did so. What rubbish! No, what happened was much more straightforward.

'Once again, we set out for Crete. The crew we had used before were waiting for us, although they pretended not to be – probably on instruction from Hercules. They were genuinely pleased to see us and to hear that the long and arduous cattle drive had been concluded successfully. I expect that only I knew that the real objective of the expedition had been to introduce a new religion there that did not tolerate human sacrifice, as well as propagate Hercules' new alphabet. After a short delay to buy and put on board the ship the necessary supplies for what we hoped would be a short voyage, we loaded the pens for the Rams and Hercules' chariot, which we had brought with us. I noticed that there were only two sheep pens, but kept quiet after catching Hercules' eye. Clearly, he might be taking three but only two would be making the journey to Mycenae. No doubt Hercules would tell me his plans when he was ready to do so.

'The short sea journey passed quickly and we were soon edging our way, against a contrary wind, along the Libyan coast towards the place which Hercules said was our destination. As usual, his navigation was perfect and we soon saw the islands known as the Gardens of the Hesperides. The uses to which the islands were put were varied. Some were partly gardens in the true sense, but some were for pasture and on parts of them many crops were being grown. Then I saw them – as handsome a flock of sheep as you would see anywhere, grazing quietly in a large field!

'With a speed that left me gasping, Hercules and two of the men had waded through the water, caught three of the Rams and carried them back to the ship. No alarm was raised and there were no shepherds in evidence. Two of the Rams were put in one pen and the third in the second pen. We turned the ship around and sailed back the way we had come, this time with the wind blowing strongly behind us. On instructions from Hercules, the Captain sailed the ship past the point where we had first sighted land and the Hercules called me over.

' "The third Ram I am taking to the shrine of Ammon-Zeus at Siwa for sacrifice," he said, "and then I shall be travelling to

Egypt, as I have much to attend to there. I could not tell you of this before because, for various reasons, it is very important that some people are not aware of my movements or my intentions. I would very much like you to accompany me on this journey and be my charioteer. I have also asked the four men you no doubt identified as warriors among the crew to accompany us for our protection. They do not yet know where we are going, but they were with us on our previous expedition and are thoroughly trustworthy."

'I had indeed noticed them board the ship just before we left Crete, but assumed that they were merely acting as bodyguards. I now realised that they had a wider role. Of course, I agreed to accompany Hercules – what else could I say? It was an exciting prospect: to visit one of the most famous and remote oracles in the world at Siwa, and then to Egypt, whose reputation for sophisticated living was worldwide. I had difficulty in curbing my excitement.

'Night fell and we beached in a remote spot to sleep. Guards were posted but no strangers disturbed our sleep that night. I could not sleep, but that was for a different reason! We were all awake before dawn. The crew were anxious to get started and none of us knew how long it would take us to reach the point of our departure. Hercules indicated that it would be at Paraitonios where we could buy horses and pick up a caravan travelling to Siwa.

'We arrived at Paraitonios at dusk. Clearly we could do nothing until morning. We decided to stay on board, although it was somewhat cramped. Hercules took two of the warriors to check on the location of the horse traders and to find out when the next caravan was leaving for Siwa.

'They were soon back with the good news that they had already agreed to purchase six chariot horses and ten riding horses, to be paid for and collected the following day, and that the next caravan to Siwa was leaving in a few days' time. The leader of the caravan was known to the horse dealer and would be in Paraitonios the following day. Hercules would be introduced to him and the dealer thought that he would be delighted to have a professional escort riding with his caravan. The additional riding horses were explained. The Ram would have to travel in the chariot in a makeshift pen – the ones on the ship were far too large to fit in the chariot. Hercules and I would take turns to drive the chariot and ride on horseback with the warriors. The extra horses would either be tied to a vehicle in the caravan or some to the chariot and others on a leading rein. Hercules explained that the caravan would be a mixed group and would move quite slowly as it had to keep together, both to avoid anyone getting lost in the desert or some of the travellers being picked off by bandits.

'The following morning, we said farewell to our crew and we watched them sail on their way home. They would look after the two Rams for us until Hercules arrived to claim them. He warned them that it would be some time before they saw him again. With some help from one of the warriors, I assembled the chariot, which we had offloaded from the ship just before it sailed, while the others accompanied Hercules to pay for and collect the horses, and meet the caravan leader.

'By the time the chariot was assembled, Hercules and the others had returned and Hercules and I put the chariot horses through their paces. All but one were acceptable and that one was returned to the dealer and exchanged for one that ran perfectly with its chosen companion between the shafts of the chariot.

'Hercules and I later met the caravan leader. He was as helpful as we had been told he would be. He would be leaving with a large caravan in five days' time, just before dawn, and would be pleased to take us with him for a reasonable fee, which Hercules paid there and then. He told us that although, in normal circumstances, the journey to Siwa took no more than seven days, this was a large – and therefore slower than normal – caravan and would take at least a day longer. It was also possible that adverse weather conditions, such as a sandstorm, could force the whole caravan to take shelter for several days until the storm blew itself out.

'The five most important items to take with us were water, some fabric to provide a shelter (such as a tent), water, food and water! As we were taking horses, as well as a ram, for us to have plenty of water was very important. The horses would need water at least twice a day or they would die. Humans also needed a lot of water in the desert and, until we reached the oasis at Siwa, which was huge, there was really no source of water on the route unless it rained. About two thirds of the way there was an abandoned settlement called Gara where poor quality water might be available, but it was best not to rely on it as bandits sometimes polluted the water supply, whether deliberately or accidentally he could not say.

'We were then shown the meeting point for the caravan and promised to be there by no later than dawn on the fifth day. Our companions were pleased that we would soon be on the move and we drew up lists of the supplies we needed, including water. When we had calculated the volume and weight of these supplies, we realised that every horse, apart from those drawing the chariot, would have to carry something. Hercules considered this carefully and decided that we would have to take some additional animals with us purely as "pack" animals. He had been told that the best animals for this purpose were the large, rather ungainly animals we had already seen near the market. We understood they were called "camels" and could travel long distances in the desert without needing water, a very valuable characteristic. We decided to purchase three of them to carry most of the water and the tents we would buy. All these purchases were made the same day and we gradually became acquainted with these strange animals, learning how to load and unload them, and even ride them. One of them had a rather tempestuous nature and would bite you if you got too close, but the other two were obedient and quiet and had obviously been used and trained as pack animals.

'The four days after we met the caravan leader passed quickly in buying the stores we needed and learning how to pack and load them on the animals we had. After taking some local advice, we found that the loading capacity of each camel was far more than we had thought and, apart from skins of water, the horses were not called upon to carry more than a tent each. We also learnt that the supply of liquid was likely to be supplemented on the journey by goats' milk. This was because some in the caravan would be taking female goats to sell in Siwa and their owners would be more than willing to sell the milk to anyone in the caravan prepared to pay for it. This was welcome news, particularly as we felt that, towards the end of the journey, the water would be not too pleasant to drink.

'On the fifth day, we were all awake well before dawn. Within a short while the animals were loaded, the horses harnessed to the chariot with Hercules and the Ram safely secured on board, and the warriors and myself astride our horses, with those animals entrusted to our care at the end of a halter. We made our way to the town square, where a large crowd of people and animals had clearly been gathering for some time. Dawn had still not broken but the leader was moving among the crowd, checking that all those who had enlisted with him were there, collecting his fee and handing back a token of some sort. Hercules commented that the token was to tell the group in which order they were to travel. Soon the leader reached us and greeted Hercules warmly. As this was our first time and we were a relatively lightly loaded and compact group, he suggested that we took the lead with him, which we accepted with alacrity. The alternative of bringing up the rear was quickly rejected as we realised that we would see little and be blinded with dust raised by the column in front of us during the journey.

'Therefore, accompanying the leader, we led the long caravan out of the square into the desert beyond. Looking back after we had left the town, I could see the long tail of the caravan snaking behind us in a fairly orderly fashion. Soon we were in the desert and much of the column disappeared in the sand dust raised by such a large group of plodding animals. As the caravan leader had predicted, our progress was slow. We merely ambled along at the pace of the slowest. At first, this was irritating but when the sun rose in the sky and we began to feel the midday heat, we were very happy at the slow pace. Shortly after midday, we reached an area where there were some sand mountains to the west of the track we were following. These, we later found, cast a pleasing shadow as the sun sank in the west. It was obvious from the abandoned water containers and other debris that this was regularly used by travellers as a stopping place. It took a long time for the whole caravan to join us. We had already watered and fed the animals and ourselves before the last of them arrived.

'The leader warned us that this was only a temporary stop to avoid the hottest part of the day. When we had rested and the sun had begun to sink close to the horizon, we would move off again for a short while to another resting place, which was a little more welcoming than this one. We decided to change horses at each stage and so, instead of resting, we harnessed two different horses to the chariot and transferred their burdens to the horses that had originally drawn the chariot. The warriors did the same. As we had unburdened each animal when we arrived at this halt, it was no extra task to change the horses and we decided to rotate the duties in this way for the rest of the journey. The leader told us that this was what those with spare animals invariably did. We noticed that some in the caravan, particularly those near the rear, did not even unburden their animals at all during these short midday stops. Their animals, mostly camels, did not seem to mind, but I was not very impressed!

'At a signal, the caravan moved off, with the leader and ourselves in the van. I was amazed how hot it was as soon as we emerged from the shadow of the sand mountain. I was now driving the chariot, and Hercules riding a horse. Although the chariot horses were quite careful to avoid the occasional boulders in the track, they did not seem as aware of them as the horse I had been riding. I experienced a few nasty jolts before realising what was happening: I had expected a more comfortable ride in the chariot than on horseback, but, in this terrain, that is something I never experienced. Hercules confirmed my experience. He was enjoying his ride on horseback and I could see that I might have a problem persuading him to resume chariot duty! I jest – we took it in turns throughout that journey and the next.

'Shortly after sunset, the leader brought the caravan into a large, flat area where there were vestiges of habitation, including the remains of primitive shelters. We were allocated one of these. It comprised a continuous mud-brick wall, no more than three cubits high at any place and sometimes no more than two, surrounding on three sides a hollowed-out area some twelve cubits square. It was barely large enough for all of us. There was no room for any of the animals. We had been warned that, despite the extreme heat during the day, the nights in the desert were very cold. Fortunately all the animals, apart from the Ram, were local and presumably were accustomed to these huge changes in temperature. We tethered the Ram under the chariot, which we left outside the compound, partly closing off the entrance, and built shelters along the outside of the walls of the compound, using some of the tents and poles we had brought, for all the animals. The difficult bit was to make the roof high enough to accommodate the camels when standing up. They normally rest either on their knees or fully prone, whereas a horse does not rest on its knees, although it sometimes dozes standing up.

'I remember the difficulty we had in doing all this, and feeding and watering the animals and ourselves in the pitch dark. There was no sunlight to illuminate our tasks and the moon had not yet appeared. Still, as the cold night air descended, we realised that our actions in providing the shelter first had been right. We had brought a little dry wood to make a fire and were able to light this with the assistance of another caravanner, who, being part of a much smaller group, had already settled down to cook a hot meal. Whilst some of us raised a covering of tents for our accommodation, the rest of us prepared our food and settled the animals. Soon, the twinkling of fires was seen throughout the camp and strange cooking smells were wafting past our noses. We thought it prudent to set a guard and so we took it in turns through the night, only one at a time, so that most of us had a good night's sleep. The last man on duty was charged with waking the rest of us when he saw the leader stirring and then start preparing the animals and packing up the tents.

'This pattern of the day was followed for the remainder of our journey to Siwa. There was no sandstorm – indeed, no storm of any kind – and we were not aware of any dramas further down the column, although no doubt there were some. We did reach the former settlement at Gara and stayed overnight there. The leader was right to be doubtful about the water. There was an oasis there, a small one, but the water did not taste pleasant, according to one of our warriors who was brave enough to try it. Still, we had no need of it as our water supplies, if beginning to taste a little tired, were more than sufficient for our needs. We were now barely two days' ride from Siwa.

'And, suddenly, there it was! Many people who have not travelled in the desert think it is a flat expanse with little or no features. This is not so. There are solid rock formations that rise out of the desert to a considerable height, and there are other, apparently stable and equally large mounds, but these are made of sand which, if assaulted for a few hours by a strong wind, will migrate and change their appearance completely. This and the fact that there are few obvious permanent features to use for guidance when crossing the desert are what make it so dangerous. This was why the first sight of Siwa was so remarkable.

'We climbed laboriously up a slippery sandy slope. As we crested the top, we saw in the distance a range of hills glowing a golden pink in the strong sunlight. In front of them, and much closer to us, we could see another object strongly reflecting the sunlight. This, the leader said, was the huge lake that formed the oasis and gave life to the large area around the city of Siwa. As we descended the slope towards the city, the citadel of which rose up in front of us like an island out of the sea, the land in front of us turned green – a vast forest of trees that, as we approached, slowly metamorphosed into individual trees of every sort. There were palm trees with dates, olive trees, lemon trees, fig trees and pomegranate trees. The cool of their shade was in such contrast to the heat of the desert surrounding them. It was an unbelievable experience, virtually indescribable and, at first, it seemed to be but an illusion. The leader, who of course had seen it many times, was moved and humbled by our wonder. He admitted that he had possibly become too familiar with it to succumb to its magic but freely acknowledged that it must be one of the world's wonders. As we progressed towards the citadel, which was lost to view as soon as we entered the groves, we felt that this was a place fit for the gods to live in.

'Although the track we were following was wide and clear, and we could probably have found our own way to the citadel, we felt bound to stay with the caravan – not that it now needed what little protection we could offer – until journey's end. Hercules smiled at our emotions. Whilst he did to some extent share them, he wanted to see where the caravans assembled and to make enquiries for our onward journey to Egypt. I had heard him discussing this with the leader, who said that he had never been on that route to the east. He only knew the route between Siwa and Paraitonios. He said there were regular caravans to the east but he understood that there were two routes. Did we know which route we wished to travel? Hercules did not answer, whether because he did not know or because he did not wish to disclose his intentions. I could only guess the latter. Later, as I shall relate, Hercules admitted I guessed correctly.

'When we emerged from the thicket of the forest, our lengthy caravan wended its way slowly through the mud-brick houses lining the track. Palm trees still flanked the track on both sides, more for shade than their fruit, I guessed. Eventually, even these trees disappeared and we approached an impressive large, open area at the foot of what was clearly the walled citadel of this amazing place. The caravan finally came to rest just to the left of the main gate. We took our leave of the leader after he had given us advice on where to find safe lodgings for ourselves and our animals and where to ask about the departure of caravans to Egypt. I, with one of the warriors, was deputed to find lodgings while Hercules and one other warrior went in search of a caravan leader. The other two warriors were left to guard our belongings and the animals, who were contentedly being fed and watered by the warriors when we left, Hercules and his companion on horseback and the warrior and I in the chariot.

'We were offered several pleasant places to rest, the best, I thought, being a short distance back along our entrance route in a shady spot. I therefore agreed to take it for that night and such further nights as we might decide to stay. The owner was talkative and I did not disabuse him when he suggested that we would be going back the way we had come. He was very impressed by the chariot and, realising that we would pay well for his services, he did not insist on my making any payment there and then. I must say I preferred to leave such dealings to Hercules and was quietly amused when I thought of the impact that the bulky muscularity of Hercules would make on our host!

'Having organised our accommodation, we returned to the place where we had left our group. As I had expected, a slightly impatient Hercules was waiting for us. I explained what I had arranged and he seemed pleased. He said that he had found that a caravan "going in the right direction" would be leaving in approximately seven days' time and he was to meet the leader of it the next day to discuss terms. He then drew me aside and said that he wanted us to approach the Temple of Ammon-Zeus, which was in the citadel, to discuss a certain matter. This was confidential and was not to be discussed by me with anybody else. In the meantime, the warriors were to take the animals, including the ram, to the lodging place, where we would join them. We would leave two horses in the care of one of the bystanders while we went into the city, which appeared to be equally unfriendly to horses as to chariots. One of the warriors would have to drive the chariot. This was arranged and, after helping them to assemble the animals and chariot into a small caravan, they trotted off, led by the warrior who had accompanied me to our lodgings driving the chariot.

'Hercules and I then found a trustworthy-looking bystander to look after our horses for us while we went into the citadel. This, we could tell, was a common custom here, as there were a number of single men squatting on the ground close to horses tied up to wooden stakes in the shade of the city wall. On the way up the steep streets of the city to the Temple, Hercules explained that he had come here to sacrifice the Ram to Ammon-Zeus in thanks for his life and for the favour of the next enterprise in Egypt, of which he declined to give me details. As we approached the Temple, two priests appeared at the door and barred our entry. Hercules was discomfited. Controlling his anger, he asked the senior priest if he knew who he was and whether he was welcome or not. The priest replied that they knew he was Hercules; whether he was welcome or not would depend on what he desired.

'Now, it is a tradition at Siwa that only kings can enter the Sanctuary and I presumed that this was what Hercules was about to ask. However, he knew that there was an outer room in the Temple that led to the sanctuary, so he persuaded the priests to allow us to enter the Temple and sit in the outer room. Hercules made it clear to me that he wished to have a private conversation with the priests, so I agreed to wait outside where the shades were now lengthening as the sun sank in the west.

‘Hercules emerged quite quickly from the Temple and, from his face, I could see that he felt he had been insulted and had not been granted his wish. The senior priest followed him out, and, motioning to him, called him to the Temple door, where they had a brief, whispered, conversation. This time, it seemed that an agreement had been reached. On the way back down to where the horses were, Hercules seemed relaxed and satisfied, but we did not discuss the events that had just passed. We collected our horses and rode off to our resting place, discussing everything but our visit to the Temple.

‘The following morning, Hercules was up early. I rose, too, as I suspected he might need my help. At first, he was rather sullen, but his natural good nature leavened his moodiness and he told me of his plans for the day. Simply put, the Ram was to be prepared for sacrifice at the Temple. The priests would carry out the ritual slaughter alone – Hercules could not be present because he was not a king. However, and this was the compromise agreed at the door of the Temple the previous evening, if Hercules would then wear the Ram’s flayed fleece over his naked body, he could enter the Sanctuary and seek the guidance of the great Zeus. He therefore proposed to give the Ram a ritual washing, with my assistance, and drive it down to the city in the chariot, leaving me with the chariot while he delivered the Ram to the priests for the sacrifice. The priests would then arrange for the Ram’s fleece to be removed and flayed and have it ready for Hercules the following morning. And so it was. We delivered the cleansed Ram to the Temple priests and Hercules returned the following day on his own. He never told me all that happened in the Temple that morning, but he was allowed into the Sanctuary and had his dialogue with the Oracle of Ammon-Zeus. He also told me that he had received the answer he needed to proceed with his plans. What these were would be revealed to me later, but it clearly related to some project in Egypt.

‘The next task was to plan our trip across the desert, eastwards to Egypt. This would be more difficult as it was much further, but there were a number of oases along the route and some mud-brick accommodation available for travellers. Unfortunately, both of these “luxuries” terminated about halfway along the route.

After that point, there were no oases and no accommodation until the cities of Egypt were reached. We asked Hercules how much further it was to Egypt than the route we had taken from Paraitonios to Siwa. He told us that it was at least twice as far, possibly more. With favourable conditions, it could take at least ten days for a fast caravan to traverse, a slow one would take much longer. He had already met the leader of the next caravan travelling in that direction and he was pleased to tell us that it would be a small caravan and the leader intended to move it at a faster pace than the one we had travelled with from Paraitonios. He estimated it would take little more than ten days, possibly less. Hercules said he thought the leader was being too optimistic and we should plan on at least twice as long and ensure we had supplies for twenty days. We would leave in a week.

'Whilst we all thought ourselves, after one journey across the desert, experienced in desert travel, we were in for a shock. Our journey across to the Great River of Egypt was quite different from the journey to Siwa. The latter had been along a well worn track, comprising mainly sand and some rock. It had been hard on the feet of the animals, but they were used to it. The track eastwards across to the oasis known as Bahariya soon presented us with problems. The first day was like those we had already experienced, but the second day we encountered a gritty surface that was an omen of what was to come. The leader had warned us of what to expect so we had brought with us some "boots" of cloth to cover the feet of the animals and cushion them from the worst of the stones. We passed through a desolate place where there were standing columns of stone, which must have been nearly one hundred cubits high, with their bases so eroded by wind and rain that they appeared on the point of collapse. Some of our small caravan even rested in the shade of these monstrous features but we kept our distance from them, fearing a gust of wind could cause a catastrophic collapse!

'The next day, we were warned by the leader to equip our animals with boots and not to take them off until he told us. If they fell off, they should be replaced immediately. Within a short time we saw why he had given us this advice. The track passed through a flat wilderness where sharp fragments of minerals pierced the surface. If a man were to walk barefoot, the soles of his feet would quickly be torn to shreds. Hercules and I decided to ride together in the chariot and free one of the horses to take part of the load of one of the others. The warriors discussed with Hercules the wisdom of dismounting to save the horses but Hercules pointed out that he would rather have a lame horse than a warrior with an infected foot. The horses, with their native cunning, soon learnt how to deal with the problem. They walked in someone else's footsteps! Thus we progressed slowly and painfully until at last the leader told us we had passed through this section and could take the animals' boots off. After a few more, dreary, burning hot days, we reached the oasis at Bahariya.

'Having ensured we were settled in comfortably, Hercules announced the following day that he had a task to perform and expected to return within six days or so. If he had not returned within eight days, and we had not received a message from him, we were to assume he would not be returning and to make our way back to Crete as best we could. There I was to collect the Rams and sail back to the Peloponnese, and deliver them to the High King at Mycenae without further explanation, except that he, Hercules, had not returned from a visit he had said he would make to a friend in Libya. I was not to mention the visit to Siwa nor this side trip to Egypt.

'I was alarmed, but did not say anything until we were alone. I pressed him to take me with him. We would travel faster in the chariot to his destination (he had indicated he would go on foot) and I would be ready to bring him back at the conclusion of what was obviously a dangerous mission. He was touched by my concern and said that he would think about my offer.

'Later in the morning, he called me to his tent and told me to get myself and the chariot ready to leave if I still wanted to come with him. I was delighted and said so. He then produced a wig of black hair and told me to put it on. I did so with a grimace. He looked at me quizzically, nodded and told me that would do. He then admonished me to wear it at all times and not ever to let it slip to reveal my golden hair. Mystified, I agreed and, with the wig still atop of my head, went to prepare the chariot, horses and myself. Of course, in my excitement, I had forgotten to ask how far we were going and how many spare horses I needed to take. Ashamed to go back and ask, I prepared two spare horses as well as the two I harnessed to the chariot and, all ready to go, presented myself at Hercules' tent.

'He approved my preparations and said that we would make the journey in easy stages. He had obviously planned this journey in detail already and, as I later discovered, had arranged overnight stops on the way. At the first, only a short run for the horses, they were only expecting Hercules on his own but they soon adjusted to my presence and that of the horses, although they had some difficulty in finding them stabling at such short notice. We had no such problem later on, so I presume a message was sent in advance warning the future hosts of the increased size of the party.

'On the third day, I felt some tension arise in Hercules and I sensed that we were getting close to his chosen destination. By now, we were in the middle of the delta of the Great River of Egypt. Up to this point, we had avoided large settlements but I could see on the horizon a large town which I later learnt was called Busiris. I also learnt later that the king who ruled here was of the same name and called himself the king of Egypt. He was not the only King in Egypt at that time. The whole of Egypt owed allegiance to the great Ramses II, but his palace was many stadia away, nearer the source of the Great River. As we approached the town, Hercules asked me to pull into the side and stop under a tree. It was early evening and there were not many people about.

'Hercules warned me that we were now in great danger. King Busiris was a fanatical worshipper of the god Osiris, who, he said, demanded the human sacrifice of a red- or blonde-headed man. Now, Egyptians were almost exclusively black-haired, so they were not endangered by the King's policy. Although many disagreed with human sacrifice, they were afraid to speak out. This barbaric practice was not carried out elsewhere in Egypt, but Busiris, supported by his priests, was adamant in maintaining it. The victims were usually unsuspecting Greeks who traded with the kingdoms in the delta – indeed there were a number of Greek settlements to the north, including Pharos. He was now going to offer himself as a target, so I must not intervene when he was arrested on entering the city. Provided I kept on my black wig, I should be protected from arrest, but it was best to avoid all contact except with those he had arranged to act as host. We then, in the gathering gloom, approached the city and stopped at a farm a short distance outside the walls, where we were welcomed, fed and given accommodation for ourselves and the horses. The chariot was hidden in one of the farm buildings and Hercules told me not to bring it out until he returned. If he had not returned within three days, I was to assume he was dead and return the way I had came, maintaining at all times the wig disguise.

'Next morning, Hercules woke me early. He was now going into the city, on his own. He would prefer that I stayed safe in the farm until he returned, but knowing my curiosity, he would not object if I chose to follow him at a discreet distance to see what happened. He again stressed that I should not intervene, as it would be fatal for me and, possibly, for him also if I did.

'We left the farm separately, on foot. By the time we approached the city gates, we had merged with a steady stream of people who were mostly moving towards the city, presumably for work or to make purchases in the markets there. Hercules, with his flashing blonde hair and striking physique, was hardly invisible. He towered over the crowd of local people with their small build and black hair. He would have been less obvious on his own, but then I knew that his objective was to be seen.

'They were waiting for him at the city gates. At least four heavily armed guards seized him and dragged him off into the city. The locals did not seem surprised and I noticed a number of the crowd who had been walking close to him quietly dispersed in different directions after Hercules had been captured. I followed one of them, whom I thought I had seen exchanging a few words with Hercules when he was well outside the city limits, at a discreet distance. However, as I turned a corner, I lost him. Realising that he may have noticed I was following him, I decided to pretend that I was going along this route for my own reasons and carried on walking as if nothing had happened. To no avail. Within paces, I was suddenly surrounded by a silent group of men, hustled through the nearest doorway and down some dark steps into a dank basement. Here, two men held me tight by the arms while a third tried to interrogate me in a language I did not understand. I replied in Libyan, deciding that this was probably safer than Greek, as I did not know into whose hands I had fallen, and protested that I had lost my way, intending to go to the market to buy some food. They clearly did not believe my story and I thought my last day had come when a fourth man emerged from the darkness in front of me and asked me in Greek if I knew Hercules. His accent was Cretan and I decided that I would risk telling the truth. I admitted I knew Hercules. Stepping forward, the fourth man looked in my eyes and, with a quick movement of his right hand, removed the wig from my head to disclose my flaming red hair. Laughing, he told the two holding me to release me. When they had done so, he carefully replaced my wig and led me upstairs to a room at the back of the house. Calling for some drinks for us, he motioned me to sit and we conversed in Greek.

'Cautiously, at first, I explained that I was Hercules' servant and had helped to bring him to this city. He had warned me it would be dangerous for me and had told me to wait for him and not to get involved. I had been shocked when I saw the guards seize him at the gate and wondered what was going on. The Cretan, who did not give his name, was a little disbelieving at first and questioned me on what I thought Hercules was doing here. I told him that I thought it had something to do with human sacrifice, to which Hercules was totally opposed. At this, the Cretan's face looked grim as he admitted that Hercules' mission was indeed concerned with the misguided religious fanatics in the city who supported human sacrifice to the gods. This was against the view of the majority, who wanted it stopped. The only concession that had been made so far was to prohibit the sacrifice of local people and kill unsuspecting strangers instead. Hercules had been wise to insist that I wore a wig: strangers with red hair were the preferred sacrificial victim! He had believed my story as soon as he had seen my hair because Hercules had told him of me and nobody who had disguised his red hair with a black wig would be unaware of the problem and dangers he would be facing in this city.

'The Cretan was clearly not sure what to do with me. It was obvious to me that he was involved with Hercules in a plot to overthrow the present King and his priests. I had walked into his trap – he was the man I had followed – and I would probably be captured by the King's men if I was unlucky. At this difficult stage of the action, he did not want to expose any of his men for fear of compromising the whole enterprise. I realised that my curiosity had led me into folly, and, as Hercules had warned me, had put his life, as well as my own, in danger. I told the Cretan so and apologised for the embarrassment I was causing him. The Cretan was quite relaxed about it: he said that, if Hercules had thought I would be indiscreet or foolish, he would have told me to stay at the farm (he knew about the farm, then), but he had not. Therefore, he had obviously thought that I could be of some use to him in the city.

'The Cretan then told me the bare bones of the plan: Hercules was to let himself be captured and prepared for sacrifice. At the moment of sacrifice he would burst his bonds, seize the sacrificial knife and slay the King and the priests and, supported by those who would have infiltrated the congregation in the Temple, announce a new regime where the future worship of Osiris, who had been killed by the red-headed Set, would no longer be celebrated by the slaughter of innocent strangers. According to legend, Set had been killed by Osiris' son, Horus, but Set had been guilty of murder. It was a religious travesty to celebrate that by killing an innocent and unsuspecting foreigner! It was also bad for trade. The majority of trade was now with the Greeks who had a predominance of blonde- and red-haired people.

'After hearing a little of my exploits with Hercules, the Cretan realised that I was to be trusted. He therefore invited me to join him in the Temple with the other conspirators. My task, with others, would be to protect him whilst he roused the crowd to support the new regime. Others nearer the altar would ensure that King Busiris and all the priests were killed and that Hercules was protected. We now had to await the news of the staging of the sacrifice, which should be on the following day, the date of the annual sacrificial ceremony.

'I passed an anxious night, wondering how Hercules was, but also excited that I was to play an important role in another of Hercules' triumphs. At least, I assumed it would be a triumph.

Like the Cretan, I could not accept the possibility of failure.

'I was woken early with the news that all was progressing as expected and that I should be ready to move off to the Temple shortly before dawn. I dressed quickly in the garments provided and ensured my wig completely covered my hair and looked natural. The Cretan looked approvingly at my outfit. He considered I would merge well with those in the Temple precinct. The main point of interest would be the sacrificial ritual about to take place on the great altar, which was, in accordance with the traditions of the day, set up in front of the Temple, the inner sanctuary being reserved for the more private rituals that only the priests and the King attended.

'I followed the Cretan and his protectors into the square in front of the Temple. Although it was still early, the square was crowded and the Cretan's protectors had to be quite forceful in establishing us in the spot previously chosen by the Cretan: to the right of the altar, with a good view of it and close to an exit route if all went badly wrong.

'After what seemed an age, the priests filed in, followed by, I presumed the King. Then the captive Hercules was brought in by four men and bound tightly, lying on his back, to the altar. I was close enough to see that he was completely relaxed: he was the most extraordinary person! Because I knew him so well, I could, even at this distance, feel his latent power. I was surprised that the priests and the King appeared completely oblivious to the danger to which they were exposing themselves. It is possible that they had not heard of Hercules, or, if they had, did not realise that it was Hercules they proposed to sacrifice. The gods must have blinded them.

'There then followed some elaborate chanting, which neither I nor most of the assembled crowd, to judge from their restlessness, understood. At last came the moment. The priest dressed in the most ornate garments, whom I correctly identified as the King, took a long-bladed ceremonial knife from one of the attendants and, side on to the crowd so that they could clearly see what he was doing, raised the knife with both hands above the body of Hercules so that the blade was pointing directly at Hercules' throat. An expectant hush fell upon the crowd. Suddenly, without any apparent preparatory movement, Hercules rose from the altar, his bonds fell asunder, he snatched the knife from the hands of the King and slit his throat, the blood spurting all over the altar as he fell to the ground. At lightning speed, before they could react to the astonishing turn of events, Hercules moved among the startled priests slashing and stabbing with the long sacrificial knife. Many fell dead on the spot, others died a lingering death as the blood poured out of them. Nobody stirred to help them.

'As soon as the slaughter was complete, men from various parts of the crowd – who had clearly been placed there by the Cretan – formed a protective shield around Hercules and called on the Cretan to address the crowd. Telling me to come with him, but at a distance, and go straight to Hercules, the Cretan leaped on to the altar surround and, in their language, told them that the days of Busiris' tyranny were over and that it was the famous Hercules who had liberated them. By this time, I was at Hercules' side. He was surprised, but pleased, to see me. Led forward by the Cretan, he accepted the plaudits of the crowd, who, I could see from my vantage point, were being urged along by groups of men placed strategically throughout the crowd. I could also see that there were men guarding all the exits to the square and anyone trying to leave was intercepted.

'When the cheers of the crowd for Hercules had died down, the Cretan outlined what was going to happen. I later understood that the Cretan would be Regent until a new king was elected. As a foreigner he could not be, and did not want to be, king. All the previous servants of Busiris would be spared if they swore allegiance to the new regime, which would be based on respect for all foreigners and the cessation of human sacrifice. This speech was loudly acclaimed by the people, by this time recovered from the shock of the coup and acknowledging the return to normal values and behaviour.

'It was some time before a blood-stained Hercules and I were able to take our leave. By the time we left, the bodies of Busiris and the priests had been removed. I noticed some other bodies, from the further corners of the square, were removed with them; presumably these were some of those I had seen earlier trying to leave the square immediately after Busiris and priests were slain.

The crowd were oblivious to this. As the Cretan's supporters moved among them, the crowd's enthusiasm for the events that had unfolded before them grew. I heard later that only a few of Busiris' entourage had preferred death to swearing allegiance to the new order, so what Hercules had enabled was in accord with the popular wish.

'The people were now being allowed to disperse but many were reluctant to go, preferring, I supposed, to participate in discussions with their friends on the new situation. This was seen as a mark of confidence in the Cretan and themselves and promised a good outcome, which indeed is what happened. At this point, at a signal from the Cretan, a band of his supporters came across to where we were standing and motioned us to follow them. They led us to what I later discovered was the King's palace where Hercules bathed and was given clean clothes. Whilst I helped bathe him, he told me a little of his ordeal whilst in captivity. He knew in advance that they would not harm him much physically, because the god would not be pleased to accept a damaged sacrifice, but they had not treated him well. Those guards were later found and forced to apologise to him, Hercules asking that they be relieved of further punishment if they swore to support the new regime, which they all did. Hercules felt that it was Busiris' regime that had brutalised them, not their own nature. An admirable sentiment!

'We remained in the palace for a few days, as guests of the Cretan. At Hercules' suggestion, heralds were sent to all the Greek communities in the delta and beyond, including Pharos and Panopolis, also known as Chemnis, to advise them that the tyrannical regime in Busiris was overthrown and human sacrifice abolished. Satisfied that he had fulfilled his task, Hercules decided to return to the farm, where we stayed for one day and night before mounting the chariot and setting off south.

'However, we did not return direct to the Bahariya oasis. Hercules wanted to visit some of the Greek colonies along the Great River, inland. So we travelled south along the riverbank, stopping at various settlements on the way. The most important of these was Panopolis, which was several days' drive south. On the way, Hercules refounded a small Greek settlement, which later became called Heracleopolis in his honour. This is now a flourishing city, I understand.

'Of course, Hercules was feted wherever he went – his fame had preceded him. The Greek communities, some of which had experienced considerable difficulties, were boosted by his arrival, and his exploits were exaggerated for the benefit of the Pharaoh's officers. Although the Egyptians were reasonably tolerant of foreigners, they did have spates of religious fervour. One of these had occurred some hundred years earlier when a Pharaoh had changed his name from Amenhotpe to Akhenaten, changed the official religion from that of Amen (Ammon) to Aten, slaughtered all the priests who would not accept the change and moved the capital from Thebes, many stadia north to a new city he called Akhetaten. We saw the ruins of this on our journey, and, as it looked interesting, crossed the river on a boat to see it. What I found particularly interesting was that nobody wanted to talk about him. It was as if he had never existed, but the remains of his city were visible, which could not be denied. We decided it was best to ask no questions, merely to visit the ruins of what had obviously been intended to be a great city.

'Now I saw many wonderful monuments and buildings during my visit to Egypt. Hercules told me of fantastic sights he had seen, of great pyramids in the sand that were said to be tombs of past Pharaohs, all faced with beautiful marble. But here, at Akhetaten, the quality Hercules spoke about elsewhere was missing: there were still remaining some beautiful paintings on the plaster of the walls still standing, but the brickwork was poor and the buildings had obviously been erected in a great hurry. It was a dismal place. Hercules told me that Akhenaten's successor had moved the capital back to Thebes and readopted the old religion. I was not surprised. The new city of Akhetaten would not, I thought, have inspired anybody. Nor would the Pharaoh Akhenaten!

'After visiting Greek settlements further south, Hercules received a friendly warning that court officials were beginning to have their attention drawn to their distinguished visitor. Hercules admitted that he had not been too discreet making these visits so soon after the dramatic events in Busiris. Whilst the most likely outcome could be an invitation to Thebes to meet a senior official – or even the Pharaoh himself – it might not stop at that. We could find ourselves politely restrained and it could take years to free ourselves. Violence would not be tolerated and even Hercules would have difficulty in overcoming the level of force the Pharaoh had at his disposal. Hercules' reaction was immediate – to leave straight away, which we did, using routes away from the Great River, which we had been advised to do to avoid the possibility of interception. At the end of the second day, we had reached the Bahariya oasis, where the others were now rather anxiously awaiting our return. Hercules had sent them a message to advise that the mission had been accomplished and that we were now off to pay a visit to some of the Greek colonies, but our party wished to start the long journey home and complete the task set by Eurystheus.

'Their anxiety was fuel to Hercules. In no time, camp was struck and we were on the move to the coast. As our ship was awaiting our return in Crete, we needed to find transport across the sea. We therefore made for Pharos, an island to the west of the delta of the Great River, which was ruled by a Greek dynasty friendly to the Achaeans. We were warmly welcomed by King Proteus and were soon on our way to Crete in one of the King's ships, leaving the camels and all our horses behind except two chariot horses, with which I had become besotted! Our chariot was taken apart and loaded on board the ship and Hercules accepted my plea to keep the two horses "because we would need them to draw the chariot when we arrived in Crete" as I had put it. The other horses were gratefully accepted into the king's stables. I know not the camels' fate.

'On arrival in Crete, we disembarked and sought out the Rams. These were quickly found and, rejoining our crew and the ship, we sailed across to the port of Tiryns, presenting ourselves and the Rams in due course at the High King's palace in Mycenae. As before, Eurystheus had no idea what to do with what he had ordered Hercules to get for him and handed them back! Hercules had patently been expecting this and arranged for the Rams to be returned to Libya.

'Now, before I advise you what Hercules' next, and last, task was, I will tell you what Hercules told me when we were alone in the Egyptian desert on our speedy return to the oasis, where our colleagues were waiting for us. I already knew what the next task was because Hercules had told me!

'You remember that, at the beginning of this story, I had told you that Hercules knew that the tasks he was being set by Eurystheus were in fact what Apollo had ordered.'

I nodded.

'Well,' Iolaus continued, 'he now told me that the tasks had been agreed in advance between Apollo's chief priest and himself, except that they had not expected Eurystheus to disallow two of the completed tasks and force Hercules to carry out two more. This was why two of them were not as close as the others to the original aim of destroying the female murderous cults – he and Apollo simply could not find, in the short time they had to consider it, two additional worthy causes. But, as Hercules had argued, there was some advantage in having some tasks that did not have the same objective, as this would confuse people and make it less likely that the true purpose of the tasks would be discovered. I was, of course, staggered to find that Hercules had known all along what he would be asked to do and, in fact, had himself suggested most of them, as he admitted to me. No wonder he was so well organised and friends and resources had mysteriously appeared at the right moments to make completing the set tasks, not exactly easy, but at least possible!

'Hercules was a little embarrassed when he told me about his role in the deception. I thought of Eurystheus, who had been becoming more and more insufferable as Hercules' successes mounted. He realised some time ago that his bullying of his cousin was damaging his own reputation and enhancing that of Hercules. If he found out that Hercules had tricked him by arranging all the tasks in advance, his anger would know no limit. He would also be sure that Hercules was plotting against him and wanted the throne. I knew that Hercules certainly did not want the throne but could not deny that his successes, coupled with Eurystheus' own attitudes, were in fact undermining Eurystheus. If the people found out that Hercules had all the time been making a fool of him, the popular ridicule released would hound Eurystheus out of his kingdom, whether Hercules would accept the crown or not.

'I was just beginning to see the humorous side of the situation when I caught Hercules' eye. He was driving the chariot at the time, which had made it easier for him to tell me the truth as he had to keep his eyes on the horses and the terrain. It was just a fleeting glance and I saw that he too saw the humorous side of it. I burst out laughing and Hercules joined me. He had to stop the chariot as he was shaking with laughter and the tears were streaming down his face so that he could no longer safely drive the chariot. We were incapable for some time. As soon as the laughing stopped, one of us had just to mention the High King's name and we burst out laughing anew.

'At last, our mirth came to an end. Hercules forecast the High King would not know what to do with the Rams and would return them to Hercules, who had already sent a message to the owners (who had been aware in advance of the "theft") that two of the Rams would be returned, the other having been sacrificed at Siwa to Ammon-Zeus.

'Over the rest of the journey to the oasis, Hercules then told me of the next task. This was to rescue his friend, Theseus, King of Athens. Hercules told me that Theseus was a womaniser and frequently got himself into trouble on this account. Before he became King, he had been attracted to the beautiful daughter of Tyndareus, King of Sparta, called Helen. She was then a child, not yet ten years' old. This had not stopped Theseus, with his constant drinking companion, Pirithous, King of the Lapithae (a people of Thessaly), from kidnapping her and taking her to Athens. When Theseus had sobered up, his mother, Queen Aethra, called him in to see her. When he did so, he found the young Helen sitting next to Aethra, who berated him for this latest escapade. As it happens, Aethra was rather enamoured of Helen and did not need much persuading from her son, Theseus, not to return Helen to her father immediately. Instead, Aethra offered to take Helen into hiding, away from Athens, until she was old enough to consider becoming Theseus' wife. This would be an advantageous marriage for Theseus as Helen was likely, under the matriarchal system then in place in Sparta, to be the heir to the throne and, on her father's death, as Helen's husband, Theseus would become King of Sparta as well as of Athens. Being ambitious for her son, Aethra also wished this, but did not want her son to be accused of unacceptable behaviour. Helen, perhaps a little overwhelmed by the greater opulence of her surroundings at Athens compared with Sparta, apparently did not object to Aethra's proposal and so arrangements were made for Helen and Aethra to leave forthwith with some servants for a city called Aphidna, approximately 175 stadia away in the north of the country, close to the coast and looking out towards the southernmost tip of Euboea.

'But Theseus and his mother had not appreciated the level of the scandal they had created and the depth of Spartan feeling. Within days of Helen's departure with Aethra, Helen's elder brothers, Castor and Pollux, were at the door of Theseus' palace with an armed force, demanding Helen's return. Theseus quickly found there was no support from the people for what he had done and they certainly did not want to fight the Spartans over it. So he promptly welcomed the two brothers into his palace and sent a messenger immediately to his mother requesting that she bring Helen back to Athens. He entertained the brothers, saying that Helen was staying at the palace as Queen Aethra's guest and she would be brought in shortly so that they could take her back to Sparta.

'Of course, as Helen was nearly 200 stadia away and this distance was effectively doubled because the messenger had to deliver the message first, it was some time before Helen appeared with Aethra back at Athens. I don't know what Theseus said to appease the angry brothers' impatience but Theseus was charming when he wanted to be and, I am told, managed to keep the brothers from killing anyone before Helen eventually appeared. Helen was pleased to see them and quite prepared to go home with her brothers, but her obvious affection for Aethra, which was clearly reciprocated, to some extent allayed the brothers' fear that something unacceptable had happened. So, on this occasion, Theseus escaped any punishment for his crime.

'The latest escapade Theseus engaged in with Pirithous was a disaster. In Epirus, many stadia to the west of Athens, there is an oracle sacred to Ammon-Zeus at a place called Dodona. Traditionally, this was founded at the same time as the Siwa

Oracle by priests who had left Egypt at the time of the religious upheaval I was telling you about earlier. Dodona lies in the country of the Molossi, and their king was called Aldoneus. He had a beautiful daughter called Persephone, who certainly lived up to her name, which means "destroyer"! Theseus persuaded his friend, Pirithous, to go with him to Epirus to seize Persephone and bring her back to Athens. Unfortunately for them, Aldoneus heard of the plot. The pair of rogues were caught and flung into prison. There was worse to follow. Although Theseus had been a popular ruler, the people did not approve of his philandering. This opposition had been exploited by a rival, Mnestheus, who could claim a distinguished heritage as he was descended from Erectheus, the sixth king of Athens, who had reigned for over fifty years. As it became clear that Theseus was unlikely to return soon, and Mnestheus ensured that the people of Athens would not pay any ransom to free him, Mnestheus persuaded the Athenians to appoint him King in preference to any of Theseus' children. If Theseus, a friend of Hercules, was to have any prospect of regaining the crown of Athens for himself and his children, it was imperative that he return to Athens as soon as possible.

'As Hercules had predicted, the final task given him by Eurystheus was to free Theseus. But, as this was a political act and could be construed as an interference in the affairs of Athens, it was announced as something quite different. The story was put out that Hercules was to bring back Cerberus, the fierce dog that guarded the land of the dead, Hades. Now this was a very clever trick because the name of Aldoneus' dog was also Cerberus, and, the significance of which I will relate later, he had a beautiful golden coat! Strangely, the lie has stuck and, in Hercules' lifetime, many fantastic stories were told of his exploits in the underworld and how he fought and subdued Cerberus to bring him back to Mycenae. However, the stories are silent on what happened to him after he was handed over to Eurystheus. If he really was such a fierce dog, he would not have been welcome anywhere. But no version of this story that I have heard addresses this problem. How gullible people are!

'Obviously, for such an apparently monumental task, Hercules had to prepare himself specially. He chose to present himself at Eleusis to be admitted to the Mysteries performed there. However, admission was restricted to Athenian citizens, which Hercules was not. This difficulty was overcome by his being adopted by an Athenian called Pylius, who I suspect was a member of an Athenian faction who knew what Hercules' true mission was and wanted Theseus restored to the throne. Even after this, Hercules had some formal hurdles to leap – his personal history was not without blemish and so he had to purge himself of his past crimes. I have since discovered that, as Hercules had not been born an Athenian, he could not be admitted to the main Mysteries. Instead, a special ritual, called the Lesser Mysteries – to distinguish it from the original rituals which were renamed the Greater Mysteries – was invented for him and later adopted for all new apostates to the shrine.

'As you know these Mysteries are each celebrated annually at Eleusis, which is some one hundred stadia west of Athens, in honour of Demeter, the goddess of corn and harvests. Hercules never fully explained the conflict here: Demeter represented the ancient matriarchal culture and was the mother of Persephone who was seized by Pluto and taken down to be his wife in the underworld. You know the story of the bargain between Demeter and Pluto whereby Persephone is allowed back to Earth for the six spring and summer months, in return for which Demeter allows the crops to grow for the benefit of the human race and the animals. Anyway, I thought it would be one of the religions that Apollo and Hercules would want to destroy, but it appears that, certainly at this stage, they felt that it was too strong to challenge. This particular cult did not seem to be aggressively asserting itself. It was more of a contemplative, and restricted, cult, which did not interfere with others or actively seek to recruit adherents. Still, it was curious because the significance of the "golden dog" was that it was a symbol of Demeter and Hercules' actual mission was seen as a slight to Demeter. Eurystheus' later ownership of the golden dog was seen as the domination by the new patriarchal order over the matriarchal.

'Apart from the visit to Eleusis, little of interest occurred on this Labour. We paused at Dodona to make a ritual sacrifice at this other shrine to Ammon-Zeus, the "twin" of Siwa, and two places less alike, despite the common foundation, would be hard to find. I was very impressed, however, by the oracular oak tree, which was a magnificent specimen and had a magic about it. As you know, the oak tree is the symbol of Zeus because, it is said, he gave humans the acorn to eat. I did try eating them once!

'On our arrival, the Palace of Aldoneus was open, and as Hercules told me afterwards, the release of Theseus to him had been agreed in advance, on payment of a large sum of money. Pirithous was dead, apparently having died in captivity of natural causes. A colourful character but Hercules thought that Theseus would be better behaved without his wild companion. He felt that Theseus' escapades were about Theseus showing off to Pirithous. Now he was gone, perhaps Theseus would settle down and fulfil his promise as a good ruler in Athens. At the palace, we were also introduced to Cerberus. A large hunting dog, he was boisterous but not threatening. He knocked me over once or twice – because he was so friendly, not because of aggression. It was important for me to bond with him because he was to accompany me in the chariot on the long drive to Mycenae whilst Hercules and Theseus rode on the horses we had brought with us. Cerberus and I developed a good relationship. When he felt bored with riding, he would put his front paws on the rail at the front of the chariot where I was standing and make a mewing noise. I soon learnt that this meant he wanted to descend from the chariot on to the track and run alongside for a while. I would slow down a little and he would jump off the open back of the chariot. When he had had enough, he would simply drop behind the chariot and leap on to the platform. For such a large dog, he was very agile and well balanced in all that he did – except when jumping up to lick your face! You will gather that I was sorry when the time came to hand him over to Eurystheus who, for the reasons I gave you earlier, was only interested in him as a trophy.

'Hercules was now a free man again. He decided to return to Thebes and I travelled with him. Theseus had already left for Athens with some friends who had been awaiting him at Tiryns. They had been told by a swift messenger sent from Aldoneus' Palace before we left that Theseus had been freed and would be in need of them at Tiryns when we returned.

'We had only been at Thebes for a few days when we heard that the Athenians had refused to take Theseus back at all, not even living there, let alone as their King. He was forced to seek sanctuary on the island of Scyros. What particularly hurt was that his family, including his mother and his children were allowed to stay in Athens, but it was some consolation that Mnestheus announced to popular acclaim that, although Theseus was banished, his children would succeed to the throne, if the people wished it, on his (Mnestheus') death. And so, this labour partly failed in its main objective, although the dynastic succession now seemed guaranteed and would be through the male line.'

'Rather a sad end to the story, then?' I remarked.

'Yes,' responded Iolaus, 'but worse was to follow. At first, the King of Scyros, Lycomedes, welcomed his distinguished visitor. Encouraged, Theseus, as usual, made a spectacle of himself to such an extent that his host felt ridiculed. There were rumours that Theseus had even seduced the King's daughters, but this was never admitted by the king or the daughters. The King was quite crafty and concealed his true opinion of his guest from Theseus, so that, when the King suggested they go for a walk along the cliffs together, Theseus suspected nothing. What happened next is disputed. Theseus' friends affirm that Lycomedes encouraged Theseus to approach too near the edge of a precipice, on ground that the King knew to be unstable and either pushed him over the edge or encouraged him to go out so far that the ground gave way under him and he fell to his death on the rocks below. Others say that Theseus was warned not to go too near the edge, but, true to his brash character, he ignored the advice and fell to his death through a tragic accident. Certainly, the King expressed all the sorrow one would expect at such a tragic death. If he was responsible for it, it was not obvious.'

'Theseus was not really a nice person, was he?' I enquired.

'Yes,' Iolaus replied, 'I am afraid I must agree to that. He was a bully, careless, vainglorious – he could be the very worst of men. You will remember that he virtually killed his own father, Aegeus, by "forgetting" to change the black sail for a white one on the ship bringing the young men and women back to Athens from Crete, which he had promised to do to signify that his expedition to kill the Minotaur had been successful. Aegeus, thinking that his son was dead, threw himself off a cliff into the sea and died not knowing of his son's success. And, of course, he cynically abandoned Ariadne on Naxos, when she had helped him find his way in and out of the maze to kill the Minotaur by the use of a spool of thread. On his father's death, he became King of Athens.

'And then a transformation seemed to come over him: for a while he was an excellent king. He transferred all state affairs, except for the control of the army (of which he remained the sole general) to a democratically elected council and allowed the council to pass laws governing a wide variety of social, business and family matters. These moves had universal popular support. Many admired him for this and gave him the credit for the achievements of the council. I have come to the conclusion that he was just lazy. It was only because there were some very able Athenian citizens at the time who took the leading positions on the council that so much good was done.

'Of course, Theseus soon became bored and went off on numerous military expeditions. When these no longer attracted him, he joined up with the worthless Pirithous, as I have already told you.

'You will be pleased to know that his sons are much better than he, and that I have just heard from them that, should you wish to visit Hercules' mother – my grandmother – Queen Alcmena, we would be very welcome guests at their palace in Athens for as long as we like. I have been warned, I should tell you, that the Queen is very old and frail. We had better go soon or we may be too late.'

I vowed to put my affairs in order promptly and let Iolaus know the following day when I would be ready to set sail for Athens.

On this, we parted.

Athens

I now had much to do. First I had to design and make a distinctive piece of jewellery fit for a queen! I had nothing of this calibre in stock – most of my special pieces were made to order anyway – and Queen Alcmena would be insulted if I were to offer her some common trinket that she had already seen worn by another lady of Athens. I did, however, have some pretty items already made, or which my assistant could make up within a few days, appropriate for one of the Queen's handmaids or an Athenian lady – but something really regal demanded my personal imagination and application.

After puzzling over the problem for a while, I remembered seeing a gold necklace and brooch, both of which I was told had been made in Crete many years ago. Although it was old, the design was timeless and the workmanship as good as anything I had ever seen. It would be a real challenge to reproduce these and I doubted if Queen Alcmena or her entourage would have seen anything like them. The individual rosettes of the putative necklace were probably originally used to ornament the hem of a garment. I decided to make the rosettes larger than the originals I had seen, which would not only make the necklace more elegant but would also conceal its origin. The brooch would be complex, incorporating, as had the original, two bees delivering honey to their hive. I would represent the honey by using the granulation technique – making small balls of gold and attaching them individually to a background plate, also of gold. I would adopt this technique to adorn the edges of the bees' wings, their heads and their bodies.

I calculated that after I had shown my assistant how to make a rosette I could rely on him to make the remaining thirty or so required for the necklace. I could then devote the whole of my time to the brooch. The complete task should be finished within two weeks. I sent a message to Iolaus advising him that I would be ready to sail to Athens at any time after those two weeks had passed. Within a day, I received a message back from him to say that we would sail for Athens on the twentieth day. This was excellent news. I had been given a little more time than I thought I needed, so I could be a little more deliberate in my work and supervise my assistant a little more closely than I had originally intended or thought I had time to afford. My early close supervision of my assistant was rewarded. It was not until his third attempt that his rosettes reached the standard I sought, and by then three days had passed. In between my supervisory visits, I had been able to design the brooch but had not been able to start any of the manufacturing work. The outcome was that the quality of the design was enhanced and the manufacturing process easier because the extra time had allowed me to amend my original design ideas to reduce or eliminate technical manufacturing difficulties. Still, work has a nasty habit of filling the time available and both pieces were not finished to my satisfaction until the day before we were due to sail for Athens!

The following morning saw me, accompanied by my wife and children, on the familiar quayside to board a waiting ship. Iolaus was already on board and welcomed us to the cabin we would share on the voyage. After a few tearful farewells, my family went ashore, we slipped our moorings and were soon at sea. The voyage was uneventful and we enjoyed brisk and favourable winds which, although we called at a number of ports on the way, guaranteed arrival at the port of Athens, Phaleron, on the tenth day after leaving Olbia. Not being a frequent sailor, although not normally suffering from the landsman's malaise, I was pleased to be on dry land again! Phaleron port was even busier than Olbia, so it was a pleasant surprise to be welcomed very soon after tying up at our berth by a party of men sent by Queen Alcmena to greet us and help us find our way to the palace in Athens. It would have been a long and dusty walk, but horses had been brought for us and a wagon for our baggage. So we entered the famous city of Athens in style.

I had never visited Athens before but, of course, had heard about the grandeur of the setting and the King's Palace. Mycenae I had seen, which, with its massive walls and imposing entrance, was impressive, although less so than Tiryns, because the latter rose up from the surrounding plain and nearby sea shore whereas Mycenae nestled on a hilltop, encompassed on three sides by higher peaks. I suppose I was expecting Athens to be a combination of both. How wrong I was! Knowing that Athens was but twenty-five stadia from the coast, I had expected to enjoy my first view of the city's famous Acropolis from the sea. But there were mountains in the way and it was only at the end of our journey on the approach road that the awesome loftiness of the Acropolis struck me like a hammer blow. Although expected, as it had been described to me many times, the actual physical appearance was mesmerising. Like Mycenae, it was surrounded by mountains higher than itself but, unlike Mycenae, it appeared to be detached from its loftier neighbours and, indeed, seemed to dominate them. This impression was enhanced by the suddenness with which it was revealed. On the approach road, we were surrounded one minute by hills on all three sides that we faced – the port was still visible behind us – the next minute we were gazing up at a huge slab of apparently impregnable rock with tall precipitous sides and huge imposing walls with structures atop built with material from which the blinding sun rebounded straight into our eyes, forcing us to look away and shade our faces with our hands. Theseus and his predecessors had certainly chosen the site of the capital of their kingdom with care!

We paused to drink in the view and allow the wagon with our baggage to catch up with us. We had easily outpaced them on horseback. Although the track was reasonably smooth, it had been uphill all the way from the port and the cart was carrying more than just our possessions. There had obviously been tasks, involving the collection of some other merchandise, which our welcoming party had discharged before our arrival. We were still absorbing the view of the city when the cart caught up with us. The men in charge could see how impressed we were and were rather amused by it. After a short rest for the wagon's horses, we proceeded up to the main gate where the party leader was instantly recognised by the guards who waved us inside without delay. After passing through a number of gates, we arrived at the foot of a long flight of steps that led up to the Acropolis itself and the King's Palace. Pausing only to remove from my baggage a small leather pouch, which contained the gifts for the Queen and some small pieces of jewellery for her entourage, I accompanied Iolaus and an armed guard up the steps, leaving the men who had met us at Phaleron to bring up our baggage and stable the horses. It was a long climb, although I was glad of the exercise after being on board the ship for so long. We paused, gratefully, several times on the way up to drink a fruit-flavoured liquid that, miraculously, had remained cool despite the hot sun. I later learnt that it was stored underground in a cellar beneath the Acropolis itself. At last, we reached the top, and our guard suggested we admired the extraordinary view whilst we gathered our breath. This we did in the shade of the portico of a conveniently nearby temple. The natural slope of the rock surface of the top of the Acropolis concealed all but the roof of the palace from where we were, so it was not until we had crested the slope that we saw the palace for the first time. This was known as Theseus' Palace because he had remodelled it during his kingship. Surprisingly, he had allowed the Athenian citizens to build their homes close by. Our guard led us to the steps at the entrance to the palace and handed us over to a colleague standing at the foot of the steps, who had clearly been awaiting our arrival.

He quickly showed us to our rooms at the rear of the palace. These had a magnificent view to the north and a rather frightening overlook of the precipitous cliffs which lay immediately below the palace. To the right, we could just see a conical mountain, that we later found was called Mount Lycavitos. It was clearly higher than the Acropolis but, seen from this distance, it did not appear to have the space at the top to accommodate a city the size of Athens. Presumably, this was why the palace and the city were sited on the Acropolis.

Our baggage soon arrived and so, after a quick change of clothes and a wash, we advised the guard that we were ready to meet our host.

Although we were in Athens to see Queen Alcmena, she was here originally as the guest of the then King, Theseus. But Menestheus, the present King, had seized the throne some years previously when Theseus had been imprisoned. This Iolaus had related to me on our voyage. We had heard that Menestheus had confirmed Queen Alcmena's revered status and, indeed, had supported her and the sons of Hercules against the threats of Eurystheus. I hoped to hear more of this during our visit. Knowing that the King would be interested to meet us (as we, him), we expected that he would greet us first, leaving us to pursue our conversation with Queen Alcmena later. Iolaus had brought appropriate gifts for the King, leaving to me the honour of presenting my gifts to his grandmother, Queen Alcmena. We understood that Menestheus had never married – indeed, he had been one of the unsuccessful suitors for Helen, now Queen of Sparta – and had already decreed that, on his death, the crown should go to one of Theseus' sons, Demophoon, who had acted as regent for a while during Theseus' absence and detention and before Menestheus seized the throne for himself. By the time of our visit, Theseus was already dead. It was a prudent decision of Menestheus to nominate the rightful heir as his successor, as it prevented factions being created amongst the people of Athens. I found that the Athenians were well satisfied with the liberality of Menestheus' reign and applauded his desire for a smooth succession.

In fact, we did not meet the King until later. We soon discovered the reason. We were ushered into a small reception room near the main audience chamber, where we were introduced to a very frail old woman, Queen Alcmena. I was, rather too visibly, shocked when I saw how frail she was and stammered an apology for our intrusion. But she greeted Iolaus with a brisk warmth and an embrace that belied her years and, turning to me, she thanked me for bringing her beloved son's right-hand man and grandson to Athens. I, too, was blessed with her warm smile and strong embrace. She asked me what I wished to know, and I told her that anything she could tell me about her son Hercules' early years would be most interesting. I explained that Iolaus had already told me in detail about the Labours, which I had found fascinating, and I now wished to put his later life into the context of his youth and upbringing. The Queen said that she would do her best to satisfy my thirst for knowledge, adding that she still felt privileged to be the mother of such a distinguished man.

'You may be wondering why the King is not here to greet you,' she said. 'This is because of me. As you can see, I am old and frail and cannot sit and talk for long. So the King and I agreed that it would be less taxing for me if I saw you first and started my story, rather than tiring myself out with some formal royal greeting that he would be obliged to give you.'

'My dear Queen,' Iolaus responded, 'we fully understand and we are both very grateful to you for agreeing to see us. You must tell us as soon as you feel tired and we will stop. I would warn you that my friend is a relentless questioner and he will want to know every small detail that you can recall!'

'You know,' replied the Queen, 'that is just what I need! I shall not live many more days and I have been looking forward to this moment ever since you wrote to me asking me if I would see your friend to talk about my son. I hear so many silly stories about him, but the tellers of these yarns are not interested in the truth. It will be a pleasure to unravel for your friend what really happened.

'You know about my first husband, Amphitryon, and how he accidentally killed my father, Electryon?' I nodded. 'Well, you probably also know that I insisted that Amphitryon, who at that time was King of Troezen in Argolis – one of the dependents of the High King – should avenge the killing of my eight brothers before I would marry him. As my father had been called back in the middle of his punitive expedition to recover his stolen cattle and punish the thieves by my husband-to-be, I could not rest until all my brothers had been avenged. Had the Aetolians not stolen my father's cattle, none of this would have happened, and I therefore blamed them also for my father's death. My dear Amphitryon, as soon as he heard what I had to say, left immediately to carry out my wishes. He was, I know, shocked at what had happened, but, curiously, I think I did the best thing I could for him. He knew I loved him but he also knew I loved my brothers and, now my father was dead, he realised the responsibility for retribution lay on him – and him alone. My surviving brother was, at that time, far too young to accept the responsibility.

'Amphitryon was away for some time. Strangely, a great calm had engulfed me as soon as he left. He had taken with him our bravest men. I knew instinctively that he would be successful and would return safely. I was not in the least worried about his safety. And return he did, having despatched my brothers' killers. True to my word – I had said that we would be married on his return, successful – we were married the very evening he returned to Thebes. But, first, as my father was dead, he was anointed King. In our eyes, at that time, a newly anointed King was to be treated as a god, but only for one day! I think this tradition has been misunderstood by some who suggested that Amphitryon was not the father of Hercules, but his father was Zeus! We consummated our marriage that night and I soon found that I was pregnant. Later I discovered that I was to be the mother of two boys.

'Now I must tell you about my husband's inheritance. He was the rightful heir to the High Kingship of Mycenae through his marriage to me and the promise of my father, who was the rightful High King. However, my uncle, Sthenelus, seized the throne, claiming that Amphitryon was tainted as he had killed my father. I knew that my uncle had not liked my father's agreement with my husband – and I suspected then that he had collaborated with those who stole my father's cattle and was partly responsible for the death of all but one of my brothers – so his actions were not altogether a surprise. We also found out that there were some senior commanders who, despite my husband's military achievements, preferred an older man to lead them. So, rather than fight for our rights, we decided to accept the position on certain conditions, which were quickly agreed.

'The main condition was that, if we went elsewhere without argument, and did not challenge the right of Sthenelus to be King, the first son to be born from either marriage would be recognised as the heir to the High Kingship of Mycenae. As my husband and I knew that I was pregnant, and we believed that Sthenelus' wife was not, we were content with the arrangement. This proved to be a serious miscalculation. We soon heard that Sthenelus' wife, Nicippe, had become pregnant. Discreet enquiries indicated that her pregnancy commenced about two months after mine, so we were confident that, if I produced a son, he would be the acknowledged heir as the firstborn.

'As I expect you know, although I had two sons, they were both born the day after Nicippe's son, Eurystheus. He was two months' premature and only just survived his first years. Many stories were told at the time about the intervention of the gods, some of whom, it was claimed, delayed my twins' birth and brought forward that of Eurystheus. The truth of the matter is that we were confident that, if one of my twins was a son – we realised quite early that I was having twins – the "race" was won. So, we were happy for nature to take its course. Naturally, and foolishly, we had assumed that Sthenelus and Nicippe would also allow nature to dictate the outcome. We did not imagine that they would endanger the lives of the mother and child by inducing the birth artificially – which is what they did.

'However, we were conscious that, as we knew I was pregnant when we made the bargain, we had not been completely honest in the matter and the outcome was, perhaps, the gods' judgment on us. So we accepted the position. By this time, my husband's accidental killing of my father had been atoned and he had been installed as King of Thebes and made very welcome by the citizens. Our two sons, Alcaeus and, of course,' she said, turning to Iolaus, 'Iolaus, your father Iphicles, were strong and healthy – so what more could we want?' She paused, glancing at me with a mischievous look in her beautiful grey eyes. 'You have a question?' she asked.

'You said the first of your sons was called Alcaeus? Do you mean Hercules?'

'I knew that would surprise you,' she responded with a smile. 'I did not say he was the first – Iphicles was, in fact, the firstborn because Alcaeus was the larger baby and it was easier for the midwives to bring out the smaller baby first. Yes, Alcaeus was later – much later – renamed Hercules, but he was named Alcaeus first and he was known by that name for most of his early life. I will tell you later how his name was changed and why. He was named after my father's elder brother and my uncle because, at the time, we thought he would be the heir to the High Kingship. At birth, we recognised that he was the stronger of the two, so we concealed from the start that he had been born second. By the time we discovered that Nicippe's son had been born earlier, the deception had gone too far and we decided not to tell the truth. By then, we felt that it did not matter but, of course, it did mean that Iolaus' father was wrongly disinherited. As the years passed, we grew more than a little concerned at our deception. Reflecting back on my life, I realise my husband and I made many mistakes, but we paid the price.'

She paused and suddenly turned from being animated and outgoing into a more reflective and withdrawn frame of mind. Iolaus immediately stood up.

'We have tired you and now we must leave you to your memories. Thank you so much for sharing these family secrets with my friend and me. I knew most of what you told us but I have never heard it before in a continuous narrative and this has made a greater impact on me than I expected.'

I mumbled my thanks, rather overcome by Iolaus' abruptness. Iolaus moved across to his grandmother and kissed her on both cheeks. She raised her hand to stroke his left arm, waved goodbye to me and we left the room without delay. As soon as we were outside the reception room, Iolaus burst into tears. To minimise embarrassment, as there were palace staff continually passing by about their business, I grasped his left elbow with my right hand and guided him swiftly to our nearby rooms. By chance, his room was the nearer so I ushered him in. He detached himself from my grasp and fell on the bed, face down, and wept uncontrollably for some time. After what seemed an age – but was probably only a few minutes – the weeping merged into sobs of decreasing intensity and frequency. Eventually he sat up, turned his blotched, tear-streaked face towards me and, holding out his hands, urged me into his embrace. From that moment there was an indissoluble bond between us. I had shared his grief: the family he had lost, the hero he had served who was gone, the sorrows and regrets of his beloved grandmother, how different things might have been, the injustice of the world and the greed of men. He did not need to explain. I knew his inner turmoil, and respected him for the way he usually controlled his emotions. He never again found the need of such a release and we never discussed it. But the experience lit a fire between us that was never after extinguished.

We were sitting side by side on the bed when there came a knock on the door: a servant summoning us to meet the King. I asked the servant to allow us to prepare ourselves and return after a decent interval to lead us into the King's presence. This he did, Iolaus remembering (as I had forgotten earlier when we met Queen Alcmena) the gifts he had brought for the King. Fortunately, I also took the gifts I had brought for Queen Alcmena. In view of what she had said when we met, we did not think she would see us again until the following day but, when we walked into the grand audience chamber, she was there, sitting beside the King. As soon as we entered the chamber, she stood up and came towards us. Leading Iolaus by the hand whilst I followed close behind, she graciously introduced us both to the King. He was not only courteous, he was clearly very pleased to see us, particularly Iolaus. As I discovered the next day, they had met many years ago in very different circumstances.

After a short discussion about our journey from Sardinia and our ports of call on the way, we had the opportunity of offering the gifts we had brought. At the request of the King, my gifts to Queen Alcmena were offered first. She was delighted by the necklace and I was rather chastened by her instant realisation that smaller versions of the rosettes had been used many years ago to decorate the hems of Cretan royal garments! As she was related to the Cretan dynasty, and had visited Crete many times, she (erroneously) thought that I had used this source deliberately in recognition of the association. I maintained a discreet silence on the matter! She also recognised the theme of the brooch, as I had expected she would. Again, she was clearly charmed by the gifts and insisted that I pinned the brooch to her shawl there and then. The affection she showed me through her eyes as I carried out this service told me all I needed to know of her natural warmth and humanity.

Iolaus' gift to the King was a surprise to me. It was an ancient dagger wrapped in a recently made leather sheath. Iolaus said that the dagger was at least two hundred years' old and had been given to him by Hercules himself. It was early Achaean in origin and of the finest craftsmanship of its time. The handle was beautifully carved bone and the blade was made of bronze with delicate images of three lions running down the blade on each side, made of thin cut out plates of gold fixed to the blade with niello, which formed a striking black background to the yellow golden lions and the delicate traces of landscape incorporated in the scene. Before the King could protest at the magnificence of the gift, Iolaus thanked the King for his support for the family of Hercules, of himself and, particularly, of Queen Alcmena since the death of Hercules' great friend, Theseus. I feared that the reference to Theseus would anger King Menestheus, but not at all. Iolaus knew his man!

'Thank you for your generosity,' the King said. 'I am very touched that you should give me this beautiful dagger, which has such a strong place in your heart. I know of your fierce admiration and affection for Hercules and that you would not part with anything he gave you lightly. I will treasure this all the rest of my life and pass it on, at the appropriate time, to my successor who, as you know, is planned to be Theseus' son Demophoon. He, I am sure, will revere this treasure as much as I.'

Iolaus responded. 'Most worthy King, your support for my lady Queen Alcmena, mother of Hercules, alone fully justifies the gift and I know that Hercules himself would be pleased at my recognition of your unswerving affection for her and her family. But let us now not dwell too much on the past. Let us hope that there are days of glory for us all in the future and that we, and those we love, will prosper.'

A sentiment to which we all concurred.

A little while later, led by a servant, we left the audience chamber for the small reception room where we had earlier met the Queen. The room had been transformed from a relaxed meeting room into an intimate dining room. Apart from the servants, there were two of the King's officials and one of the Queen's ladies waiting to join us at the table. Halfway through the magnificent meal, with the King's permission, the Queen and her lady left the table to retire to bed. Before she went, the Queen arranged to meet us in this room at an agreed time the next morning.

After the Queen had retired, we found that the King had a real sense of humour – if a trifle earthy at times! – and we could fully understand how the people of Athens had taken to him. Theseus had originally been regarded as a good king and was famous for encouraging the people to take charge of their own lives. He had only reserved to himself foreign policy and the command of the armed forces, leaving the people to manage domestic affairs as they saw fit. Before I met Menestheus, I could not understand how the Athenians could possibly reject Theseus in favour of anyone else. But, listening to Menestheus, and adding what I knew of Theseus' behaviour in the last few years of his life, I began to see that the Athenians had grown tired of Theseus' unreliability. It was not much help having control of domestic policy if the King retained control over the army and navy but was never there! What made it worse was that the people knew where he was – chasing after young ladies with his friend Perithous. Menestheus was clearly not a ladies' man, but he had similar democratic views to Theseus. He therefore was an acceptable and effective successor to Theseus and, because he was unmarried and had no children, the Athenians could look forward to an unchallenged succession to Theseus' son – a proposition that Menestheus himself had made. No doubt the Athenians thought that the lesson they had given his father would not be lost on the son!

The more I got to know the King, the more I liked him. He had his humorous side, but, when he was serious, he was not only sensible but realistic. I felt that it was a pity that there were not more Kings like him – particularly in Argos! Iolaus was vastly amused at my 'idolising' Menestheus, but he agreed with my conclusions. He confessed that he had left Greece for Sardinia because he despaired of the quality of Kingship among the Achaeans whom, he thought, were petty and vindictive. His view was that it would all end in disaster. He was right, of course.

The following morning we resumed our discussion with Queen Alcmena. She had no difficulty in remembering where we had reached the previous day and, after an appropriate greeting, plunged directly into narrative.

'As I said yesterday, Iolaus' father was the firstborn, but, as he had been brought out artificially to make the birth easier, we saw nothing wrong at the time in claiming that the stronger of the two babies was the elder. Indeed, the difference was so marked that we were not sure if Iphicles would survive childhood. Happily we were wrong on that. Alcaeus – I shall call him that until he formally changed his name – from the start dominated the household, but he was a happy baby, if rather hungry! He grew up fast and strong and everybody loved him. Later, there was a story that he had killed two serpents with his bare hands when he was only a few months old. According to the tale, the serpents had been sent by Hera, the wife of Zeus, to kill him. I am afraid both these stories are untrue. As I have already said, Alcaeus was as much my son as his brother. Hera had no reason to kill him as he was not the progeny of Zeus. Indeed, as we shall see, he later identified himself with Hera so why should she seek to destroy him?

'Obviously, we realised that, although he was not to be the High King, Alcaeus would be someone special. We therefore wanted him to have the best possible upbringing and education. Iphicles shared this in his early years but it was soon obvious that he could not keep up with his brother's phenomenal physical and intellectual development, and so separate arrangements had to be made from around the age of ten... You have a question?' she asked me.

Apologising for my rudeness, I said, 'I had heard that one of the elements of the agreement between your husband and your brother-in-law was that the son born second would have to serve the other for ten years. Is this right? From what Iolaus has told me, I believe this is not true.'

A rueful smile passed over Alcmena's face. 'Once again, my husband and I are probably to blame for this story. My memory is not so good and I cannot at this moment remember all that happened. It may come to mind when I reach the relevant part of the story.' Here she paused, before continuing. 'To answer your question – no, such a promise was not made. It would have been rather grotesque, do you not think, to commit an unborn baby to slavery?' I hastily agreed.

'I was talking about the steps we took to ensure that Alcaeus' talents did not fail to develop for lack of proper training,' she continued. 'We took advice from all over Greece and engaged the best: Autolycus, Odysseus' grandfather, taught him to drive a chariot – he also briefly taught Iolaus later – Castor, the son of King Tyndarus of Lacaedemon and brother of Pollux and Helen, taught him the arts of war, Eumolpus, who later became High Priest of the Mysteries at Eleusis near Athens, taught him to sing and play the lyre, Eurytus, King of Oechalia in western Greece taught him to shoot with a bow and arrow – with disastrous consequences – the centaur Cheiron taught him philosophy and morals, and Linus, a Theban from Boeotia, taught him literature and, fatally, tried to teach him to play the lyre in the temporary absence of Eumolpus. So you see he had the best teachers and they generally found him the best of pupils, if rather demanding at times! As Iolaus knows, he really was a melodic singer and a beautiful lyre player. He often took refuge in music when events or people conspired against him and he needed to be tranquil and focus his thoughts.

'We were first alerted to the violent side of his nature when Eumolpus had to return to Eleusis for an extended period on the order of the then King of Athens, Erectheus – which later led to a estrangement between them – and Linus, who considered himself a master lyre player, decided, without consulting us, to take over the lessons. The problem was that his style and method of playing were completely different from that of Eumolpus. Alcaeus had learnt Eumolpus' methods and was happy with them – he wasn't going to be told to play differently by another teacher. Linus was angry with Alcaeus for not doing as he told him and beat him with a stick. I think this happened several times, even after Alcaeus had warned him to stop and leave him alone to practise playing the lyre the way Eumolpus had taught him. The next time Linus struck Alcaeus, Alcaeus retaliated by hitting Linus over the head with the lyre, which killed him. This was the first we knew about the problem and it came as a great shock. It was our fault, really; we should have thought about what might happen when Eumolpus left, but we didn't. Anyway, Alcaeus was now of age and was prosecuted in court for murder. He consulted Cheiron and put together his own defence which he conducted admirably himself. I can still remember his eloquent speech when he pointed out that while he much regretted the consequences of his actions, he had suffered serious assaults from Linus several times, had asked him to stop and had only struck Linus in self-defence. Alcaeus, with some help from Cheiron, had discovered that the legal principles of a man called Rhadamanthus were generally accepted as being fair and just throughout Greece and had been particularly adopted by the Achaeans. Rhadamanthus was a Cretan by birth but left Crete as a young man, and, over a number of years passed through mainland Greece and the islands close to the shore of Asia Minor. He made a great impression, to such an extent that he was anointed King of many of the eastern islands and some Greek cities in Asia Minor. He was admired for his wisdom and impartiality in administering justice. One of his most important principles, which was adopted as a law by many cities, was that it was legitimate to resist force with force. As this law had been adopted by the city of Thebes many years previously, Alcaeus pleaded that it applied to his situation. The court, who had heard evidence of the previous assaults by Linus and the warning given by Alcaeus, accepted the justice of his defence and, much to our relief, acquitted him.

'However, we knew immediately that we had a problem – as did Alcaeus – and it was he who came up with the solution. He loved the open air, animals and the study of the heavens. And so he volunteered to become a herdsman until he reached the age of eighteen.

'My husband found him a herd he could manage and I scarcely saw him for the next few years. Of course, in the early days, my husband visited him frequently and paid trusted servants to look out for him. He also sent me regular messages, from which I concluded that he was really enjoying himself and, what was important for us, was keeping out of trouble. During this period of his life, he developed a deep knowledge and affection for animals, particularly cattle and horses. As Iolaus knows from his own experience, Alcaeus had an uncanny way of communicating his thoughts to bulls, cows and horses. Unless they were troubled by an illness – when their behaviour could be a little unpredictable – Alcaeus could nearly always get one of those animals to obey him. He explained to me once how he achieved this. Basically, he said, it was a matter of transferring knowledge and self-confidence from human to animal. It was of prime importance never to betray their trust. This was particularly vital with horses, of which he was especially fond, as they performed so many useful tasks for men. If you betrayed them, he once said, they will always remember and never forgive. Unfortunately, they sometimes take out their vengeance on someone who has not wronged them. Alcaeus explained this by saying that they seemed to taint all mankind with the cruelty they have experienced from one member. He was always very cautious when he met a mature bull or horse for the first time. He claimed to know within minutes whether or not an animal had been mistreated and if kindness could now redeem it. If he felt not, he would have nothing more to do with the animal. He was invariably right in his judgment.

'The two other things he learnt from his year as a herdsman were knowledge of the stars – and, through that, navigation – and philosophy. The latter arose because he had already been taught to think, partly by the unfortunate Linus, and he had the opportunity to develop his thoughts with little interruption. I don't think he would have achieved as much in his later life as he did without serving this unusual apprenticeship, which was complementary to his abilities and his previous training. Of course, he also honed his military skills, killing predators to protect his herd and wild animals for food. He enjoyed his independence and his self-reliance. Later in life, he never expected anyone to do anything for him. He was always prepared to see to all his own needs and the needs of those who were with him at the time. You must have noticed that, my dear Iolaus?'

'Yes, indeed,' responded Iolaus. 'He had high standards, particularly on food. He often told me quietly when he was being entertained in high places how badly the food had been cooked and how much better he could have cooked it himself.

'Seeing my disbelief on one occasion in my early days with him, he told me precisely what was wrong and why, and proved it to me on the next occasion we were alone by cooking the same dish himself. The taste and texture differences were incredible!'

Iolaus continued, unable to hold himself back from praising

Hercules. 'His empathy with animals, particularly cattle and horses, was phenomenal. Only he could have masterminded driving a huge herd of cattle halfway across the world as he did. No wonder Eurystheus was so sure that Hercules would fail when he gave him the task of stealing the Cattle of Geryon and bring them back to Mycenae. The way he gained the trust of horses was awesome. I had always considered horses to be unreliable. He told me that this was not so. It was the humans, he said, who were unreliable. Horses were by nature very trusting, relying on the instincts and experience of their elders in the herd. Man was treated as an elder and instinctively trusted, he said. I agree with you that Hercules believed that, when and if that trust was misplaced, the animal betrayed would never trust the person responsible again, and some horses would never trust anybody again. Hercules was able to assess very quickly whether a horse new to him could ever be trusted. This depended, he said, to some extent on how long their trust had been developed before betrayal and whether they had been let down only once. The problem was that a horse's anger, which was usually mingled with disappointment, could be very deep seated and might not emerge for years when an unexpected event would trigger a violent reaction. But I am interrupting the flow of your story. Please continue, my dear lady.'

'Thank you,' replied Queen Alcmena. 'I was glad of the respite you gave me and it was very interesting to hear what you had to say. You spent many years with him and faced many dangers together, so you really knew him better than I. As so often happened with Alcaeus, he decided his own future. On returning to Thebes, just after his eighteenth birthday, he heard that a wild lion, the Lion of Nemaea, was ravaging my husband's herds and those of our close neighbours, both to the west and to the east. The Lion appeared to have two favourite lairs, one in Mount Helicon to the west and one in the Cithaeron mountain range, to the south and east of Thebes. His presence on Mount Helicon was causing the greater upset because the Thespians, who lived in the city of Thespiae at the foot of the mountain, worshipped at a temple to the Muses at the mountain's summit and, when they held their festival, they did so in the constant fear that the Lion would strike. They also held a somewhat wild festival to Eros at the foot of the mountain by the sacred spring of Hippocrene. As I expect you know, the spring is supposed to have first risen from the spot that the winged horse, Pegasus, struck with his hoof, the word "Hippocrene", meaning "the horse's fountain". King Thespius was keen, for all these reasons, to have the Lion killed, but, as he ranged over a large area, he was difficult to catch. A large band of heavily armed men roaming over the same area hunting for the Lion would not have been welcome, and a single person or a small band would have been endangering their lives and nobody was prepared to take the risk.

'Naturally, as we realised later, this was an ideal first task for the young Alcaeus. I hardly recognised him when he returned to Thebes after his largely self-imposed exile: he was so tall and strong. Dressed in rough clothes, he looked quite savage, although he had kept his "palace" manners despite spending so many years with animals and country people. First, Alcaeus went to Thespiae to meet the King and be shown where the Lion had last been sighted and where the latest killings had occurred which appeared to be his. His visit was short, because he concluded that the Lion had left the area and the time of the Festival of Eros had almost arrived. The King pressed Alcaeus to stay but he wished to go after the Lion, whom he thought was now somewhere in the Cithaeron mountain range, which was a vast area to cover. However, he did stay one night, which many years later gave rise to a preposterous story, which I will not repeat. Alcaeus did leave hurriedly the following morning, but not for the reasons given by some: he only wanted to track and kill the Lion.

'It took him many days to find the Lion. He only succeeded because a local shepherd reported to him a sighting of the Lion high up in the mountains, above the snow line. Once he had found the spot identified by the shepherd, Alcaeus was able to identify the Lion's footprints in the snow and track it. The first we knew of his success was when he returned to Thebes, surrounded by an admiring crowd – which he clearly enjoyed! I was terrified when I first saw him striding down the street because he had skinned the Lion and was wearing its pelt over his body and the Lion's head, with the upper jaw and the teeth still in it, wagging loosely over his head. At first sight, it looked as if the Lion had eaten him and was walking on its hind legs! As soon as he realised my fright, he took off the Lion's skin and handed it to a bystander to look after for him. He also passed over the huge club he later told us he had used to stun and kill the Lion. The club was made from a whole uprooted olive tree, a close-grained, very hard, wood, which was traditionally used for expelling evil spirits. A practical and philosophical choice!

'That evening he told us how he had found, tracked and killed the Lion. The skin he had brought back showed the enormous size of it and I feared for him as I knew this success would lead him into many and more dangerous adventures. But he had lost his heritage and I began to realise that he would never be satisfied with a conventional life. He would have to pound his own path. This, of course, he largely did, although that was not always apparent at the time.

'When the news of Alcaeus' exploits became known, we were, as I had feared, flooded with requests for him to kill this wild animal, right that wrong and so on. We tried to restrain him, or at least make him see for himself how people were trying to exploit him. He did listen, but, again, events took over and the next escapade was typical and really settled his future.

'Some years earlier, a group of Thebans had accidentally killed King Clymenus of Orchomenos, a city on a lake, a day's ride west of Thebes. On his deathbed, the King demanded that his sons avenge his death. His eldest son, Erginus, raised an army and attacked Thebes and surprised and defeated the ill-prepared Thebans, who had no choice but to sue for peace and accept the demands made by Erginus. This was that the Thebans had to pay an annual tribute of one hundred oxen to atone for the killing of his father. Alcaeus knew nothing of all this but, by chance, he was on the road from Orchomenos to Thebes when he met a group of strangers travelling towards Thebes. Noticing that they appeared to be rather officious, Alcaeus asked them what their business was in Thebes. They replied that they were messengers from Erginus to remind the Thebans that the tribute was due shortly. Unfortunately, one of the messengers then said that the Thebans were lucky that Erginus had not lopped off the ears, nose and hands of all the Theban men for the injury they had done by killing his father. Pausing only to enquire, sarcastically, whether Erginus really wanted such tribute, Alcaeus promptly amputated those very parts from all the messengers and sent them back to Erginus with their severed body parts hanging from their necks.

'Of course, Erginus was furious when he heard what had happened. The messengers were, in fact, heralds and, as such, provided they did not behave aggressively, they were entitled to safe conduct on their mission. It could be argued that, by making the remarks they did, they forfeited their right to immunity. Certainly, that was what the Council of the Theban citizens felt. However, the Thebans had been disarmed by the Orchomenans on their previous defeat by Erginus, and, when they received a demand from Erginus to hand over to him the person responsible for the "outrage", failing which he would invade their country and take retribution, the Council had really nothing to say.

'The Council did the only thing they could in the circumstances. They invited Alcaeus to their deliberations and asked him what he proposed to do about the situation he had created. They made it clear that they supported what he had done, but were in no position to resist a military onslaught by Erginus, which would undoubtedly cause death and injury to many Theban citizens. Alcaeus had the answer.

'In anticipation of Erginus' and the Council's reaction, he had earlier sounded out the young men of the city. They had agreed to join with him to fight Erginus and his army. One of them had pointed out that, although the citizens had been disarmed, the gods had not been. By this, he meant that many of the temples were adorned with shields, spears and swords and no-one had thought to remove them. Here was a ready-made armoury in waiting!

'Faced with Alcaeus' resolution, his growing reputation, and the strong support of some young men who came into the Council chamber with him, they authorised Alcaeus to raise an army to protect the city against the threatened attack and sent Erginus' herald back to his master with the blunt message that Thebes would not surrender anybody and, if Erginus wanted to pursue the matter, he should do it in person by coming to Thebes himself. This response was not quite what Erginus expected and, predictably, it enraged him still more. No doubt this was what Alcaeus had calculated when he advised the city fathers on the wording of their reply. Erginus was so keen to take vengeance that he did not pause to find out a little more about his opponent and whether the Thebans had found a local source of arms. Alcaeus, meanwhile, had already recruited a small army of young, well-armed men and, before Erginus had even left home, Alcaeus' force was already encamped on the road from Orchomenos to Thebes waiting for him. Alcaeus spent the several days it took Erginus' force to reach him training his young men and planning with them in detail how the enemy force would be trapped in a narrow pass, through which ran the only good road between the two cities. Scouts posted along the road kept Alcaeus informed of the progress of Erginus' army, whereas Erginus had not bothered even to send an advance party to warn him of dangers ahead, so confident was he of total victory.

'The annihilation of Erginus' force by Alcaeus' small band was sudden and complete. I am not familiar with military tactics but I am told that Alcaeus' rehearsed plan worked perfectly. The enemy were taken totally by surprise and some fell dead, I understand, before they had time to draw their swords. Erginus himself and many of his leading warriors were killed – most by Alcaeus. Very few escaped back to Orchomenos. As soon as the survivors reached their city, they found Alcaeus on their heels. Without any preliminary, Alcaeus demanded entry to the city. When the gates remained closed to him, he smashed them open and killed all who tried to bar his way to the palace. On arriving at the palace, which by then was empty, he ransacked it and set it on fire. The hastily assembled City Council sued for peace, which he granted on the terms that they paid tribute of two hundred oxen annually to Thebes, twice that which they had forced out of Thebes. This they gratefully accepted as the alternative to death or slavery.

'But Alcaeus knew that, in his haste, Erginus had left for Thebes without his chariots and cavalry, which had been told to follow. Alcaeus' scouts had located them encamped in a valley halfway from the city to the pass where Erginus' force had been defeated. Now, the valley was not very close to the main route between the cities and their location was not known to the Orchomenans, who had assumed that their mounted force had suffered the same fate as their infantry, so this part of Erginus' army were not yet aware of the defeat of the main force.

'Alcaeus took a small group of the best soldiers with him to where this mounted force was rested. Timing his arrival at dusk, Alcaeus was shown by his scouts the layout of the camp before darkness fell. Noticing that the horses were tethered on the eastern – Theban – side of the camp, and the wind was in the west, he decided that the best plan was to wait until the camp was quiet, remove the horses and steal through the camp in small groups, killing the soldiers as they slept. As he explained to me afterwards, the horses had to be removed first because, as they were downwind from the camp, they would sense his force's approach and would give the alarm by whinnying. He was concerned that any noise from restless horses would be enough, despite it being against the prevailing wind, to reach the camp and alert the enemy. The Theban scouts and Alcaeus knew where the few sentries were that had been posted. Some were guarding the horses but the majority were guarding the camp. Although few in number, they had to be killed first.

'My husband, and Alcaeus' father, Amphitryon, had joined the expedition and together they killed the horses' guards and removed the horses without any horse being alarmed sufficiently to make any unusual noise. I heard from those who returned from the enterprise, which, sadly, my husband did not – he alone was killed in the assault on the camp – that Alcaeus led the horses away in small groups by himself, handing them over to others when he felt they were far enough away from the camp for any noise the horses then made not to be heard. It must have taken him a very long time. I believe it was almost dawn before all the horses had been removed and the attack on the camp could begin.

'Most of the enemy were killed as they slept but Amphitryon was surprised by their leader, who it appears was awake and with a sword in his hand when Amphitryon approached his tent. No one really knows what happened, but there was a fierce combat between them that ended in them both being mortally wounded. Alcaeus was heartbroken and brought the body of his father back to Thebes for burial accompanied by a small advance party. The remainder, in sombre mood, arrived two days later with the horses and the other spoil they had taken. Of course, the Thebans were overjoyed when they heard the news of the great victory. Only a few, including me, had the loss of a loved one to mourn, so there was general rejoicing but I was not expected to join in. Still, I had to be pleased at the victory of my son and that my husband had died bravely fighting alongside him in a good cause. I just felt empty.'

This seemed an appropriate place to suspend our talk, which we did. Iolaus and I again expressed our thanks to the Queen for her kindness in recounting so vividly what was really the story of part of her life and which was bringing back so many sad memories. She graciously acknowledged our concern but added that, in some ways, it was helpful to her to talk about these past events to her grandson and his friend. She knew we really cared for the people she was talking about and she had rarely had the opportunity of rehearsing these stories in such sympathetic company.

Rather reluctantly, we agreed to accede to her request to meet again later in the day. Iolaus and I both felt that the Queen was tiring herself too much, but she insisted on continuing after what was to be only a short break. I believed then, and this was borne out by subsequent events, that she knew she would not live much longer. She was anxious to tell her story before it was too late.

Of course, I was curious to find out what had happened when Alcaeus was at the court of King Thespius, on which the Queen had declined to comment. I could tell from the little smile that had flickered across Iolaus' face when the Queen made her comment on the 'preposterous story' that he knew to what she referred. I had heard some tale about the King's fifty daughters and Hercules but this was my opportunity to hear the full story, so, when the Queen had retired and we were left alone in the room, I asked Iolaus.

'The Queen mentioned Hercules' visit – I'm sorry I can't think of him as "Alcaeus" – to Thespiae but declined to elaborate. I seem to remember some rather scandalous tale about what took place during his visit – a rather incredible one, I believe. Do you know what actually happened?'

Iolaus smiled broadly. 'I knew you would want to ask about that,' he said. 'According to the story circulating a few years after the events, Hercules – I agree, I also have difficulty in thinking of him as Alcaeus – was pressed by the King to stay in the palace overnight. The King had fifty daughters and I am sure that he wished to have Hercules as husband to one of them. However, Hercules was only a young man at that time and with little experience of women. He also was at the beginning of his adult life and emphatically not ready to settle down to married life. It may be that Thespius realised this and, under the pretence of it being an obligatory part of the Eros ritual, which was about to be celebrated, suggested to Hercules that it would be in order for him to sleep with his eldest daughter, Procris, in the hope that she would bear Hercules' child. Hercules always denied to me that this did happen, but I was never too sure he was telling the truth about this. He certainly could not be blamed if he did accept the opportunity offered, as I am sure the lady would have been willing!

'However, this possible incident was soon expanded. One of the versions of the story has Hercules staying at the palace for fifty nights and, unknown to the King but through the collusion of Procris and her sisters (except one who declined to become involved), taking each of the daughters to bed on consecutive nights! According to this version, all the daughters had sons, two of them having twins. Of course, this version of the story unravelled when it became clear that Hercules had only spent one night in Thespius' Palace, as he had quickly found out that his quarry had departed south east to the Cithaeron mountains. Then, the story was that Hercules had slept with them all and made them all pregnant in the one night! That is why the Queen called the story "preposterous". She is right. But that does not mean that there not a grain of truth in it. I believe there is, and I think the Queen does, too, but she will never admit it!'

Curiously, I knew of another story, in which these supposed fifty sons of Hercules had joined Iolaus, their uncle, in Sardinia, and he had not mentioned another story, which suggested that the daughter who declined Hercules' attentions became a priestess in a temple, founded by Hercules himself, dedicated to his own worship. I imagined that Iolaus had not mentioned these absurd rumours because they clearly were fantasies. Remembering the flash of annoyance Iolaus had shown on a previous occasion when I had made a naive comment, I decided not to pursue these thoughts with him.

Time passed quickly and we were soon again closeted with the Queen to hear the next part of the story.

'Creon took back the throne on my husband's death, but, so as not to upset Alcaeus' apparent right to be King, and reflecting the popular opinion of him after his successful exploit in killing the rampaging lion and his expedition to Orchomenos, offered him the hand of his daughter, Megara, in marriage. He consulted me about this proposal and, at his request, I talked to Megara herself. She was aware of the proposal – Creon had discussed it with her – and she had no hesitation in telling me that she would be honoured to be the wife of my son. I had no doubt that she would be a good wife to him – but I was concerned that he would not be a good husband for her…' She paused and a few tears crept down her cheeks. Iolaus instinctively moved towards her to comfort her, but she held up her hand, motioning him to remain where he was.

Continuing she said, looking directly at Iolaus. 'This part of Alcaeus' story is as painful for you as for me. The events I am about to relate both made him and undid him.

'As both parties were more than willing, I told my son that the proposed marriage had my full support. The ceremony was elaborate as it became a double wedding: Alcaeus marred Creon's eldest daughter, Megara, and Iolaus' father, Iphicles, married his youngest daughter. At first, my fears were not realised: Alcaeus and Megara were very happy together and I had soon had grandchildren. In the meantime, Alcaeus, who had been made "Protector" of Thebes by King Creon, had not been inactive, militarily speaking. He had been called out to defend the city against an onslaught by King Pyraechmus of Euboea, an ally of Erginus. He too was utterly defeated and was killed. After this, no human dared challenge the new power at Thebes. But, unfortunately, the manner of Pyraechmus' death was inappropriate.

Alcaeus, presumably in a fit of anger, ordered his defeated enemy's body to be torn to pieces by being tied between two wild ponies. This was barbaric. When this became generally known, there was universal revulsion. Alcaeus, after basking in unprecedented public favour, found this sudden reversal of fortune very difficult to take. He became uncommunicative, reclusive and even surly. He felt the gods were angry with him. Perhaps they considered that he had been given so much and was ungrateful. I could see his mind was disturbed, but had no idea of what would happen next…'

Here she paused again to recover her composure. We both knew the tragedy of what happened next. Iolaus himself had been present and was scarred by it, although his later close companionship with Hercules and the passing of many years had softened its impact. We implored the Queen to pass over this episode but, anxious to tell her story in full, she continued.

'Alcaeus' grandchildren were playing some war game in the garden adjoining the part of the palace in which we lived. Some other children, friends, were there, too, including Iolaus and his two brothers. The children were being very noisy, shouting and screaming and totally absorbed in their play. Suddenly, Alcaeus rushed out of the palace towards them, sword in hand. The children thought their famous father was joining them for play. Iolaus, the oldest, knew better. He, by chance, was a little apart from the others, near the door by which his uncle had entered the garden. He saw the manic look in his uncle's eyes, dodged his flashing sword and ran indoors to get help. By the time the servants and I arrived, all the children were dead, slaughtered by my son, father to some of them. Alcaeus, still possessed, was building a funeral pyre from uprooted trees, wooden fences, anything that would burn and we were powerless to stop him throwing the dead children's' bodies on the pyre. It was a terrible sight. We recognised that there was nothing useful we could do. The children were dead and, if we interfered, we would join them in death.

'And so we just waited until the storm abated. Gradually, his madness left him and sanity returned. Looking around him, at the dying fire, the half-burnt children's' bodies on it, and the bloody sword in his hands, the enormity of what he had done fell on his consciousness. He collapsed on the ground, the sword still in his hand. Thinking it now safe to approach him, I ventured to his side and gently removed the gory sword from the grip of his right hand, speaking gently to him all the while. A servant came silently up to me and relieved me of the sword. Alcaeus fell into my lap, convulsed with sobbing.

'We remained like that for some time. Creon and senior court officials came to see what the problem was but I waved them away. There would be time enough later for explanations and expiation. The important objective now was to remove him from the scene of this terrible act, try to understand its meaning and restore my son's sanity. At last, the sobbing and convulsions ceased and I, with help from two of the servants, led him away to his room. As soon as he was inside the room, he told us to leave and slammed and bolted the door. I left the servants there with strict instructions to give him all he asked for (except weapons) and to let no one near him. I arranged to send servants regularly to his room over the next week to relieve those on duty and they kept me informed. Apart from reports of occasional bursts of sobbing and the sound of furniture being thrown against the walls, little was reported to me. Or to Creon, of course, who was as concerned as I about the fate of our grandchildren. Alcaeus did not ask for any food, although water left outside the door was taken, apparently when no one was looking. I think the servants, who admired him, just let him know when they were taking a walk!

'Creon and the court officials wanted a full explanation. Iolaus, as the only witness, was questioned many times, weren't you?'

'Yes,' replied Iolaus. 'They wouldn't leave me alone. I was very young at the time and I hardly saw anything. Anyway, I ran for help directly – as I kept on telling them – so I wasn't there. I am quite sure that, if I hadn't seen him coming at me, I would have shared the fate of my brothers and cousins. There seemed to be a thought that I had survived because I knew about the event before it happened. As if he would have told me in advance! I wasn't particularly close to him at the time, although we did become great friends later, as you know.'

'Yes,' responded the Queen, 'your support and friendship was one of his most valuable possessions, as he frequently told me. I suppose that getting to know him as well as you did as his charioteer, in what was probably the most testing time of his life, must also have helped you come to terms with the tremendous harm he had done to your family and mine?'

Iolaus nodded. 'I came to see what a complicated – yet simple – person he was. Complicated because his brain always seemed to be working on not the next problem, but the one after that, and simple because he lived by the simple principles of loyalty to those who were loyal to him and to whom he owed loyalty (whatever their attitude to him), being honest in all his actions and honouring his word. He had great difficulty in understanding anyone who did not believe what he said, doubted he would fulfil his promises or reneged on a promise they had made to him. The last upset him most, as you know only too well!'

The Queen smiled ruefully. 'Indeed, I do know. But I can see your friend is waiting patiently for me to return to the story! Anyway, after about a week, Alcaeus opened the door of his room and rejoined the world. He looked a wreck. His wife, Megara, was still in shock, so I had arranged with the servants to be the first to be told when his sanity returned. They were only too keen to come running to tell me, as they did not know what to do with him! I had already discussed with Creon what we should recommend to him when he retuned to normality, so Creon kept all the court officials out of my way for the first crucial days after Alcaeus had emerged from his self-imposed incarceration.

'The crimes he had committed were too great to be overlooked. He had no explanation and was as shocked as we were by what had occurred. So far as he could recall, no prior event had triggered this outburst and he could think of no reason why he should kill his own children. He accepted that he needed help and expiation. I had agreed with Creon that he should be encouraged to go to consult the Oracle at Delphi for advice on how to make atonement for his crimes. The legal authorities, advised by my friend and future husband, Rhadamanthus, had agreed that Alcaeus, being obviously temporarily mad when he committed his terrible crime, was not responsible for his actions and was therefore not liable to the normal criminal sanctions, provided he sought and accepted the appropriate spiritual guidance – which the Delphic Oracle would provide.

'Alcaeus immediately accepted the advice and, within days, was on his way to Delphi with a small, armed escort. Creon, with a subtlety I had not expected, persuaded me to go with him. This was a very wise decision. News of the infanticide had preceded us. The people along the way, who days before would have acclaimed him as a hero now hurled insults – and even stones – at him. My presence alone on occasion prevented a riot, during which harm would undoubtedly have resulted. Alcaeus, prior to this, would have reacted angrily to the people's contempt but he was now so crushed with his guilt that I do not think he would have resisted had the crowd attacked and killed him.

'Gradually, the word spread that Alcaeus had been driven mad by the gods – what man in his senses would kill his own children? – and, overwhelmed by his loss, was on his way to Delphi to find what he must do to appease the gods that had maddened him. The last part of our journey was, happily, free of demonstrations, although I was always alert for trouble.

'We were very kindly received by the Chief Priest at Delphi and I was allowed to share accommodation with my son. Two days passed before the Chief Priest told us that we were to consult the Oracle the following day, which was the seventh of the month. I expect you are both aware of the rituals that precede consultation?'

We nodded.

'It followed the usual practices and, of course, Alcaeus and I were both in the formal procession to the sanctuary to hear what answer Apollo had for Alcaeus.

'Now, as you know, the Pythian, seated on her tripod out of sight of the suppliants, is in a trance and Apollo speaks through her in a language only one of the Prophetai, the priests of the temple, can interpret. I did hear some mumbling from behind the screen where, I understood, the Pythian was seated, but it was quite unintelligible to me. As a woman, I was not allowed to be as near to the sanctuary as my son, but I could still hear the Pythian speak in her trance. I found it hard to believe that any helpful response could come from such doubtful utterances – indeed, the Oracle was notorious even then for issuing misleading or ambivalent responses. Alcaeus and I were therefore prepared for an unclear, perhaps even contradictory, response.

'We were accordingly amazed with what the Priest told us: his madness had indeed been visited on him by the gods, but without the permission of the King of the gods, Zeus. Zeus had therefore put Alcaeus under the protection of his wife, Hera, in recognition of which he was to adopt the name of Hercules, which means "the Glory of Hera". Whilst he was acquitted of the guilt of killing his, and his brother's, children, he must nevertheless submit himself to his cousin Eurystheus, the High King, and carry out the ten tasks that he would set. On the satisfactory conclusion of those tasks he would have expiated his guilt and would be freed of his servitude to Eurystheus. I was bitterly disappointed with this ruling and I could see that Alcaeus – Hercules – was also. We accepted the name change and welcomed the protection that his adoption by Hera brought to him, but neither of us could see the justice of his being punished for what Zeus himself accepted he was not responsible.

'We had a dilemma. The Oracle had spoken, more clearly than usual, and we could not challenge it. Indeed, it would be very unwise to challenge it. We talked through the night and could see no solution. As dawn was breaking, we at last fell asleep.

'When I awoke the sun was high in the sky and my son was not to be seen. He must have awoken before me and gone out into the fresh air so as not to disturb my sleep. I washed and dressed and, as I too walked through the door, I saw Hercules walking up the slope from the Castalian Spring, one of the holiest places at Delphi and where we had purified ourselves the day before. I could see that he was changed. The deep gloom had left him and there was a revived sense of purpose about him. He was reconciled to his fate. I was glad, though puzzled. What had caused him to change his opinions so dramatically from those we exchanged during our long discussion the night before?

'He could hardly wait to tell me. An hour or so after dawn, having had only a short sleep, he awoke to see the Chief Priest at the open door, motioning him to follow him and urging him not to wake me up. Seeing that I was sound asleep, and knowing that our armed party were nearby, he did as he was bid, pausing only to tell one of our "guards" that I was now alone and he was to look after me while he went with the Chief Priest. First, the Chief Priest led him to the Castalian Spring, where we had the previous day purified ourselves by washing our hair, hands and feet in the smaller of the two pools. This time, Hercules was required to strip, put on a white shift provided by the Chief Priest, who was similarly attired, and accompany him into the larger pool where, joining hands, they immersed themselves under the water. All the time, from the moment their feet touched the water to stepping out, the Chief Priest was mumbling a prayer. For the first time after they had met at the door of our room, the Chief Priest spoke, telling Hercules that he was now cleansed of his crimes. He then drew Hercules aside and led him to a small hut nearby where a cloth to dry himself was draped over a chair, as were, neatly folded, the clothes he had divested before plunging into the pool. The Chief Priest told him to dry himself, get dressed and await his return.

'This he did, in some mystification. The Chief Priest soon returned, dressed apparently in a new white shirt. At the Chief Priest's invitation, Hercules walked outside with the Chief Priest and strolled slowly away from the sanctuary with him while, in a low voice (to avoid being overheard Hercules presumed), the Chief Priest explained the nature of the tasks he was to perform for Eurystheus. He was first sworn to secrecy. Eurystheus himself was not to know. Eurystheus would be told by Apollo's messengers what tasks to set and would have no idea of the hidden purpose.

'The Chief Priest said that Apollo was concerned at the continuation of the barbarous practice of human sacrifice and the growth of aggressive, murderous, female cults. The tasks Hercules would be set were to be primarily aimed at eliminating or at least discrediting these practices. There was also another hidden aim but Hercules would not tell me what this was. I expect that it was not only his promise to the Chief Priest to keep his mission secret but the nature of it which prompted his silence. He never did tell me, but I deduced later that it was to overthrow the female domination of kingship with male succession. This latter policy was, perhaps a little surprisingly, in places popular with women as well as men. The female "regime" was not popular with the elder daughters because, as I am sure you are aware, it was through the youngest daughter that the crown descended. This was essential to extend the range of fecundity and the prospect of heirs. You should view Hercules' "Labours" in that light. But, I expect Iolaus has already told you this?' she concluded, turning to me.

I confirmed that he had. 'Yes, Iolaus has told me the hidden agenda, although it is hard to see how some of the tasks fit in to this. What also puzzles me is that Zeus appears to be your son's patron and my understanding is that his matrimonial indiscretions – to put it in mild language – often led to arguments with his wife, Hera. Whilst I believe the worship of Hera has, for a long time, not involved the sacrifice of human beings, only animals – but excluding cows for some obscure reason – and I have no knowledge that her priests supported the rights of female succession, I find it hard to believe that your son's mission was jointly approved by Zeus and Hera.'

'What a shrewd man you are!' commented the Queen. 'I came to the same conclusion, and once asked Hercules to explain how the differences between Zeus and Hera were put aside. He thought a while and, thoughtfully, suggested that either they jointly wanted to claim some propriety over him or the Chief Priest of Apollo had lied. He always inclined to the latter view. It helped to confuse, so was probably justified!

'I was relieved now at the outcome. Hercules was comfortable – I won't say happy – about his immediate future, and so was I. It was a little difficult explaining to Creon and the court on our return to Thebes why the edict of the Delphic Oracle did not dismay us more than we pretended. Hercules had already broken his vow of secrecy by telling me part of the hidden agenda, and we had agreed that neither of us would say anything about it when we returned to Thebes. Although it appeared a terrible punishment for what was acknowledged not to be his fault, Hercules had been declared cleansed. This was the best outcome. Provided the tasks set by Eurystheus were reasonable – and surely, we argued, he would seek divine guidance on the tasks he should set – Hercules' reputation must be enhanced. I also privately said to Creon that it would keep Hercules busy and out of our way for a good many years, a sentiment which, from a mother, sounds rather heartless, but I was sure in my own mind that this was likely to be in his own best interests. Posterity will judge whether or not I was right about that.

'Incidentally,' she continued, turning to me, 'you seem to be unaware of the reason cows are never sacrificed to Hera. You may not realise that the majority of our cults originated in Crete many years ago. When the civilisation there was destroyed by successive earthquakes and flooding, the people were ruined and they blamed their gods. The priests fled for their lives to Egypt, taking with them their beliefs and religious practices. They were fortunate, because, soon after their arrival, Egypt entered on a long period of prosperity and they adopted these new cults as their own and adapted them to their customs. One of these was to identify a god with an animal: on royal tombs and inscriptions you will see animal heads on human bodies – even their rulers were sometimes represented in this way. The cult figure of Hera adopted the head of a cow in Egypt and this association remained when the cult fled persecution in Egypt to the Eastern Islands and mainland Greece many centuries later.'

It was again time to suspend our talk. I already knew the next part of the story. Although the Queen believed that she might have something to add to what Iolaus had recounted, she accepted that he knew far more about the 'Labours' than she did.

Iolaus and I had noticed how much more tired she was looking as our talks progressed. We were concerned and said so. She agreed that the process of telling us about the past was proving more tiring and upsetting than she had expected, and readily agreed to Iolaus' suggestion that, when we met the next day, she would tell us about Hercules' life after the 'Labours' and what happened immediately after his death. As this would include the destiny of Eurystheus, I must confess I was looking forward to that.

We were well entertained that evening by King Menestheus, who had, after his initial hospitality, left us very much to do as we wished. He had made it clear that we were free to come and go as we pleased and we took advantage of this several times, exploring the compact city on the Acropolis and the infant settlement at the foot, on the western side, which was enclosed by the Lyromid Wall. We quickly discovered one – or rather two – of the reasons why the Acropolis had been chosen for the site of the city of Athens. Its defensive nature was obvious, as was its relative closeness to the sea for food and movement. Although the solid rock made any cultivation, except in pots, virtually impossible, there were, however, two natural springs that provided copious flows of water and which had not, in living memory, ever failed.

The denseness of the building development added welcome shade should our wanderings take us out in the full-day sun. This was not oppressive because everywhere there were large pots with plants, flowers or shrubs, which not only softened the sharp edges of the, mainly stone, buildings but also, particularly in the evenings, issued a heady, languorous, mix of perfume to the air. There were attractive small fountains dotted everywhere, most of which were open to use by any passer-by for whatever purpose the water was needed at that moment – drinking, watering plants or animals and even cooking and pottery making.

We made a visit to the top of the hill, which had caught my eye on arrival, called Lycavitos. This was some distance away from the east side of the Acropolis. When we had suggested to Menestheus that we would like to visit this hill, he said that, whilst it should be quite safe for us to go there, it was outside the protection of the city guards. As we could be seen by our clothes to be wealthy foreigners, it would be sensible for him to provide us with an armed guard for our protection. This he did, and we experienced no problem – apart from climbing the steep slopes of the Lycavitos Hill! It was considerably higher than the Acropolis and, from its summit, gave us an outstanding view of the Acropolis and the surrounding countryside. There was a military camp of some sort at the top and the guards were pleased to see us and direct us to the best views. I imagined that they did not have too many visitors. This they confirmed. I think they felt rather isolated. However, they showed us with some pride a mirror signalling system they used to communicate with the other military establishments nearby. Whilst we were there, a message came from the signal station on the roof of the King's Palace on the Acropolis. The King was enquiring about our safe arrival. I suspect he was doing this mainly to give us a demonstration of the system. There were also ready-made beacons to light in the event of a hostile attack. The lighting of the beacons would alert all the nearby watch stations far quicker than would be possible by mirror-signalling each one, as we readily agreed.

After a most enjoyable half day spent in the company of these guards, we slowly descended to the foot of the hill to join the track back to the city. Here we found two chariots awaiting us – sent by Menestheus, who thought that we must be tired from our day in the hot sun and would welcome a ride back to the Acropolis, where we would face another stiff climb back to the palace. He was right! Iolaus and I were very relieved to be able to relax for a little while before attempting our final climb of the day.

If I had one reservation about Athens, it was just that, somehow, climbing down from the Acropolis' plateau to the, relatively, flat area below made little impact. You reached the Nine Gates of the main entrance to the city almost without noticing it. But, climbing back into the city was another matter entirely. I was not surprised when Menestheus told me that the city had successfully resisted many enemy assaults already in its relatively short history. I could not help comparing it with Mycenae, Thebes and Tiryns. All those cities had well protected entrances but, apart from Mycenae, none had the additional protection of being built on a virtually impregnable hill. Mycenae, it was true, had steep slopes on two of its sides, which the towering walls on top made almost unassailable, but the main gated entrance was approached by a gently sloped paved roadway, up which it would not be difficult to drive a battering ram right to the gate itself. This was not possible at Athens. The outer gates could be assaulted in this way. Even they were well – and better – protected than the entrances of Mycenae and Thebes but the access to the Tiryns' main gate exposed unwelcome visitors to attack from above on both sides and was particularly difficult to storm.

Farewell to Alcmena

The next morning I awoke early. I quickly realised that, although it was still dark outside, there was much activity inside the palace. Opening the door of my room, I saw servants rushing about, apparently aimlessly, carrying lit torches, items of clothing and other objects that I could not identify. Turning towards Iolaus' room, I saw that the door was ajar and, pushing it open, I saw that he was already dressed and gone. Taking a flaming torch from within his room, I went back to my own room and dressed quickly. Managing to waylay a female servant in her headlong rush towards the royal quarters, I asked what was happening. She was clearly distraught and, through her tears, motioned me to follow her, which I did.

We soon reached the destination, which, it transpired, were the quarters of Queen Alcmena. As I reached them I saw Iolaus and he beckoned me over to him. Releasing the servant who had guided me, I thanked her and she went off quickly to carry out whatever task she had been designated to perform.

As I approached Iolaus, I could see that he had been weeping and knew immediately that Queen Alcmena had passed away. This Iolaus confirmed. The Queen had died in the night, peacefully, in her sleep. He had already spoken to King Menestheus who had, on hearing the sad news, decreed a three-day period of official mourning, at the conclusion of which there would be funeral games in gratitude for her life. We were both expected to stay for the games, returning home afterwards on the most convenient ship.

I gave Iolaus my condolences on his sad loss and, with his assistance, had a brief audience with the King to do the same and express my grateful thanks for being invited to participate with the Royal Family and citizens of Athens in the period of official mourning and the celebratory games. Knowing that the King had much business to attend to, as soon as politeness allowed I excused myself and left the chamber to seek out Iolaus.

He agreed that we should aim to leave Athens as soon as possible after the completion of the funeral games planned for his much loved grandmother. We felt that, as the palace staff would be heavily engaged in making arrangements for the Queen's funeral and the funeral games, it would not be right to ask them to enquire about our travel arrangements back to Olbia. After making some discreet enquiries of the Chief Steward, he helped us arrange a return trip to the port of Phaleron, where we could enquire personally on sailings back to Olbia. Although it was a short distance to the port, we were not familiar with local customs or the areas where robbers were active, and the Chief Steward was very helpful in directing us to those who could advise us on such matters and even arrange for us to join an organised group if that appeared to us to be the best course. By discussing our plans with the Chief Steward, rather than unilaterally making our own arrangements, we avoided any misunderstandings or the possibility of a search party being mobilised if it was suddenly discovered that we were 'missing'. After we had made arrangements to join organised parties to and from Phaleron, we also gave the steward who had looked after us the details of our expected time of departure and return to the palace.

All went smoothly. The group we joined on the downward trip were rather dour and restrained but friendly enough and, anyway, the distance was not great so we soon reached the destination and parted. At the harbour, we quickly identified the agent's shop we had been advised to try first to book our return sailing. The officials there were very helpful, and knew who we were. They had heard of Queen Alcmena's death and were suitably sympathetic. She was a great favourite with the Athenians, which included those who lived in Phaleron.

The agent knew of a ship that was expected to arrive later that day and was scheduled to leave for Olbia within ten days of arrival. This was the only ship available at that moment, of which the agent was aware, which was travelling the complete distance to Olbia. Despite the apparent ease with which we had booked our outward passage to Phaleron, we were told that it was generally quite difficult to be able to book passage on one ship for the whole journey. Normally it was only possible to complete such a voyage by using several ships, sometimes spending days ashore waiting for the next ship to arrive. So we were very fortunate in being able to book our passage on the one ship. The agent assured us that this particular ship had passenger accommodation that was at least as good as that on the ship we had used on our outward journey. Supported by these assurances, we had no hesitation in commissioning the agent to book our passages. This he did, promising to send a message to the palace when the ship had docked and advising us when to present ourselves for embarkation.

As we had concluded our business more quickly than we had expected, we had time to spare before we needed to return to the meeting point, where we would join the party returning to the city. We fleetingly thought about, but rejected, returning on our own as being too risky. The weather was warm and sunny and so we enjoyed a few hours of real leisure. Latterly, we placed ourselves within sight of the meeting point and we were surprised how soon the time for our return to Athens arrived. This time, the group we joined was lively and humorous. The uphill slog passed unnoticed, our full attention being on the wide-ranging and, occasionally hilarious, conversations that we enjoyed with our companions, the beautiful landscape we passed through and the heady scents that impinged on our senses. All too soon, we reached the foot of the steps to the Acropolis, where the party divided. The smaller portion climbed with us, somewhat wearily, up the steps to the top, where the final separation came. We were the only members staying on the north side.

Arriving back at the palace, we notified the Chief Steward of our safe return and the day on which we expected to be called down to Phaleron to prepare for embarkation. He thanked us for this advance notice, as it enabled him to make arrangements for staff to be available to convey us and our baggage down to the quay. On hearing the name of the ship we would be travelling on, he confirmed that it was indeed a comfortable ship for passengers. Fortuitously, the same ship was bringing some goods for the palace, so those staff who took us down to Phaleron could also bring back the palace consignment. We were pleased to learn this. We did not wish to create too much extra work for the palace staff. It was satisfying to know that they would have been making the trip down to Phaleron anyway.

The three days of official mourning passed. During these, the funeral was held. To my surprise the Queen was not buried in the royal burial ground on the Acropolis, nor even in the official burial ground for noble Athenians at the foot of the Acropolis. After the religious service, her body was placed on a carefully constructed wooden pyre, which was lit by eight priestesses dressed in full-length white robes.

I learnt later that the Queen's ashes were put into an urn so that she could have her official burying place in the Temple of Zeus Olympios at Thebes. This was apparently what she had wanted and Iolaus, who had been consulted after her death, had felt appropriate. As it was no more than 300 stadia from Athens to Thebes, Iolaus accompanied the urn on its journey to Thebes and participated in the ceremony in the Temple there. The party did not leave until after the funeral games had been held but Iolaus returned to Athens long before we had notice that our ship had arrived at Phaleron and we should proceed to the harbour to prepare for embarkation.

The funeral games were a great spectacle and a great success. Because of his prowess and his close relationship with the Queen, Iolaus was invited to be the main official at the games, chairing the panel of judges who awarded the prizes to the winners. He had politely declined to enter the chariot race, claiming that he was now too old for such strenuous activity. He was, of course, loudly acclaimed when he appeared on the rostrum to award the winners their garlands.

In addition to the chariot races – there were several over different distances and one for the older veterans – there were foot races, archery and discus-throwing competitions. I am no expert in foot races, but was impressed with the accuracy of the competitors with their arrows in the archery and those who threw the discus such a long way. Perhaps, I mused, their discus was lighter than ours? And so, it was all over.

Sadly, the Queen had died before finishing her story. However, Iolaus had reassured me that he also knew about the later episodes which the Queen would have related, although he conceded that he would probably have a rather different perspective to the Queen's. Now was not the time to pursue this so I contented myself in the time left to us by writing up the notes I had taken of our discussions with the Queen. I had just completed this task when we heard that our ship had arrived in port. The Chief Steward summoned the staff and we made our way again back down the hill to Phaleron.

On arrival in the docks at Phaleron, we were taken straight up to the ship and to our quarters, where we deposited our baggage. We were then conducted to the Captain's quarters. On the way to his cabin, I was impressed by how well armed the ship was, and enquired about this from the Captain. He explained that although, on this occasion, he was part of a small fleet, he often had to sail alone or with only one or two other ships. He therefore liked to be prepared for an attack and he confided that some of his crew had been warriors, including experienced archers. I felt that we were in good hands. The Captain explained that, although he was happy for us to be on board, we would not be sailing for a few days to allow the fleet, including his own ship, to finish unloading and then load fresh cargo. Even then, adverse weather conditions could delay our departure.

Return to Olbia

We were both exhausted – mentally, physically and emotionally – after Queen Alcmena's death and were anxious now to be on our way home. The Captain pointed out that, as his ship was part of a small fleet, the readiness of his ship was not the only consideration. Departure might be delayed by the default of others or, as he had already warned us, by adverse weather conditions, as it was now early autumn.

As it turned out, our departure was one day later than expected, because of adverse winds. It was a slow journey, as not only were the winds generally unhelpful, there were also ports to visit to unload cargo. At some, our fleet was diminished, either because our Captain was not prepared to wait while one of the accompanying ships completed unloading or it was not travelling further with us. Among the few memorable ports of call was Tiryns, whose massive walls and a citadel crowned with a magnificent palace celebrated the imagination and ingenuity of its builders. It was fitting to be reminded that this was the birthplace of Hercules. Due respect was paid to him by all visitors, including the few passengers on our ship.

Dulled by the interminable voyage and the withdrawn characters of the Captain and his crew, on top of our sad experience in Athens, Iolaus and I grew apart. Although we had no disagreements or arguments, by the time we disembarked at Olbia we were barely speaking to each other. Although not hostile, we had certainly lost that easy friendship that had developed during our time together in Athens. However, towards the end of the voyage, I did manage to thank him sincerely for all his efforts in arranging the visit to Athens so that I could meet his grandmother. The sincerity of my gratitude and the recollection of his gracious reception at Athens must have touched him, as his farewell in Olbia was more friendly than I had begun to expect. It was but a brief spark to lighten the gloom of his mood and as I arranged for my baggage to be unloaded and transported to my home, I realised that I might not be privileged to hear more from Iolaus of the adventures of his distinguished uncle.

Immersion in my business, developing some of the design ideas I had been stimulated to imagine during my visit to Athens and the return to the chaos of normal family life soon banished my gloom. Within a few days of my return, I was perusing my notes of the conversations with Iolaus and Alcmena. Apart from the rest of Hercules' life, I identified gaps in what I had already been told: what happened to Mnesimache? Iolaus, when telling me about the Fifth Labour, the cleaning of the Stables of Augeas, had promised to tell me her story. And what was the truth about the death of the High King Eurystheus and his grandmother's involvement in it? I had to know.

A month or so after our return, I resolved to make discreet enquiries from mutual friends to find out Iolaus' present mood. At first, the responses I received were discouraging and it was clear that those friends who met him shortly after our return had found him deeply melancholic. This they attributed to the death of his grandmother, who was, as I appreciated, his last living close blood relative. Then I realised that most of these friends had only encountered Iolaus shortly after his return. None had spoken to, or even seen, him recently. Believing Iolaus' spirit to be strong and outward going rather than introspective, I felt that recovery to some level of normal behaviour would not be long delayed after his return.

I therefore decided that a 'chance' encounter, possibly on the docks – which I should be able to engineer by finding out when he was expecting a shipment – was the best strategy. I discarded a direct approach to him at his home or in the street near his house, as it would look contrived and invite rejection. I had no wish to upset him nor to be rebuffed in pique. It was a little while before I received news of a shipment he was expecting and, by good fortune, I was expecting a small consignment myself at about the same time, although on a different ship. As I had legitimate cause to be visiting the docks and enquiring about the arrival of my ship, it was not difficult to elicit casually information on the arrival of other ships, including the one Iolaus was expecting.

When I was finally able to get arrivals information, it happened that the exact timing of the arrival of my ship was not known but Iolaus' shipment was due in two days' time. I was told that my ship could arrive on the same day, although it was more likely that it would arrive several days later. It was not hard to pretend that I was in urgent need of the goods being consigned and persuade the wharf manager to suggest that a daily visit would not be inappropriate!

I had just arrived at the wharf to enquire about the arrival of 'my' ship when Iolaus appeared with his servants to take delivery of his property from the captain of a ship about to tie up at the wharf. I was relieved when Iolaus greeted me warmly like an old friend. In a short conversation we speedily re-established our former cordial relationship. He gave no apology for his recent aloofness and I did not refer to it, preferring to react positively to his present obvious good temper. We briefly recounted what we had been doing since our return and I delicately introduced the subject of our visit to Athens, where ladies' comments had encouraged me to design some new pieces. To my excitement, Iolaus suggested that when I had some examples made up he would be delighted to see them and give me his reaction. I readily agreed. As I already had made up a few pieces and others were in an advanced stage in my workshop, we made an appointment to meet at his home at midday in four days' time. We then parted amicably, he to attend to his shipment and I to my workshop.

Armed with a small selection of the Athens-inspired jewellery, including one based on a brooch worn by Queen Alcmena, I arrived at Iolaus' house at the appointed time. His demeanour was as it had been on the wharf some days earlier: warm and friendly. He expressed great interest in my work and instantly recognised the inspiration for the brooch, which he praised as being an improvement on that worn by his grandmother. As I had hoped, this reference led him back to Hercules and what he called 'the unfinished business' between us. I was delighted as I had not been looking forward to broaching the subject with him; it was much to be preferred that he raised it first, as he had done.

'It was most unfortunate that Grandmother died without telling you all she knew,' Iolaus said with a detectable tear in both his eyes, 'but I know most of the remainder of the story and she would not have enjoyed telling you about some of the terrible events in which she participated, about which you must be very curious.'

I admitted that I was.

'Still,' Iolaus continued, 'there is much more to relate. I think there are some episodes I promised to recall when I was recounting the stories about Hercules' Labours?'

'Yes,' I agreed. 'During your account of the Fifth Labour, there was a mention of Mnesimache, daughter of Dexamenus, King of Olenus. I gathered it was not relevant to the tale of the Labour, but an incident did occur involving them and Hercules at that time.'

'That is right,' confirmed Iolaus. 'Hercules and I called on King Dexamenus on our way back to Tiryns from Elis. He agreed with Hercules that, if Augeas' son, Phyleus, preferred that his father be not deposed in his favour, then so be it. During our first meeting with Dexamenus, Mnesimache came into the chamber. It was clear to me by the way they looked at each other that Hercules and Mnesimache had some affection for each other. Quite how much I was to find out much later. At this time, Hercules was married to Megara who, as I expect you know, became my wife at Hercules' own suggestion after he divorced her. When he returned to King Dexamenus' kingdom in Olenus some years later, Hercules was a single man. But he had some other adventures prior to that, which I should recount to you.

'On our return to Thebes, it was all too obvious that Hercules' marriage to Megara, Creon's daughter, was over. I don't think either of them could forget Hercules' terrible slaughter of their children and there had been a very long separation during the many years of the Labours. They both thought their relationship was doomed. This was most unfortunate because I think that originally they were genuinely fond of each other, but mortals cannot fight the will of the gods. But I was very surprised when Hercules suggested that I take his place as Megara's husband. She was older than I, but I was very fond of her and (apart from Hercules himself) was the only survivor of that terrible day when all her children and two of my brothers were killed. So, we had considerable empathy and could weep together for our lost past – which, I am afraid, we sometimes did. Anyway, I accepted that it was best for them that they should separate.

'By this time, Megara's father, Creon, was dead. With no sons alive to protect her, a separation from Hercules would blight her future life. I felt that I had a duty to help and at that time had no ties myself. I resolved that if Megara was willing to marry me, I was more than a willing husband. Hercules gave me permission to speak directly to Megara and I found her gentle, understanding and captivating. I fell in love with her and she with me. The difference in our ages meant nothing. Hercules was delighted and he told me that I had lifted a great burden from him, for which he would be always grateful. I protested that, while I was delighted to be of assistance to him, Megara and I loved each other, so we were not planning to be married purely for his benefit! At this, he was even more pleased. Hercules' divorce and my marriage were quickly arranged, and Megara and I had many happy years together. She died some years ago now and I did not remarry. Sadly, we had no children but because I led Hercules' children and others here to a happy life in Sardinia I am frequently addressed as "Father". I expect you have heard me greeted in this way?'

'Indeed I have heard that expression used by some of your contemporaries,' I replied, 'and wondered at its derivation. Thank you for the explanation. What did Hercules do next?'

'I suspected afterwards that Hercules had already planned his next move,' responded Iolaus. 'Sadly, this had very tragic consequences. Eurytus, the son of Melanius, King of Oechalia – a city state in the mountains of northern Aetolia, roughly halfway between Thebes in the east and the Ionian Sea in the west – was proud of his archery skills. He offered the hand of his daughter, Iole, to anyone who could beat him and his four sons in an archery contest. Hercules took up the challenge and won easily. Eurytus, claiming to be outraged at Hercules' treatment of Megara, considered him an unsuitable consort for his daughter and on these grounds excused himself from fulfilling his promise. A little later, by now in a drunken state, he also claimed that, as Hercules was bound to Eurystheus, he was a slave and not a free man and so was not eligible to win the prize offered. He therefore insisted that Hercules left empty-handed, which Hercules did.

'It happened that Iphitus, one of Eurytus' four sons, did not agree with his father's decision and pressed him to honour his promise. The other three sons supported their father with the outcome I have already related. Some time later, some of Eurytus' oxen were stolen and many, including Eurytus and the three sons, thought that Hercules had stolen them in reprisal for being cheated of Iole. Iphitus refused to believe that Hercules was responsible and volunteered to go in search of the stolen oxen. In fact, a well-known thief, Autolycus, had stolen them and changed their appearance, so that not even their owner would recognise them. Unfortunately, whilst he was driving the oxen away, he met Hercules who, always ready to strike a bargain, asked if they were for sale. Autolycus, keen to get rid of them, named a price that Hercules couldn't possibly reject. Hercules then drove the oxen back to Tiryns where he pastured them in a meadow close to the fortress.

'A few days later, Iphitus, whose offer to go and search for the oxen had been accepted, met Hercules on the road to Tiryns. Iphitus had taken this route because he had been following what he correctly identified as the oxen's tracks which, much to his dismay, led towards Tiryns where he knew Hercules was living. On meeting Hercules, he politely enquired of him if he had seen the stolen animals and gave a description of them. Hercules did not recognise the description as applying to the animals he had bought and denied any knowledge of them. However, knowing that Iphitus had supported his right to Iole against his father, Hercules offered to help him look for the oxen. After several hours of fruitless searching, it was now late afternoon and Hercules suggested to a tired Iphitus that he accompany him back to Tiryns for a feast, an offer which Iphitus gladly accepted.

'About halfway through the meal, when the drink had loosened their tongues, Hercules began to realise that Iphitus suspected him of stealing the oxen. Throwing the table over, Hercules gripped Iphitus by the right arm, led to the citadel wall and stood him on the parapet where he would have a clear view of the pasturage where the oxen Hercules had acquired from

Autolycus were grazing. Disclosing that he now knew he was being accused as the thief, Hercules demanded of Iphitus that he look around him and identify the stolen beasts. Iphitus admitted that he could not see them and, in a rage, Hercules, shouting "Then you have accused me unjustly!" hurled Iphitus from the ramparts. He fell some sixty cubits to the ground and died instantly with a broken neck. Of course, a crowd gathered and I was called. Realising that Hercules was seriously drunk, and knowing something about the dispute with Eurytus, I guessed what had happened. After first making arrangements for Iphitus' body to be taken to a secure place, I hurried Hercules away to his quarters nearby.'

Iolaus paused and took a deep breath. The recollection of this tragedy was clearly very painful for him. I resisted the temptation to make some banal remark and kept silent. After what seemed a long time, he sighed, apologised and suggested that he call for some refreshments. While waiting a short while for this to arrive, Iolaus started talking about his business and the large cargo which was about to be unloaded.

'It will take two to three days for my people to check this consignment,' he said, 'so it has occurred to me that, if it is convenient for you, we could meet again over the next two days to give me time to tell you the rest of my story about Hercules. What do you think?'

'Splendid!' I responded. 'My workshop staff have enough work in hand to keep them busy for the next day or so without any need to consult me, and I heard this morning that the ship with my cargo is expected to arrive no earlier than two days' hence. It would therefore be very convenient for me to hear the remaining episodes in Hercules' personal history in the meantime – if you feel able to do so. By the way, the thief you mentioned – Autolycus – is that the same man whose daughter married Laertes, King of Ithaca, and who bore him Odysseus?'

'The very same,' he rejoined. 'Returning to my story… you must forgive my occasional moments of weakness. I really care about my uncle and his reputation. He was so talented and his basic nature was kind and gentle, but he loved wine, although it did not reciprocate his affection! I tried and succeeded many times in preventing him from drinking too much but I could not always be by his side. I was mortified by the Iphitus incident because I was in Tiryns at the time. I was aware that he had bought these oxen and I asked him their source but he gave me an evasive reply. This was not like him: he was usually very honest and straightforward with me, so I suspect he knew there was something wrong about them, although he did not know they had been stolen – he would never be knowingly involved in a casual theft. I am sure that he did not know until much later that these oxen had been stolen from Eurytus and that they were the animals being sought by Iphitus. When sober, he would have treated Iphitus as a friend because he knew that he had supported him against his own father. Unfortunately, when drunk and feeling the finger of suspicion was being pointed at him for a crime he did not believe he had committed, his reactions were always violent and totally predictable.'

'What happened next?' I enquired, hoping steer Iolaus back to the story. 'I imagine that you had to send a message to Eurytus to inform him that his son was dead and then talk to Hercules?'

'Yes,' replied Iolaus. 'But it was a little more complicated than that. First, the authorities had to be informed of the death and there were too many witnesses to avoid Hercules being implicated. I was given a day to get him sober and deliver him to the authorities to explain what had happened. At that stage, although Hercules had been seen to throw Iphitus down from the ramparts, it was not known why he did it. It did not take long for the whole story to emerge and for Hercules to be revealed as the innocent victim of a professional cheat. However, that did not excuse his killing of Iphitus. The oxen were returned to Eurytus and, in accordance with custom, Hercules was fined and required to do penance.

'But Hercules' troubles were only just beginning. Eurytus refused to accept any payment for the loss of his son. Although the payment was made, it does not appear to have reached Eurytus or his family. Nobody seems to know who got it. King Neleus of Pylos refused to sponsor Hercules' purification as Eurytus was a friend and neighbour. However, one of the King's sons, Nestor, supported Hercules' application. Although

King Neleus would not change his mind, he made it clear that he would not oppose his son sponsoring Hercules' purification elsewhere. Now Deiphobus, the grandson of Theseus, reigned in Sparta and was a friend of Nestor's. He was pleased to be able to give Hercules some repayment for the help he had given to his grandfather. The purification of Hercules in the temple of Apollo at Amyclaes in Sparta was soon arranged and executed.

'Hercules, however, was still in turmoil. I think Iphitus' family's refusal to accept the compensation upset him and prevented him from achieving closure on the third-most distressing event of his life. So, after taking advice, Hercules went to consult the Oracle at Delphi on what he should do to calm his spirit.

'I did not accompany him on that journey, so I can only tell you what he told me and what extra information I gleaned from those who went with him. All my sources agree that it was made clear to Hercules on arrival that he was not welcome and would neither be admitted into the sanctuary nor permitted to consult the Oracle. Hercules thought it significant that the Pythian, a woman priestess, appeared to be in charge. The priests of Apollo were nowhere to be seen, although it was usually they who controlled the access to the Sanctuary and the oracular processes. The Pythian was normally only involved in uttering the oracular response and did not generally come into direct contact with visitors. The main reason given by the Pythian for refusing Hercules access was because he was a murderer but, by this time, Hercules had complied with all the conditions laid down for purging him of the guilt of the murder: the payment of compensation and purification. Hercules thought there must be another reason for the blunt refusal. After some discussion of events on his return to Tiryns, Hercules and I concluded that either there was a political motive that we couldn't fathom or, more likely, the female Pythian, in the absence of her male superiors and aware of Hercules' recent anti-female cult activities, was taking some spiteful revenge on their behalf.

'The abrupt refusal gave rise later to stories that Hercules lost his temper and threatened the Pythian. As time passed, the stories became even more exaggeratedly pro-female and anti-male, which tended to support the conclusion to which we came on the underlying reason for the refusal. Hercules openly admitted to me that he did use strong words and was quite insulting to the Pythian but denied ever using any physical violence against her person or against the sanctuary itself. One of the later circulating stories suggested Hercules had attempted to carry away the sacred tripod and had only been prevented from doing so by Apollo himself! This was always denied by Hercules.

'His show of defiance did, however, produce an outcome. Hercules stayed overnight in the area and the next day received a message from the Chief Priest to call on him at the Sanctuary, which he did. This time, the Pythian was not to be seen – only the priests – who said that there had been a misunderstanding and he would be permitted to consult the Oracle, subject to the usual rituals being observed. On the completion of these, Hercules was led into the Sanctuary, where he heard the Pythian's response, which is unintelligible to all but the priests. The Oracle's decree was that Hercules had to be sold incognito as a slave for one year if he wished to purge his guilt. Without hesitation, he accepted the decision.

'On returning to Tiryns, Hercules was advised that he had been sold to Omphale, a queen of Lydia in Asia Minor. Two attendants from Delphi accompanied him there and accepted the agreed payment from Omphale, which was intended for Iphitus' dependents. But this, too, was declined by his family.

'When he returned to Greece over a year later, Hercules told me of his experiences in the service of Queen Omphale. He did not know how Omphale had heard of his availability – she never told him – and he was convinced that, at the beginning of his servitude, she did not know who he was. Her country was overrun by bandits and predatory and fierce wild animals. Her husband had been killed in circumstances that Omphale preferred not to talk about. Hercules subsequently learnt that her husband had lusted after a young priestess he had seen whilst out hunting in what have been renamed – in memory of him – the Tmolus Mountains, chased the priestess and assaulted her. She hanged herself in shame. To avenge her shame and death, her fellow priestesses chased him into a field where there was a wild bull, who gored him to death.

'Within weeks of his arrival in Lydia, Hercules had cleared most of the bandits out of the country. Those whom he had not killed fled the area. News of his exploits reached beyond Lydia and Omphale soon discovered the identity of her distinguished slave. Not surprisingly, Omphale was physically attracted to Hercules and, from the way he talked about her to me, he also found her attractive. When he sailed away, he certainly left behind him a broken heart and some permanent reminders! I have heard mention of several children and not all were born to Omphale. Hercules was understandably a little coy on this subject and I have had to rely on hearsay to some extent.

'There was one particular story about his stay in Lydia that surfaced some time after his return. This concerned an allegation that Hercules had worn women's clothes and did women's work. I asked Hercules about this and he thought it very amusing.

' "You know," he asked me, "that in Lydia they still cling to the matriarchal tradition?" I nodded. "Well," he continued, "this means that the regal authority rests with the queen and not the king. On occasion, however, the queen may want her consort to wield the regal authority and their traditions recognise this possibility. What happens is that the king puts on the queen's robes and is automatically invested with her authority to carry out state duties. One day, Omphale and I decided to make a dawn sacrifice at a temple of Dionysus some distance away from the palace close to the royal vineyards and pray for a bountiful crop. It was early in the season and we knew that one of the vineyard workers' huts would be empty so we planned to spend the night there.

' "At this time, Omphale was pregnant with our first son. Because it was not seemly for a pregnant woman to make this particular sacrifice, but it had to be carried out by the sovereign, we agreed to exchange clothes. As we wished to make the sacrifice at dawn, we decided to exchange clothes before we went to sleep – on separate couches so as not to impair the validity of the sacrifice – which we did.

' "Unknown to us, Omphale had a male admirer who had been following us all the way from the palace. I awoke in the middle of the night to find a strange male body in the bed with me. He had a beard so I knew it was a man. In the dark he had apparently identified the clothes I was wearing with Omphale and assumed it was she who was wearing them! At this stage, he was at the bottom of the bed. I gave him a mighty kick with my right foot, which propelled him out of the bed and across the room. He ended up embedded in the turf wall on the opposite side of the room where the impact dislodged some metal cooking pans, which fell on his head with a loud crash. The noise awoke Omphale, who called the servants who had accompanied us and were sleeping nearby to bring lights.

' "When we saw this poor fool spread-eagled on the floor, with cooking pans over him blinking in the light – and rubbing his badly bruised body – we and our servants could not help laughing uncontrollably. We all agreed that this was one of the funniest sights we had ever seen. The intruder limped outside while we were laughing at him and we decided to let him go. We never saw him again. I think he is the author of the various stories about my dressing up in women's clothes, which, of course, are completely untrue!" '

'Hercules was now fully restored to his former self-confidence and vitality. As I feared, his interlude in Lydia had given him time to think. He now had a strategy for "righting a number of wrongs": a visit to Troy to rescue Hesione and demand his prize horses from Laomedon and a punitive visit to King Augeas at Elis. A fearful dread crept over me when I heard his future plans.'

Troy

'You will recall that,' continued Iolaus, 'on returning from his limited participation in the Expedition by the Argonauts, Hercules passed by the city of Troy and rescued Hesione, the King's daughter, from a terrible fate. He also killed the monster that had been terrorising the country.

'Well, Hercules decided that his first task now that he was relieved of his, effectively, self-imposed servitude was to avenge the duplicity of King Laomedon and the citizens of Troy. He realised that he could not take on a whole city's population by himself alone, so he set about raising a small army of friends and supporters.

'Now, Troy and the Trojans were not very popular with many Greek sailors, particularly those who had sailed on cargo ships that had ventured into the waters near Troy. This was practically unavoidable if the ship was sailing between Thessaly – and anywhere north of there – and the eastern Mediterranean, including Egypt. The alternative routes via Crete or the islands were not really feasible for most voyages. Although the King and the ruling Council of Troy had agreed with their neighbours, including the High King of Mycenae, that they would suppress the pirates who infested their waters, they did not in fact do so. On the contrary, there was evidence that they encouraged the pirates in return for a share of the spoils. It was also believed that some of the "pirates" were actually Trojans and there was a strong rumour that at least one of them had a very close connection with the Trojan Royal Family.

'Consequently, when Hercules let it be known discreetly in the right quarters that he intended to sack Troy and avenge himself on the King for his perfidy in his personal dealings with him, he had little difficulty in raising a substantial force. I myself went on this expedition so I can vouch that many distinguished warriors were members of our force: Peleus, King of Thessaly –

the father of Achilles – and Telamon, his brother, King of the island of Salamis and father of Great Ajax were but two of the most illustrious to accompany Hercules. I must not forget to mention Oicleus, who later died nobly defending the beached fleet at Troy. All together, a formidable force of approaching one thousand warriors sailed in eighteen warships against Troy under the command of Hercules.

'In order to achieve an element of surprise, individual ships of the fleet sailed from different ports at different times. We did not meet as a fleet until we reached the island of Scyros where the King, Lycomedes, was a friend of Telamon, who guaranteed his confidential support for our venture. Lycomedes himself was no friend of the Trojans: he relied on supplies of necessities and luxuries – including the much-prized lapis lazuli – from the Blessed Sea and the East. These cargoes had to run the gauntlet of the Trojans and their allies and subjects who had colonised both sides of the Hellespont. Supplies that did get through frequently had an extortionate surcharge levied on them. Some disruption to the ruinous practices of the rapacious Trojans and their King would be as welcome to Lycomedes and his sailors as to the mainland Achaeans.

'Hercules' plan was to launch our attack from the island of Tenedos, which was some two hours sailing away from the shore by the walls of Troy. He suspected that there would be lookouts on the island who would have some means of signalling a warning of any emergency to guards on the walls of Troy itself. It was essential that these lookouts be disabled before they could send any message. As the arrival of a large fleet of longships (as warships were known to distinguish them from the smaller merchant ships) would indicate an imminent attack, it was agreed that Hercules would sail half a day in advance of the rest of the fleet so that, if the lookouts did spot us, they would think it was only one ship sailing towards them and might wait before alerting their colleagues on the mainland. There was a risk that our ship would be attacked by pirates, which could be more than an inconvenience. They would soon see that we were a warship and not an unarmed merchant ship and would probably not choose to pick a fight with a ship likely to be full of armed men and nothing much worth stealing.

'All went well. We arrived off the island of Tenedos in the small hours before dawn. The weather was calm but there was little moon. We saw no fires on shore and concluded that there might not be any lookouts awake on the side of the island facing us. This part of the coast faced southwest and the buffeting by the prevailing winds over many years ensured there were no obvious landing places – which was, presumably, why there were no lookouts. But, as always, Hercules had the answer. One of the crew he had selected for his ship knew the island well and directed us to a cove where we anchored offshore, close to beetling cliffs. The roar of the breakers hammering the rocks at the foot of the cliffs was so loud that we could hardly hear ourselves speak. But it would also prevent any sound of our arrival being heard.

'The sailor "guide", Hercules and three of the oarsmen threw a raft overboard and paddled to the base of the cliffs. As dawn was now breaking, we were able to follow their progress up what appeared to be a narrow track leading to the cliff summit. One of the men, who had been carrying the raft, stopped whilst the others cautiously went over the top and disappeared from sight. Within an hour, Hercules and the two men who had accompanied him reappeared and gave us the signal to sail into the island main harbour, where Hercules would meet us with his men and the raft. Hercules had calculated that the time he would need to complete his task of dealing with any lookouts and for us to sail round to the harbour would be close to the time it would need for the rest of our fleet to catch up with us. He was right. As we rounded the east point of the island on the run into the harbour, we could see, on the southerly horizon, several masts close together, which could only be our colleagues.

'On approaching the harbour, we saw nobody except Hercules and the three men who had accompanied him. As soon as they saw us, they launched the raft and paddled quickly out to come alongside. We hauled them in with the raft and immediately turned about towards Troy. By this time, the first of our fleet was close enough for us to signal to them that Hercules had dealt with the Tenedos lookouts and we proceeded undetected to beach the ships under the walls of Troy, where we disembarked, except for

Oicleus, who was directed to stay behind and guard the ships with two men while we quickly advanced on the city.

'We were soon spotted by the guards on the walls and curtain on the west side of the city. The alarm was raised, but it was clear that they had not had any warning of our approach until then. As we approached the city, we could hear the pandemonium within. Later we learnt that Laomedon had armed all the citizens to resist our attack whilst he led a group of them, armed with weapons and burning torches, to destroy our ships. Hercules ordered us back to the shore to protect our ships, but, had it not been for the bravery of Oicleus and his companions, we would not have got there in time. His stout resistance – to the death – enabled us to relaunch the ships and put them safely out of reach of the Trojans. Seeing that his stratagem had failed, Laomedon ordered his force back to the city and, despite having to fight his way through some of our force – who were too far away from the shore to help relaunch the ships – he managed to regain the main gate and return to the city.

'The ships were brought back to shore so that most of the force could be disembarked again. This time, several men were left aboard the ships, which were tied together in groups to make it easier for a few men to manoeuvre them and then moored offshore where the water was deeper than an average man's height.

'Now Telamon's father, Aeacus, had been involved in the reconstruction of the walls of Troy when Laomedon became King of what was then a desolated city. It was reputed that Neptune and Apollo were invoked by Laomedon to assist in this task on the promise of sacrificial offerings. Whilst most of the walls were built with divine assistance, Aeacus was assigned responsibility for that part of the wall known as the curtain on the west side. When it became clear that Laomedon was not going to pay him for his work – he also denied the gods their offerings – Aeacus introduced a hidden flaw in the construction of the curtain wall that meant it could be breached at that point without too much difficulty if you knew where the flaw was. Telamon had been told by his father about the flaw and how to breach the wall.

'I am not sure whether Hercules knew about this. Certainly he picked out the west wall as the place for the assault he now ordered and he allowed Telamon to take the lead. Then a strange thing happened. The night before the assault – it took us all day to assemble the equipment to stage the assault – I was awoken by a distant rumbling and the ground I was lying on moved. I jumped up in alarm and I heard a similar reaction from my colleagues who were nearby. "The gods are displeased with us," I heard someone say. I was not so sure. I accepted that the death of Oicleus was unfortunate, and could indicate the displeasure of the gods, but we had Neptune and Apollo on our side, surely? They would not be supporting the Trojans after the way they had been treated. There were no more rumblings or ground movements, so we all went back to rest until dawn, which was not long coming.

'As usual, when some violent action was about to take place, Hercules was busy bustling about, encouraging everyone to get ready so that he could start the assault on the walls of the city as soon as possible. As I have already said, Telamon led the way, straight to the west wall. I thought it looked a little different in the dawn light from what I had seen the previous day, but I could have been mistaken. Whatever Telamon knew about the construction of the wall, he certainly knew how to make a hole in it! Despite the attempts of the Trojans to stop his team working on the wall by dropping stones on his team, even boiling water, we ensured that they had an effective protective cover, harassed those on the walls above by shooting arrows at them and making diversionary assaults elsewhere so that the Trojans could not be sure where the main attack would be made.

'Much sooner than we had expected, Telamon and his team had made a large enough breach in the wall for us to enter the city. Hercules led the way with Telamon in close attendance. I believe that Hercules himself killed Laomedon and all his sons except Podarces, whom, he remembered, had protested his father's refusal to honour his promise to reward Hercules when he rescued Hesione and slew the sea serpent. The city was then put to the torch and the houses of the rich ransacked. I played my part in all this, but without much pleasure, and refused my share of the plunder.

'The women were spared but kept as captives, as is the custom, and Hesione was treated honourably. She pleaded for the freedom of her brother, Podarces, and this Hercules granted to her on condition that she ransomed him. She did so by giving her golden-threaded veil to Hercules. Thereafter, Podarces was always known as Priam, which means "bought" or "ransomed". Surprisingly, Hercules then appointed Priam King of Troy, an appointment he, even more surprisingly, accepted, considering the city was now a burning ruin. I suppose it looked a great deal worse than it really was but the walls and main buildings would take many years and much effort to rebuild and repair. Still, I must admire Priam and his citizens. They restored Troy to its former glory within a very short time. Hesione, herself now in Hercules' thrall, was offered to Telamon as his consort, which seemed at the time to be mutually acceptable. Sadly, they parted some years later, although Hesione bore Telamon two sons, Teucer and Trambelus. After he had re-established Troy as an important city, Priam swore that he would claim the return of his sister and made many unsuccessful attempts to do this. It became an unfortunate obsession, which reopened and kept alive the conflict with the Mycenaeans.'

Return to Elis

'Flushed with his success at Troy, Hercules was keen to raise a force to dispense a similar level of retribution on King Augeas of Elis. A few of those who had accompanied him to Troy also volunteered for this new expedition but Hercules raised most of his force from Tiryns and the neighbouring city states. It was about this time that I realised that Augeas was one of the Argonauts who had accompanied Jason on his quest to recover the Golden Fleece from Colchis on the eastern shore of the Blessed Sea to back his claim to the throne of the Thessalian city of Iolchos. He lacked neither courage nor friends, as we soon discovered!

'On this occasion, the intended victim, Augeas, was not unaware of Hercules' plans. Forewarned of the planned assault, he raised his own army and appointed his two nephews, Eurytus and Cteatus, as generals to organise the defence. Eurytus, too, had accompanied Jason on the *Argo*, and was an experienced warrior. Just as we were about to launch the campaign, Hercules was afflicted by a fever.

'By this time, we were already in Elis and, a few days after Hercules fell ill, we suffered a heavy defeat from Augeas' forces. Many of our warriors were killed, and my father, Iphicles, one of the hundreds seriously injured in the encounter, had to be carried off the battlefield. Although he survived for some time afterwards, he never fully recovered his health and died in my arms during one of my visits to him in Arcadia.' Iolaus paused.

As it was getting late, and we had already agreed to meet again the following day, I suggested that this might be a good point to suspend our discussion. I was also appreciative that Iolaus was no longer a young man and recollections of past events and old friends, now departed, could be emotionally very tiring for him. His appreciative glance at me when agreeing to a pause until we met tomorrow at mid-morning, told me that my instinct was right. Pausing only to thank him for his hospitality and his staff for the excellent refreshments they had brought, I said my farewell and hurried on home in the gathering gloom.

When we met on the following day, we greeted each other like the old friends we now were. Iolaus, with little preliminary, took up the story.

'I was telling you yesterday about our disastrous first assault on Elis. This was a rare defeat for Hercules but he was remarkably philosophical about it. He regretted the loss of life and injury among his supporters, but we assured him that we had all accepted there were risks in the enterprise, we were all volunteers and had to be prepared for whatever fate and the gods threw at us. While we were debating what to do, we were told that the Corinthians had ordered that the fighting should stop as the Isthmian Games were about to start. As you know, it was a tradition that, during the Games, all fighting should be suspended so that athletes from all states could participate in the Games without fear of assassination by their enemies.

'In fact, the calling of a halt suited us quite well: we had suffered a severe defeat, our leader, Hercules, was still not well and we needed to withdraw our shattered force. To be able to do so without the constant threat of ambushes or assault by the Elians and their allies was a great benefit. During our withdrawal, we learnt that king Neleus of Pylos had sent warriors to help the Elians. This angered Hercules and he vowed to avenge this as well as Neleus' previous refusal to purify him after he had thrown Iphitus from the walls of Tiryns because of his alliance with Iphitus' father.

'Our force then dispersed. Hercules and a few others, including me, travelled to Olenus, a port on the north coast of the Peloponnese where we were made very welcome by King Dexamenus, a long-time friend of Hercules, who disregarded his close relationship (by marriage) with the mother of the two generals Augeas had appointed to manage his army and repel that of Hercules. I suspected at the time that his actions reflected mainly his wish to secure Hercules as husband to his beautiful young daughter, Dejanira. As she was besieged by many admirers, her father had promised her hand in marriage to whoever was the strongest. The arrival of Hercules was timely, as the competitions to select the strongest suitor were about to commence. Hercules was, by this time, fully recovered from his malady and had no difficulty in winning the various competitions: archery, running and chariot driving, I recall. The hand of Dejanira was awarded to Hercules by her father, who arranged a lavish marriage celebration. Both then and later, I was aware of a strong affection between them. It was very sad that it should all end so tragically several years later.

'Hercules now took his new bride to Tiryns, whilst I travelled to Pheneus in Arcadia to see my father, who was resting there recovering from his wounds. On my arrival, I was distressed to find him weak and despondent, but, by the third day of my visit, he had recovered some of his old optimism. I was pleased at his positive reaction and when, a few days later, Hercules arrived, accompanied by his bride and his mother, Alcmena, with his latest plan, I had no hesitation in leaving my father in the good hands of those around him. He was, of course, very pleased to see his mother, who would ensure that he was well looked after.

'I understood from Hercules that his sudden arrival was partly a direct result of the actions of King Eurystheus, who had accused Hercules of trying to mastermind a coup to depose him and take the throne for himself. He would not listen to Hercules' denials and, with the support of the Council, ordered him out of the whole area of Argolis, which meant that he could not reside in his home city, Tiryns. Hercules explained that he had brought Alcmena so that she could visit her son, my father, and be companion to Dejanira while he was away on campaign. He had heard that the Elians had decided to attend the Isthmian Games at Corinth and were at this moment preparing to go there. They would be passing nearby, as their route would take them through Arcadia on their journey to Corinth, and there should be good opportunities to ambush them at some point.'

'But what about the ban on such action during the Games?' I asked. 'Surely, an attack would be in breach of this?'

'I asked Hercules the same question,' Iolaus responded. 'His reply was ingenious, I must say, and, as subsequent events proved, accurate: "By the time the Elians get within my grasp, the competitions at the Games will be over," he said. "They are only intending to attend the religious ceremonies at the close of the Games. The ban on fighting only applies to the competitions: no state at war can send competitors to the Games, so the tradition is that all wars are suspended during the competitions. The religious ceremonies are separate. In addition, as I have been banned from my country, I am officially stateless and therefore not bound by the rules."

'I protested that I still thought the embargo on military activity should still apply, but others, more knowledgeable about such matters than I, agreed with Hercules' interpretation. As time was short, I dropped my argument.

'It was not difficult to agree on the best place for an ambush: the Elians would have a number of choices on which was the best route from Elis to the border of Argos, which was to the east of where we were. By the time they reached Nemaea, a town that had good reason to be grateful to Hercules as he had killed the fierce Nemaean Lion, the mountains around forced them to follow the road through Cleonae. It was there that we laid our trap. This time we were successful: Augeas and his two generals were killed along with many of his warriors. The remnants we rounded up and took them back in chains to Elis.

'When we reached Elis with the prisoners and a sizeable force, Hercules consulted those of the Council who dared meet him, and agreed with them that, providing they would grant him reasonable spoils of war for the insulting behaviour of their King, and accept Phyleus, Augeas' son, as the new King, he would release the captives and leave. They readily agreed to this and immediately sent a herald to Dulichium to tell Phyleus that his father was dead and that the people wished him to return to Elis as their rightful King. Hercules sent a personal message, too, to reassure Phyleus that it was not a trap. Hercules had made it clear that he and his force would stay until Phyleus had returned and wished him to go.

'In the meantime, his warriors needed accommodation whilst he, I and the senior warriors took rooms in the palace. Obviously, some of our men were offered accommodation by the newly widowed wives of the Elian warriors. This gave rise to a story that Hercules suggested to the widows that, in order to repopulate the city after the heavy loss of life in the battle, they each select one of his force to take to bed. What happened was that, as we were in residence for some time, friendships did develop between some of the widows and members of our force, particularly those who had no existing attachments. Most of these became permanent relationships. When we finally left, being sped on our way by a grateful Phyleus, our force was less than half the size it had been when we arrived! As Hercules remarked to Phyleus when the level of this affiliation became clear: "You have a group there who will be loyal to you, and I suggest that you employ the best of them as personal bodyguards" – which is what he did.'

'The Elians may have compromised with Hercules, but I heard their allies were not so happy,' I interjected.

'You mean Molione, the mother of the two generals?' Iolaus queried.

'Yes,' I said. 'I heard that she complained to Eurystheus and demanded compensation from him for the loss of her two sons, who were not, in fact, Elians. I presume they got a brusque answer?'

Iolaus laughed. 'Yes. I heard Eurystheus denied all responsibility for the actions of Hercules and pointed out that he had banished him some time previously. And there the matter might have rested but Molione decided to take the matter further and approached the Corinthians for support, claiming that the ambush at Cleonae was illegal as it took place during the Games, that Eurystheus had wrongly denied liability for the payment of compensation and that the Argives should be banned from attending the Isthmian Games in future until the dispute was resolved to her satisfaction. Of course, you know that the Isthmian Games is one of the most important and prestigious in the whole of Greece, so it would have been a serious blow to Eurystheus' prestige if Molione's plea had been successful – which it wasn't. The Corinthians were not going to alienate one of the most important kings in Greece because two adventurers had lost their gamble with fate!

'When negotiating with the Council at Elis, Hercules had

indicated that after giving his warriors a modest share of the spoils agreed with the Council, he would dedicate the remainder to Zeus at Olympia and establish there a four-yearly festival of Games and religious observance. As you know, Olympia is not far from Elis and, as soon as Phyleus was reasonably settled, Hercules and a group of us visited Olympia to mark out the ground for the various facilities and temples so that work could begin as soon as possible.

'Olympia is a magical place. I can well understand why Hercules chose it as the site for his temple to Zeus and the location for celebratory Games. Of course, the site had bewitched others before Hercules, although, by the time Hercules became seriously interested in developing it, only vestigial remains of the earlier attempts were visible: a few holes in the ground where wooden posts had been were the most obvious signs.

'As soon as we arrived there, Hercules and I stood on the southern slopes of a wooded hill, which Hercules said was called the Kronion, after the great king of the gods, Kronos, who was overthrown by Zeus. When I asked him why he used the name of the past king of the gods, he said that it was not his name for it – it was the name already attributed to it by the previous developers of the site. Indeed, looking more carefully at the ground beneath our feet, I could see traces of a stone building and, scraping away the earth, I quickly uncovered a primitive terracotta figurine that Hercules thought could be several hundred years old.

'But Hercules was not interested in the past – only in the future and his vision of it. Despite the evidence that the earlier developers had kept close to the slopes of the Kronion, presumably for protection from unwelcome visitors – the north winds and flood waters from the two rivers (which met south of the flat site in front of us) – Hercules wanted his Olympia to spread over the plain.

'His enthusiasm was infectious. He soon had us marking out sites for a magnificent temple to Zeus, an almost as imposing one for his consort and Hercules' nominal patron, Hera, a running track, facilities for the athletes and the officials and, of course, for the priests and priestesses who would serve the two temples. Some say that he founded the Olympic Games at this time and participated that year in the first of those Games. Although that is not strictly correct, it is true that he communicated the idea of the Olympic Games during that visit and initiated the preparations for them. It was not until the following year's summer that the inaugural games were held on what was, by any standards, really a building site. Having entrusted his plans and the spoils from Elis to a man he had appointed to supervise the work, Hercules and our group left for the port of Cyllene, a naval station on the west coast of Elis facing towards the islands of Samos and Ithaca – not the inland Arcadian mountain and village of the same name that was the reputed birthplace of Hermes, the messenger of the gods.'

Pylos

'On arrival at Olympia, we met the rest of the force to accompany us to Pylos. Whilst we were at Olympia, they had made their leisurely way to Cyllene and, as requested by Hercules, had made arrangements to buy provisions for our next expedition and secure transportation. We learnt that we were much indebted to Phyleus, who had built up very friendly relations with the authorities at Cyllene whilst in voluntary exile on the island of Dulichium in the Ionian Sea, which traded with the mainland mainly through Cyllene.'

At this point, Iolaus paused and I could see that he was rather uncomfortable about the next part of the story. He soon explained his reticence.

'By this time, I had become rather sickened by all the killing. Neleus' refusal to purify Hercules at his request was based on his local alliances, as was his support for King Augeas. The Elians considered themselves at this time rather superior to the Pylians and were quick to take offence. They had the resources to make Neleus' life very difficult. Although his palace was protected against attack from the sea – the palace was built at the top of a steep slope leading down to the port and the shore – there were no defences on any of the three landward sides. The palace had been designed and built by Cretans following the Minoan pattern, where land-based attacks by your neighbours were very rare, and you only normally needed protection from a pirate raid, which would always come from the sea. Even allowing for that, I have always believed that the Pylians were dangerously complacent and the sudden, but surely not unexpected, attack by Hercules proved my point.

'Anyway, I told Hercules what I felt and reminded him that one of Neleus' sons, Nestor, had supported his request for his father to purify him and should therefore be spared. As it happened, Nestor was away in Laconia when Hercules' force attacked Pylos and was not involved.

'Hercules could not conceal his disappointment that I did not want to accompany him to Pylos but graciously suggested that I travel with the party to the point of disembarkation at which point, if I still wished to return to Thebes, I was free to do so. He would sound out a few others who might like to accompany me. They would provide me with some protection. I was grateful for his concern and my gratitude mollified his temper, so that, when we arrived at our destination and I reiterated my request to leave, he was extremely pleasant about it and, as he had promised, provided me with a sturdy and sizeable band of warriors to accompany me home.

'This means, of course, that I cannot tell you much about what happened at Pylos. I certainly cannot give you an eye-witness account! Hercules later gave me a brief account, partly, I suspect, because he wanted my approbation. Neleus himself had not been killed, but allowed to abdicate in favour of the only son left alive after the slaughter, Nestor. Apparently, he returned just as Neleus surrendered his palace. This was fortunate because Hercules and his party had not started to ransack the palace and its surrounds. My views about this expedition were well known. The spoils already taken from Elis had been substantial so in the end the men were satisfied with that. They neither needed nor wanted any more to carry home! I like to think they remembered what I had said and I think Hercules would have found it difficult to justify burning the palace when he had only just agreed with Neleus that he should withdraw in favour of Nestor – and Nestor had just arrived fortuitously to accept his heritage.

'So, although most of the stories about the campaign say that Hercules burnt the palace to the ground, this did not actually happen. I do know that Nestor built a magnificent new palace alongside the old one, so that Neleus' original palace became just a wing of the whole complex. I believe the old palace is now mainly used to house visitors. It retains most of the original features, such as a banqueting hall and an impressive reception area.

'Hercules did not tell me that a firm friendship had developed between himself and Nestor, although this soon came to my attention. I suppose Hercules was reluctant to tell me in case I was upset by it. I was more than happy to rely on my kinship with Hercules as the foundation for our relationship – I did not want more.

'It was about this time that the whole of the area known as Messenia, including its main city, Messini, also called Ithome, came under the authority of Nestor. It was rumoured that Hercules had given it to him. This was probably true. The acquisition enabled Nestor to become a very rich man and able to afford the very best craftsmen to build and adorn his new palace. He also developed some fine stables and well-trained horses, for which he became famous.'

Sparta and at Home in Calydon

'The next expedition for Hercules was to restore his friend, Tyndarus, to the throne of Sparta. Tyndarus had been driven out some years earlier by his own brother Hippocoon. By this time, the army he had gathered together for his expeditions to Elis and Pylos were dispersed and the warriors had returned home. Hercules therefore had to raise a new army for his assault on Sparta. This did not prove difficult: there were a number of cities, and their rulers, who had good reason to wish ill on the Spartans, and particularly their present usurping King. One of the closest of their neighbours, who had suffered much at their hands in the past, were the Tegeans, whose city of Tegea was one of the most important in Arcadia. Their King, Cepheus, and his twelve sons, were enjoined by Hercules to join him in an assault on Sparta. To Hercules' surprise, they were not at first willing to enlist, but, after Hercules had given Cepheus' daughter a charm, with instruction on how to use it to scare off any who attacked the city while her father and brothers were away on campaign, they reluctantly agreed.

'Although the attack was successful, and Hercules' force suffered few casualties, Cepheus and all his sons were killed in the battle. Hippocoon and all his sons were killed and Tyndarus was restored to his throne.'

'Tyndarus married Leda, did he not – and Leda was the mother of Castor, Pollux, Helen and Clytemnestra?' I interjected.

'Quite right,' Iolaus responded. 'Helen later inherited the crown of Sparta through her father, Tyndarus, and her sister married Helen's husband's brother, Agamemnon, who was the eldest son of Atreus, the rightful King of Mycenae. But that was some years after the period we have been discussing. However, your question does emphasise the importance of what Hercules did. The effects of many of his actions lasted for several generations.

'It was now time for Hercules to abandon his wandering life and return to his new wife, Dejanira. Over the next few years, I saw little of Hercules. What I heard about him did not encourage me to seek him out. Whilst I could understand his frustration in not having a kingdom of his own, his father-in-law Dexamenus, King of Olenus, and the King and citizens of Calydon in Aetolia, where he now lived with his wife and family, treated him as a hero and he wanted for nothing.'

'What rumours did you hear about him?' I enquired.

Iolaus frowned. 'Oh, the usual ones about Hercules striking people in his cups and killing them with a single blow. Sometimes, the storytellers really let their imaginations go: in one story I heard, Hercules (sober this time) had raised a finger to admonish a servant and accidentally caught him on the temple. The blow is supposed to have killed the servant instantly!

'Hearing these stories, I was becoming very concerned about his well-being and managed to secure an invitation from his father-in-law to join him in a visit to Calydon to see his daughter and grandchild. I knew that Hercules was likely to be there, and I was keen also to see his young son, Hyllus, who had been born to Dejanira some time earlier.

'I was made very welcome by Oeneus and Dejanira – Hercules was out hunting. He had been told that I had been invited and the news had met with a somewhat mixed reaction from Hercules. I wondered if his absence was an indication of his disapproval of my visit, possibly because I had not asked him first. In fact, when we later met, after some awkward first few moments, he seemed genuinely pleased to see me. When we sat down to eat, he told amusing stories of some of our adventures together, seeming (to me, who knew the facts better than the rest of his audience) to exaggerate in my favour my modest contributions to his various successes, particularly when on his now-famous Labours.

'It was in his telling of these stories from the past that I detected a restlessness in him. I had suspected this was what I would find. He was a wanderer and always would be. He would never settle for long to a normal domestic life, especially one without challenging responsibilities. And here I also became aware of Oeneus' ambivalence in his attitude towards Hercules. You could see that he admired him and was proud to have such a distinguished son-in-law. But he was also afraid of him, as a potential rival. Hercules, I soon found out, was more popular than the King. He was also more visible. The King, who had endured the ignominy of being thrown out of his kingdom by his own brother's sons and had only been restored to his throne by his grandson Diomedes after several years of exile, visibly lived in fear and rarely was seen in public.

'This was a double tragedy. The people much preferred him to his brother's sons, who had ruled them with a ferocity they did not care to recall, whereas Oeneus was generous and kind and, more importantly, just. Whereas his brother's sons had allowed those of wealth and importance to behave as they liked, unchecked, Oeneus punished those who broke the law and protected those who were, unjustly, oppressed by others – whatever their respective status. However, his aloofness deprived him of the knowledge of the public's respect for him and, although his council tried to keep him informed of the citizens' high regard for him, he did not believe it in his heart to be true. This fed his natural melancholy and, a few years later, oppressed by this, he abdicated in favour of his son-in-law, Andremon. Oeneus sadly died on his subsequent journey to Argos a short time later.

'I think Oeneus was also disappointed in Hercules' disinterest in matters of government. He may have hoped that Hercules' marriage to his friend Dexamenus' daughter would awake some latent interest in Hercules in government, but it clearly did not. I was not surprised. Hercules was a man who liked to be doing things physical. He was as shrewd a man as I ever met in judging the character of men (although not so with most women) and was famous for his impartiality. If he could have tamed his temper, he would have made a good ruler. Most of those who knew him, including me, thought that, as he grew into middle age, he would mature and become wiser. Sadly, he did not, although, as you will hear, his life was cut short before its natural end. And so, Oeneus wisely abandoned his original idea of regarding Hercules as a possible successor.

'Sensing most of this, my time at the court of Oeneus was

therefore rather unsettling. Nevertheless, I had some memorable moments: Hyllus, barely a year old, was enchanting and he and I, over the years, became great friends, as I shall tell. Dejanira was besotted with Hercules, who loved her too in his own way. I felt she was too forgiving, but that was her nature.'

Assault on Ephyre

'I managed to have a little time alone with Hercules. It was as I had feared. He was bored. After some hesitation, he told me, in confidence, of a plan he was developing to raise an army of Calydonians and attack a neighbouring city. They had supported the usurpation of Oeneus by his nephews. With little persuasion, he offered the name of the city: Ephyre in Thesprotia, ruled over by King Phylas, who himself had commanded a force supporting the insurrection against Oeneus and had, with his troops, been involved in atrocities against loyal Calydonians. He must have thought, after several years had passed, his kingdom being several days' march north-west of Calydon across many independent territories, the Calydonians would not dare – or bother – to take revenge. How wrong he was!

'Rather against my better judgment, I allowed Hercules to talk me into accompanying him on the expedition. I know – I was a fool! But I wanted to make my own judgment on what was likely to be best for Hercules and I felt that he would only really be himself on campaign, not in a palace surrounded by servants and his wife and son.

'As I had expected, as soon as we started on the preparations for the expedition, Hercules was a changed man. Vitality replaced the lethargy I had earlier noticed and the spark returned to his eyes. His good humour came back, too, and we soon resumed the conspiratorial relationship we had enjoyed all those years ago in my youth.

'There were two main tasks: to determine how we were going to reach Ephyre and how many men we would need. The latter would determine the amount of equipment and supplies we would need to purchase and would also affect the former, to which there were two aspects. A large force could not easily traverse through the independent states that lay on whichever land route we took from Calydon to our destination. If we went by sea, we would be constricted by the size of the fleet we could hire and the capacity of the ships. Capacity would affect not only the number of warriors (who would also need some sea-going experience) but the amount of supplies we could take with us. After seeking the advice of King Oeneus' Chief Steward and Dejanira, we concluded that it was not feasible to take any of the possible land routes. Whichever route we took, we would have to cross territory where the rulers were on at least friendly terms with the ruler and people of Ephyre. Even if we received permission to traverse their territory, the size of our force would indicate that it was a punitive expedition and any request for passage would ignite immediate speculation on what was our objective. The news of our activity would quickly reach Ephyre and any element of surprise would be lost.

'We accordingly concluded that the better prospect was to go by sea. This was a relatively easy option because Calydon was on a navigable river, the Evenus, which flowed into the sea at the mouth of the Gulf of Corinth, less than one hundred stadia down stream. Ephyre itself was close to the sea coast, on a navigable tributary of the River Acheron. We would have the choice of disembarking at or near the mouth of the River Acheron, or sailing upriver and disembarking closer to our target. An advantage was that we could make the choice when we arrived, not before we embarked. We also made another early decision. The boats we would use would be purchased and manned by sailors we selected. By doing this, we avoided having to give the boat owners or the sailors any guarantees and would have the boats available for a swift withdrawal if our campaign was unsuccessful. This strategy would also limit the number of those knowing where we were going. If we hired the boats, the owners would want to know this information and we could not give it without risking our lives.

'Hercules decided that a force of 200 men would be sufficient, which, assuming the warriors would take regular turns at the oars, meant that we could carry them in six longships with a professional crew of some fifteen to twenty men on each boat. Although we would not expect the sailors to fight, they would be required to guard the ships and could assist the warriors in an emergency.

'Hercules' reputation ensured a flood of applications for both warrior and sailor vacancies. We were able to recruit some very experienced fighting men who, like Hercules, only felt really alive when fighting and could not settle down to ordinary life. The quality of leadership we found was so high that Hercules had no difficulty in choosing six outstanding captains, one of whom could be put in charge of each ship. The responsibilities of each captain included the procurement of a longship and the selection of the crew and the warriors to sail in it. This left Hercules only the task of finding the funding for the ships and organising and funding the supplies. To ensure nothing was overlooked, he asked each captain to appoint a deputy, who formed a group to list all the equipment and food they would require. At this stage, only the captains and their deputies were told of our destination. The remainder of the force were only told when we were at sea.

'I observed to Hercules on their lack of interest on the destination. He responded by commenting dryly: "Well, they just want to fight and share the spoils!" That summed it all up perfectly.

'At about this time, I started to encourage Hercules to think about his future life. I thought it unlikely that he would ever settle down to a normal family life and he was not suitable for kingship – which he didn't want it anyway. After a certain amount of bluster, he did agree finally that I was right and he shouldn't just drift from one situation to the next. When we were a day or two into our voyage, I suddenly had what I (and Hercules) thought was a brilliant idea. Hercules would consult the Oracle at Dodona and ask them for advice on what to do.

'Now, the Oracle of Ammon-Zeus at Dodona was established long before that at Delphi and was no further than 300 stadia from where we were going. With chariots and a light accompanying force of armed horsemen, it would be possible to make the return journey from Ephyre to Dodona in a maximum of three – possibly two – days. The terrain was mountainous but we had little doubt that the road to Dodona would be reasonably good and we should be able to make good time. As a regular route, it would probably be reasonably free of bandits, but we would need to take a strong armed guard for our security. With this decision made, Hercules selected the fifteen men to accompany us, who were all good horsemen, and we counted on being able to "liberate" a chariot or two at Ephyre with horses, if required, to add to the two chariots we had brought with us. But first we would have to win the forthcoming battle.

'We arrived off the coast near the mouth of the River Acheron late in the evening, having halted two days previously at a remote spot to exercise the horses and the troops on board to ensure everyone was fit and ready for the onslaught on Ephyre. At that point, we had sent a small group of heavily armed men, with the chariots and horses, along the coast so that they would reach the river before we got there. Their instructions were to find out if there were any manned guard posts along the coastline that could give warning of the arrival of our fleet and disable them.

'As we approached the river mouth, we identified a previously agreed signal from our shore party that indicated either that they had found nothing or that they had neutralised it without triggering an alarm. One of our fleet pulled close to the shore and some of the party came aboard. After a brief discussion with Hercules, the men returned to the shore and Hercules announced that they would move cautiously up the Acheron to the junction with the tributary on which Ephyre stood, clearing any lookouts as they went. They would then wait for us there as they would need help to cross the Acheron at that point. The tributary joined the Acheron on the right bank and they were on the left.

'Our fleet of six longships moved slowly up the river, helped by a slight favourable tidal current and a brisk westerly wind – sent by the gods, we believed – which enabled us to use our sails as the main source of power. On the rare occasions when we needed to use the oars, they were carefully muffled with cloth so that little sound could be heard on shore. We sailed in single file, well spaced apart, but with each ship linked by a light rope to the next to ensure we kept together, hugging the left bank so closely that we could occasionally hear the muffled clatter of the horses' harnesses. I have to admit, even now, that I felt the excitement of it all: the physical challenges of unexpected events and the accompanying camaraderie that added to the intoxication of the adventure. I could well understand that some who had experienced this way of life found it very difficult to give it up. But, I knew that destruction can be wrought in a moment, creates great hardship and the damage can take years to repair. Sometimes it is never repaired. Lives lost can never be recovered. Is this what the gods want? Is this what we want?

'Soon we reached the junction of the two rivers. The first ship turned up the tributary, called the Cocytus, and anchored on the left bank at a convenient point. The others anchored close to the left bank of the Acheron, the first two quietly embarking the land party, excluding the chariots and horses, who went up stream to a place where they understood they could wade across the river. This they did and we soon learnt that they had met up with the first ship. By that time, another land party had been ferried to the right bank of the Acheron and made their way up the Cocytus opposite to where the first ship was anchored. Hercules now had to decide whether or not to disembark at this point or ease the ships upstream and disembark later. The moon was due to rise in a short while and, although the sails were down – and would remain down – the ships would be easily visible from the shore and the only quiet way of easing the ships up stream was for men on shore to haul them using ropes. Hercules rejected this because it would tire the men out and take too long.

'The decision was taken to disembark the majority of the warriors. The crew, assisted by two warriors on each ship, were instructed to turn the ships around and wait in the middle of the Acheron channel for our return. As the tributary was quite wide, it was decided to transport the chariots and horses to the right bank so that they could assist in the assault. It was not thought likely that any opposing force on the left bank would have any influence on the outcome of our imminent assault. However, before the chariots were transported or the majority disembarked, the land party scouted upstream almost to the city walls to check and eliminate any outposts there might be. We soon had a report that there were no manned outposts, although there did appear to be guards on duty at the city gates, which, amazingly, were open. Open fires could be seen through the gates and a few armed men could be seen walking about.

'This was all reported to Hercules, who immediately ordered the fleet to pull over to the right bank of the Cocytus and disembark the warriors. With some difficulty, the chariots were loaded on to the first ship, the horses on to the second, and thus the chariots and horses and all the warriors assembled on the right bank and advanced quietly to the city gates.

'As we attacked through the open gates, the moon came out, which made our task the easier. The attack came as a complete surprise and, within a very short time, King Phylas and many of his soldiers lay dead or wounded. We suffered only a few minor casualties. The city elders surrendered the city and our warriors took their rewards. Hercules' "prize" was King Phylas' daughter, Astyochia, by whom he fathered a son, Tlepolemus, who later became a king in Rhodes.'

Dodona

'Hercules made arrangements for the city of Ephyre to be governed. One of the captains we had brought with us, with some of the men he had enlisted, undertook to recruit from those in the city and train them as new guards to replace those killed. When all the details had been settled, I reminded Hercules of our plan to visit the Oracle at Dodona.

'We quickly assembled a small group of warriors, who were supplied with horses, but took only one chariot. I resumed my old position as charioteer to Hercules. Less than seven days after we had captured Ephyre, we clattered out of the city through the gate we had entered and went swiftly on our way to Dodona. Before we left, we had discovered that the best route to Dodona was to follow the track upstream alongside the right bank of the river Acheron. The alternative route would take us to the west and would involve us crossing a range of mountains. This we would avoid if we followed the Acheron to its source, which was not far away from Dodona.

'First we had to cross the Cocytus. We were directed a short distance upstream from the city and found the indicated crossing, where we had no difficulty in fording the river. We then followed a track due east, which brought us to the walls of Pandosia, on the right bank of the Acheron. We avoided the city and circled to the north, soon finding the track running north to Dodona, which we reached well before midday.

'Dodona, I found, was a beautiful, peaceful place. I suppose this was partly because of the contrast with the blood-stained and restless place of tragedy I had just left. But Hercules felt it, too, and so did some of the warriors we had brought with us. So it can't have just been my imagination.' He paused here to order us some refreshment.

'I have never been there,' I said, trying to contribute, 'but I have heard about it. The word "simplicity" is one I associate with

Dodona, but I have never had a satisfactory explanation. Can you tell me what impressed you most about it?'

'Certainly,' responded Iolaus. 'First, the location. The sacred grove lies in the middle of a long, fertile valley, protected to the north by an impressive mountain range, the main part of which is crowned with the double peak of Mount Tomaros. The sacred site is surrounded by growing crops of corn and lush, grassy meadows grazed by flocks of goats and herds of shambling cattle. Until you are close to the sanctuarial grove, you cannot tell where its boundaries are – indeed there seem to be none as the goats wander into the sacred grove apparently at will. This blending of every day life with the supernatural emanates an unbelievable tranquillity.

'Secondly, there are virtually no buildings. The sacred place is a grove of trees with only a simple sacrificial stone altar in the middle by the sacred oak tree. The only indication that you are looking at the sacred tree (there are other oak trees in the grove) is that this particular one is surrounded by a circle of small bronze cauldrons on tripods. Those and the altar identify the location of this sacred place.

'To get back to my story, by this time we had reached the edge of the sacred grove. A tall man, dressed in a flowing white robe but with no shoes on his feet, emerged from the grove and politely enquired as to our business there. I stayed in the background while Hercules explained to the priest that the reason for his visit was to consult the Oracle. On hearing what Hercules' enquiry was – his future – the priest indicated that he should return at dawn the following day, alone.

'We retired to join our colleagues and break the news to them that, as we had expected, we would not be starting our return to Ephyre until late the following day. We then set about finding ourselves a sheltered spot to erect the tents we had brought with us. It was clear from the many makeshift stone walls close to the grove that visitors were expected to see to their own arrangements. Unlike the other religious sanctuaries I had visited, there was no army of leeches offering you services you didn't want and expecting you to pay ridiculous prices for necessities, like water and kindling. We understood that the priest, and his predecessors, had made it clear many years ago that the sacred site was not to be contaminated by such activities. Fresh water was available from a number of springs nearby, as was enough wood to light a fire for warmth or cooking.

'I ensured that Hercules was ready well before dawn and accompanied him to the edge of the grove, where I left him. On his return some hours later, he told me what had happened.

'When he arrived, three priestesses met him and led him to an area beyond the grove, towards the mountains. Here there was a shady pool fed by a bubbling spring. Hercules was required to strip except for a loincloth and immerse himself fully in the water. One of the priestesses gave his head a little push downwards to ensure that his body was totally covered! He was then led out by the same priestess to where the other two were waiting to dry him with soft linen cloths. When he was completely dry, he was led, barefoot, back to the grove where the priest was waiting for him. The priest then took him to the altar in front of the sanctuary, where a tethered goat was waiting, which the priest expertly despatched on the altar, the blood draining into grooves in the altar that then fed into four small bronze cauldrons. Moving to the sanctuary, the priest placed each of the four cauldrons, into which the goat's blood had poured, on an empty tripod, so that the circle around the sacred oak was now complete. With Hercules standing immediately behind him, the priest, facing the oak tree but outside the circle of cauldrons, struck one cauldron a sharp blow with a stout cane. This sent a vibration around the circle that, so I understand, will continue indefinitely until it is stopped by something interrupting the passage of the vibration.

'After the vibrations had circled the cauldrons several times – Hercules detecting the different sounds of the cauldrons holding the goat's blood from the other, presumably empty, ones – the priest motioned to Hercules to stand in front of him and, at his signal, touch a cauldron and stop the vibration's passage. At that moment, the leaves of the oak tree shivered with a whispering rustle. Hercules admitted to being very impressed.

'Following a brief prayer, made facing the altar but with his back to the sacred oak, the priest then led Hercules away to where the priestesses were waiting with his clothes. When fully dressed, he joined the priest who was sitting on a stone bench, near the sacred pool where Hercules had been purified earlier. The priest invited Hercules to sit down next to him and explained what the message from the Oracle had been.

'Hercules wouldn't tell me what future the Oracle saw for him, but it had given him a message that affected me. The Oracle foresaw a difficult and dangerous time for all those descended from or related to Hercules himself after his death. I gathered this would not be long delayed, although Hercules seemed to think it was a distant prospect – certainly his actions after our return to Calydon indicated this.'

'But what did the Oracle forecast for you?' I blurted out before I could stop myself.

Iolaus laughed. 'Well, after warning of tough times ahead, which I and the fifty sons Hercules had by the daughters of Thespius would survive, the Oracle said that I should take them to Sardinia and found new colonies there. On our return to Calydon, I realised that I could do little more to help Hercules, particularly as he wouldn't – or felt he couldn't – tell me what the Oracle had said about his own future. And so, accompanied by a message from Hercules, I set out on the journey back to Thespiae to see King Thespius. I arranged to pass through there on my way to Thebes, which is the closest main city.

'I was courteously received by the King, and met the sons of Hercules. They, and their mothers, were dismayed by the message I brought from Hercules, which was not in fact quite the same as he had told me. The Oracle had decreed that three sons should go to Thebes, seven stay in Thespiae, and the remaining forty go with me to Sardinia. As the sons were still very young, I suggested that, as the Oracle had not specified when we should go, we should defer any migration at least while Hercules was alive. This was agreed and, after a short stay, I moved on to Thebes.'

Moving On

'I can tell you little of Hercules' activities over the next few years, as I was not involved personally,' said Iolaus. 'What I do know is that he settled down for a few years at Calydon with his wife, Dejanira, and their son, Hyllus, and I understand that he enjoyed being with them as Hyllus grew up. He particularly favoured his eldest son, Hyllus, and they grew very close. As Hyllus approached maturity, he wanted to travel with his father and, much as I had done before him, he became, at a very young age, Hercules' companion on his expeditions. It was from him I heard about Hercules' death, as he witnessed it.

'However, before we come to that, I can tell you that, after a long (for him) period of quietude, he was prey to his demons again and after accidentally killing one of King Oeneus' servants he decided he had best leave Calydon on voluntary exile. On his way to Trachis, which is some 450 stadia to the north-west of Thebes, he and his family had to cross the River Evenus, which was in full spate with the spring rains. Hercules carried his son across the river on his back and, leaving his club and bow and arrows with Hyllus on the far bank, swam back for Dejanira. As he reached it, the centaur, Nessus, arrived and, claiming to be the local ferryman, offered to ferry Dejanira across the swollen river.

'Hercules accepted and was already more than halfway across when he heard the screams of his wife as Nessus tried to rape her. Reaching the far bank, Hercules retrieved his bow and, arming it with one of his poisoned arrows, aimed and fired it at the recumbent Nessus, who must have been well over two stadia away. On being struck in the middle of the back by the arrow, he fell to the ground bleeding profusely from the wound. With his dying breath, he told the recovering Dejanira to remove his blood-soaked tunic and keep it in a safe place, observing that his blood had the power of reclaiming a husband from other women. Dejanira did as Nessus had suggested and concealed what she had done from Hercules. Unknown to her, of course, Nessus' blood was contaminated with the poison from Hercules' arrow.

'Hercules and his family, after no more alarms, eventually arrived at Trachis, where King Ceyx gave them a warm welcome and promised to assist Hercules' purification from the, now, two killings he had made: that of the servant at Calydon and the more recent one of Nessus. This was accomplished and Hercules and his family remained at Trachis for a number of years. Two further children were born to Hercules by Dejanira at Trachis: a son and his only daughter, Macaria, making three in all.

'After Hercules had been living at Trachis for some time, I received an unexpected message from him, asking me to meet him. He gave no indication of why he wished to meet me. As I had never visited Trachis, and I wished to see his family, two of whom I had not seen, I acquiesced on condition that we met there. He agreed and the meeting took place some days later.

'As a close relative of Hercules, I was made very welcome by the King and his staff. The room I was offered must have been at least as good as the royal chambers with its own bathroom! I had heard that such a luxury had been installed by Nestor in his new palace at Pylos for his Queen, but this idea of having a room set aside especially, and uniquely, for bathing was certainly novel at this time among the Greeks. I must admit that I enjoyed the experience and did not consider it at all "effeminate", as some said. I was pleased to meet Dejanira again after a gap of a number of years and I was impressed how, despite the difficulties she must be experiencing in coping with her husband's eccentricities – and worse – she clearly loved him deeply. Her three children were a credit to both of them. They benefited from the attention of both their parents and I heard that they had recently had a visit from their grandmother, Alcmena, who had taken up residence at Tiryns. But Hyllus was the favourite of Hercules and I could see why. Now about twelve years old, he was a tall and handsome young man. He was alert, obedient without being subservient as he was ready to question anything he did not fully understand, athletic with skills in horse riding and archery – which must have pleased his father – and, also like his father, knew how to express himself, whether in private or in public. I predicted a fine future for this young man. We shall be meeting him again before I finish my story.

'Soon, Hercules and I were alone and he told me what was on his mind. He had received a secret message from Delphi saying that Apollo wished Hercules to do something for him. The son of the king of Itonus, a city in the south of Thessaly, a man called Cycnus, was interfering with the passage of cattle bound for sacrifice at Delphi. He was doing this by levying a varying toll on the drovers who, not having anything to offer except head of cattle, and no credible defence against Cycnus' armed bands, had no option but to yield up some of the cattle. The cattle did not belong to them but to Apollo! Sometimes, Cycnus' greed led him to seize the whole herd, particularly if the drovers had been killed by the armed men because they had resisted their assault.

'Now it so happened that Cycnus was so arrogant about his skills as a chariot warrior that he had issued a challenge that he would give a valuable prize to anyone who could beat him. Apollo had proposed that, to conceal his real motive, and justify killing Cycnus – who himself had killed many who had taken up the challenge but lost – Hercules should accept the challenge, provided I was prepared to support him as the charioteer.

'I was more than a little nervous at this suggestion. I had not driven Hercules in a chariot against such a skilled opponent ever before. Fortunately, I had revisited and refreshed my skills on the visit to Dodona and still frequently drove a chariot, although merely as a method of travelling between cities on good roads, not in an arena that I did not know, and that would no doubt have deliberately tight corners to upset the opposition, and with which our opponent would be very familiar. I said as much to Hercules. As I knew, he had his own brand of arrogance, and dismissed my fears. So I was forced into the only alternative: find out myself how dangerous this venture might be.

'The reassuring thing for me personally was that, although the losing challenger invariably was killed – and his head exhibited on a pole in the nearby Temple of Ares – the charioteer was normally allowed to leave unharmed. At least, if I could avoid being killed by an accident in the arena, I was likely to survive, whatever the outcome! This meant that there were some charioteers around who had participated in a contest. Pausing only to tell Hercules not to issue a challenge just yet as I had not yet made up my mind to be his charioteer, I started making enquiries about previous challenges.

'I soon had the names of two charioteers and managed to see both of them. One blamed himself for his sponsor's failure and was rather a pathetic creature wallowing in self-pity. He gave me nothing I wanted. But the other had approached the task in much the same way as I intended to do. Prior to his sponsor's challenge, he had managed a clandestine visit to Itonus to take measurements of the arena in which the duel would take place. He confirmed my suspicions: the corners of the arena were subtly tighter than normal, and, in addition, the overall length of the arena was slightly shorter. A charioteer used to the normal measurements, and without having had a trial run, would be at a disadvantage. This charioteer gave me the measurements, which he fortunately still had, and advised me to mark out an arena to these measurements for trial runs before travelling to Itonus. He gave me two other useful tips: always keep my chariot under an armed guard who never slept on duty, and ask to be allowed a trial run on the course. The first was to counter interference with the chariot to make it unstable – my informant knew this had happened to some challengers. The second request would be denied, as this would "damage the course" but I would be offered an alternative arena. This alternative was to the normal measurements and was of little value in getting used to the particular profile of the course on which the actual contest would take place. However, a perfunctory trial run on this course would convince Cycnus that his devious plan had not been discovered by his opponent.

'I thanked him profusely for his advice, swearing him to secrecy and paid for the detailed measurements he gave me. On returning to Trachis, I told Hercules that I wanted to practice on a competition track on my own first, to get used to it and then with him on board in the full armour he would be required to wear as one of the rules of the challenge. Only when I was satisfied with the results of these trials would I confirm that I was prepared to act as his charioteer in this dangerous encounter, and only then could he tell Cycnus that he was accepting the challenge. Hercules was inclined to ignore my wishes but I reminded him that Apollo himself had told Hercules that I was to be his charioteer and must have known that I would want to be properly prepared to have some guarantee of a successful outcome. With rather bad grace, he accepted defeat.

'The following morning, he came to see me. When I told him what I had learnt from the former charioteer, Hercules was quite contrite and offered to help mark out the course with me on some land close to the city's own course. The King had offered us the use of his course for training and was quite hurt when we declined. However, when we explained the reason and, later, he drove a chariot himself on both courses, he realised how right we were!

'Hercules and I quickly realised that the small adjustments made by Cycnus to the course were expertly conceived. The shortening of the arena upset the rhythm of horses trained to race in a normal stadium and the slight adjustment to the radius of the corners meant that horses (and charioteers) used to racing to the limit would find they had run out of space and would end up hitting the side bank and probably turning over the chariot, with disastrous results for both the horses and those in the chariot.

'My analysis was that these modifications had a very serious consequence. Well-trained racing chariot horses and charioteers would be expecting a standard course and would find it hard to adjust to the actual profile of the course. By the time they had adjusted, Cycnus would have decapitated the challenger. I decided that, to give us a reasonable chance of success on the course, I would have to train new horses for the chariot rather than, as I had intended, use experienced ones. At this stage, I was not even sure if I needed to have a new chariot made with a slightly narrower axle. I was not keen to do this as Hercules was used to fighting in a full-sized chariot and, anyway, our smaller chariot might be disqualified if we were discovered!

'My judgment was right: a slightly smaller chariot would have been slightly easier to manoeuvre but Hercules, with his great bulk would have been less comfortable. After a few weeks' trials, I had broken in the horses to their task and I had acquired the skills needed to negotiate the tight corners without destabilising Hercules. We were ready to accept the challenge.

'The rest of the story is quickly told. As forecast, our request to have a test drive on the course was denied and the course offered was to the normal dimensions. To avoid suspicion, I cantered around it a few times, without travelling at full speed. It certainly felt different from the course I had been using for training. There was an attempt to interfere with our chariot during the night, but the guards we had posted prevented this. Cycnus could not deny there had been an attempt to interfere with our chariot as, in accordance with our instructions, the guards waited until the intruder had started to loosen a bolt before arresting him. Still, it was amusing to be able to force Cycnus into making a grudging apology. Being forced to make an apology clearly upset him and this was just what we wanted.

'The contest was over quickly. On the very first run, the collision between the two warriors resulted in them being both thrown to the ground. Before Cycnus had even got to his feet, Hercules was thrusting at him with his spear. Cycnus bravely fought back, but the outcome was never in doubt after the fall and Hercules' spear into Cycnus' body was fatal.

'There was a stunned silence from the crowd who had gathered to watch what they thought would be the demise of yet another poor stranger. A few swords were drawn and some heavily armed men entered the arena and walked towards Hercules. I called on Hercules to mount the chariot, but he declined and faced the advancing group, the spear in his hand dripping Cycnus' blood. I think it was the sight of Cycnus' blood that convinced them it was a lost cause. Just before they came within reach of Hercules' spear, the leading man turned, sheathed his sword and walked back the way he had come. The others followed. Hercules then remounted the chariot and I drove us slowly to the exit, where our men were waiting to escort us back to the stable block in which we had been accommodated overnight. We decided to leave immediately, which we did. We later had a message from Cycnus' father, apologising for the reaction of some of his people to his son's defeat and death. I later discovered that the father was old and in fear of his son, who behaved just as he wanted, to the dismay of his father, who knew how obnoxious he was. Privately, he was not sorry that his bullying and cheating son had been killed, but he obviously could not admit this publicly.

'By the time we arrived back in Trachis, there was a message waiting for us from Delphi congratulating us on our success. They certainly had an excellent information network!

'I decided to return to Thebes after a few days of rest and celebration. When I took my leave of Hercules and his wife, I did not think it was a farewell, but I never saw either of them again alive. I will now tell you of the final events of Hercules' life.'

The Death of Hercules

'I expect you remember that Hercules won an archery contest organised by Eurytus, King of Oechalia, but that the King refused to give Hercules the prize, which was the hand of his daughter, Iole, in marriage?' I nodded. 'Well, Hercules now decided, after a gap of several years, that he would avenge the insults hurled at him by Eurytus at the time, and claim his prize – even though he was now happily married to Dejanira.

'Hercules had no difficulty in recruiting a rabble of adventurers to go with him and duly took the city, killed Eurytus and his three remaining sons (Hercules had already killed Iphitus, his other son) and seized Iole. There are conflicting stories about Iole's relationship with Hercules. Some say that they were attracted to each other but there is also a fantastic story that Iole tried to kill herself to avoid falling into Hercules' hands by throwing herself from the walls of the city. Her life was reputedly saved because her voluminous skirts were filled with air as she fell and gave her a soft landing!

'Whatever the truth, Iole became Hercules' property, but he sent her with the other enslaved Oechalian women back to Trachis to be in the custody of his wife, Dejanira. From what happened next, it would appear that Iole intimated somehow that she found Hercules attractive, and that Dejanira felt she had a rival.

'Hercules, in the meantime, had left Trachis to visit Mount Oeta, which overlooked and was to the south of Trachis, in order to make a thanksgiving sacrifice to Zeus for his successful expedition to Oechalia. His son, Hyllus, went with him. Hercules then prepared an altar in the sacred grove near the mountain summit and, realising that he had forgotten to bring the special cloak and tunic he normally wore on such occasions, sent a servant back to his wife at Trachis to collect them from her.

'When the servant arrived, Dejanira remembered what Nessus

had told her to do if she ever felt she was losing her husband to another woman. Fearful of Iole's possible influence on Hercules, she quickly found Nessus' blood-stained tunic and rubbed some of the blood on to the inside of the tunic she was sending to Hercules. Wrapping it up securely inside the cloak, she gave it to the servant instructing him to give the parcel to Hercules personally and unopened. This he did.

'Hercules, by now absorbed in thinking about the rituals he would have to perform, opened the parcel, took out the tunic and put it on. He then sacrificed the prime bulls he had brought and lit the fire he had prepared, casting incense on the fire. By now, the heat from the fire had released the poison from the blood smeared on his tunic. As soon as the poison touched his skin, he felt a severe burning sensation and tried to tear off the tunic. But it had stuck to him and could not be removed. He tried to douse the fire in the tunic and on his body in a nearby stream, but this made it worse. In agony, he overturned the altar and tore up some of the sacred trees. Finally, he recognised that his death was near and called on Hyllus, who had been watching the torment of his father with open-mouthed horror, to help him so that he could place himself on the fire – which would now be his own funeral pyre.

'Hyllus did as he was bid. As soon as Hercules' body was engulfed in the flames, there came a clap of thunder from above and a lightning strike hit the middle of the pyre, scattering it over a large area. Smoke rose from where the pyre had been and those present claim they saw, in that smoke, a shadow of a chariot, drawn by four horses with a revived Hercules holding the reins, ascending upwards into the sky. In a moment, the vision was gone. No physical remains of Hercules were ever found.

'Hyllus brought the news of Hercules' death back to Trachis. Dejanira, quickly realising she had been duped by Nessus and that she had unwittingly killed her husband, committed suicide.

'When the news reached me at Thebes, I was deeply shocked and distraught. Knowing of my close relationship with Hercules, Hyllus himself came as the bearer of the sad news. I soon discovered that he had come not just to share his grief but also to tell me of Hercules' last words, from which we could both take some comfort.

'At first, when Hercules felt the burning sensation, he accused his wife of deliberately wishing to destroy him. Hyllus refused to accept this and, in his dying moments, Hercules rescinded the unkind things he had said about his wife and accepted that she had been tricked. He admitted that the Oracle at Dodona had told him that he would "die at the hands of a dead man". He now realised that Nessus was his nemesis. His last words were to ask Hyllus to thank all those who had helped and befriended him over the years. I was very pleased to find that he had been granted time to say some very kind words about me personally and his real friends.

'The reaction to his death, and the manner of it, gave rise to many thanksgivings for his life's achievements. Some, of course, such as Eurystheus, welcomed it, but the majority view was that he was an exceptional man who would be much missed. Before long, altars sprang up – even temples – named in his honour. Today, there is hardly any significant city without one – and all these cities claim that he visited them and achieved some marvel for them.'

We both kept silent for a while. Then, my curiosity overcame my reticence and I dared to ask a final question.

'But that was not the end of the story, was it?' I said. 'I know you and the children of Hercules came to Sardinia, but there were some events leading up to that, were there not?'

Eventually, he told me. But that is another story…